Dark Tales from a Dorset Rectory

unearthly happenings at the edge of the everyday world

by J.R. Armstrong-Gregson

I0690517

Dedicated to Julie, who put up with all this.

**Published in January 2025 by emp3books Ltd
6 Silvester Way, Church Crookham, GU52 0TD**

© **J.R. Armstrong-Gregson 2025**

ISBN: 9781910734599

www.emp3books.com

Also by J. R. Armstrong-Gregson:
The Roman Army over Time

(writing as Gavin Armstrong)
Red Hound: The making of Cuchulainn
King over the Water
Clearances: a morality tale of the Old West

Contents

FOREWORD

As aficionados of the ghost story will soon realise, this volume owes much to *Ghost Stories of an Antiquary* and its sequels, the writings in this genre of the scholar Montague Rhodes James, Provost of King's College, Cambridge, and then Eton College between 1905 and 1936, and briefly Vice-Chancellor of the University of Cambridge. They follow James' advice that such stories are most effective when set in the not too distant past (though a century earlier than most of his), and like his they tend to focus on the world of the lone seeker after academic or religious knowledge – with the ultimate message that some things are best left undisturbed.

Incidentally, I originally called this collection *Ghost Stories*, but changed it to *Dark Tales*, in recognition of the fact that only a minority of the pieces actually feature conventional "ghosts". It is the case that many of James' stories contain revenants, demons and other spirits rather than actual ghosts, including the best "ghost story" in the language, "'Oh, Whistle and I'll Come to You, My Lad'".

The earliest of these pieces is the one entitled "Waste Ground", which took its geographical setting from the fact that I had been living in Dorset for some years. Towards the end of the writing, the Reverend Theophilus Hale, MA (Oxon), Rector of St. Mark's, Stoke Armitage, literally rode into the story, unexpectedly, and took charge of it, a state of affairs which continued as he stayed on to be the common point of reference, and often the subject matter, for the rest of the collection. My thanks go to him.

WASTE GROUND

Even for an Anglican clergyman of his time, the Reverend James Dawlish had little sense of the spiritual; indeed, even his notions of basic morality were somewhat fluid for someone in his chosen calling. His entry into the ministry had been decided upon not from any spiritual promptings or a sense of vocation, but from his perception of the established Church as being a route to financial security and social advancement which involved little more than being austerely pleasant and accepting the niceties of a respectable and comfortable existence. The mainspring of his not inconsiderable activity was the promotion not of the Gospel but of himself, and this had propelled him from being the son of a modestly successful Bristol tailor to becoming, via diligence rather than brilliance at the local grammar school, a commoner at St. Jude's College, Oxford, where his industry and willingness to please his betters had enabled him to secure a reasonable degree while establishing several worthwhile connections, despite his lack of funds and social adjuncts. And so it was that, after only a brief spell as a town curate, he had been appointed to the parish of St. George's, Charton, through the good offices of his old college friend Lord Tolworth, whose uncle the Earl had the living of Charton in his gift.

The young parson, riding a borrowed horse, approached Charton from the east, on which edge of the village his new church and vicarage lay, on the south side of the lane which further along became the High Street, with its inn and a few shops and businesses. It was a late afternoon in October, and he urged the beast on in his anxiety to be at his destination well before nightfall. Unusually, he had not yet seen the place, there having been no time for the usual preliminaries, as the Earl had wanted the post filled as soon as possible after the sudden death of the previous incumbent. He had only had time to organise the sending ahead

3

of the two trunks of his effects, the box of books and the few small pieces of furniture which made up his possessions and to arrange, by letters to two prominent parishioners, the engagement of a housekeeper and a maid – the terms he used for them, though in truth both servants lived out and were employed for only a few hours a week, the one mainly cooking and the other doing some cleaning and the firelighting.

The sun was quite low, just above the thinning trees, as he reached the outskirts of the village, dazzling his eyes a little; he took in a tower in the Decorated style, nave windows of the early English period and a Tudor porch sheltering the entrance, but he rode straight past the walled churchyard with its pair of great yews to the vicarage, which he knew to be next door. It was a small but tasteful brick residence, dating from the early days of the first King George, and probably quite unlike most of the other buildings in Charton, some of whose thatched roofs and stone walls he could see above the hedgerow ahead. He was relieved to see a light on and smoke rising from the chimney; he had sent instructions for the housekeeper to await his arrival and to have a meal ready for him, and these orders had clearly been acted upon – a good portent for the future. As he pulled up at the gate and dismounted, a short, stout woman who had obviously been watching for him, bustled out of the front door, followed at a much slower rate by a tall, sallow man wearing the leather apron associated with smiths and farriers.

"Mistress Williams? I am the Reverend Dawlish. You have been preparing for my coming, I see."

"Yes, your reverence, that's I. We're right glad to make your acquaintance, sir. Now if you'll come with me, sir, Williams 'ere will take your 'orse around yonder to the stable while you get yourself settled."

4

The silent man, who appeared to be her husband, led the animal away behind the house while the clergyman followed her up the path to the front door, between lawns passable but for patches of moss, flowerbeds now largely reduced to brown tangles and four gaunt apple trees still laden with unpicked fruit. He noted with satisfaction the symmetry of the façade, and passed inside, where he delayed his inspection of the house until he had partaken, in front of his own fire, of the coarse but filling mutton and dumpling stew which had been simmering for rather too long. As he ate, he gazed out of the dining room window, which looked out onto the front garden on the side of the house nearest the church. Although the light was failing, he immediately became aware of a curious feature which disturbed his sense of order: the wall which separated his garden from the churchyard did not, as one might have expected, run squarely down the forty feet or so to the lane, keeping parallel to the side of his house, but actually cut across his line of vision, as though angled away from the church, so that his view ended with an obtuse angle rather than with his front wall square on to him.

While Mrs. Williams cleared away, amidst profuse apologies for the meal – "it were somewhat that would keep till you came, you see, sir" – the vicar inspected the rest of the rooms briefly, by candlelight. All seemed satisfactory, though the thought of the truncated view from his dining room continued to vex him oddly until, after Mr. and Mrs. Williams had departed in some haste, he fell into bed and slept dreamlessly after his long day of travelling.

The following morning, the clergyman awoke late, and became aware of voices elsewhere in the house – probably the Williamses. He hastily rose, splashed water on his face from the pitcher on his table and dressed. Pulling back his curtains, he looked down at his new front garden, and was at once struck by a feature which he had not noticed the evening before but which deepened his puzzlement about his garden wall – properly so called, because, looking on it from above, he saw that it was not, in fact, also the wall of the churchyard. The ancient lichened blocks of the latter made a right angle with the lane, whereas the slighter and more recently-built wall surrounding his plot was separated from the older boundary by a few feet, and moved away from it as they approached the road. The two walls thus enclosed a narrow strip of land, roughly in the shape of an elongated funnel, which appeared to be densely overgrown.

When he had hurried downstairs he found Mrs. Williams berating a small but heavy-featured girl, whom he judged was probably usually pale, though now she had ashes smudged across her face – the result of an unsuccessful attempt to blow up the fire in the dining room.

"I be very sorry about this, your reverence, but Mary do 'ave 'ad a little accident with the fireplace, Mary being she and your maid to do the cleaning and bits, sir. What be ye a-thinking of, girl? Curtsey to the gentleman, there, tongue-tied, be ye?"

The girl looked at the floor as she bobbed; her lips appeared to move, but no sound emerged.

"She'll be fine once I've instructed her properly in 'er duties, sir. Now be off with you as there's no point now the gentleman be 'ere already."

Mr. Dawlish ascertained that the domestic accident was limited to the region of the hearth, and he sat at his table while Mrs. Williams brought him his breakfast. After eating, he began to empty his trunks and set out his books in order on the shelves in the study. The furniture, fabrics and kitchen and tableware, he understood, were generally the property of the vicarage; the personal belongings of his predecessor, he learnt, had been packed up by the Williamses and despatched to his next of kin, a cousin who lived in London and whom they had never seen in Charton. The housekeeper apologised when he pointed out that she appeared to have missed a few items: he had noticed a couple of volumes in a drawer in the study, a wide-brimmed hat on top of a press, and so on. She explained that it had been done in a great hurry, and that she feared more would come to light – especially in the church, as she had not had access to the vestry. When he had spent some time determining with the woman her duties and the girl Mary's and the precise timing of them, she left, to return later to make his supper, as he was dining with Colonel Johnson, the most notable of his parishioners.

Towards the end of the morning, Mr. Dawlish pulled on his riding coat, hat and boots and went out to the stable to saddle the horse, which he had to do himself as Mr. Williams did not appear to be a regular member of his staff. He rode out into the lane and through the village, noting the principal features – The Black Bull inn, a duck-pond, the bakery, the blacksmith's – and nodding or raising his hat to the few people he saw on the way. The Manor House, the imposing edifice of sixteenth-century origin where the Colonel lived, was on the far side of Charton, but he reached it at an easy walk in under a quarter of an hour. After a pleasant repast of game and claret, followed by a lengthy session in which he felt himself to be in the position of Mrs. Williams or Mary being instructed as to his duties but during which he restricted himself to his practised acquiescence, he returned home as he had come. The Colonel's requirements were not extreme or unexpected: nothing obviously Papistical, but at the same time nothing tinged with low-church Dissent. Learning that his new vicar had not yet been inside the church, the Colonel assured him that it had been kept clean and was ready for use the following morning; the vestry, however, had been kept locked for the month which had lapsed since the death of the last incumbent and he could not comment on it. The Colonel found the key after a brief rummage in the drawer of his desk and entrusted it to him.

Mr. Dawlish paused at the front of his house, and his gaze was drawn again to the curiously arranged walls between it and the churchyard. He urged the horse to the gap between them, and stood up in the stirrups to survey it from the highest vantage point.

Each time he looked at this spot, it made less sense: now he saw that the two walls did meet, at their further end, and did not enclose a path. The churchyard formed a regular rectangle, with fields behind; the wall around the vicarage formed a smaller rectangle, except that the wall nearest the church was angled into his garden, touching the churchyard wall at one corner but then leaving a triangular strip which widened as it approached the road to the front. This strip was the length of the vicarage plot, perhaps fifty or sixty yards, and where it opened onto the lane was about six yards wide. It was choked with curled brambles, nettles higher than a man, all manner of weeds and grasses. What purpose it served, the vicar could not determine, and this only increased the disproportionate sense of irritation he felt. He ascertained that it did not mark a watercourse; it had obviously never been a footpath, as it had always been blocked at one end; it was too narrow to have contained a cottage or any kind of building. It seemed to him that it was almost certainly, from its position, part of the vicarage property, and he resolved to find out why it was marked out in this way and why it was allowed to interfere with the view from his house.

It being Saturday, Mr. Dawlish was mainly occupied for the rest of the afternoon in putting the final touches and adding some specific references to the sermon which he had been turning over and rewriting for several years for his first service in his own parish. As had been arranged, Mr. Shaw, the verger, arrived at the house as the sun was starting to set, to introduce himself and show the new man around the church building. Over tea, Mr. Dawlish managed to conceal from his verger the fact that he had been on site for

8

twenty-four hours without even venturing into the church, sensing that this fact would be all over the parish by morning and not to his credit. Mr. Shaw was obviously an enthusiast: he wondered if the vicar had noticed the subsidence in the south aisle, the fine foliage on the capitals of the westernmost pair of arches in the nave, the interesting medieval glass in a particular window, and so on. At last, Mr. Dawlish suggested they should go across so that they could have the features before them as they talked, which would divert attention from his own responses, or lack of them.

The last glimmers of daylight were failing as they entered the building, and the verger lit a pair of lanterns so that they could appreciate some of the details in its dark corners. They looked at the brass monument to an early Armitage, one of the family who had lived at the Manor for some three centuries before the Colonel's father had bought it, and the even older recumbent effigy resting on an awkwardly sloped shelf in a long niche in the wall of the chancel. The verger explained some of the peculiarities of the acoustics in the building, and demonstrated some from the Jacobean pulpit. He identified the occupants of the more prominent pews, and sketched in their positions in the community. The only thing that really concerned his listener was where the Colonel would be seated and how he should direct his speech to make the best impression at that point. At length, the vicar, feeling that he had done all that he needed to do to appear gracious and interested, thanked the verger profusely, and accompanied him back to the house in a manner which suggested that their meeting had come to an end. As they walked, Mr. Shaw indicated, in the north-eastern corner of the churchyard, where the late vicar, Mr. Wise, had been interred, under a large Celtic-style stone cross. Mr. Dawlish noted that the monuments tended to be crowded together at the eastern side of the church, with very few up against the wall which adjoined, or almost adjoined, the vicarage garden; he asked the verger if there was any particular reason for this, and was told only that "the ground was probably better for burial there". At the house, while trying not to appear to be rude, the vicar did not give the verger an opportunity to sit down again, but helped him to his stick and said goodbye.

When the man had gone, he realised that he had missed an opportunity to investigate the vestry with someone who knew his way around it. He really had to check that everything was in place for the morning, in the way of vestments and plate, so that he could present himself in the best possible light before the Colonel, so he decided to return to the church with the key. Taking up a double candlestick that came to hand and a tinderbox, he hurried back across, pausing in the porch to light the candles. He was not a superstitious man, nor even an imaginative one, but he was conscious of feeling less comfortable now in this dark place than he had felt only a few minutes before, in company. This church was distinctly colder and damper than the one he had left behind in town; it held a silence which was not punctuated by street noises from outside, and a darkness that was not compromised by lights from neighbouring inns and houses shining through the windows. He suddenly felt more alone and more vulnerable than he had ever felt – yet not alone, and more vulnerable because of it: the shadowy place itself and its atmosphere, like a permanent holding of colossal breath, seemed almost to be another entity, both watching and enclosing him.

He tried to shake off these thoughts as he gave an involuntary shudder, and proceeded to the vestry door. He turned the key and entered: it was little more than a large cupboard. Fortunately, there was a supply of candles near the door and a pair of sticks, so he lit two from the ones he carried and set them up on an old high desk. He opened the press and the chest and found a quantity of vestments in good repair and clean; chalice and plate were in need of some polishing up, but that could wait for the morning and the verger. Blowing out the extra candles, he locked the door again and returned to his sermonising as speedily as was dignified,

10

passing as he did the black void of the entrance to the incomprehensible strip of waste ground between the walls.

The Sunday communion service was not quite as he had visualised it, though the church was full, both because of curiosity about the new pastor and because the ritual of letting others see one's Sunday best and criticising theirs had been suspended for the past five sabbaths. The organ seemed to be tuned to a lower pitch than was now fashionable in towns; the choir lacked refinement, though they made up for it with volume; most disappointingly, his thoroughly prepared and rehearsed sermon did not seem to create the interest and approval he had been expecting. Perhaps he had included too many of his carefully-gathered Latin tags and quotations for the taste of this rustic congregation; perhaps in his later years Mr. Wise had been in the habit of delivering a shorter address than was now the fashionable norm. Whatever the source of the problem, he sensed restlessness and lack of attention as his discourse went on, and when he observed Colonel Johnson barely suppressing a yawn he decided to omit his analysis of references to building and construction in the New Testament, and conclude. Outside, afterwards, few of the villagers tarried to do more than wish him a good morning, as a strong wind was getting up, bringing dark clouds and whirling weakened leaves from the trees, but the Colonel assured him that the service had been conducted "perfectly adequately".

When all had gone, the Reverend Dawlish re-entered the empty church, and smiled wryly as he remembered his discomfort of the previous evening: this morning had been the real test, and he felt he had passed, though not with distinction. He disrobed, put on his hat and coat and hurried home across the churchyard as best he could against a strong wind; in the lane, a gust lifted his hat off as he tried to hold his coat-tails down, and spun it into the vegetation which filled the strip of waste ground. Muttering things not entirely in keeping with his position and the day, he pushed his way in and tried to reach in and seize it as it bobbed on a viciously-barbed tendril. Brambles caught his coat and nettles stung his hand as he stretched towards it, just out of reach. He pushed in, feeling the compressed undergrowth resisting him, like springs pressing into his chest and thighs. The hat nodded as though laughing mockingly, inches beyond his grasp. A stray tendril of bramble was dragged across the back of his hand, raising a row of bloody dots where the veins were close to the surface. He abandoned the task, but then found it hard to disentangle himself from the clutching plants. Striving to unpick barbs from the shoulder of his coat, he felt a stocking catch on a thorn; when he bent to free it without ripping it, a strand whipped across his face, stinging and grazing. Maddened, he pulled himself away suddenly, leaving strands of fabric and hair behind; he looked around hastily, his face red with the smart and with embarrassment, to ensure that no-one had witnessed his failure; but his gaze returned to the overgrown patch, and hardened into an angry scowl. This was no longer just about an eyesore which offended his sense of order and symmetry: it was about something which opposed his will and now taunted him.

That night, and for most of the nights to come, he relived those few minutes in his dreams, extended to agonising length; and in time the brambles would become as clutching hands and the thorns as cruel claws.

A couple of days later, Mr. Dawlish was carrying out a more thorough examination of the contents of the vestry, and discovered a drawer of papers. Amongst the documents were several maps and plans relating to the area and the parish, evidently accumulated over the years or perhaps collected by Mr. Wise during his long residency. There was a map of the county dated 1695, and another, much earlier, which seemed to make a special feature of roads and defensive features: Mr. Dawlish speculated that it might date from around the time of the Spanish Armada.

12

There was an elegant sketch and plan of the church and vicarage made by the diocesan architect, stamped with the arms of Queen Anne, and an older plan of the village showing individual plots and the names of the occupants, marked 1665. But the feature to which he attended on several documents was the strip of ground at the boundary of his garden and the churchyard. The architect's drawing of the early 1700's, which depicted the thatched house which had been the previous vicarage, indicated a passage between two walls which might have been a farm track, but the 1665 plan indicated the churchyard wall as the boundary between the two properties; a dotted line, angling away from it but clearly within the garden, perhaps marked the line of the lesser wall.

However, a detailed but crudely-executed plan of the church property which bore a name which he recognised from the list of previous incumbents – he had been vicar in the later years of Henry VIII's reign – simply showed a straight line between the two plots. Whatever its purpose, the triangular strip had apparently been marked off with the inner wall at some point between the middle of the sixteenth and the middle of the seventeenth century. If that ground had once been part of the vicar's garden, it could be so again, with just the clearance of the wild growth and the demolition of that ridiculous wall. That would show it who was master here now. For the first time, he smiled, albeit grimly, as he walked past its shadowy entrance on his way home.

When Mrs. Williams brought him his solitary supper that night, he asked her if it was known in the village why that piece of land was walled off in that way. She shook her head; she had not been brought up there, having come to Charton when she married Williams, but she had lived there more than twenty years and had neither heard anything about it nor given it a thought. But Williams was native to the place, like his father and his grandfather, and she would ask him.

The next day, Mr. Dawlish, who had slept fitfully between dreams of the bramble patch, hoped for some news from her at breakfast; then at dinner; and finally, as she cleared away after his tea, he could contain himself no longer and, at the risk of seeming foolish, he asked her if she had questioned her husband about the waste ground.

"Well, your reverence, sir, I did ask as you said to, but not getting much of a reply, if it please you, I didn't think it worth the repeating. Williams says, sir, that there be reasons for most things but we don't always do right to be trying to find 'em out. No, sir, I don't think he knows anything about it, and if he don't, nobody do. It's just one of those things best left alone, if you ask me, sir, as Williams says, begging your pardon."

Two days later, he paid his weekly visit to the Manor House. He took tea with the Colonel, and as they discussed the domestic arrangements at the vicarage and certain small alterations and improvements Mr. Dawlish intended to put before the parish or the diocese, he introduced the subject of the garden wall, as a minor issue and not one which had come to sit malevolently at the back of his thoughts throughout every day. His first aim, to learn why this excrescence had developed, was frustrated, as the Colonel seemed to know even less about it than Mrs. Williams – in fact, until Mr. Dawlish pointed it out, he had never really noticed it except as a clump of wilderness between two civilised enclaves, part of his internal geography since boyhood. Not that he was really local; his father had moved down from Bath and purchased the Manor House after the extinction of the Armitage family, when he was two years old, and much of his time since had been spent away at boarding school and then with the army, mostly overseas in Canada. In his second aim, however, the vicar was successful: he could have the Colonel's backing if he chose to apply for the restoration of the garden to its original and intended shape and dimensions – as he phrased it.

The same formula, avoiding any suggestion of his irrational animosity towards the waste ground (which had eventually given up his hat, thanks to Williams' skill at fishing with a long-handled rake), was used in his subsequent applications to the Earl's estate manager and the diocesan clerk of works, neither of whom seemed very concerned; he had to supply a sketch-plan of the current and proposed situations, but, as there was clearly no question of any other rights being involved or any other freeholder having an interest, he was given a free hand to do as he wished. His manner improved; his dreams became for a short period less tortured and less frequent.

Having made inquiries through Williams' connections in the village, he had come to an amicable arrangement with a local farmer: as soon as they could be spared from the land for the winter, two labourers would be provided, with tools and a cart, to clear away the undergrowth of the waste ground, and then to dismantle the superfluous garden wall. In return, the farmer would keep for his own use most of the stones – a small price, given that the vicar would have paid to have had them hauled away.

In mid-November, the two men arrived at the vicarage very early in the morning, armed with billhooks, scythes and stout leather gloves and leggings, and at once they attacked the waste ground with vigour. Mr. Dawlish had hoped that Mr. Shaw, the verger, might have been on hand to supervise the work, but he could not require it, as it concerned the vicarage and not the church directly. Within an hour, they had cut back six or seven yards, loaded the material onto the cart and were taking it away to be burned; Mr. Dawlish watched with satisfaction from his bedroom window, and then returned to composing his next sermon. Towards the end of the morning, when he was beginning to think of Mrs. Williams coming to prepare his meal, he heard a rapping at his front door;

15

he looked out, and saw it was one of the workmen. He opened the window and asked what he wanted.

"Please you to come down, sir. Jethro 'ave 'ad accident, like, and we do 'ave found some'at over yonder."

Half way into the waste ground, at a point about level with the back of his house, they had partially uncovered a block of dark stone. It had been revealed when Jethro's scythe had struck it, sliding off and grazing his leg: the injury would have been much worse if he had not been wearing stout leggings. The block appeared to be rectangular, its longer sides being as parallel with the converging enclosing walls as they could be. Its exposed short end was perhaps a yard broad and nearly as high, with a space about a yard across on either side – allowing it to be walked around. It seemed to be only crudely worked. Jethro, his wound roughly bandaged, was sent home, and Mr. Dawlish instructed the remaining labourer to continue the clearance, while he watched. After another ten minutes he had exposed a slab some five feet long, devoid of any inscription or decoration; if worked at all, it was just as it had been cut from the quarry rather than being shaped.

After the man had taken a break to eat bread and cheese and Jethro had returned with his leg bound up, the rest of the strip was soon cleared, as it narrowed to virtually nothing as the two walls converged, and this darker, confined end was less densely overgrown.

In Mr. Dawlish's mind, the mystery and problem of the waste ground had been cleared away like the weeds only to be replaced by a new puzzle more tenacious than the brambles – that posed by the stone block. Was it a natural feature, or had it been put there deliberately? Had the enclosure been put up around it, or had it been dumped there because the existing patch was vacant? Several initially attractive answers soon had to be abandoned by logic. It could not have been put there to block access, as it was too low and could easily be walked around, and it could not have been specifically to prevent access by vehicles as the strip led nowhere. It was very unlikely that it was left over from any building work, as the stone did not seem to be like any stone used in the church or the walls. It seemed improbable that anyone would take the trouble to bring such a large piece there without a deliberate aim, yet it had clearly been cut, albeit roughly, and so was not just a natural rock outcrop. Perhaps the wall which excluded it from the garden had been put up simply because an incumbent had become sick of the sight of it; but this was unlikely, as it would scarcely have been visible from the house, being on a level with its back corner. The vicar was inclined to think that the erection of the garden wall, sometime between the reign of Edward VI and the Restoration, was in some way connected with the stone, perhaps with its arrival.

And then there was the question of what to do with it. Leave it as a feature in the new garden – perhaps levelling the top to make a seat? Mr. Dawlish decided to be rid of it as soon as the wall was down and there was room to take it up: it was not an attractive feature, it looked as though it would be very hard to carve, and he associated it with the malevolence he had perceived in the brambles which had surrounded it, as if guarding it.

As it was a private vicarage matter, Mr. Dawlish had not been expecting the parishioners to be much concerned about his clearance works, but he was surprised at how very little interest they seemed to take: The crowd outside the church after the service on Sunday seemed, if anything, to disperse more quickly than usual, hardly anyone glancing at the cleared waste ground as they hurried away. Mr. Dawlish ascribed this to the coldness of the morning. The Colonel was prepared to spend a few minutes inspecting the site. He had no explanation of the stone slab to offer, it never having been visible before in his lifetime, but he pointed

17

out to the vicar that the ground level of the newly exposed area would be several inches lower than the level of the garden, which had been planted up and fertilised for many years since the dividing wall had been built. Mr. Dawlish expressed gratitude for the advice, although he had already noted the difference and was looking out for possible sources of topsoil with which to reduce it.

The following week saw the careful dismantling of the garden wall and the removal of the stones to the farm where they would be reused for new pig-pens. Although this act achieved the reincorporation of the waste ground into the vicarage garden, Mr. Dawlish's discomfort if anything increased: his garden was now bounded on one side not by a defining wall but by a depression covered by moss and the remains of weeds, and the grim stone slab was now visible every time he went outside instead of lying hidden. He realised there was little he could do about the state of the strip with winter fast approaching – the turning over of the soil, along with careful weeding and the removal of loose stones, being a very long job which would have to wait until the Spring – but the stone could be removed at once. The farmer was unwilling to extend their arrangement to this task, and refused to provide men and cart for the job even when Mr. Dawlish offered a generous sum in payment; this was curious, as his argument that they were now busy throughout the winter seemed contrary to what the vicar knew about farming practices, but he put the reluctance down to the fact that one of the men had already been injured working in the waste ground. Enquiries in the village for men willing to spend a day or two raising the stone and carting it away met with no response. As November ended, he resigned himself to having to wait until he could procure workmen from elsewhere.

Although he cultivated the acquaintance of well-connected people assiduously, it would be true to say that the Reverend James Dawlish had no close friends; and so it was that his first visitor at Charton did not make the trip expressly to see him but merely called in for a night in the middle of a journey elsewhere. Dr. Stephen Richardson, Fellow of St. Jude's College and a contemporary of Mr. Dawlish as an undergraduate, was on his way westwards from Oxford at the end of the Michaelmas term, and he arrived in Charton in the early afternoon. After some refreshment, in the middle of their conversation, Mr. Dawlish was pointing out some features of his new home when he found himself apologising for the state of the front garden and describing the strange stone slab; he immediately felt somewhat embarrassed at bringing this detail up as though it was the most pressing matter in the world, but Dr. Richardson seemed genuinely interested and asked to be shown it. Putting on hats and coats against the raw air, they went out and walked around the stone. Mr. Dawlish was expounding some of his theories about its origin when his friend interrupted him.

"Oh no, it is impossible that it should be a natural feature of the place. This area is chalk, and this rock is granite, which is only found at a great distance from here. Even allowing for the fashionable theories about rocks being moved by the action of water and ice, this stone could not have come here except by the deliberate action of man, and that with considerable effort. It is a very hard material. Whoever put this here intended it to last until Judgement Day."

They then began to speculate about how deeply it might be embedded and so how much effort would be required to prise it up. His guest appeared to share his interest in it, if only out of politeness, so Mr. Dawlish fetched a spade from the stable and found a spot along the edge of the slab which was not an impenetrable tangle of roots; with an effort, he forced the blade into the hard ground and dug out a small amount of soil. After a second attempt, they peered into the scrape which he had made: the stone ended only a couple of inches down, and there was soil beneath. They tried another spot on the other side, with exactly the same result: unless the stone was tapered on the underside, it had been merely laid on the surface and had settled a little by virtue of its weight and the action of rain softening the ground. It would therefore be comparatively easy to move.

"If it were not for its unfinished state," commented Dr. Richardson, "the other side of that wall would perhaps be a fitter setting for such a piece of work." A sudden gust of chill wind as the sun set made them both shiver.

That night, the dream returned: the vicar saw the slab again covered with brambles, and as he pushed into it, the brambles turned to hands, as before. But now they seized him hard and pulled him into their midst and down, towards the slab, and towards a face which, mercifully, passed from his recollection within moments of starting to awake. And so it would be every night: he would remember and recognise the face when in his dream, but forget it completely when he returned to the waking world.

About three weeks before Christmas Day, just as the first flakes of snow began to flutter down tentatively from a leaden sky, four men arrived from Sherborne, the nearest sizeable town, with a cart and some tools and stout wooden poles. The offer of a free granite slab to be carried from only a few miles away had tempted a monumental mason to take the stone off his hands; the idea had come to the vicar as a result of his friend's dry joke. The men dug holes on opposite sides of the block, straight down and then inwards so that they would meet in the middle and create a tunnel under it. They then did the same further along, and passed ropes through the tunnels, which they tied together; a single rope then lashed these loops together and was passed over a pulley suspended from a structure of poles erected over the block. By hauling on this rope, the men lifted the slab straight up. Their cart was backed into the waste ground from the lane, through the gap which would later be closed off with some of the dismantled stones from the garden wall which had been kept back; it was taken right up under the suspended slab, which was then lowered. The men took down their poles, loaded them onto the cart and drove off slowly with their load.

Mr. Dawlish stared at the patch left behind, a depressed rectangle of bare earth amidst the wrecked vegetation, edged with the exposed roots and stalks of the weeds which had thriven in the shelter of the stone. He did not feel the triumph he had expected to feel; perhaps that would come when order had been restored here and it was covered over with lawn and flowerbeds. He shivered from the cold and went indoors to his fire. That night, his nightmare was so bad that he woke up with a scream and hastily scrambled to light two candles, which he left burning for the rest of the night, though he could not recall exactly what had scared him so badly.

The next day he heard the shocking news. Although moving at a slow walking pace, the horse had slipped, presumably on some ice, on a slope of the Downs near Wooton Glanville; the stone had shifted in the same direction and the cart had turned over. The slab had landed on two of the men, who had been sitting on that side and who had been thrown to the ground: One had had both legs crushed and was likely to lose them, and the other had died instantly from severe skull fractures. The driver had a broken arm and ribs; the fourth man was lucky to have sustained only a sprained ankle, and had been able to hobble to the nearest house for help. The shock of the cart overturning and the sickening crunch of the falling slab came so vividly into his imagination that the vicar cried out, where he stood in the churchyard, and fainted to the ground; the parishioners who had brought the news carried him into his house and put him on his bed, still in his clothes, to recover. He awoke to find it dusk already; Mrs. Williams would be coming very soon to prepare his evening meal. His curtains had not been closed. He got off the bed and walked across to attend to this; he happened to look down into his garden and the lane; it had snowed while he had slept, and the rising full moon lit up the white coating and made it seem like inverted day rather than night, with the brightness below and the darkness above. He pulled the curtains together.

When the housekeeper was preparing to leave, her husband appeared at the house to collect her, as he had the night before; this was a new development, and Mrs. Williams herself seemed not to have expected it. When Mr. Dawlish suggested that it was because of the harsher weather and the danger of his wife having a fall, the grim farrier said merely, "mebbes", which Mrs. Williams apologetically expanded. He saw them out and down his front path, really so that he could stand for a moment at his front door looking at the wintry scene, which stirred even his dull sense of wonder a little. He noted, from the footprints in the snow along the edge of his garden, that the farrier must have come in through the gap in the front wall rather than by the gate.

His dream that night was different: so much he knew when he awoke in the early hours and shivered by his candles. The rapidly-fading memory of near-sleep was of the slab in the waste ground still, but now it was devoid of brambles; nor was it a snowy, nocturnal scene, but one lit by the brightness of a setting autumn sun, with lush green grass around the stone. There were other strange features: the garden wall was not there, and behind the slab was a thatched building which he did not recognise. As he walked towards the slab, he became aware of someone sitting on it, facing away, though he could not raise his eyes against the low sun to see it clearly. When he reached the slab, the figure turned, and that was when his own muffled cry roused him from the vision.

A letter arrived the following morning from the Reverend Theophilus Hale, rector of St. Mark's, Stoke Armitage, a parish close by, and it was handed to Mr. Dawlish by Mrs. Williams as she passed almostly silently into the kitchen, evidently in more of a rush than usual. He noted smudges of ash on it, and wandered into the parlour with a vague idea of asking Mary to be more careful, only to find her not there and the fire struggling to catch. Mrs. Williams followed him in:

"I be very sorry, sir, but you see as 'ow we be a bit short-handed this morning, as they say, and I be trying to make the breakfast as well as light the fire."

"And why is that? Is the girl ill, or just unreliable?"

"Oh no, sir, don't think badly of 'er, though she is not what you might call regular ill."

"Well, an explanation, if you please, of why my staff are not at their prescribed duties."

"You see, sir;" and there was a pause, not the pause of one who had no words – Mrs. Williams was never such – but almost the opposite; the pause not of one feeling inferior and embarrassed, but of one trying to be kind by limiting what could be said. "She 'ad, like, an accident as she was coming in in the dark this morning, sir; a fall, as it might be, where the stones are out at the front; well, sir, she says she was pushed over by some ragamuffin a-'iding in the shadows, and there was a struggle and she was scratched on the face, but she got to the door and we patched her up and Williams took 'er 'ome just a few minutes ago. She was very shaken by it, sir, and I doubt she'll come again in the dark."

"Pushed over, on my own doorstep? By a, a ragamuffin? I have never heard of such an outrage! What sort of a place have I come to? Does she say who it was?"

"No sir, and from 'ow she describes the attacker, it weren't nobody that she might recognise, but something she imagined in the dark, in her fear. I doubt there be anything as might be gained from questioning 'er, sir, and 'er nerves is still bad, poor thing."

Muttering angrily to himself that he had thought to have left such behaviour behind in the more squalid parts of the town, with some scathing comments about the dangers of secret gin-drinking, he failed to grasp the inconsistency in the cook's account. He opened his letter as Mrs. Williams, relieved at being pressed no further, returned to firelighting and cooking.

In the letter, Mr. Hale apologised for neglecting to make contact with his new colleague sooner, pleading indisposition from a recent fever. Wishing Mr. Dawlish well in his new post, he suggested a meeting in the near future for social purposes as well as for discussion of matters of concern to them both; Mr. Dawlish felt no need of either, but, conforming to the etiquette expected of him, sent a reply to the effect that he would be very pleased to receive Mr. Hale the following week.

The attendance at communion that Sunday morning was a little thinner than it had been, even allowing for the absence of the Colonel and his family, who were visiting in Bath, but the presence of less than a dozen at vespers, usually well attended, came as a shock. The congregation hurried away into the darkness at the end of the service with their lanterns, but the vicar did manage to catch the verger and asked him if there was any particular reason for the poor showing that day. The man made some uncharacteristically hesitant remarks about the cold and the drawing in of the nights, but seemed unable to meet the clergyman's gaze and to be anxious to be off himself. Mr. Dawlish was deep in thought and unaccustomed self-doubt as he made his way into the lane and then through his gate: surely it could not be anything he had done, anything he had said in the sermon that morning, which had offended them? He slept especially badly.

It snowed again that night, and when Mr. Dawlish ventured out to take morning prayers in the church he was displeased to see that he had had trespassers in his garden – probably had been having them unawares for some time: for there were lines of footprints in the snow running from the lane, through the gap of the waste ground and along the side of his house. They went both into and out of his garden, and down the lane into the village. He surmised that the locals were using the gap to cross to the fields behind the church, vaulting his back garden wall, and had probably been accustomed to using the waste ground for this purpose for generations. He chose not to remember that the strip had been quite impassable before it was cleared, and not to notice that at least one set of prints appeared to go across the front of his house and round the further corner, but he resolved that the gap should be blocked off as soon as possible, even if the season was not suitable for the construction of the section required to complete his front wall.

Two loafers were soon recruited from the inn to pile up the stones which had been kept for this purpose into a low barrier connecting the existing wall and that of the churchyard. It would not stop a serious trespasser, but was at least a sign that the route was not authorised. Nevertheless, that night the vicar was awoken by the sound of the stones being disturbed, as though someone was climbing over them; he chose not to investigate, for fear of appearing ridiculous, confronting his own parishioners in his nightgown.

In the middle of the following morning, Mr. Hale arrived at the vicarage; he was fifty years of age, and had been at St. Mark's for a little over twenty of those years. His bluffness was more a result of a quick and sometimes impatient intelligence than of a lack of courtesy, and his stoutness more from time spent in study and devotion than from indulgence. He paused in the lane for a few moments, looking thoughtfully at the alterations Mr. Dawlish had made to the front of the vicarage – he had been a frequent visitor in the days of Mr. Wise – as his horse snorted hot breath into the frosty air. The two clergymen were soon installed with a glass of wine each in front of the fire in the study. As Hale had not met Dawlish before, he had nothing against which to measure his present demeanour, but it was clear that the new vicar seemed nervous and was probably suffering from lack of sleep – whether from anxiety over his new duties or from some other cause he could not tell. The older man soon brought up the subject of the changes in the garden, allowing his host to go on for some time about what he had discovered from the old plans, how the weeds and the garden wall had been removed, and what his intention was concerning the gap at the front. For some reason he did not understand himself, he omitted mention of the granite slab, until Mr. Hale mentioned hearing about the unfortunate accident of the cart and then listened in attentive silence while Mr. Dawlish described the finding, the appearance and the fate of the stone. When he had finished, Mr. Hale suggested that they should put on hats and coats and go outside to inspect the work.

They walked down to the pile of rubble blocking the gap, and both men looked keenly at the footprints in the frozen snow, which to Mr. Dawlish seemed more numerous than they had been the day before. Without speaking, Mr. Hale strode back along the line of tracks which ran between the churchyard and the house, and Mr. Dawlish followed, with some reluctance. The tracks did not lead to the back garden wall and into the fields; with several running to and from the lane and two sets circling the house, they all stopped and started at a point in line with the back corner of the vicarage. The place where the slab had been. The snow here was all disturbed and muddied by some activity there had been at this spot.

Mr. Hale noticed the strange expression on his host's face. "What is the matter? Whose footsteps are these?"

Mr. Dawlish admitted he did not know, and, as his teeth chattered from the sharp frost, he clumsily told of the mystery of the nightly visitors; he also felt compelled to mention the significance of that spot, the previous location of the slab, glad for once in his life to have someone in whom he could confide what might seem foolish told in another setting. Mr. Hale again looked thoughtful, and they returned indoors.

"I know nothing of the curious stone you found; from what you say about the state of the place in which it was discovered, I suspect no-one living had ever seen it until that day. I do not believe Mr. Wise knew of it; certainly he never spoke of it. But I do know that he would never have disturbed the strip of ground between his land and the church, even though it is technically part of the vicarage grounds and it has been a blighted wilderness all my time here. When I questioned him once as to his enduring of such a blemish next to his well-tended garden, he told me that he had been solemnly instructed by his predecessor to leave it strictly alone, though he was given no reason for this curious injunction. He understood the message had been handed on from one incumbent to the next, time out of mind, and no doubt he would have passed it on to you had he not died so unexpectedly."

Mr. Hale's story both intrigued and disturbed Mr. Dawlish, though he could think of no reason why the waste ground should have been preserved in this way. When his guest had gone, promising to return at once should he need any help, he walked slowly round to the side of the house and stared for some time at the footprints. They were considerably smaller than those he himself would make, and, while not those of an unshod foot, lacked the clear shape which the impress of the heel and sole of a boot or shoe would show. He moved to the spot where the stone had lain on the surface. He must have slipped on one of the footprints which had partly melted and refrozen, making a small slippery patch of thin ice, because he suddenly fell headlong onto the ground, where the snow was churned up and mixed with the earth beneath. He lay for a moment winded and shocked by the pain of having banged his forehead and nose, though this was mitigated by the soft snow, and his eyes were blinded with tears; then he began to ease himself up – but he could not: he felt that the snow, or rather something in the snow and earth, held him, gripped the front of his coat, then pulled his chest and face down. He could not raise his head; he could see nothing, and he began to fight for breath as his mouth and nose filled with the snow. He felt he was being drawn into the ground, and suddenly his forgotten dreams came to him from his subconscious mind: the hands in the brambles, the figure seated on the slab, the face of something unutterably ancient and evil and twisted out of all human form by that antiquity and iniquity. He felt himself sucked into the earth, out of the realm of air and light and all that was wholesome.

Mr. and Mrs. Williams had found him lying unconscious by the side of the house, face down in the snow and half-suffocated by it, when she had come (now always accompanied by her husband when she went to or from work) to prepare his dinner. They had looked for him when they found the front door open and no-one inside; the brawny farrier had carried him into the house, and now he found himself propped up against a chair, on the floor in front of the study fire, wrapped in a blanket. Mrs. Williams was chafing his frozen hands back to life, and then applied a glass of brandy to his mouth. The spirit, to which he was not accustomed, burnt his cracked lips. Mr. Williams was standing watching him, and then produced the longest speech the vicar had yet heard from him:

"There be things as be best left alone."

28

Mrs. Williams turned impatiently and hushed him briefly.

"There, there, sir, pay no mind to Williams. You do 'ave 'ad a fall on the ice and it knocked you back, and you've got a chill from lying out there, sir, but you'll be fine once you've got warm again and 'ad a bit of a rest, I'm thinking."

The vicar could do no more than nod a little, and then took some more of the proffered brandy, which this time made him cough.

"That's right, sir, you get that stuff out o' your lungs."

The next two days, which Mr. Dawlish spent in bed, were divided between fevered dreams of the now-accustomed kind and wakeful periods in which he was troubled by fears born of the nightmares and the night-time. However, thanks to Mrs. Williams' ministrations and an encouraging visit from Mr. Hale (who questioned the housekeeper in detail about the incident but did not mention it in the presence of the victim), on the Sunday morning, the last of Advent, he felt physically strong enough to take the communion service, though his spirit was scarcely up to it. The congregation was again disappointingly sparse, but he consoled himself with the thought that some might have assumed he was too ill to hold the service, and that the return of the Colonel in the next day or two would set the example needed to ensure a better turn out for the Christmas period. In the late morning, while he was still resting from his exertions, Mr. Hale returned, with Williams the farrier and Mr. Shaw, the verger, and made what seemed to him an absurd suggestion.

"Williams here went into Sherborne the other day and noticed that the stone slab which you had removed from the garden here is still lying by the roadside where the cart overturned. I have made enquiries of the mason who was to have had it, and he is adamant that he wants nothing more to do with it, as he deems it to be ill-omened after – what happened. As far as he is concerned, it belongs to anyone who cares to move it. I have come to propose to you that it should be brought here and put back where it came from."

He finished briefly, with no explanation, and Mr. Dawlish felt that there was much unsaid. He protested that it was a ridiculous idea: it was no longer his worry, it was down to the mason who now owned it to clear it from the road, and he would have nowhere to put it in his new garden. Mr. Hale indicated that he was missing the point, but was unwilling to explain himself; instead, he urged Mr. Dawlish to ride out with him, if he felt at all strong enough, and see the stone where it lay. Mr. Dawlish tried to dismiss this idea, but the others joined in persuading him and in his weakened condition he submitted, as he would clearly get no peace until they had done this.

"Tell me, Mr. Dawlish," said Hale, "did you notice an inscription or other marks on the stone?"

"No; nothing at all."

"But you did not get to see the underside?"

"The underside? What would there be on the underside?"

"Perhaps nothing; perhaps not."

The two clergymen rode out along the snowy road for a few miles, until they came to the slope near Wooton Glanville; here they slowed, as the way was quite treacherous and it had snowed several times since the accident, though there was no disguising the great piece of stone which lay part on the roadway and part in the hedgerow beside it. It was almost devoid of snow; Mr. Dawlish could see how it might not cling to the sides, but was surprised the top had only the lightest dusting on it. Mr. Hale, however, explained that he had already been to see it and had actually swept it clean; the reason for this was to become clear.

"The stone actually turned over in the course of the upset, so that the side now uppermost is the one you have not seen, which was previously in contact with the ground. You should also know that the villagers had preserved certain ancient stories concerning it which had, as far as I am aware, not been related to newcomers until Williams came to me with them. You must excuse him: he felt that he did not want to trouble you in your illness, but he was concerned because of his wife's frequent presence at the vicarage. You shall understand presently," he added, as the other looked alarmed.

Mr. Hale dismounted and took from his saddle a short-handled brush; he advised Mr. Dawlish to remain mounted so as to have a better view. He brushed vigorously at the top of the slab, and indicated to the other that he should look at the exposed area. At first, he could see nothing on the roughly cut surface beyond some gouges and marks amidst the natural blemishes and the adhering spots of snow and ice, but when Mr. Hale began to move his fingers round these in one direction they resolved themselves into shallow, crudely carved letters. There had indeed been an inscription on the slab, but on the underside. Mr. Dawlish strained to read: *Whatsoever ye shall bind on earth shall be bound in heaven: and whatsoever ye shall loose on earth shall be loosed in heaven.*

"Matthew, chapter 18, verse 18."

"Exactly so," said Mr. Hale.

This was on the central part of the slab, and was the most carefully executed part. The rest was done less precisely and less deeply, merely scratched onto the hard rock as though in a hurry. Mr. Dawlish continued to read as Mr. Hale brushed at the rest. At one end of the slab, what one might term the top, was the injunction from Exodus, *Thou shalt not suffer a witch to live*, followed by the initials AG and the date *Anno Domini 1650*. At the bottom, *And I will cut off witchcrafts out of thine hand.*

"The prophet Micah, I believe."

"Indeed."

"But what does it all mean?"

"In the absence of any documents from the period, it is of course hard to tell, but I think we can safely assume a burial which could not be permitted in consecrated ground, and which could not even be countenanced on any other land, private or common. I would take the first and last parts of the inscription to be in the nature of a criminal charge, or at least a justification for what was done to "AG", if that refers to the one convicted rather than to her judge. Assuming the former to be a woman, of course."

"I begin to understand..."

"We may perhaps go on to surmise a pastor setting an example of Christian charity by donating a piece of his own garden – or perhaps just being desperate to dispose of the body somewhere, in the face of general hostility."

"But if the burial was so hurried and so furtive, and of a wretched outcast, why would someone go to the trouble and expense of such a massive monument?"

Mr. Hale sensed that Mr. Dawlish had not quite grasped the implication of the central section of text.

"I should think it is not really in the nature of a monument, as we should understand the nature of a monument to be – a memorial or commemoration. Hence the fact that it is set so far back from the lane and has been walled off and abandoned." Mr. Dawlish still expressed puzzlement. "Perhaps, perhaps the verse from Matthew is not so much an article of faith as a, for want of a better word, a charm. Perhaps the function of the stone was to keep something in. Or, more exactly, to keep it – down..."

The events of the past few days, the footprints, the nocturnal scrabbling on the stones, his own experience on the ground, all suddenly leapt together in Mr. Dawlish's mind to make an awful coherent sense, and he gave a faint cry and swayed in his saddle as though he would fall. Mr. Hale caught his reins and held a hand up to his side to steady him. He dismounted shakily, and Mr. Hale continued to prop him up as they stood in front of the menacing shape.

"We can only guess at the terrible events which led to this outcome, in the dark days around the Great Rebellion, but those alive at the time clearly took the matter seriously, as we now see they had good cause to do, in the light of your recent experiences. I suggest that we do what we can to return things as closely as possible to how they were, and hope that these troubles will pass."

Mr. Dawlish, who had been shaking his head in astonishment, nodded his consent, and they remounted, the older man leading the younger's horse and watching over him as they returned to the vicarage. Mr. Dawlish retired to his bed again, and Mr. Hale entered into earnest discussions with Williams and Shaw, overcoming their reluctance with suggestions of what might befall if they did not act swiftly to put matters right. It was now mid-afternoon, and the sun was already sinking, so that it was too late to do anything that day, but the word was spread around the village that no-one should venture out that night (as they had in fact been avoiding doing since the slab's departure), and Mr. Hale stayed at the vicarage. Mr. Dawlish's night-terrors were dreadful, and he fell asleep only as the dawn broke.

As soon as the sun was fully if weakly up, a team of village men, led by Mr. Hale, Williams and Shaw, set out with their stoutest cart, and they manoeuvred the slab onto it with great effort. As they commenced the return journey, a snow storm blew up, a blizzard in their faces as though trying to slow them until the early dusk should fall. They persevered, and brought the block back to the vicarage, where a group of women and children had been shifting the stones blocking the gap; the cart was backed into the waste ground and the stone was tipped out where the snow had been scraped back to reveal the depression it had previously made.

The following day, the Colonel returned, and Theophilus Hale and the verger went to the Manor House to explain what had happened. They all went at once to the vicarage, and lengthy discussions were held, the results of which included the writing of long letters to the Earl by both the Colonel and Mr. Dawlish and the departure of the latter by coach, with his few possessions but without a word to anyone except his fellow cleric and Mrs. Williams, on Christmas Eve, just as a curate known to Mr. Hale arrived to cover the Christmas services in Charton.

Some weeks later, Mr. Hale received a brief and somewhat stilted letter from Mr. Dawlish, thanking him for his assistance and assuring him that his nerves had largely recovered. The Earl had taken some responsibility for what had happened to him, and he was about to depart for Derbyshire to take up a tutoring position for which his patron had recommended him. Meanwhile, the granite slab had been repositioned exactly on the spot it had occupied. Some of the stones taken from the garden wall had instead been built into an enclosure three yards square, one side being the churchyard wall, all around it. This was later topped with spiked railings, within which brambles grew tall again, and it has never been entered, from that day to this.

TO BE A PILGRIM

Of all the itinerant dissenting preachers of the period covered by these chronicles, the one held most in odium by the official clergy of the country was probably Pilgrim Brown – though, in truth, the lack of sincerity behind the rhetoric which he displayed and which they despised was less dangerous to their position than the genuine zeal of some others. His very name was scorned as an affectation, though none knew if his parents had christened him thus, perhaps propelling him into his vocation, or if it was a kind of nickname acquired from his calling. The Reverend Hale was not alone in surmising that he had devised it himself as a kind of distinctive title and had actively encouraged its use; indeed, to his most devoted followers at the height of their faith, he was simply "The Pilgrim".

His method of progress across the country was not unlike that of a medieval pardoner, though without the authorisation of the established Church. Securing an introduction from one village to another, he would set up as a wayside preacher in some prominent spot and by sheer verbal and emotional force and the striking dramatic tricks of a ham actor he would attract and fire up in their quest for salvation a number of the locals, who would spread the word; thus, a crowd, as much in search of entertainment as of enlightenment, would attend his "revival" at a prominent spot by a nearby river, stream or lake. Amidst much singing of psalms, cries of alleluia, and a constant stream of loud sermonizing from Mr. Brown, volunteers would be ducked under the water and pronounced saved – for a second, very public baptism outside the established Church was a central tenet of his eclectic but quite consistent theology. The allure of the forbidden, the political overtones of the radical and the colour which he injected into proceedings attracted large numbers, especially of those who felt themselves marginalized by the genteel Anglican institution: the labourers, the independent artisans and the small shopkeepers. After between a week and a fortnight of baptismal sessions, bouts of preaching and large-scale picnics laid on by his new followers, during which time attendance at the local church might fall to as low as a fifth or even a tenth of the norm, Pilgrim Brown moved on again, taking with him substantial "contributions" to assist in his missionary work.

However, Brown always looked to move to quite a remote parish, rather than taking the obvious, efficient route of travelling from one place to the very next. He seemed to seek for a new stage where he would be unlikely to meet members of previous congregations and where news of him would be unlikely to precede him except in its newest gloss. The reason for this was simple: the seed which he spread was not such as strikes a root and takes hold, but that which springs up and soon withers on shallow soils and stony ground; and the reason for this was Brown himself, for there was no care for the fledging community of faith he left behind, no successor in his stead, no epistles of guidance. Sometimes, a few disillusioned disciples would try to follow him, but would never be able to trace his movements; nor could they pass on warnings to future victims. Meanwhile, the flame which he left at his departure flourished for perhaps three or four weeks, before beginning to fade for lack of sustenance; when it became clear to his converts that he would not return or even contact them again, which might take them some three months or more to grasp, the drift back to the parish church began, and within half a year it was as if he were only a dream, insubstantial and yet disturbing, his independent existence proved only by the diminution of their assets and the increased haughtiness of the betrayed vicar.

Many parts of Brown's performance were in the nature of set pieces which he would use in most places, while being careful not to repeat himself until his next village. For example, the local clergyman would often keep an eye on the revival at a distance, thereby inviting Brown to hold him, or rather a popular caricature of him, up as an example of the failings of the established Church, especially the institution of the tithe, which was bound to rouse popular sentiment when Brown laced his speech with half-remembered Biblical phrases which made it sound learned and convincing. If the man appeared on horseback, as if a landed gentleman, then he dealt Brown the trump card. This happened when the Reverend Tall of Travely rode to the river and sat for a while watching the baptisms from the bank.

"For believe me, my brothers and sisters in the risen Lord, there are those amongst us who would have us believe that they speak for Him and that they represent Him amongst us. But do they take up His cross and live as He did, in poverty and humility? No indeed, but they ride on fine horses and live in large warm houses which could house many, and eat great dinners which could be shared out amongst the hungry poor. Pride, and greed, and gluttony! What kind of inhuman monster can consume a tenth of what a hundred or two hundred or three hundred families can produce by the sweat of their brows? Let them beware the coming of the winnower, the fire which shall consume the weeds...."

The Reverend Tall could not take any more of this very thinly veiled assault, especially when many of his flock followed the Pilgrim's gaze and began to jeer at him; he wheeled away and spurred back towards his vicarage. But not all parishes responded in quite the same way, and Brown was disappointed when he tried the same line at Stoke Armitage: the people became quiet when he started to preach against the alleged misconduct of the clergy, even mention of the tithe failing to arouse their anger, and when they followed his eyes up the bank to where Hale sat quietly on his horse they seemed to bow their heads and look embarrassed, both at being found out by their rector and at apparently condoning by their silence what was being said against him. For once, Brown faltered, and only when his near-silence had been achieved did

Hale turn his horse around slowly and trot away. That revival never caught fire again, and Brown left two days later. On the following Sunday, Hale addressed a full congregation on the subject of the Father's capacity for forgiveness of folly, using the parable of the prodigal son as his text. The rector was relieved: he had endured the Pilgrim's visitation with only minimal harm to his flock, and should never have to suffer it again. Another few months, Hale supposed, and Brown would have visited all the parishes in the diocese which he could safely enter ahead of negative publicity, at which point his practice was to shift to another diocese.

And so he was more shocked than surprised to find Pilgrim Brown waiting for him at the vicarage after Sunday Eucharist, at about the time he would have expected him to be journeying across the country in search of more "contributions". The man was wearing a long coat into which he had tucked his beard and a broad-brimmed hat, in an effort to avoid recognition, and had slipped into Stoke Armitage at a time when he guessed that everyone interested in matters spiritual and likely to recognize him would be in the church. He stood up, twisting his hat in his hands, as Hale entered the study into which the housekeeper had shown the visitor.

"I apologise for this intrusion at your busiest time of your week. I am –"

"I am well aware of who you are, sir, and of what you are. Pray make your business brief." Hale did not encourage him to sit again.

"I had expected some hostility, sir, given my reputation amongst your class," Hale raised his eyebrows, "but I also know who you are and I believe that when you have heard something of my story you will not be entirely unsympathetic to my plight."

"And what do you presume to know of me, sir, given that we never met before and even now have barely exchanged fifty words?"

The preacher paused for a moment and looked down briefly before resuming. Hale noted that his accent was northern, perhaps Yorkshire; he had indeed wandered far. "What I know of you, sir, stems from the fruits of your works; from the fact that it was in this parish above all others in this diocese that my labours were in vain. This I ascribe to the fact that the incumbent, unlike too many of his calling, is a worthy man who cares for each of his flock, no matter how humble, making my assistance unnecessary."

"Assistance, man!" Hale could contain himself no longer, and avoided recognition of the compliment. "Have you any idea of the harm you cause, stirring up congregations, making them dissatisfied with their Church, dividing them from their pastors, and then abandoning them? Do you think that is producing – fruit?"

"My mission is to spread the word of truth, not to administer an organization. That I have to leave to men like – to others."

"Does it ever occur to you that when Our Lord Jesus Christ spread the word of God on earth He was careful to leave behind a body of men appointed to nurture what He had planted? That when St. Paul had passed through a country and left a group of converts behind, he took pains to keep in touch and continue his teaching of them through epistles, so that they should not be left without a guide? The Apostle of the Gentiles was not in the habit of taking a collection and then disappearing without a word."

"You know something of my mission, then?"

"Mission, you call it! Sir, every clergyman in the country knows what you do. Would that their congregations heeded their warnings too, and stayed away from your heinous gatherings."

41

The amateur preacher suddenly slumped back down into the seat from which he had risen, hands and hat between his knees, his head bowed. For a moment neither man spoke or moved, but a cloud descended on the scene in place of sharp discord.

"Sir, I have not come to debate the rights and wrongs of my mission with you, but on a quite different matter, and I ask you to hear me out, in your capacity as a minister of the Lord whose spiritual learning is greater than mine and whose experience is fuller and more settled and hence sounder than mine." The tone had changed. Hale sat down, leaning forward a little, still saying nothing but affording the man an opening. "Firstly, you may not be aware, since I did not stay long enough in your parish, that a regular part of my mission is normally a service of healing, which, according to numbers, may be appended to a preaching or held as a service in its own right."

Hale's anger returned, redoubled. "Healing, man! You delude the sick by pretending to heal in the Lord's name, like a quack doctor or medicine-seller? This is becoming blasphemous – "

"Please, I do understand and can sympathise with your outrage at the idea. I assure you that I have never claimed to be a healer, at least, not as a result of any powers of my own. If the Lord chooses to heal one who believes in Him and calls on Him during one of my services, so be it; how can that be sinful on my part?"

"And do the people chance to make contributions of money as a result of these – opportunities for the Lord? I believe I understand. Pray continue with your account."

After a short pause, the Pilgrim recovered his composure. "The healing starts with the singing of a psalm by the whole field," that being his usual word for his congregation, "the sick and those who have brought them or accompany them. I then pray at some length for the forgiveness of sins and the restoration of the body, and while more psalms are sung I tour the field to visit each of the sick in turn, to inquire of their afflictions and pray over them. At the end, we have a final prayer and they disperse."

"Do you lay hands on the sick, in the manner of faith healers?" Brown nodded, and so did Hale, slowly. "Most enlightening."

"Now, because mine is an itinerant mission and I seek no fixed place in which to lay my head, I rarely hear any more about the outcomes of these services. However, about six weeks ago, I was in a parish of this diocese – I believe the incumbent's name was Tall, but the name of the village eludes me; so many different places."

"Travely, the parish of St. Barnabas."

"Yes, that was it. There was a healing service, on the Saturday concluding my first week there, and about sixty people had turned up – perhaps a dozen of the seriously afflicted with one or two attendants each, and a score of individuals with lesser ailments. We began as usual with a psalm and prayers and then I went around the crowd, exchanging a few words with the individuals and spending some minutes with the little groups. One couple, very poor it seemed from their attire, had brought a boy of about six with them: he was quite lively and perfectly normal, but he had been blind for over a year, as a result of a sharp, delirious fever he had suffered. He could remember what familiar things looked like and the colours, but he had no vision whatsoever. As the case seemed hopeless – there was no way they would ever be able to afford medical attention, even if such could have helped – I could only encourage them to show patience and accept the trial the Lord had given them to bear in His name. Although they had obviously heard this many times before, it seemed to be a help to them to share their tragedy with another and encounter sympathy. I held the

43

boy's forehead in my span as we prayed together, and I moved on. When I had completed the round, we prayed again and began the last hymn. That was when I became aware of sounds of distress towards the back of the crowd, and a commotion starting; the hymn broke down as more and more people directed their attention to the source of the disturbance, and the sound of loud and excited talking replaced that of singing. I was standing debating within myself what to do when the crowd opened and the poor family were projected towards me. The little boy seemed distressed, burying his face in his mother's skirt, and the parents did not know what to say; indeed, they did not seem to know what they felt, but happiness seemed uppermost. "Oh sir, he can see! Little William can see again!" And it was true. He could tell the number of fingers put up, and describe people, and identify colours; he could not look for very long, as the unaccustomed brightness seared his eyes and the whirling images made him giddy, but see he certainly could. I called upon the people to thank God for what He had done, but they called out, "Miracle!", and that was when I became anxious, and determined to seek your advice. I am only a humble worker in the Lord's vineyard; I do not have powers, and I do not seek them. I would not know how to use them justly. To have been given this responsibility is a burden I do not want."

He was, unaccustomedly, struggling to find the right words, and Hale softened again, even finding fault with himself for hasty judgement; he would have assumed that the man would have sought to make capital out of his new reputation as a miracle-worker. But he maintained a measured and detached tone.

"I feel that you still presume too much in believing that you have been singled out especially by the Lord. The cure came some considerable time after you had set hands on the child, and not immediately. I have heard of similar cases: a failure in a sense or limb can suddenly right itself after a long period, even when suffered from birth. The cure is not always permanent, in fact, and the impediment can return, even more tragically. It may be in this case that the excitement of the crowd and the unaccustomed noise released something in the child – presumably with God's blessing, but not necessarily through your intervention. If you have been given a sign in this, it is perhaps not that you are so favoured but that you should not even risk simulating the true healer, but concern yourself only with the salvation of the soul. This bartering with God, of faith for good health, smacks to me of the Papists praying to their statutes for prosperity!"

And so Pilgrim Brown was sent on his way with stern injunctions not to presume to heal and to content himself with spreading the gospel and praising God, if such was his wish; his ego was perhaps a little deflated, but justly so. However, Hale was disturbed to see that his advice had been flouted when, three weeks later, Williamson, the verger, brought him a fortnight-old copy of the Messenger, the newspaper of a small town twenty miles away which his sister there passed on regularly. The most prominent piece in it related how, only a few days after Brown's meeting with Hale, a local man who had suffered from a paralysed tongue for years, following a severe infection, had suddenly been able to speak properly again in the middle of one of his preachings – beginning with a great "Alleluia!". The man's speech, which had been little more than an incoherent slobbering, had sudden become normal, apart from the effects of disuse, and was gaining in articulation by the hour. The article made no use of the "m"-word, but its tone was serious and laudatory. Hale was saddened to see that his words had gone unheeded, and that Brown's apparent change of heart had so soon reversed itself into publicity-seeking. So he was very surprised when the man appeared again at the rectory, under cover of darkness, looking haunted and distressed rather than triumphant.

"He was the cousin of the owner of the newspaper, and the story was ideal material for publication; there was no way I could have prevented it coming out, though I begged them to keep it quiet. God knows I did not want it to happen again; it was not even a healing service – following your advice, I have given those up. Look at me: I am practically a fugitive; even where I have perhaps let down the people in the past by moving on, all has been forgotten apart from these cures, and I am pursued by crowds begging for healing for themselves and others. You cannot imagine what it is like to open your host's door in the morning and find a mob of cripples and blind men, parents holding up sick infants and children carrying parents on stretchers, all crying out for your help, when you know there is nothing you can do for them. You try the back door, but there is a group waiting there too; all you can do is run and try to get past them as they screech and clutch and tear, and as you get away – for at least they are all aged or lame or short of breath – you can hear entreaties turning into demands and finally into curses at your meanness."

The Pilgrim was now sobbing into his hands. From the state of him, he had apparently had few chances to wash or shave for some days, and sleep and food had been in short supply too; he was almost spent. Hale softened yet again. He slipped out to the kitchen and returned with a tankard and the remains of a pie, which the Pilgrim fell on without a word, eating and drinking as he continued to weep. At length, he finished and thanked Hale, who suggested they pray at once for spiritual strength and assistance. Brown nodded assent and knelt; Hale lit a candelabrum on the sideboard behind them and turned back, making the sign of the cross. "Lord Jesus Christ, who knowest the fallible condition of man, we call on Thee to look down in Thy infinite mercy on these humble sinners and bring peace to their troubled souls. Our Father, who art in heaven, hallowed be Thy name – "

A sudden and terrifying change came over the Pilgrim; instead of joining in the paternoster, he made an inhuman rasping sound, combining the growling of a dog and the spitting of a cat, though much louder and deeper. He lashed out at Hale, but from his kneeling position he only succeeded in falling on all-fours. As Hale took a couple of paces back and reached out for the heavy candelabrum, the Pilgrim looked up at him, snarling; his jaws fell open, and a rough voice came from him, though none of his organs of speech seemed to be involved.

"Enough of a torment to have to endure hearing this fool ranting on about the Nazarene for hour after hour; without you joining in – and you actually believe in what you say, which makes it intolerable!"

The Pilgrim writhed and shook, like a dog drying itself, and a stream of the foulest language Hale had ever heard poured out of his mouth; some of the words he knew from the alehouses of Oxford, some he had come across by accident and could guess an approximate meaning for, but some were entirely unknown to him. The Pilgrim's eyes rolled in his head, and he strained upwards on his knees, his hands clawing the air. Hale stepped back again, brandishing the candle holder and shouting "No!" repeatedly in his panic. He frantically looked about him for some other means of defence, should it come to that. The Pilgrim fell silent, but began to shuffle towards Hale, who saw with horror that only the whites of his eyes showed. Faith came to his aid, without his thinking it. He pulled the two long candles out and threw aside his one substantial weapon: he held one candle in each hand and crossed them before him, stepping forward as he did so and calling out, "In the name of Our Lord Jesus Christ, withdraw!" The thing that had been Mr. Brown threw up its arms, howling hideously, and fell backwards with shock, striking its head on the floor. It lay still. Hale risked peering over; the face had returned to the normal appearance of the Pilgrim. He knelt and prayed earnestly for several minutes, then brought water and revived the man. As he recovered, Hale helped him to a chair; his head had been banged quite severely and he had a lump, and his knees hurt greatly from the strain of the awkward backwards fall on them, but otherwise he seemed to be as he had been before the seizure.

"What happened? Did I faint? I seem to have had a bad fall. My head – "

"I am afraid you have suffered rather more than that. I hesitate to use sensationalist language, but, from the little I know of such matters, it would appear that you may have been the victim of a case of what is known as demoniac possession."

Even after a lengthy description from Hale of what had happened, repeated, Brown could not take it in.

"But how could that have been inside me, surrounded by prayer and godliness all the day?"

"It must be a very strong and malicious demon, and it seems to have strong powers of resistance to hearing the name of the Lord and seeing His symbols – especially as it senses insincerity in your use of them. But at least we know that true faith and sincere prayer, exercised with a little courage, can overcome it. You have not had such an attack before?"

Brown shook his head. "Not to my knowledge. But perhaps, as you say, this is the first time it has had to confront true religion." Nevertheless, he still did not really understand or accept Hale's interpretation of events and so was not yet properly afraid. "I must have had some sort of fit and fainted. My head hurts."

Hale shook his head in turn. "It won't do, man; you need help to get rid of an evil that is no part of you but is within you." At once the Pilgrim's face changed, and Brown sprang from the chair, straight into the air without the use of his arms for support. His hands fastened around Hale's throat and his legs were wrapped around his waist. Hale fell backwards, fortunately onto the cushions of the settle; had he fallen to the ground and been stunned or even winded it would have been all over with him. Struggling desperately, he tried in turn to throttle his opponent, but Brown's bottom jaw dropped open and his neck seemed to expand by inches, and the great cavern of a mouth breathed a foul sulphurous vapour into the rector's swelling face. Hale's legs were still free: kicking against the settle, he rolled the two of them off it onto the floor, so that he was on top. The blow loosened Brown's grip for a moment so that Hale could take a breath and reach out a hand to the fireplace; he grabbed whatever he touched first and brought it down smartly on Brown's forehead. The object came into view: it was a small log. He hit him twice more, and that was enough. Anxiously checking that he had not injured him seriously, and relieved that he had not been forced to use an iron poker, Hale disentangled himself.

When Brown came round, he was surprised to find that his ankles had been firmly bound together with a curtain-tie; his head hurt abominably, and he could feel a large plaster on his forehead. Although it was dark, he understood himself to have been carried or dragged into St. Mark's church, and to be sitting slumped in the front pew. Shortly, he could make out the high arches of the windows through which shone stars and moon. In front of him, sitting on the sanctuary steps, was Reverend Hale, with a book in his hands. The double candelabrum was on the floor next to him, making a small pool of light. He noticed his waking and spoke: "I am sorry about the cord, but I need to slow you down a little, should you, or that which is within you, decide to attack me again. Pray do not attempt to remove it. What do you last remember?"

"We were talking – no, we were praying; I am not sure why. I was kneeling and you lit candles."

"Just so – we were praying, and that is precisely what caused the evil to take over your body. What happened in the next few minutes – "

"No, wait. Oh my God!" Confusion and horror struggled in his face as some thought troubled him and was put aside with great difficulty. "What did you mean – attack you again?"

"I don't suppose you remember it, as you were not in control then. No; well, sufficient to say that you had me by the throat and I was within an inch of my life; I am afraid that I had to use force to save myself – hence the pain in your head."

Brown groaned and clutched his brow. "I do have an idea of something of the sort happening – but as one might recall a bad dream, as a general emotion and a hazy picture, not clear and full like a real memory of the past. I seem to remember us grappling and falling to the ground, but not why we were behaving so out of character, and the very fact that we were fighting, and so fiercely, makes it unreal and fantastical. Wait; there was something about a demon. That was not part of the dream – you were telling me that I was possessed by a demon. I must have dreamt it. Dear God, what is going on?"

Standing, Hale shook his head sadly. "I am sorry, but it was, and is, no dream. I believe a malicious, destructive spirit has taken up residence inside your body, and from time to time it takes over. It requires firm and immediate action."

"But I don't understand. Surely such things only happened in Biblical times? And why would it choose me, when it could inhabit a true sinner? Living a life of preaching and praying must be torment for it. It makes no sense."

Hale snorted. "You have just explained it yourself. You do not believe yourself to be a sinner – you see yourself as a saint, when really there is no sincerity in your religion. You are the perfect vehicle for this thing, travelling around giving false hope to the people. Turning them against the Church. Building up the Pilgrim until the day when his little world is brought crashing down. It may be that the healing came from this source rather than a divine one, so as to discredit religion in the long run."

Taking up the light, Hale walked around the sanctuary, lighting in turn candles which he had set up wherever he could: candles in short candlesticks and domestic holders placed on the altar, candles in tall candlesticks lined up around the walls, stumps of candles just within reach on window ledges and in odd niches. Behind them, overhead, the clock struck two. As each candle reinforced its neighbours and was reflected in the glass of the windows and the brass of plaques and containers, the entire chancel of the church was slowly illuminated until everything below three or four yards high was clearly visible, including the standing cross on the altar and the larger version on the wall behind; above, the shape of the huge cross hanging from the ceiling pressed down towards them from the surrounding gloom.

As soon as he had taken all this in, Brown felt himself slipping away into a state somewhere between consciousness and unconsciousness but from which he would remember very little, and that so fragmentary and meaningless as to be rejected by his waking brain out of hand. Hale saw the change on his face, this time mixed with fear induced by the setting, and faced up to it in language which chimed in with the fragments of prayer and scripture with which he interspersed his words. "Knowest thou where thou art? The very house of God!" A growl. The being was strong and determined, but it was not in fact very intelligent and did not always understand the details of its surroundings or the capabilities of the body it inhabited. It attempted to spring up and

51

clamber over the pew to get at Hale, without realising the significance of the cord round Brown's feet, and the man crashed down on the kneeler between the seats. It began to drag itself along to get to the end of the row, but Hale appeared there, holding aloft the cross and torch.

In truth, Hale did not really know what he was doing. He had never experienced anything like this before and had never paid much attention to the business of exorcism. All he could do was employ appropriate words and rely on faith to overcome evil. He was not being courageous so much as desperate: he was mortally afraid of what he was facing, but sensed that he had not to show weakness in the face of the fiend. Ultimately, at the back of his mind was the knowledge that he was standing in his own church, in the house of God, and was as safe there as he could possibly be from the forces of evil. And yet the thing seemed able to survive and even thrive there....

"I command thee and bind thee in the name of the living God whom all must obey, good and evil, living and not living, of this world and others." The thing thrashed around in its confined space in the pew, swearing and cursing, until Hale began to fear that it must be doing Brown serious harm. "I command thee be still!" And he pushed the cross close up to the twisted face as he shouted his commands over and over until it subsided and lay panting. "Tell me thy name! By the power of Our Lord Jesus Christ, who cast out the unclean spirit Legion, I command thee to name thyself!" This took some more time, as the thing knew as well as Hale did that having its proper name would give him some power over it. At length, having writhed and cursed itself weary, amidst blasphemies and expletives it shouted out what sounded like "Shamset".

"Shamset I name thee and bind thee by the power of the living God to answer me. What dost thou in the body of our brother Brown? How camest thou there and for what end, Shamset?"

Hale's interest was partly academic and partly practical in wanting to understand the nature of the thing with which he was dealing. The spirit was more amenable when its name was used, and it began to speak more freely, as though to itself, in between bouts of hideous gurgling laughter and volleys of obscenity and with many sudden changes of pitch and volume. Hale tried to follow and remember as much as he could hear and understand.

"Some of us attend on human emotion... drawn by emotion, passion, erotic or religious... food for those without feeling... inspires us empty, drives us... the empty feeding on feelings... and at such a moment of noise and emotion I passed into this world of senses and into this creature whose soul was so thin despite his loud words... room for me and me empowered by empty voices and desires." From this, Hale surmised that the thing had actually entered Brown during a preaching session, drawn by the energy of the crowd. "Where least expected, safest from detection and from harm; but the cost – his ranting about his master... every word burning... and the symbols and the singing and the torment, but not all the time, not like hell, and at least his words are empty; not like here, in this cursed place... and sometimes I am me. I say to him, mock them, the fools... make them beg and give... fill them with vain hopes, empty and precious, then leave them... make pain... disappointment... then faithless, empty, alone. He thinks he does good. I mock him."

Hale felt he understood enough, and began to worry that the thing might be regaining strength and planning its next move. He moved to the altar, and took up blessed water to sprinkle; the demon seemed to understand and began to drag Brown upright, but Hale was on him at once with his cross and prayers, and the Book of

Common Prayer. During the time when Brown had been unconscious, he had marked certain passages appropriate for such purposes, and he proceeded to read them out. The clock in the tower told the half hour and then three o'clock before he had finished the struggle. He would force the thing to be quiet, then endure a blast of energy which blew out some of the candles. He would terrify it with the name of God, then be appalled by a stream of abuse from it. At one point, it succeeded in lifting Brown two yards into the air, but Hale forced him down again into the pen formed by the pew before Shamset could launch his body at him as a missile.

"Shamset, thou unclean thing, thou hast no place with a Christian soul inside a human body. Be gone from within him, and from this world, and return to the place of damnation prepared for such as thee!"

Hale had often wondered exactly what happened when demons were said to be cast out, as in Biblical times: did they simply vanish or fade away, or could they actually be seen leaving the body? If the latter, which way did they go? Downwards seemed more appropriate if less spectacular than upwards. Now he had an answer, even if based on only one example. The thing seemed to give up as Brown collapsed again with exhaustion, and actually left his body in something approaching a material form, as well as giving up its hold on him. Hale, who had ventured very cautiously into the pew to check on the state of Brown, saw a dark shape draw out of the upper part of the man and pass partly through and partly over the front of the pew. It seemed to gather briefly in front of the chancel, being perhaps a yard high and a yard off the ground. Hale rushed round to get a better view, but he only saw its back for a couple of seconds before it disappeared. It had temporary substance but was not solid; was like a very localised gas, perhaps, but did not seem to be material as we understand it. If one looked directly at any part of it, that part seemed to fade to

54

nothing and only the parts in one's peripheral vision remained undisturbed. It seemed black, darker than the surrounding shadows, and roughly rounded, though it had no clear definition and seemed to be in permanent motion around its edges. It had what seemed to be thin limbs, how many he could not be sure, which first bent upwards and then turned down and splayed out to the sides, rather in the manner of a large spider or crane fly. Before he could be sure of anything much, it shimmered darkly and was gone.

Hale sprinkled the blessed water on the spot and made the sign of the cross repeatedly. He then returned to where Brown lay in the pew, groaning: the violent movements of the demon had battered and twisted him painfully, leaving bruises, sprains and pulled muscles, but there were no serious or permanent injuries. He helped Brown up the aisle – he could hardly walk or speak – and sat him in the porch, then went back and extinguished the candles. Locking the church door behind them, he all but carried the man across the churchyard and into the rectory. Exhausted, he could not face the stairs with his burden, and made him as comfortable as he could in front of the warm cinders in the sitting room, on a pile of cushions. One trip up and down for blankets, and then Hale went to his own bed and fell on it clothed as he was. He was awakened – it seemed minutes later – by the sound of the housekeeper coming in to make breakfast and lay the fires. He could not move fast enough to prevent her from finding Brown on the floor, but managed to limit her to one short shriek. He explained as far as he could, without any mention of demons, how he had struggled overnight for Brown's soul and swore her to secrecy for the few days that he would need to be with them to recover. (Not only did he want to prevent hordes of the Pilgrim's enthusiastic current supporters, vengeful former followers and miracle-seekers from besieging the rectory, but also he wished to avoid awkward interviews with the Archdeacon and the Bishop for sheltering the renegade and performing an unauthorised exorcism.) She accepted this, though doubtfully, in that prayer, no matter how intense, does not leave one bruised and with bumps on the head. It was politic and practical for Hale to share the secret with the verger Williamson as they prepared for the morning service, which Hale passed though almost in a daze, though moved from time to time to peer about in case there was a giant black spider lurking in the shadows.

After the service, he slept for a couple of hours, and by mid-afternoon Brown was awake too, though aching and pensive. They spoke at length about what had happened and in particular what Brown should learn from it, and it was clear that the man had had a major change of heart and would not be continuing in his former way of life. Williamson called in, and mentioned that Zebulon Nye, a local poacher, was deep in his cups at the Black Horse and telling all who would listen that St. Mark's was haunted; that he had been out very late (for what purpose he did not say) and had seen lights at one end of the church; that he had gone to investigate but had been stopped by hideous noises which had driven him off in fright. In the course of the next service, Hale apologised for any noise which may have disturbed parishioners living near the church, late at night, but repairs to the organ were best done at a time when it would not inconvenience anyone – which was true, and did not commit him to having had any such repairs done.

The next Sunday morning service was much more dramatic, the time of the full congregation being chosen for the appearance of a chastened Pilgrim Brown, introduced rather as Jack Brown when Hale led him out of the vestry after a brief sermon. Much quieter and less assertive than before, a thoughtful Brown announced that he was giving up his mission; that he had realised that his methods and his own character were inappropriate for such a role; that he had sought spiritual direction from Reverend Hale, and that as a consequence of this (and this was news to Hale) he had decided to return to his native York, where he still had family and friends who could help him start afresh. In that large city he hoped there would be opportunities to resume his former occupation. He went on to ask the parishioners to extend his apologies to any they should meet who had been misled by his activities, and to pass on to them his encouragement to seek their salvation within the organised Church, as Christ had apparently intended in setting up His own. Finally, he wanted it to be known that he had no healing powers whatsoever and that any cures which may have happened during his services were accidental, or at least not caused by him – which the people took to mean that he ascribed them to divine intervention, which was very far from what he and Hale believed.

The next day, when he felt sufficiently recovered from his ordeal and was about to take his leave, Hale asked him out of curiosity what his previous occupation had been in York – "gravedigger"; and the origins of the Pilgrim's mission suddenly became clear. Hale wished him well with all sincerity as he left, and not far away, though in a different part of the universe of things, an ancient entity known as Shamset waited at the boundary between worlds. Though it had not actually experienced feeling in itself, it had briefly been in contact with those who did, and had been close enough to understand the difference between their form of life and its own; and it was resolved to return as soon as opportunity presented itself.

ROOT AND BRANCH

The most eminent resident of the neighbourhood of Stoke Armitage, the parish of the Reverend Theophilus Hale, was probably Major-General Sir George Henry Randall, who had inherited Randall Court from his father after service in Ireland and Canada and was the twelfth of the name to be master there. An active man who had chosen the infantry over the cavalry because he preferred using his own legs, he had never taken to the sport which traditionally fitted his situation, namely riding to hounds; instead, in retirement he favoured the combat sports which had been the basis of his own professional skills and the team games with which he had promoted the fitness and organisation of the troops under him. He personally coached the sons of some of the local gentry in fencing, in the long gallery of the Court, and the sons of some of the local artisans in boxing, on a roped-off wooden dais behind the house; he sponsored the most successful cricket club, known as Randall's Volunteers, in the area, and Stoke Armitage could field in total three teams, each capable of beating all-comers from miles around, thanks to the General's provision of first-class kit and insistence on an orderly and scientific approach to both batting and bowling. In his eagerness to promote sports and games more widely, he had instituted the annual St George's Day Meeting, an afternoon of competition followed by an ox-roast in the grounds. It was the highlight of the calendar after Christmas and May Day in many respects, though most of those who attended did so for the sake of the free food and drink rather than for the athletics. The General had a notion to recreate the ancient games of Greece, but was rather thwarted in this by the unwillingness of many to take part and by mischance: the running race was always won by one of the footmen from the Court, they being selected for their speed and stamina; the discus (referred to memorably as "pitching the plate") was viewed somewhat sceptically; the javelin he dared not try to introduce. More successful was "leaping", but only after a well-wisher had suggested that the element of risk and hence of excitement could be increased by staging it over a point at which, just outside the front gates of the Court, a local stream broadened and cattle coming down to drink left an expanse of churned mud on both banks. One in three competitors fell ignominiously into the mud and every year at least one would end up in the water, to the delight of the spectators.

But the General's greatest passion, still quite unusual for the time, was archery. He believed that the proficient use of the longbow not only constituted the most effective training of body and mind and the co-ordination of the two but also had been the true seed and facilitator of the British Empire. In truth, his grasp of history was somewhat vague, and he would not have found fault with Shakespeare in the matter of striking clocks in ancient Rome and cannon in the reign of King John, but he held fast to the belief that England's glory stemmed directly from the exercise of the bow – especially when practised against the French – and he did what he could to revive the ancient custom in a way not seen since Tudor times: all of his tenant farmers had to attend the Court on alternate Sunday afternoons in the summer so that they could practise at the butts with a tankard of cider while their wives took tea on the terrace above – the last detail being a shrewd move by the General to inject some competition and seriousness into the affair. And lest this anachronistic scene should seem too absurd, entertain for a moment one some twenty years earlier, in which a Major Randall attempted to teach Canadian Indians to use the longbow in place of the shorter weapon which they had already discarded in favour of firearms.

The General had studied not only the use but also the composition and making of the longbow, and so had a particular interest in yew, the traditional material. As he frequently remarked in the hearing of the rector, yews were originally planted in churchyards in order to maintain a supply of the wood for this purpose when the tree was banished from farmland because of the poisonous nature of its seeds; it followed, he would maintain, that the yews belonged more to the bowmen than to the church and were a national military, not ecclesiastical, resource. The Reverend Hale had never risen to this idea as it had never quite occurred to him what the General was suggesting and the General had never addressed him openly and directly on the subject, but it suddenly made sense after the great storm of March the third. The devastation was much less than was the case near the coast or on higher ground, but still many trees in the neighbourhood of Stoke Armitage were damaged, snapped or completely uprooted in the terrible winds of that day. Those around the church were largely spared, but a particularly old and spreading yew, undoubtedly rotten in some places and overstretched in others, had lost a large branch, which had smashed through the churchyard wall and lay blocking the lane outside. The General arrived at the rectory at the end of the same day, risking the final gusts in order to lay a kind of moral claim to the timber; in short, he would guarantee to have the lane completely reopened the next day and the wall rebuilt the day after, free of charge, in return for the branch itself. The rector agreed without hesitation, indeed with gratitude on behalf of the village, for the job of simply moving the great limb would have outweighed its value as kindling, so the General did not need to explain his motives. It was only later that Hale remembered the link to his passion, and learnt that a guard had been placed on the lane all that night, and then he filed away the idea that the General owed him another good turn in the future.

True to his word, the General had the branch dismembered and removed piece-meal the following day, but not in a random hacking and hauling; the sound wood was carefully separated from what was rotten or shattered and carried to the Court for storage, before the rest was crudely cut up and either carted away or given as kindling to any local people who turned up. Unfortunately, whatever its merits as material for longbows, the wood of the yew did not prove very satisfactory for domestic fires: the first and only time the Reverend Hale's housekeeper used it, the rectory was filled with smoke and the cracking and spluttering once the fire had taken hold recalled musketry practice. Gossip around the village had more serious stories to tell: one child had been struck on the arm and burnt by a smouldering thumb-sized fragment, and a piece said to be bigger than an apple had flown out of one fire and smashed a mirror. All over Stoke Armitage for the following week garden fires consumed not only debris and leaves but unwanted yew logs burnt safely in the open.

Unfortunately, the great limb itself was found to be too diseased and twisted to be of use for bows, but a shoot from it, eight feet long and nearly straight, was sound and of exactly the dimensions the General required; fortunately, it had been growing upwards and had suffered no damage in the fall. The General viewed the rest of the tree wistfully, but it was sound enough, and sounder now that a diseased limb had been removed; in any case, its total loss would have ruined the symmetry of the four great yews at the cardinal points of the compass around the church. In fact, as the General guessed, the yews and the enclosure they marked out pre-dated the church, their twenty-foot girth proclaiming an age of at least a millennium and a half as against the less than a millennium since the foundation of St. Mark's. He had the torn part of the damaged tree cleaned up and sealed, and consigned it to the care and use of future generations.

Almost a year passed, the precious yew bough having been stored in the stables of the Court to dry. At last, the General could contain himself no longer and began work in order to have the bows ready for shooting in the spring. Having already successfully made bows from ash and elm, he had no qualms about undertaking the making of the bows himself, initially assisted by the man he called his forester, otherwise the gamekeeper, who contrived to strike the back of his left hand a firm blow with a mallet while driving in wedges, which put him partly out of action with bandages and slings for a fortnight. The shoot was split lengthways into four staves, from each of which a bow six feet long would be made. It was a pity that it was timber from a branch and not a trunk, said the General to all his visitors as they were taken to see the work in progress, as the latter was always much stronger and more reliable. If any of his visitors chanced to express any interest in this idea, the General would recite the doggerel of part of a medieval tale of Robin Hood in which Little John was let down by such a bow and captured.

When the four bows were finished, the General tested them at length and declared them all to be good, though differing a little in quality and temperament. The best he kept for himself; of the next two, one was dispatched to his son, serving in India, in the vain hope that he would finally take an interest in archery, and one was kept at the Court for the use of distinguished visitors. The brief use of it was also allowed as a special treat, as the General saw it, for any of the tenants who distinguished themselves at the Sunday shoots. The fourth bow, despite the General's declaration, was disappointing and weaker in the pull, and so it was not that much of a sacrifice when he offered it back to the church, to hang on the wall next to the memorial to Sir Henry Randall; he had been favoured by Henry the Eighth, himself a keen promoter of the longbow, and had first built the Court out of the ruins of a small priory, a victim of the Dissolution. The rector was quite content with this: he was not being obliged to use the thing himself, and had sufficient antiquarian interest in it to compose, with the General's help, a brief account of the longbow and its part in medieval history, which he wrote out on a card to mount beside it. At a little ceremony one Sunday afternoon, during a brief but torrential storm, the bow was officially presented by the General to the rector and accepted by him, with short speeches on both sides, and was set in place on two brackets, tilted across a blank section of nave wall. The verger and two of the General's tenants, in sporting outfit and bearing bows and quivers, were in attendance, and many of the villagers not present would have remembered that moment equally clearly, for it was when a bolt of lightning struck and all but demolished the woodshed of Jacob Potts, in which much of the discarded yew wood had been kept for kindling. Nothing of that was heard distinctly inside the church, for Mr. Spaulding, the new schoolmaster, had struck up a toccata on the organ as the men congratulated themselves on the aptness and dignity of the church's latest decoration. In time, another card bearing sketched copies of medieval pictures of archers and a display of several replica medieval arrows provided by the General were added to the exhibit.

Although the Reverend Hale would not have been aware of it otherwise, something of a renewal of interest in archery was taking place in some parts of the country, amongst those with the resources and leisure to pursue it. For some, it was merely a passing Romantic fad, akin to the predilection for castles and abbeys appreciated only as atmospheric ruins, or to the dream of Arthurian chivalry in which every detail was emblazoned with heraldry; for a few, though, it was becoming a serious sport as well as an exercise in tradition. About a month after the completion of the bows, the rector's housekeeper disturbed him while he was working on his sermon, to announce a Mr. and Mrs. Crowthorne of Exeter, with a query concerning the church. The rector was somewhat vexed at the interruption, but in recognition of their supposed long journey and their interest in St. Mark's, he had them invited into the parlour for tea, and ordered some refreshment for the coachman and horses waiting outside. He soon ascertained that Mr. Crowthorne, a Devon squire, was one of the breed of new archers, who had met General Randall at several events and had suddenly thought of taking up his open invitation to visit, while passing quite close on his way home from visiting his wife's sister near Blandford. Unfortunately, they had called at the Court only to learn that the General was in Bath for a week; Mrs. Crowthorne had expressed an interest in looking in at the church before moving on, and there they had found the longbow exhibited. Hence their appearance at the rectory, in the expectation of finding another toxophilite. Reverend Hale had to disappoint them in that respect, but was able to make up for it in some degree by granting a request that Mr. Crowthorne might take down the bow and try it out.

Returning to the church with the rector, the visitor mounted a chair and took down the bow, which had a string in place but was unstrung, so as not to damage it, and so the first thing Mr. Crowthorne did was to string it for use. In case, dear reader, you are unfamiliar with the simple mechanics of this exercise, I would explain that the bowstring is shorter than the wooden bowstave, otherwise it would not bend the bow. Near each end of the stave is a groove round it, and at each end of the string is a loop to go round a groove; with one loop round one groove, the bowman must contrive to bend the stave sufficiently to be able to slip the other loop into place at the far end. Mr. Crowthorne went for the simple method of putting the strung end of the bow into the side of his foot and pushing down on the upper limb of the bow, to bend it down to the higher loop. Despite straining at it, he was a couple of inches short, and cheerlessly smiled to cover his embarrassment. "These traditional bows have so much greater draw weight than our modern ones!" he explained. He slipped off the lower loop, and put the upper loop round the upper limb of the stave, so that it slipped down to the middle of the bow; then he put the lower loop back in place round the lower groove and pushed the bottom of the bow into the side of his foot again. This time, his straining to bend the upper part of the bow downwards was so that he could push the upper loop up the limb and eventually hook it round the groove. He strained, his face tensed and his cheeks bulging, but he could not quite get it where he needed it. He relaxed, then started again; this time Mrs. Crowthorne moved forward and was reaching out to help him, and then the awful thing happened: with a great crack, the bowstave split just below Mr. Crowthorne's knee and the two parts flew in opposite directions, the short one flat to the ground with a slap and the longer one up into the air, where a jagged edge ripped its way up Mrs. Crowthorne's dress from around her waist up her right hand side to deliver a mighty blow to the underside of her outstretched arm, which was thrown back over her head. She staggered backwards and fell to the ground, Reverend Hale springing forward just in time to prevent her head from striking the flagstones. Mr. Crowthorne meanwhile had been thrown forwards by the sudden removal of the resistance to his pressure, and had landed on his face on the floor; his nose was bleeding profusely, probably broken, and as he helped the stunned but moaning man onto the chair Hale was horrified to see one of his front teeth broken off close to the gum. Because of the bleeding, he risked leaving them for a while and hurried out into the lane, where he found two labourers lacking immediate labour and sent them at once to fetch Doctor Thompson as a matter of urgency.

In retrospect, it could have been worse. If the longer broken stave, for example, had followed a trajectory perhaps an inch or two from that which it followed, it would have laid Mrs. Crowthorne's cheek open and taken out her eye. The material of her dress had slowed the flying limb down as it tore it, and it had been thick enough to prevent the sharp edge from touching her skin; all she had to show for the incident was a badly bruised arm and a ruined dress. Mr. Crowthorne had fared worse: his nose was not quite straight thereafter and he never found a satisfactory way of filling the gap in his smile, though these long-term problems were as nothing compared to the agony he went through having the smashed remains of the broken tooth and root removed so as to stabilize its partner and prevent rot. They were obliged to stay in Stoke Armitage for three days while Mr. Crowthorne was attended to and recovered sufficiently to resume his journey. He was all for awaiting the General's return in order to confront him with the results of his handiwork, but Reverend Hale, who, feeling some kind of indirect responsibility for the accident, put them up for the period in the rectory, managed to calm him, in return for a promise to explain to the General on his return in detail what had happened and what the result had been.

When, a few days later, Hale had finished his story and handed over the broken stick, the old soldier looked very concerned. He examined the break carefully, and leaned on the longer part. He knew that, as he said before, a branch stave was weaker than a bole stave, and that that stave had been the least satisfactory of the four, but there was no way in which such a thing should have happened. Possibly after many hours of solid use, but not so soon – quite impossible. He promised to write to Mr. Crowthorne, whom he recalled well, at once, and suggested to the rector that he should take down the rest of the exhibit when he returned to the church. Hale recognized that the old soldier was indeed unaccustomedly shaken by what had happened, and what had nearly happened, and blamed himself for it entirely. He urged him to sit for a moment, and said what he could by way of comfort, unconvincing though it seemed even to himself, being composed of expressions such as "complete accident", "no-one's fault", "no serious harm done", conventionally linked together. He thanked the priest for his solicitude, but as far as Randall was concerned, it was his workmanship which had been faulty, his egotism which had put it on display and therefore entirely his responsibility that two innocent people had been injured. There was a modesty and a quietness in his voice and his manner which Hale had never heard before, and he was convinced that, as he had suspected, there was a different Randall behind the confident bluff sportsman, who had been a true leader of men as well as the driving force behind them.

As already mentioned, archery had for some time been enjoying something of a fashionable revival in the world outside Stoke Armitage, and clubs had formed in several parts of the country. One, indeed, met sometimes as close as Thorningley Castle and

Lord Thorning was officially its president, though only because his house was such a picturesque backdrop and his hospitality was generous; his interest in the pursuit was very limited, and he entertained the archers mainly in the hope of keeping his reclusive wife in touch with society. The real force behind the club was Sir Reginald Shawcross of Croxton Minor, a retired colonel of infantry and author of *From Senlac Hill to Bosworth Field: the Conduct of Warfare in Medieval England*, who regularly turned up in medieval costume of green as Robin Hood at the meetings of The Merry Men of the Forest, as the club was called. Despite the democratic overtones of their name, the group of about a dozen was divided into senior members, who could provide grounds in which they could shoot, and junior members, who were not so fortunate. Sir Reginald himself had created at Croxton Minor a lawn a hundred and twenty yards long by thirty wide as a butts, surrounded by a crenelated wall in grey stone and with a matching pavilion in mock-Gothic style at one end where the families of members could take tea while watching the sport. A slender tower twenty feet tall rose from one corner of the building; it contained only a spiral staircase, to allow a servant access to the top, where he could hoist a flag of the club's emblem another five yards aloft during shooting.

Some two months before, presumably because word of his interest in the sport had spread, General Randall had received a general invitation from The Merry Men to attend one of their shoots, with a view to becoming a member; although not a particularly sociable man except when presiding over events firmly on his own ground, the General had felt quite pleased to be asked and had sent a tepid but affirmative reply. This had now caught up with him, and along with the rector's tale of the broken bow there had been awaiting his return from Bath a formal invitation to join them on Midsummer's Day at Thoringley, as being the most convenient meeting of their programme for him to attend. Indeed, the invitation was still on the desk in front of him when Hale came with the broken stave.

68

The meeting was only a few days off. In a sudden rush, almost of panic, the General thrust the invitation into Hale's hands and asked him if he would accompany him, as his guest. Something was wrong, he felt: the way the yew branch had snapped off, Joseph's accident with the mallet and now the Crowthornes; he was not superstitious, but he felt uneasy about it in a way that was definite but undefined, if that was possible. The rector was taken aback, but the General carried on; it was not just that the rector was the nearest person to hand, but he felt that he could understand what was going on more than anyone else and he knew that he could rely on Hale's – the word he finally used, with some fumbling, was integrity.

"I felt like this sometimes in the woods in Canada. Oh, do not imagine anything like what is left of our English woods, a few trees between fields with a pretty village behind; there the woods are deep forest, never cut by man, stretching for mile after mile after mile, the same in all directions, so that you could imagine yourself as the only walking man amidst a million identical trees. No clearings, no dwellings, only faint paths crossing and recrossing each other and all with the potential to lead you back to exactly the same place if you wandered. And yet you knew that all around were hundreds of animals, thousands of birds, millions of insects, all unseen and yet all perhaps watching you. And Indians, perhaps, friendly or unfriendly, waiting and watching in their patient, inscrutable way. And perhaps something else, older and darker, watching and waiting in the blackness between the trees. While the birds were singing, your horse was snorting and the men marching behind you were snapping twigs and rattling their kit, it was fine, it was normal; but if you got ahead of the column and stopped, sometimes the great silence would fall, and you knew that everything in the forest was holding its breath, focused on you, and waiting for the oldest and darkest of them to make its move. That is how I have felt since bringing the yew staves into the house."

The mundane conclusion of this anecdote surprised Hale. "You feel uneasy because of the bowstaves?"

"It is ridiculous, I know. Since the branch came down in the storm over a year ago and I stayed awake most of the night in anticipation of acquiring genuine English yew, I doubt I have had an uninterrupted night's sleep, except for the past week in Bath. It has been worse since we moved the timber from the stables into my workshop at the back of the house, and worse again since the completion of the work. Sometimes it is a dream which I cannot recall on waking; sometimes a noise in the house or outside; sometimes it is for no reason at all – though an owl has taken to perching somewhere just outside my window and hooting most of the night. I can't see the beggar, and shouting at him has no effect except frightening the servants; I have even fired a few arrows in his direction, but to no avail." A long silence followed. "Do you think I am – unwell?"

"No, I do not think so. The Church does not admit of such a phenomenon as a run of bad luck theologically, but we know from our experience that it can happen, perhaps simply because in the course of the hundreds of possible outcomes which befall us every day there are bound to be occasions when several bad ones fall together, just as several good ones may. It just so happens that, in our limited perception of things, more bad outcomes than good ones have so far attended these bowstaves, which are merely pieces of wood, after all. It is equally natural that you should feel responsible in some way because you have taken charge of them, but I doubt that there is any connecting cause for these unfortunate events, and it is most certainly not you."

Even so, Hale agreed to accompany the General to Thorningley at Midsummer, so that on that day three horsemen approached the great tower of Thorningley Castle from the direction of Stoke

Armitage: the General, the Reverend Hale, and Joseph the forester, who had slung over his shoulder a great leather bag in which were several bows, though he had been instructed not to bring Sir George's new yew bow – which did not displease him, since he still cursed it for the injury it had caused him in the making. Several figures in twos and threes could be seen wandering around the vicinity of the castle, but one standing as though on watch at the top of the great entrance staircase bounded down and across to greet them with great energy. If this action alone had not been enough to tell Hale that it was not Lord Thorning, the man's costume would have confirmed it. He wore a very loose, open-collared linen shirt, over which there was a curious green jacket, also open-collared, cut off at the sleeves and buttoned down the front. This reached half-way to the knee, and below it were stockings, in the old style but green. Short tan boots of soft leather, a broad matching belt holding the jacket in and a matching guard round the lower left arm, of the kind which Hale had learned to call a bracer, completed his extraordinary outfit, except for the strangest thing of all, which gave to the clue to his assumed identity: a short woollen garment round his neck and over his shoulders, of brighter green than the rest, had no apparent purpose until he turned and it was seen to be a hood hanging down behind, rather as in academic dress. It could only be Sir Reginald.

"Have I the honour of addressing Sir George Randall? Splendid, sir, splendid! Reginald Shawcross, a Merry Man of the Forest and right glad to meet you at last! And bravo on your positively Chaucerian retinue – a Yeoman Forester and a Priest! Almost a perfect accompaniment for a perfect genteel knight! Well met, Sir Priest!" Hale reached down and had his hand wrung briefly. "You know, we need a Friar Tuck in our little band; we have several aspiring Robins and a sprinkling of likely Marions, and more than enough of Much the Miller's sons, if you know what I mean, but we are in sore need of a chaplain." Hale excused himself as a mere onlooker. "Ah well, so be it. At least we have the doughty knight to swell our ranks." Servants came forward for the horses.

At the back of the castle, Lord Thorning was standing watching proceedings with an air of melancholy dignity, content to let the Merry Men organize themselves. Beyond the terraces and flowerbeds, a field normally grazed had been cleared of animals and a swath of grass twenty yards wide and much of the length had been cut short. Six round straw targets had been set up across this, two at thirty yards' distance for the novices and one each at forty, fifty, seventy and ninety yards. To the side of the shooting area, a deer carcass was being prepared on a spit to cook over a trench where a fire was burning – the traditional roast for the club's supper. Sir George, with Hale in attendance and followed at a short distance by Joseph carrying his gear, went straight to Thorning to greet his real host and the club president. They had not actually met for several years, though they had known each other when in the service. The General had a few rough words to say about the presumption of Sir Reginald, and Hale thought it best to leave the two old soldiers to talk a while; having greeted Lord Thorning, he asked if he might visit the chapel and see the alterations he knew had been made since his last visit – mainly the ripping out of the medieval seating and panelling, to meet a more modern fashion. He smiled and nodded as Lady Thorning showed him the new work, although feeling a profound sadness for what had been lost, and then made his way back down to the field, where he found poor Joseph being berated by Sir George. It was immediately clear why: the cover for the bows had been untied and rolled out on the ground, and lying on it with the two bows of ash and wych elm which Sir George had intended to bring was the distinctive yew bow which he had reserved for his own use. The General was angrily expounding on the need for obedience and attention to detail in his service, and in the gaps Joseph was uttering apologies mixed with protestations, for he was as tall as the General and broader and knew his own worth and loyalty; all around could hear, though most affected not to. Hale laid a hand on the General's arm and stared into his eyes as he turned to him, to indicate that he knew that what vexed him was not merely supposed neglect of orders. Sir George fell silent; the crowd ceased to pay attention; Hale spoke quietly to Joseph.

"Joseph, did you know that Sir George particularly did not want you to bring the new yew bow today?"

"Course I did, your reverence. He told me not to bring it, most particular, and I was pleased at that, cause of how it had already made me thump meself wi'the mallet."

"And did you in fact bring it, Joseph? Did you take it and put it in the bag with the others and tie it up? Never mind the fact that it is lying there; did you pack it to bring with you today?"

Joseph continued to stare at the object at his feet, but he shook his head. He looked at Hale and his master in turn without flinching, shaking his head again. "No, sir, I did not pack it; I took the two other bows and tied them up but I left that one on the rack. I can see it there alone now. I even grinned at it out of malice as I walked off and left it."

None of the three raised the obvious question of how it now came to be on the ground amongst them, for it was a question to disturb each of them, especially the one who had first fashioned the thing.

An awkward silence was broken by the energetic reappearance of Robin Hood, now with a quiver on his back. "I say, a real yew bow!" He had picked it up and was examining it before anyone could stop him; "Irish wood, no doubt, Sir George?"

"Well, no, grown in our own village in fact – in this man's churchyard."

73

"Your arrival pleases me more and more, Sir George of Old England! Now it seems to me that if there is one man with a right to try out such a piece of tradition, it is a man straight out of the same legend – what do you say? May Robin of Locksley shoot the grey-goose shaft from the bow of yew?" He had already strung it and was testing its draw.

"No, I mean, it is a very unsatisfactory piece of work. I had not meant to bring it. It does not shoot well." Sir George was trying all possible variations on "no" without lapsing into the impolite. It was difficult to refuse in this atmosphere of forced conviviality without seeming churlish, and Sir George could not immediately think of a reason to refuse him with which to replace the half-formed and apparently crazy true reason for his reluctance.

"It seems good enough to me. Either you are being very modest or else you want to keep this beauty for yourself! Just let me try three arrows to see what it feels like and then I won't trouble you about it again – please?"

"Oh, if you must, but if anything goes wrong it is entirely your responsibility – understand that. Just three arrows. For heaven's sake be careful!"

"I shall. I do know something about shooting, you know."

At the shooting line, a couple of the junior members of the club whom he would call the Miller's sons were firing rather haphazardly at the closest targets. Sir Reginald strode up to the further end of the line, opposite the ninety-yard target and shouted "Stand fast" in a very commanding voice quite unlike his usual one. He took an arrow from his quiver and fitted it to the bow. He lifted it, and smoothly drew the string back to his ear; with a great noise the shaft sailed away and struck the left hand edge of the target. The more knowledgeable standing by applauded. "A good strong bow indeed!" he shouted back to Sir George over his shoulder as he began to take his second shot, adjusting his aim minutely. The arrow slammed into the target an inch or two to the left of the gold centre. "Now for it!"

"Now indeed!" muttered Sir George, unaware of how tightly he was clutching the rector's arm. He closed his eyes as the third shaft was loosed, but opened them again in relief as the sound of cheering mixed with clapping; the arrow was proudly in the centre of the target.

"You have nothing to be ashamed of with this bow, Sir George! But it needs a real test, and not shooting at stuffed targets. I say, Thorning, how wide is this field, to that oak growing out of the hedge, say? Lord Thorning had wandered over, attracted by the noise.

"Oh," slowly, thinking, "traditionally, this field was originally a hundred and eighty yards wide; but we took twenty yards out for the terrace; from where you have your shooting line there, I suppose the tree would be about a hundred and fifty yards."

"Excellent! Now what do you say to a small bag of silver against my hitting the tree from here, first time?"

"Er, yes, no harm in that. But I don't see how you can do it, not with one shot and a new bow."

Sir George broke in, "Excuse me, sir, but I did agree to just three shots with that bow, agreed reluctantly, and I must insist on its being returned at once."

Lord Thorning, who had heard nothing of this so far, looked puzzled, mostly at the General's apparently petulant attitude.

"Sir George," said Sir Reginald, "the President and I are just negotiating a little wager about whether I can hit yonder tree, and I don't see another bow here that will let me make a game of it. Surely just one more shot won't make that much difference? I haven't done anything disastrous with it yet!"

The General looked perplexed.

"Go on, George, old man. Just one, eh?" This from Lord Thorning.

"Very well, if you must, but if there are any consequences, you share the blame between you. I hope that is understood."

"Perfectly. Well, let's see: a guinea says you don't hit the tree with one shot from that bow from this shooting line. And the arrow must stick in the trunk, not get caught in the leaves or anything like that!"

"Very good."

Sir Reginald called a servant over and instructed him to go a hundred yards down the field and stand well to the side, and watch to see if he hit the tree. He took another arrow from his quiver and fitted it as he stepped up to the line and called out again. He drew more slowly, aiming higher than before, well over the tops of the targets, and paused slightly before letting go. A few seconds later, the footman was running back up the field, shaking his head. Gasping, he announced that the arrow had easily reached the distance and cleared the hedge, but had missed the tree by six or seven feet to the left.

"I failed to compensate for that pull to the side in the wretched bow," muttered Sir Reginald, dejected for the first time that day. Sir George, grateful for no worse accident, very deliberately took the bow from his hands and passed it to Joseph to wrap up and put aside until they should leave.

After a little more general socializing and disorganized practice, Lord Thorning, accompanied by a silent Sir Reginald, appeared on the terrace and announced the commencement of the competition rounds for the day, at which point the ladies and families retired to the tables and chairs on the terrace and the men proceeded to the shooting line. Hale found himself somewhere in between, on a chair behind Sir George's position. The Merry Round was the club's own pattern of contest, somewhat akin to the York Round. In it, each man shot two dozen arrows at a thirty-yard target, which were then tallied up and the target moved back to fifty yards for two dozen more; then the same number again at seventy and finally at ninety – eight dozen arrows over four distances. As there were five senior members and six so-called juniors and Sir George, they would shoot two to a target, by tradition, one senior and one junior, shooting dozens alternately. The five seniors drew lots for partners, leaving two, Sir George and Reverend Brook, the local schoolmaster and de facto curate, to shoot together.

Sir George was quite satisfied with his first dozen arrows: seven hit the centre of the target and five the next sector out. His partner had missed with his first arrow and struck a non-scoring corner of the target with his second when all were distracted by a commotion on the terrace behind, which roused the Reverend Hale, who was starting to succumb to the morning's ride and the spring sunshine. He stood and looked round: as far as he could see, a young woman was trying to make her way through the tables and chairs of the ladies but was being held back by a footman. Several of the archers called out impatiently, some less politely than others, but none seemed willing to leave the line and Hale himself, hearing shrieks including phrases that sounded like "badly injured", "perfect right to", "stupid games" and "what are they going to do about it?", hastened up the steps to ascertain the cause of the disturbance. Ordering the footman to let go of the woman, who was in what might be described as smart agricultural clothes, the dress of one who might feed poultry herself but supervise others in more demanding tasks, he took her aside and made her calm herself and moderate her voice before telling him what she wanted. The ladies resumed their tea, the gross conduct of the lower orders in general being just as valid a subject of conversation for them as any particular discussion of what the woman might say.

In brief, from what the woman told him, in between asking him to get help, and from what he had already seen, he pieced together the story of how her son Thomas, playing tag with his sisters in the next field, which his father farmed as Thorning's tenant, had been hit by Sir Reginald's arrow aimed at the tree. It had been falling to earth and hit him only in the calf, but as he was a small child it had gone most of the way through. He had passed out with the pain as the sisters had carried and dragged him back to the house, from where his mother had run to seek assistance. Without a word, Hale left her and went down to the shooting line, where he tapped on the arms of Lord Thorning and Doctor Sankey and so called them away from the game. Some further quiet but agitated discussion involving them followed at the back of the terrace, at the end of which the doctor reluctantly left with the woman, at the urging of his lordship, who returned to the competition. The archers were engrossed in the shooting, and only Sir George seemed still aware that there had been any disturbance; he briefly asked Hale what the woman had wanted, and was satisfied when told it was help with an injury on the neighbouring farm.

That would have been the end of the matter, and perhaps of Sir George's apprehension, had Doctor Sankey not returned to the castle. The competition had reached its final phase, the ninety-yard mark, and the Reverend Brook had shot his seventh dozen, the four arrows traveling the distance all missing the target. Sir George was about to take aim, when he noticed the doctor coming down the steps from the terrace, carrying his bag and what appeared to be an arrow. He watched as he walked up to Lord

Thorning, who drew back from the line and called Sir Reginald over. They were in serious but very quiet discussion again, but fell silent as the General approached them. He took the arrow from the doctor in his own shaking hand; it was bloodied, and was one of Robin Hood's grey-goose shafts.

"Who?" he said hoarsely.

"The child of a tenant, in the next field. That shot at the tree in the hedge."

"How badly?"

"Through the calf, but cutting nothing serious; a great shock and lameness for a while, but he will recover."

Sir George nodded slowly and handed the arrow back. He walked back to the line, collected his bow and other gear as though sleepwalking, and returned to take his leave of Lord Thorning, apologizing for his departure and inability to take further part in the sport of the Merry Men. He nodded briefly at some of the others – for all were now watching and the competition was forgotten – but ignored Sir Reginald. Hale followed him; he paused at the trench, where bright hot embers were roasting the venison, and he slipped the yew bow in amongst them. In the intense heat, it soon twisted and charred, burst into flame and spat and crackled as it disappeared. A few minutes later, the General, the Rector and Joseph were riding away from the castle. Not a word was exchanged until they were at the Court and dismounted; they went straight to the library where the bows were kept, and while Joseph emptied the bag Sir George took down the guest bow of yew and indicated that Hale should follow him. He paused at the entrance to his workshop, then muttered, "Too dangerous to try cutting," and instead went to the drawing room, where he found a copy of an old newspaper and a tinderbox and spills, and took some stumps of candles out of their holders, handing them to Hale to carry. They then proceeded out into the garden, behind a sheltering wall, to a low pile of cuttings and foliage ready for burning when it should be big enough. Sir George stuffed screwed up sheets of the paper into the pile, and then put the bow across the top, arranging the candles on their sides along it and carefully lighting them, leaving the spills in place as wicks. With a final spill he lit the paper. They stood back. The wax spread along the stave, creating little pools of almost indiscernible flame; some of the pieces of paper burnt well, and started leaves crinkling and shrivelling; the bowstring caught and flared up. In time, especially where the wax dripped, four or five strong flames developed, taking up twigs and charring the underside of the bow. After a couple of minutes, the pile reached a critical heat and turned rapidly into a blaze, and the yew wood began to catch fire in earnest. However, it had a final trick: it cracked down its length, and one thin burning rod two yards long leapt from the fire and fell at their feet. Sir George lifted it on two twigs and threw it back on top. "Pray, man!" It did not seem proper for Hale to hesitate through lack of suitable texts or through lack of understanding of what to pray for, so he simply started in a conventional tone and let the words have their way.

"O God our Father, hear our prayer and take from us whatever ill fortune may attend on this wood and its fellows. Let them do no more harm to man and let whatever evil may dwell within them return to its place of darkness and trouble the world no more. In the name of Christ Our Lord, Amen." The wood spat again and the flame rose up.

"Amen."

Sir George seemed to find the words completely apt, though Hale had rather surprised himself with what he said and doubted that it was sound in terms of his theology. Sir George made to move away; Hale began to follow, but was instructed to stay. The

General returned shortly afterwards with a large canful of water. They watched the fire burn down, then he doused the embers thoroughly – "just in case".

"It was worse each time; you could see that, couldn't you? A broken wall, a bruised hand, a smashed tooth, a pierced leg; you could see what was coming next, couldn't you?" Hale's silence was enough for the old soldier. Then something which both had forgotten came back to him: "I must write to India at once and warn Edward. It will barely have got there yet, and I doubt he will be in much of a hurry to try it."

About three months later, some ten weeks after the dispatch of Sir George's envelope in the opposite direction, a letter arrived at the Court from India. It was from Colonel Hurst, the commanding officer of the General's son, Major Edward Randall, and the contents of such a letter were always entirely predictable. Amidst the expressions of sorrow and the praise given to the Major as a man and as a soldier, it told in some detail how he had met his untimely end. He had taken immediately to practising with, as the Colonel put it, a bow and arrows which had recently come from England, and had started hunting with them in preference to a gun, albeit yet with little success. With a native corporal, he had been stalking buck at a waterhole when he had the misfortune to cross the path of a hungry tiger in pursuit of the same prey. Rather than take the weapon which the corporal was holding out to him, he had fired his arrow, missing the charging creature by several feet, before it knocked him to the ground. The corporal had been able to dispatch the tiger with a bullet at very short range, but in the time it took him to move a few yards out of the way and take aim it was all over with the Major. The Major's possessions, including the bow, were being returned to England.

The bow never did arrive, perhaps having been misappropriated quite early in its journey, before even reaching the ship, to cause mayhem in some Indian village. Perhaps it was soon recognized as ill-omened, and destroyed; perhaps it still survives in some part of the world, still bent on its own mission of destruction. Hale visited the Court several times in the next few months, nominally socially or as he was passing, but both men understood; Hale even understood when on one occasion virtually all Sir George said to him was, "The owl has gone". They rarely if ever thought of what had happened to that fourth bow, being limited to the more immediate grief and concerns to which the bows had brought them. Sir George gave no more thought to the yew trees in the churchyard – certainly not in terms of archery, which he gave up at once and completely, but also as regards his theory about their age and what might have preceded the Christian church within their enclosure. Hale tried to keep that casual remark out his mind also, and could never have imagined the skulls buried with the roots when the yews had been planted, so that the spirits of the dead might sit in their branches and ward off the wizards and magicians of any enemy who dared trespass. And it is as well that he could not.

WHAT REMAINS

Like many clergymen of his day, the Reverend Hale took a keen interest in natural history, as being the most obvious example of the bounty and beauty bestowed by creator on creation, and like them too his interest paradoxically extended to the collecting of specimens devoid of the very life which had first made them interesting. However, he did not share the fashionable passion for field sports, and no mounted fish, foxes' masks or deer's heads adorned the rectory at Stoke Armitage; instead, there were cases of butterflies and moths and pressed wild flowers.

However, collecting could avoid the inevitable death of the specimen altogether when manifested in the latest fashion, the acquisition and identification of fossils. Debate as to their nature was still fierce, many refusing to accept that they represented long-extinct creatures, but fossils did not yet represent to the Church of England the threat to the very roots of conventional religion which they later became; the split between science and theology over the mechanism of change in the living world was in the future, and a clergyman could still happily entertain and even promulgate the idea that a fossil was in some way the remains of an extinct ancient life-form without being charged with blasphemy. The Reverend Hale was not troubled by them at all at a theological level: it seemed to him quite obvious that something like a spiralled ammonite was basically the shell of a long-dead creature, petrified, he supposed, by a process not unlike that he had seen in certain wells and caves, whereby minute deposits of matter left by countless drops of water built up a coating on something left beneath. Whether this had happened at the time of the Biblical Flood or not did not seem to him to be a question deserving of much attention, as nothing much depended on the answer – and there seemed little possibility of a definite answer in any case.

Such things were rarely found then in his part of the country, and his collection amounted to a mere handful of specimens sent to him by friends – the shadow of a fern caught in a piece of slate, ammonites from beaches on the Isle of Wight or the coast to the south of him, an undoubted ancient shark's tooth from an improbable inland site, and so forth – so he was very pleased to receive an invitation from Canon Wycherley. The Canon had lectured on Plato and the Pre-Socratics during Hale's time at Oxford, and they had kept in touch intermittently over the thirty years which had passed since; he had retired to Dorset only a couple of years earlier, to a house on the western edge of Lyme Regis. He had long wanted to live by the sea and to be roughly equidistant from family members and friends in the cathedral cities of Exeter and Winchester, and he had found a house clinging to the wooded cliffs overlooking Lyme Bay which answered both of these requirements very satisfactorily. In his letter, he mentioned, by way of an added inducement, that the local beaches were among the most prolific spots in the entire country for finding fossils, which Hale already knew; he replied enthusiastically, and a month later, having secured a locum for his parish, he arrived at Anchors House to spend a week with his old mentor.

"And Lyme Regis is also, as it were, the site of the second birth of English Protestantism, for just down there below the trees to the east is Monmouth Beach, where the Duke of Monmouth landed to prevent the betrayal of our religion by the Papist King James." Hale said nothing, and some doubt provoked by the carnage of Sedgemoor and the Bloody Assize must have crossed his face, which made his mentor smile and continue. "Quite right, my boy – a total shambles, a pitiful business of delusion and revenge; but perhaps a noble thought lay behind it. Let us hope so, or so many died horribly and in vain."

Although only a few minutes' brisk walk from the edge of the town, Anchors House gave the appearance of being in a very remote spot, perched as it was on a ledge on the cliff face and surrounded by trees. Access to it was appropriately difficult: the rough road from Lyme into Devon across the Undercliff ran a little way behind and above it, but the final approach to the rear of the house was down a precipitous path for thirty or forty yards. A cautious rider or two men with a handcart with brakes could manage it, but no vehicle could get close; reflecting on this later, Hale realised that nothing in the house much larger than, say, a carriage clock was less than fifty years old, and the difficulty of delivery was perhaps the main reason. At the bottom of the path, when one had pulled up from the headlong descent, one found oneself on a semi-elliptical ledge which had probably at some time been deliberately cleared and flattened and which was largely occupied by the house, gravel having been spread over the rest. The garden, if such it could be called, sloped above and around the house, and straight down from a point barely ten yards in front of the building. Mostly it was covered with rough woodland and could only be traversed with care on foot, but here and there small level plots had been cultivated so as to enable the growing of garden plants. A series of steps, each formed by ramming two pegs into the ground two feet apart and setting a plank of wood upright behind them to retain a packing of earth, wound down from the front of the house for perhaps a hundred yards, visiting several such spots: one accommodated a rustic bench affording a clear view of the sea between the trees; one supported two fine rhododendrons; one, of perhaps six square yards, was packed with bulbs and corms in peat to provide a Springtime blaze of snowdrops, crocuses, daffodils and bluebells; and so on.

The house itself was a curious structure, on a quite pretentious scale but built of local materials by rustic craftsmen unaccustomed to the styles they were trying to imitate. In date and details it was clearly Tudor, but the main material used externally was a soft stone, grey when wet and paling to rusty when dry, related to that of which the crumbling cliffs of the bay were composed. The walls, especially that facing the sea, were made thick in compensation, but even so they had been deeply weathered, with distinct channels worn from the edges of windows and where drips leaked from the gutters; the surface of the wall was uneven, with dips where rain had scooped out the middle of a slab or the outer face of a block had flaked away to a depth of a couple of inches. The rectangular Tudor windows and the thick pillars framing the doors were of harder stone, and stood a little proud of walls which demonstrated the work of erosion as convincingly as the cliffs themselves.

As the position made cellars impossible, there were only two steps up to the front door, which faced the sea; there one entered a hallway two storeys high, dominated by a heavy Jacobean staircase sweeping up the opposite wall and dividing to right and left; the elaborate but clumsy balustrades continued as the edge of a landing running back towards the front of the house overhead. Above the point where the stairs divided was an upright oval niche with a shelf across the bottom which must once have supported a statue; from the ceiling high above hung an iron ring the size of a cartwheel, set around with candles and raised and lowered by means of a chain. To one side of the hall was a single very large room, one storey, or nearly four yards, high; as was typical of the house, the walls were panelled with plain dark oak boards to half their height, with rough whitewashed plaster above and iron sconces set symmetrically. The back wall featured a fireplace and chimney-breast of a size commensurate with the room, made of smooth alabaster turned grey and decorated with crude acanthus motifs and swags; a small person could stand inside it, were it not for the large iron grate for burning logs, and Hale marvelled at the effort which must have attended on bringing the larger parts of it to this spot. The other two outside walls were dominated by the rectangular windows with stone mullions and thick, often eccentric glass, giving views mostly of the trees outside but, especially in the winter, with occasional glimpses of the sea. As elsewhere in the house, the furniture was sparse but very solid, mainly of oak and of Tudor and Stuart date. This large room, which the Canon referred to as his "great hall", had probably been intended for social gatherings, and a small dance could have been held in it; now it was divided into islands of activity by a number of rugs spread across its varnished floorboards: the largest of these accommodated the settles around the fire, another an antique spinet and an elaborate music stand, a third a writing desk and armchair.

"Space," said the Canon, "space and the prospect are what led me here; good big rooms to move around in, not like hat-box college rooms or a cramped cathedral close, and the sight of the sea in all its moods. The man who made this house knew very well what he was doing: everyone else builds from choice out of the way of the weather, behind the hump of the cliff, but he planted his house in the teeth of the gale for the sake of the wild view!" It was the Canon as Hale remembered him, the most Romantically inclined of Classical scholars, who would escape from Oxford whenever he could, to walk the Cumnor hills, and who secretly preferred Shakespeare to Sophocles. Yet only now did it occur to Hale that he had been his favourite teacher because he had been the one he had most respected for his character.

On the other side of the entrance hall, at the front of the house, was a dining room with a long table with bulbous legs; behind this were kitchen, pantry and laundry room. Upstairs, the whole length of the front of the house was taken up by a solar, a long public room with large windows and again scatterings of objects: a chest of musical instruments; a day bed; a table and chairs set out for chess; some large pots and pieces of statuary. The centre portion of it, of course, connected with the grand staircase and served as part of the landing. This gallery room was the main point of the house, for the view from it was over the tops of the trees and showed uninterruptedly the bay and the English Channel beyond.

Off it, towards the back of the house, were guest bedrooms, the Canon's private suite and a room which he had converted into a fine library. Except for those which had a window at a side of the house, these rooms were quite dark, for they faced into the wooded slope; the emphasis had been on the enjoyment of a public life in the gallery, not private indulgence. The top floor of the house was quite different, something of a warren of small rooms amidst chimneys, dormers and storage areas, enclosed within mock-battlements; up there, in what had been a suite of nursery, schoolroom and governess's accommodation, were the self-contained quarters of the Hardys, the couple who had been engaged by the Canon to act as handyman/gardener and cook/cleaner. They were in their early fifties, he having just lost his job as a gamekeeper as a result of a shooting accident and the previous incumbents having decided to retire following the demise of their employer.

As he was shown round, Hale expressed repeatedly his admiration for the place and its setting, to the Canon's obvious satisfaction; many of his acquaintances had voiced reservations about the distance of Dorset from Bath, London or Oxford, about the remoteness of this particular spot, about the treacherous nature of the path down, about the gloominess of the trees, about the battered appearance of the fabric, about the impossibly old-fashioned decoration and furnishings, about the tomb-like colour-scheme – but the Canon sensed that Hale truly understood and appreciated what had drawn him here, and suddenly realized that of all his students he had been the one with whom he had felt he had most in common.

Hale chanced to surmise that the house might have been built by a sailor who could not bear to be parted from the sea, perhaps someone who had known Drake or Raleigh in the West Country, and that this was the origin of its name. Perhaps some relic of an Elizabethan galleon had once graced the gravel outside.

"An attractive vision," replied Wycherley, "but in fact the truth is even more picturesque. You will note that the name is not Anchor House, but Anchors House; it is not even that in the earliest mentions, but Anchoress House. With a certain laxity over pronouncing and not pronouncing "e" and slipping apostrophes in and out over the years, we end up with the more readily-understood version which misled you. So it is often with ancient words...."

"A hermitage?" queried Hale before the older man launched into a full lecture on word-change.

"Yes indeed. The name refers to the ancient institution of the anchorite, or anchoress in the female form, the holy hermit who lives a blameless life of utter simplicity away from the temptations of society and so gains grace for himself – or herself – and for the community whose charity supports him. Or her. In truth, the ladies seem to have been predominant in this, apparently at times being voluntarily walled up in a corner of a church, apart from a small window through which to speak wisdom and receive supplies. An interesting Papist institution, though rather too sensational for the Protestant taste, I think."

"And was there really a hermitage here?" asked Hale, trying to maintain a proper Protestant calmness and distance.

"Come with me. You have not seen the best feature of the house yet." And the Canon broke out into a huge smile which totally undercut his recent stricture. He led Hale back to the entrance hall, collecting a double candlestick on the way and lighting it, and to the side of the grand staircase, where there was a small door by the back wall. He produced a bunch of keys, selected one, and unlocked the door; stooping slightly, they passed through it and down a step, entering what was in effect a tiny room under the treads of the staircase, a little below the level of the floor of the house. It took Hale a moment to get used to the candlelight in that dark space, but eventually he took it in. They were standing on the bare earth, but within the foundations of the house. In front of them were two sections of rubble walling, meeting at a right angle; the top of the corner was perhaps four feet high. One section of wall, the one in line with the steps above and parallel to the back of the house, fell away from the corner quite abruptly and was down to the ground after about a yard and a half. The other portion, running back towards the foot of the stairs, remained at the four-foot height for nearly two yards before falling away just under the bottom step, a total of perhaps eight feet. Half-way along this longer section, starting just below the top of the walling and sticking up a foot or more above it was the broken lower half of a stone window-frame, with a central mullion. They stood in silence for a while, then the Canon spoke in what was little more than a whisper. "This, I believe, is about a half of the anchoress's cell. Certainly it is medieval – its location inside this house is enough to prove that – and the design of the window looks ecclesiastical. The previous occupants, who lived here for seventy years, through two generations, thought of anchors as you did, and imagined that this was just the ruin of an old cottage; had removing it not been such a task, they would probably have dismantled it and hung coats in here." Hale was too astonished to speak, and followed Wycherley back out, tripping on the step despite a reminder.

"Well, what do you think?"

"I think I have rarely seen anything more extraordinary. How it takes one back to another age, another mode of existence!"

"Quite, even if a Papist existence. I really meant, what do you think of my understanding of the site?"

90

"Oh, no question of it. Though why it should have been preserved in this way I cannot imagine, when the model everywhere was the pulling down of monastic buildings in order to build houses like this from their ruins."

"A very interesting question which we shall never be able to answer, I fear. My feeling is that the hermitage was in this ruined state long before the house was built, and so it was not seen as part of the great dissolution; the original builder may or may not have had Papist sympathies – perhaps he merely wished to preserve a piece of the place's heritage. I have been unable to find out much about him: his name was Alexander Crampton or Crompton; he was a wine merchant and ship-owner with property interests in Lyme, Dorchester and Exmouth. He married late in life – a woman from Axminster – and built this house in the early 1550's. He left no descendants, as far as I have been able to ascertain."

Having completed the tour of the inside of the house, Wycherley led Hale outside, clearly with a particular intention, as he had next to nothing to say about the exterior. They made their way to the back of the house, past the small stable and up a few steps in the earth like those at the front to what seemed to be sort of wooden shed or small outhouse a little way up the slope. The Canon produced his keys again, and opened the door, beckoning Hale to look in. The back wall of the shed was the cliff itself, and the ivy-covered structure was really only a kind of porch over what was inside, which was a spring of water coming out of the rocks. A slate square with a central round hole in it was fastened to the cliff, and out of it trickled a weak but steady flow. This fell into a stone tank, about a yard square, which almost filled the floor of the little building. It was perhaps a foot deep, with the beginning of a pipe just below the surface at the front edge. "This is still the source of water for the house; that pipe flows down into the kitchen. When I arrived, the pipe was lead and that plate was of rusted iron, so I replaced it all at once. Nevertheless, that spring remains, and it was the reason for the hermitage being here, I am sure. It is called Anchors Well, or properly Anchoress' Well, the simplicity of which convinces me that it is perfectly genuine and so is the story which it supports; otherwise, it would long ago have become St. Ive's Well or St. Somebody's Well and credited with healing powers, as always happens. It never dries up, and often, especially when the snow melts higher up, it can become quite a roaring little torrent. So you see, "as he locked up, "even when you merely wash your hands or take a drink of tea in the house, you are directly in touch with the ancient history of the site!" It was clear that simply living in Anchors House was enough to bring into the Canon's life an excitement greater than he had experienced even amidst the ancient spires of Oxford, and Hale found it quite infectious.

The Canon suddenly apologized for having given his guest scarcely time to drink his tea before taking him on the tour and for subjecting him to such a lecture on the place, and acknowledged the tiring nature of the journey. He would show Hale to his room at once and let him rest awhile. However, the old man paused in a slightly dramatic fashion at the foot of the stairs, before making an astonishing announcement; Hale was not fooled into thinking this was really something just remembered or regarded by the speaker as trivial, and he put his bag down on the step. "There is one thing more I ought to tell you now about this house, and that is that it may be of that class commonly referred to as haunted. In other words, occasionally things happen here which cannot be explained rationally and certain people appear to be able to see or hear things here which others cannot. I mention this because I know from things you have said before and from what others have told me about you that you are interested in such matters and may be sensitive to them. I would not like you to encounter something of the sort without warning." Hale tried to interrupt, but the Canon went on. "I shall tell you what little I know of this at dinner, but, as you might expect, it seems to concern what is in there" – he pointed as if through the stairs – "and whatever happens does so in the parts of the house nearest it. Now I have two rooms prepared for you, and you may choose. One is a rather gloomy and not very large room just at the top of the stairs here, next to my library; it has a view of the trees behind the house. The other is a more spacious room right at the other end, with a pretty view to the west out of the side window and a glimpse of the sea. Which would you have, or would you rather see them first?"

Hale grinned: "I shall have the room by the haunted staircase, if I may!" And the Canon grinned back hugely: "Good man. But I must confess that I lied a little – only that room has actually been made up and aired." And they laughed as they ascended with Hale's small amount of luggage.

The room was not as bleak as the owner had suggested: it was true that little light came in and it was almost permanently in the shadow of the slope behind, but the windows on either side of the fireplace were large and as much as possible had been done to make the room appear as bright as it could. The oak panelling had been omitted or removed and the whole was plastered and whitewashed, with predominantly cream and red coloured hangings, bed-clothes and bed-curtains. The fireplace on the back wall was again in alabaster, and the rug which covered most of the floor was a darker cream colour, tending to grey. There were two full-length mirrors, which added to the effect of lightness and spaciousness, and numerous candle holders, both fixed and portable. In addition to the bed and small tables to either side of it, there were a washstand, a large clothes-press, a huge chest, two armchairs and a table of the sort used for playing cards. Decoration was provided by a number of the small, coloured and framed prints of English architectural subjects which hung in many of the smaller rooms and some of which Hale remembered from Wycherley's rooms in Oxford. This room featured the great monastic sites of Yorkshire, shown as deserted Romantic ruins wrapped in ivy: Fountains, Rievaulx, Byland, Mount Grace.

At the end of Mrs. Hardy's dinner, across one end of the long refectory table, the Canon continued what he had so teasingly left off. "In truth, there is little to tell. The previous occupants were apparently not troubled by it at all and dismissed all talk of it, fearing only at the end that the value of the property might be affected; it did not occur to them that the idea might make it actually more attractive! Some old people in the area preserve a legend of a ghostly figure of a monk or nun or friar in grey or brown or black seen in, around or near Anchors House, with some notion of there having been a monastic building hereabouts, but none has ever quite seen it in person, having been told by someone now conveniently dead. Incidentally, hardly anyone in the town knows of the origin of the name of the house or of the ruins under the stairs, and they were unknown to the outside world until I got Sir Charles Gracechurch down from St. Simeon's College to date the stonework last year. The Hardys have heard something of the story but regard it as nonsense, though certain things have happened since they arrived which have made them wonder. So the only evidence which I have derives from two written sources and from my own experience. The older written source is an entry for Lyme Regis in an Elizabethan pamphlet on "Wonders of Devon and the West Country", from which I have the earliest spelling of the name of this house; most of the entry concerns the Cobb, or harbour wall, but there is mention of a cell in the woods once occupied by a series of anchoresses but now under a house. The "wonder" is that the ghost of one of the hermits still appears, as if looking for its former home; the writer does not seem to have been aware that it was still above ground. The more recent is a series of diary entries made by a Parliamentarian sergeant of horse in May and June 1648; he and his men had been quartered in Anchors House to defend the western edge of Lyme Regis during the unsuccessful

94

two months' siege of the town by Prince Maurice. Come and I shall show you."

Delaying the drinking of port, the Canon led the rector upstairs to the library, and pulled out of a drawer a hand-written journal of folio size, apparent his commonplace book. "In between brief accounts of the fighting, snatches of prayers and memories of home, there are references to strange happenings in the house. I have a few transcribed here, taken from over three weeks; the original is in an antique volume belonging to a retired soldier in Lyme, who showed it to me. The style, incidentally, is very abrupt, and omits many short words." The Canon leafed through the book, then started to read.

Disturbance overnight, Troopers Harries and Barnes raising alarm for fire. Claimed to have smelled smoke coming from the wooden stairs, but nothing found.

Trooper Harries reported seeing ghostly figure on staircase when returning from sentry duty midnight last night. Told not insult Risen Lord. But refuses go upstairs in dark and sleeps in kitchen.

Trooper Playfair paraded without gauntlets. Claimed taken from kit. Ordered fine and punishment, but Trooper Barnes confirmed kit often tampered with. Rooms at top of stairs have bad reputation with men. Gauntlets later found in hall.

Harries again with story, this time at pre-dawn sentry duty. Saw brown figure by foot of stairs. Ordered not to repeat nonsense to others.

Harries' story has spread. Men unwilling to sleep in rooms by stairs or in hallway.

Broke open room under stairs in case Royalist hiding place. Just remains of old staircase (sic), but found tinderbox, comb, spur taken from men. None admits having key.

"Those are the main entries. Harries, or Herries, seems to have been a very sensitive soul, by the way; he later breaks down in tears on wounding a Royalist soldier with his pistol and has to be slapped by an officer. The relevant details seem to me to be the ghostly figure, the moving of objects and the confining of activity to the vicinity of the stairs, around the ancient ruins. The apparition is reported only by Harries, and is perhaps therefore only for the chosen few, though perhaps others saw it – hence the "bad reputation". The moving of objects is not the violent behaviour of many haunting spirits, which seems, from my reading on the subject, to depend on the surplus energy of a hysterical adolescent, but appears almost mischievous as some of them are. Or at least so I thought until it struck me that the gauntlets might have been placed in the hall and the other things inside the stairs as a kind of trail to lead the men to the cell – for what purpose I cannot tell, though it clearly failed."

"Do I understand from what you say that you do yourself believe there to be something haunting this house?" asked Hale, somewhat surprised.

"I think the evidence irrefutable. One might easily dismiss the vague and general reports of local gossip, repeated in the sensationalist "Wonders", as being attendant on any old house in a remote spot, but not this document. These were soldiers and God-fearing men, not to be misled by shadows; Sergeant Traynor – that was the writer's name – starts by being sceptical but ends up accepting the story. Also, there is my own experience over the past almost two years. I must confess that I am not the kind of soul to whom apparitions appear, and I have never seen anything in or around this house. However, the longer I have been here the more convinced I have become that there is at times some presence here which cannot be accounted for by means of another person. Always I have felt this in the hallway, on the stairs, in the middle part of the gallery or in the adjoining rooms, but never in my own quarters, where I spend most time. The feeling I mean is not merely a lonely person's wish for company or a nervous person's sense of being watched, but something more, more tangible, though that is definitely not the right word. It might be a slight movement at the corner of one's vision, gone when one turns; an apparent disturbance in the glass as one passes a mirror, settled when one looks; the hint of a noise, doubted as soon as heard. Once I was sure that a string on the spinet sounded; more than once I have seen the edge of a hanging move as though brushed against, when there was no draught; on one occasion a row of books on a shelf, which had not been disturbed for weeks, all suddenly fell on to their sides as I looked at them. You could say these are just the normal effects of the settling of an old house, and many creak and groan far more than this one does, but these are more subtle than that, as though something were almost but not quite there, almost but not quite performing actions. Whether it is trying to communicate with me and failing or rather trying to keep out of my way, I cannot tell; but I feel no sense of threat from it, and believe it to be benevolent, or at least indifferent.

"More significantly, because there are other witnesses to it, are the movements of things, recalling the problems faced by the old troopers. It started soon after I had moved in: Mrs. Hardy, herself new to the house, came to me as cross as she dared be with an employer to ask me to stop moving her knives, as it was delaying her in the kitchen. When I got her to explain herself, it seemed that several times one or other of her favourite knives had been moved from where it hung, and the final straw had been a search by her and her husband which discovered the vegetable knife in the corner of a tread on the staircase. I denied all knowledge of it, of course, and asked her to show me where the knives were kept:

they were hung from a rack just inside the door from the entrance hall, in other words, at the point in the kitchen area closest to the staircase. The bread knife was still missing, I recall, and was not found until I discovered it under the stairs while I was showing Sir Charles Gracechurch the ruin. Since then, the knives have been kept safely elsewhere, but other things left accidentally on the table by that door have ended up outside it. The Hardys have come to accept that that is a peculiarity of the house, or perhaps still regard the incidents as being some peculiarity of mine, but have not bothered themselves about an explanation.

"Incidentally, though I don't keep animals myself, when Sir Charles came down last year he brought his two deerhounds with him. At first, they came in quite happily through the front door and started sniffing around the place as they do, but within a couple of minutes their attention seemed to have been caught by something at the foot of the stairs, though we could see nothing. They both approached the stairs very cautiously, then they suddenly backed off, and finally they ran into the great hall whimpering. After that, they would only cross the entrance hall at a gallop, and no way could they be persuaded to go up the stairs. During the visit, they slept in the kitchen, whereas at home they invariably spend the night next to Sir Charles' bed, and they preferred to come and go through the back door."

Wycherley proposed an early start in the morning, as, he said, the best time to find fossils on the beach was in the morning as the tide withdrew and the best spots he knew for finding them were a little way away. "I expect you will sleep soundly enough tonight after your journey, ghostly hermits or not!" Early next morning, after an uneventful night, they led their horses up the slope behind the house, to the roadway; the Canon's horse was used to this, but Hale's was reluctant and needed some coaxing. However, soon they were riding eastwards,, through Lyme Regis and beyond, to the nearby village of Charmouth, where in a break in the cliffs the little river Char cut across the beach to empty into the bay. They walked their horses on along the sand as the tide pulled back from the foot of the crumbling cliffs which mounted up on their left, exposing sand glistening in the early sunlight coming from ahead around the great dark bulk of Golden Cap before them, the highest cliff on the south coast. Ahead of them also were hurrying a couple of local men with spades and rakes on their backs, who had begun their race when there was just a narrow gap between sea and cliff and who paused from time to time to scrape at the sand or attack the cliff face itself. "Professional fossil-hunters. They sell them to visitors like you."

The Canon called on Hale to stop: here was a greyish patch of sand with some fragments of dark rock in it, where a piece of the cliff had fallen down in the night and had been washed away as mud. He explained how any fossils in the fallen fragment would be left exposed or near the surface, until picked up or buried by the next tide. "The fossils are all in the cliff, but usually can only be found on the beach below." This surprised Hale, who knew that they were commonly found on the shore and had naturally assumed they had been sea-dwelling creatures whose remains were discovered where they had died. Wycherley was unable to resolve his difficulty: "Sea-creatures they certainly were; larger cousins of the ammonites are said to live today in shallow tropical waters. How they come to be in the cliffs I cannot tell; perhaps the dead creatures were washed into the soft rock at high tide and stuck there, though that suggests that the sea was then much higher than it is now. Some say that the creatures were washed onto the land to die at the Great Flood."

They dismounted, and the older man went down on one knee and stroked the surface with his crop. Almost at once, "There!" and he presented an ammonite to Hale – a tiny thing, on the tip of his finger, but a perfect grey spiral of unimaginable age. For the next hour, they examined several such spots along the beach, finding

99

almost a dozen perfect specimens, the largest, which Hale turned up, being wider than a gold sovereign; there were also many fragments, or spirals lacking their centres, and the Canon advised him not to burden himself with such stuff. Even more numerous were the belemnites, tapered or pointed cylinders an inch or two long, grey to black in colour, some thick or bulbous and others very thin; these represented the petrified body of a creature like a razor shell, although the Canon was not very clear about this. Unable to find a criterion by which to judge them, similar to the completeness test for ammonites, Hale ended up with half a capacious pocketful of the things. At length, the Canon, to whom this pursuit was not a novelty, declared himself ready for breakfast, and they trotted back through town to the Undercliff.

Hale later found that the specimens had left mud and grit in his pocket as they had dried, and he washed them in his washbowl. Some of the frailer specimens did not withstand this treatment, and reverted to mud, but the ones closer to being stone shed some accretion and became better defined. He spread a pocket handkerchief out on the small table by the bed and laid the ammonites carefully in rows to dry, with the mass of belemnites next to them. He took the bowl down to the kitchen to empty.

That afternoon, they walked back into Lyme Regis where the Canon pointed out features of interest, such as the walled harbour of the Cobb and the assembly rooms, and they called at the parish church at the far side of the town to take tea with the vicar there – an amiable Oxford man, though more of Wycherley's generation than Hale's. If he knew about the reputation of Anchors House, which he surely did, he refrained from mentioning it, and, for the visitor's benefit, the conversation mainly concerned fossils, and in particular one recently uncovered by one of the parishioners and referred to as "the great sea creature." Wycherley explained: "As happens from time to time, a specimen rather more impressive than your ammonites, the skeleton of an entire large animal, came to light recently in the bay; it took several men many hours of digging and carting to get it out of the cliff where it was first spotted after a storm, and it has been sold to a wealthy collector in London. It is at the moment awaiting packing before transport is arranged for it, and I have already asked the finder to let us have a look at it tomorrow before it goes, if it would interest you."

This last was really a tease, as it was clear that Hale was excited at the prospect, never having seen such a thing before, though having read a couple of accounts. That night, he again slept well, as a consequence of walking and the sea air, but awoke twice. The first time, it was to be roused out of a dream in which he was standing under the stairs by the ruin, though it was as bright as daylight and he seemed to be able to see the trees and even the distant sea through the walls of the house. He turned over and fell asleep again. The second time, he was aware of a sound somewhere between a rustle and a rattle, which made him think of pebbles on the beach or gravel crunching underfoot. Someone walking on the path around the house? No, the source of this sound was inside the room, very close at hand, not far from his bed; this idea made him shake himself awake and sit up at once. The noise stopped, but not before he had identified it as the disturbance of the fossils spread out on the table – by a cat, perhaps? He got out of bed hastily, and lit a candle. Yes, they had definitely been disturbed: some of the ammonites now overlapped whereas they had been spaced out and the pile of belemnites had been spread around and a few had rolled onto the floor. He rearranged them, extinguished the candle, the smoke from which seemed to smell very strongly, and returned to bed, shaking more from excitement than fear; he lay awake for most of the remaining two or three hours of the night, but nothing more happened.

Next morning, he told a very interested Wycherley as much as he could recall as they walked back down into Lyme, and Wycherley went over the outlines of the story of the great sea creature again.

"Incidentally, I hope you don't mind me suggesting that the purchase of a small item from his shop would be a suitable gesture in return for the viewing?"

Hale agreed without hesitation.

"Good; if we were strangers, we could expect to be charged for entry into his house for this purpose, or indeed into many of the houses in Lyme where fossils may be seen. The man's name is Joseph. He has an uncanny instinct for finding the best fossils, knows exactly what can be found where along this coast and when and can distinguish between many different types of fossil which would look much the same to you or me. He has no idea at all what they are or how they came into being, but his practical knowledge is excellent."

The house, or cottage, stood close to the beach, in a small fenced plot which made no pretence of being a garden: a net was draped from poles to dry; a stack of logs against the wall was ready for the fire; a lean-to at the side was clearly made of odd planks and boards, some the gift of the sea; a few scrawny poultry scratched around a similarly improvised coop; two well-used wheelbarrows stood by the door. The low building itself appeared to be of the local soft stone, plastered and whitewashed; unlike its surroundings, it gave no hint of dilapidation, and clearly the business of fossil-collecting paid well enough for frequent paint and repairs necessitated by the battering of the wind and spray. It leaned or curved inwards towards the top, so that with the sharp keel of the thatch across the roof it looked rather like an upturned boat. Two fair-sized windows flanked the front door and two smaller ones peeked out of the thatch, indicating the number of rooms. As the Canon opened the little gate, two small barefoot children ran round from the back, and stopped short when confronted by two dark-suited clergymen; the boy stuffed a hand into his mouth to stifle a whoop, and the girl clasped her arms behind her back and drilled into the ground with one foot. The door opened, and a large, florid-faced man appeared; "I seed ye before ye knocked, your reverend! Be off and play now," this to the children, who turned and charged away; "come in, your reverend, and your other reverend."

"Thank you, Joseph, but we don't wish to intrude or take up your time. This is Reverend Hale, of whom I told you, and he is very keen to take up your offer to show him the remains of the great sea creature."

Hale concurred, expressing his gratitude, and the man, making light of the matter, led them to the door of the lean-to, which was more securely locked than the door of the house. The structure clearly served as workshop, stock room and shop. When they could see inside, Hale was aware of rough benches and shelves around the walls, on which were set out Joseph's wares: pieces of rock waiting to be opened for the treasures which might be inside them; fossils with accretions still on them; pieces in the process of being cleaned, polished and in some cases varnished ready for sale. A complete ammonite, standing on edge and fully eighteen inches across, dominated the room. However, attention was soon drawn to a sheet of rock which virtually filled the floor space and made them edge into the room carefully. It was roughly rectangular, nearly four yards long and close to three yards at its widest; the upper surface being very irregular, it was between one and two feet thick. Embedded in it were the remains of a great sea-creature, basically its distorted skeleton; the bones were of a different colour and texture from the matrix, but they were firmly set in it as though in concrete. The creature had a large round skull at one end, lying on its side; the uppermost eye socket was a ring of bone the size of a small plate, and there was a long pointed snout with ferocious-looking teeth still in the open jaws. Behind the head was a long squashed ribcage, ending in the suggestion of a tail, and sticking out at each side was a delicate spread of bones like long fingers with the shadows of fins or flippers between them. The ten-foot long creature was clearly a maritime predator, perhaps something like a dolphin, thought Hale, though it had a more reptilian appearance and the head reminded him of pictures he had seen of Nile crocodiles. He inquired of Joseph what it was, and then remembered what the Canon had said about him. "Great sea creature. Great fish, like in the Bible. I reckon it lived until Noah's flood; he couldn't have put such a thing in the ark with the sheep and cattle and such, could he?" He laughed at his joke, and the others felt obliged to join in; they certainly did not contradict him, though it was plainly no fish. Hale asked about the circumstances of the discovery, and was again puzzled to learn that it was found not on the seabed but deep inside the cliff, above the level of the waves, when a large piece of rock broke away exposing the head. As they left, he asked the price of the large ammonite, and contented himself with the purchase of a thin sheet of polished stone bearing the clear imprint of an ancient plant.

They were largely silent on the way home, amazed by what they had seen, especially Hale, for it was a new experience for him, whereas Wycherley had already seen a specimen of like size, though apparently from a different species. On their return, Hale went to his room to put his fossil plant away. Remembering the night before, he glanced casually at the table by the bed. To his great surprise and perhaps delight, there had been a change: at, as it were, the head of the collection, many of the belemnites had been picked out and arranged to form what looked like capital letters: two upright in parallel with a third between and at right-angles to them to make an "H", one upright with three shorter ones sticking out at right-angles down the right side to make an "E" and so forth. "HELP", they spelled out, with an ammonite spiral serving for the rounded part of the "P".

Overcoming his astonishment, Reverend Hale spoke aloud: "How can I help you?" He looked intently at the tabletop, then recalled that the letters had been formed in his absence, and discreetly withdrew, to gather his thoughts at a window in the corridor. Curiously, he felt no fear at this display of something so far beyond the norm, but a thrill which was that of excitement. He returned to the room a few minutes later, to find the first message dismantled and in its place "PRAYERS MASS". A pair of ammonites, one above the other, served for a rather unsatisfactory "S" but the meaning was clear enough. The priest then asked a question which had occurred to him as necessary for his safety as soon as he had left the room: "Do you accept as your master Our Lord Jesus Christ?" This time there was no delay: resisting watching, he heard a moment's scrabbling on the table, then looked. The relevant letters had been plucked from the word "PRAYER" and assembled hastily as "AYE" at the edge of the tabletop. He stood back and again spoke aloud: "Who are you?"

There was no immediate response, and he went out and walked up and down the gallery before returning. The tabletop was unaltered. He repeated the question – "Who are you? What is your name?" – and again he left the room. He went in search of his host, who was sitting in the garden, resting and watching the sea. He sat on the bench next to him and, though rendered less than fluent by his excitement, he explained at length and with much repetition what was going on in his room. The Canon's mood in response was what could only be described as great happiness: he too was excited, glad to have his belief confirmed, proud to be the owner of a genuinely haunted house, and perhaps more beside. Nevertheless, he voiced muted agreement with Hale that the spirit he had contacted was asking for prayerful assistance in passing on and that they could not in charity deny their help in ending the haunting, Papistical though the idea seemed to the Canon. "Praying for the dead, indeed!"

"But, if this is an old anchoress, she was and presumably still is a Papist through no fault of her own, having been born before the great reforming. But why, after perhaps three hundred years, has she decided to ask for help, and why ask it of me?"

Wycherley was ready with a reply: "As I have said, it, or she, appears to have – a connection, as it were, with some more than with others. You and Trooper Herries, for example. And you left her the means of communicating. Perhaps she has tried with others but failed."

Despite a great desire to see it for himself, he decided to forgo going with Hale to look at the "writing" in case he disturbed their communication with his less positive attitude towards the anchoress' faith. By the time Hale returned to his room, the other had had time to ponder his last question and had arrived at a reply.

"FORGOT."

It was the saddest thing Hale had ever read.

"What did you do in life?" He turned to look out of the window while the fossils were slowly re-arranged behind him. There was the shed which housed the spring – but no, the shed was gone, and instead a thin stream of water flowed out of a crack in the cliff and tumbled and dropped its way down a couple of feet into a rough basin made of stones, from the edge of which it was dripping. The trees seemed denser and darker; the odd touches of cultivation – a stone birdbath, the pair of Roman-style pots at the foot of the steps, the steps themselves – were missing. Then, in alarm, Hale became aware that the window frame itself had gone, and the wall of the house, and he seemed to be hovering above the scene, looking down. Fighting a rising feeling of panic, he turned back, but the room had disappeared and he was looking across the woodland and over the bay, with no sign of the Canon or the bench. He looked down to where the stairs had been, and instead, a couple of yards below him, was the mossy and neglected thatched roof of the hermitage, no longer a ruin, standing in a tree-girt clearing at the back of the ledge. It was as he would have guessed from its remains, about ten feet by five, short end facing the sea but sheltered by a few remaining trees on the rim of the ledge. In the middle of one long side, to catch the early light, there was an arched window, covered with some sort of thin fabric, and matching it on the other was a low, rectangular doorway. The one detail that was new to him was the bulge at the north-west corner, where there was a rudimentary chimney emerging above the thatch; a thin plume of wood-smoke was rising from this just in front of him.

Without appearing to move, he found himself standing at the open door, looking in. It was dark inside, there being no plaster or paint on the stone walls, but he could make out a straw mattress on a rudimentary low wooden frame along the wall under the window. In the corner to the right, there was a kind of wooden kneeler of the sort called a prie-dieu, before a simple crucifix nailed to the wall, and a shelf on which stood a few crude items of crockery. To the left, there was the small hearth beneath the chimney-breast; the light from a low fire was hidden by a wooden structure formed of a beam on four splayed legs, over which two substantial garments, one light and one dark, had been draped, producing a characteristic smell of wood smoke and drying fabric. A stool and a tiny low table to match it completed the furniture, which, though sparse, all but filled the small space. More than he had ever done before, in this place Hale understood that true contentment does not rest in material possessions, for this hovel was not poor despite the paucity of comforts; he had the strong feeling that this was a place of purpose and of joy, and he knew why a spirit might grow attached to its simple purity. He heard a noise behind him, and he turned half in expectation and half in trepidation, his heart quickening, but there was only his bedroom wall and the window there.

He paused for a moment as his pulse and breathing slowed, then walked over to the bedside table.

The responses were not always easy to read, but there was ingenuity in it when it was grasped: it was of course the curved letters that needed the work. A single ammonite, O; two ammonites, one above the other, S. An upright belemnite with an ammonite next to it, a D; a B would require a longer belemnite and two small ammonites, whereas a P would dispense with the lower one and R would add a belemnite leg.

"DOMINI SERVVS"

Hale was nonplussed for the briefest of moments, then realised that his interlocutor used more than one language. It was Latin: "a servant of the Lord".

"I shall return and do what I can for you, though you must understand that the forms of our Church are not as yours were. We can pray with you, but cannot perform the mass as you knew it."

The Canon was proving increasingly reluctant to let "his" ghost go, and he even appealed to Hale's scientific curiosity by pointing out that to have one with whom such communication had been established was undoubtedly a very rare occurrence and could lead to all manner of discoveries about the world beyond; after all, she had been there for centuries, and a few more days could not matter. But Hale overruled his tutor with the argument of Christian charity and with the fact that he had given his word; her lingering was an aberration, not the norm of the life beyond as hoped for in their religion, and should be corrected at once. Unlike the fossil bodies, the human spirit was not intended to be trapped in the substance of earth after death but to be washed away into another world as was the mud by the tide. He pushed his analogy further: it was actually the inert matter of the hermitage ruins which was the petrified shell or bone of the fossil, and the remaining consciousness of the anchoress which hovered about it was the equivalent of the fragile sand or silt which could easily be washed off – but in this case it was far more important than that to which it adhered, for it was some part of a human soul. But he agreed in part that they should try to learn more in the time remaining.

For most of the next two hours, the two men were occupied at the dining room table with a sheaf of blank paper, which the unusually silent Canon was cutting with scissors into squares of about an inch and a half; his colleague then wrote a letter of the alphabet boldly on each one, and stacked them as they went along into piles, one for each letter. These they then arranged carefully in rows on two large trays, putting heavy towels on top to hold the stacks in place. They then carried them slowly up to the room at the top of the stairs, taking pains not to disturb them, and laid out the piles carefully in alphabetical order across the bed, starting with a large supply of A's. The biggest pile was of E's, with large ones of such letters as T, S and I, small ones of such as F, J and K, and a handful of the last three letters. The Canon withdrew, and when it was absolutely still in the room Hale said, "Please use these to tell us what you can; then we shall help you on your way in peace", and followed him out. For another hour the two men sat in the vast space of the great hall almost speechless, fiddling with a late cold lunch, each unable to settle his thoughts, wishing the time to pass. At last Wycherley could stand it no more: "She," for both men now thought of the ghost as the person had been in life, "must have finished by now." His tone was closer to pleading than asserting, and they both rose and went up the stairs, opening the bedroom door very carefully so as not to cause a draught.

What they saw inside far exceeded their hopes: across the bed, across the floor, on the furniture, the squares had been arranged into strips, each containing the equivalent of two or three sentences or ideas. Most of the letters had been used. Although they were arranged in no particular order, were subject to lapses of grammar and sense and were composed in a mixture of low Latin and an English which was nearer to Chaucer than to Dryden, Hale was later able to reconstruct a continuous story out of the fragments. For the moment, the two contented themselves with careful transcription of the strips, finally picking up the squares in a sequence and placing them for future reference in a box which the Canon took to his study to lock away for safety. Hale remembered to say thank you to the room before going downstairs to fulfil his part of the bargain; but then turned again in the doorway. "One last question before you leave this place," said Hale. "I believe others have been able to see you in the past; is it possible for me to see you also?" Even as he spoke, Hale was aware of the dangers of what he was requesting and he immediately regretted asking for it. Suppose she appeared proportionately aged: would he be able to control his disgust, and if not, how might she react? She might appear as something so hideous that he might lose his mind, as some who have risked haunted houses are said to have done. Perhaps it was not to happen at all. But then there was the smell of damp sacking and smouldering wood and it was as though the air itself a few feet in front of him was disturbed and flickering – yes, there were faint touches of brown in it, which spread and became a shape, as though a shadow cast by nothing. The shape, though indistinct around the edges, was roughly that of a torso, narrowed and rounded at the top, hovering a little above the ground. For a few seconds he watched it, entranced; then it seemed to make an internal effort, and momentarily shook with a great spasm – and then he caught a clear glimpse of a face, a yard from his own but at chest-height; not withered and aged, but perhaps as she had been at her death, which Hale was later to realize had been very early. The pale, unlined face, thin from austerity, was framed by a tight wimple, covering the hair, but bright blue eyes, a small nose and a little of an unfurrowed brow were visible. The lips were parted in an unaccustomed but unforced smile. And then the vision was gone and the brown shape faded.

Wycherley was in a rather better mood now but still somewhat reluctant to part with his ghost, and even more dubious about being party to Roman prayers for the dead, but out of charity he lent his support to what Hale had devised. The Book of Common Prayer offered them little which was relevant, and this was not in the nature of an exorcism, so Hale determined to improvise as best he could. They placed a chair in the hermitage and set up on it the biggest crucifix in the house, from the wall by the Canon's bed. Two candles flanked it; they had first planned to light up the whole ruin, but then perceived a potential danger of fire under the stairs. In the absence of proper ritual items, Hale sprinkled blessed water straight from the bottle that he had with him and burned in a small metal candle-holder a few grains of charcoal and incense which the Canon kept for freshening unused rooms. He began to speak:

"Almighty God, whom all here acknowledge and adore, we beseech Thee to take to Thyself our sister here who has served Thee faithfully in this place for many generations of men and has surely earned a place of rest as her reward. Send Thy angel, we pray, to guide her to the light of Thy presence, where she can best continue her work of praise and worship." And more of the same, calling on the anchoress too to move into the light. Then the men prayed the prayers of their Church, and finally spent a while in silence. They took down the candles and cross and locked up. "Do you think it worked?" Hale shrugged, but went to his room to try a test. "Sister, are you here?" Then he saw that the fossils had already been moved for the last time: "GOD SPEED". Never again would a shadowy brown figure, or the unexplained smell of wood smoke, or disappearing kitchen utensils save Anchors House from

111

being as mundane and predictable as any other house, and all that remained of the haunting was a memory and a pile of hand-written letters which, when laid out and all cast into English, could be made, with some insertions and interpretations, to read as follows:

"I came here when the old one died, to carry on the prayer, but I died too soon and they buried me in front of the cell. (Hale assumed this would be at the foot of the present stairs.) The prayer was not finished, the work was barely started. I should have gone then, but I stayed to pray, stayed too long and forgot moving on. It was dark and cold but I stayed to sing. No-one came after me. The thatch fell in; rain and wind made my things fade away. A man came and took the jambs and lintel of my door, and the wall fell down. But the stones remained, and I became fast in this place like the stones. I needed help to go, prayers, mass, but no-one came anymore to pray here; it became a place of fear, and I stopped singing. It grew darker and colder. Then they built this house, but they were not people of God; there was noise, children and dogs, music and dancing. Once men came with Bibles and I tried to make them understand, but they had swords too and could not help me. (A clear reference to Trooper Herries and his colleagues.) Now there is peace, understanding at last, and help for me to move on out of the cold and dark. I go. There is light. Thanks be to God."

DUST TO DUST

The Reverend Theophilus Hale had long had the notion that things which creep, which make their way across the ground as we do but in a manner totally at odds with ours, are particularly repugnant to the human psyche, being, as it were, a parody of normal human, and indeed animal, motion. This peculiarity of motion, it seemed to him, was compounded by its sheer ethereal unnaturalness or, in other cases, its painful clumsiness – the impossible gliding of the snake or the laboured stumping along of the larger lizards, the one defying normal ideas of propulsion and the other being achieved, apparently, despite rather than because of its level of utility. When indulging in natural history as a hobby, Mr. Hale could more practically ascribe his species' hatred of such creatures to the ancient fear of the poison of serpent, spider and scorpion; when in a more professional, theological mood, he fancied it derived from Adam's disgust at the Enemy who had tempted him and was therefore condemned to crawl on its belly in the dust. The dust, incidentally, from which he had himself been made, and which, for his Fall, would ever after be soiled by the things which crawl and writhe in it....

And so the Reverend Hale felt a particular thrill of horror and fascination when the parishioners of St. Thomas', Oakbank, told him of the creeping thing which had entered their lanes and their nightmares. Several times they had tried to discuss it with their own minister, the Reverend Simmonds, but he had dismissed them out of hand, even angrily, condemning what he called their childish nonsense and superstition, and, knowing of his great learning and ascetic, studious ways, they had felt compelled to accept his verdict, at least verbally. But they knew Mr. Hale to be a man open to new and unconventional ideas, from a certain reputation which was spreading through the villages in the vicinity of Stoke Armitage, and so had no qualms in approaching him on the subject in Mr. Simmonds' absence. Ordinarily, Mr. Hale would have ordered them, sternly, to take the matter to their own minister and would have refused to come between pastor and flock, whatever that pastor's stance; but on this occasion, he was, at least temporarily, in the position of their pastor and responsible for listening to and calming their fears – this, quite apart from any interest he might have felt himself in their story.

The fact was that the Reverend Simmonds had been granted a long leave of absence by the Bishop, to visit the Holy Land, through which he had travelled in his student days, before entering the Church. Although the trip would be in many respects arduous, he was still a relatively young man and it was felt that the rigours would stimulate him out of the melancholy and nervousness into which he had fallen of late, much as an older man might have needed rest and tranquillity to achieve the same ends; so he had persuaded the Bishop, and he had also made out a case for the benefits to scholarship that might accrue from a period of research amongst the Jewish communities he had visited some years earlier – for his field of study, unusual among Anglican clergymen of the time, was the Hebrew language and the writings and wisdom of the descendents of Abraham.

St. Thomas' being a small parish and there being an unaccustomed temporary dearth of curates, it had been determined that Sunday services, and a subsequent weekday visit (including the possibility of an overnight stay at the vicarage in case any parishioners needed private counselling), would be alternated between the half dozen or so nearest clergymen – who took to the arrangement with differing levels of charity. Reverend Tall of St. Barnabas', Travely, who had the longest journey and favoured a leisurely start to the sabbath, arrived a few minutes before a Eucharist service put back an hour and a half to accommodate him, and departed while the parishioners were still leaving the church, having recited but the opening and closing paragraphs of the sermon he had already delivered to his own congregation; his visit on the following Wednesday for late matins detained him even less. The Reverend Hale, however, had decided that little more than than a dozen nights in total away from his own parish would spiritually deprive no-one, and when his first allotted week came around he put on a full programme of services on Wednesday as well as on Sunday, and remained on duty overnight, intending to leave early for the morning service at home.

And so it was that one Wednesday evening, as the sun was beginning to set over the vicarage orchard, as viewed from the window of Mr. Simmonds' study, he was sitting in Mr. Simmonds' best armchair, listening to a delegation of some seven or eight of Mr. Simmonds' parishioners, whose faces and some of whose names he remembered from the preceding Sunday, all packed into the small room and standing. They seemed troubled rather than fearful: the creeping thing in the lanes of which they told had done nothing to harm anyone – indeed, it seemed usually to be trying to avoid contact with them, as a rabbit will, though in its case it was prevented from hiding itself away quickly by the slowness of its motion. Their anxiety was caused, as Mr. Hale would have supposed, by the very unnaturalness of the thing and its association with the dust, as though in an abject parody of their own posture. One thing he did ascertain very early in their meeting, from their pent-up rebuttal of Mr. Simmonds' criticism that they were the victims of old superstitions, was that the phenomenon was of recent origin and not a tradition handed down and hacked about – which made their extraordinary story more plausible. "It were never knowed in our fathers' time," said a youngish man standing half in the room and half in the hall; "Nor never in ours, till, maybe, five years ago," rejoined an older man, the verger Harry Turnbull. Mutterings of dissent and assent around the room, and then the keeper of The Green Man inn told once again what would in time become the nucleus of the story as it would indeed itself be handed on to become the fabric of a legend for future generations.

115

Although they had heard it rehearsed many times, most often in the bar of The Green Man, the others listened attentively, as though straining to catch the teller out in some detail of his own tale.

Removing the film of circumstantial detail, digression, personal speculation and incorporated material, as the Reverend Hale tried to do in his head, the essence of the story was as follows. One summer's night, a few years before, two men who had been making merry in The Green Man departed for their homes while it was still quite light, going down Deep Lane. Hale ascertained that one of the men had died soon afterwards, but that the other, a farm labourer called Black, was still alive, though no longer willing to talk about his experience, or attend this meeting – indeed, he had hardly been drawn to mention the incident since the night on which it had happened. Entering the darkest section of Deep Lane, where the shadows of the high banks and thick hedges had almost replicated the night which a lingering sunset sought to avert, they both pulled up at the same moment, sensing something in their path, something which they were unwilling to approach while lacking even a name for it. They stood still and almost breathless, and strained their eyes into the darkness, overawed as even the roughest and simplest of men are when confronted by something so outside their experience. Perhaps ten paces ahead, a prostrate figure was creeping away from them along the edge of the lane, as though looking for a way off the road and into the bank. It had the general shape and configuration of a human figure, though rather shorter, and it seemed to be dragging itself along with its hands and elbows, if such it had, with a mildly side-to-side swaying motion. Something answering to a head was raised above the further edge of the creature, while a length pointing towards them suggested legs, though these did not seem to be moving of their own accord. The darkness did not allow them to determine the colour or detail of the creature, nor even if it was clothed, but they had a general sense of it being quite dark and roughly textured, and they could hear laboured breathing. After a moment's stupefaction, they turned and fled back up the lane to The Green Man, which was still open; demanding spirits in a hurry, they blurted out fragments of what was in their minds, and the shaking and even sobbing which accompanied this soon convinced the late drinkers that this was not just a trick to get free brandy. A half a dozen decided to go down Deep Lane at once to determine what lay behind the story; one or two thought there might be a poor soul struck down by sickness and needing help; one or two expected to find a lost dog or strayed sheep; and one or two made sure they had their stout sticks with them before venturing out. They returned twenty minutes later, in the true darkness of night, without finding anything, but Black and his companion, grown men as they were, insisted that the party stay together to accompany them home and then keep in a group for as long as possible until all were safely behind bolted doors.

Since then, the creature had been seen, or reported as being seen, in similar circumstances perhaps a dozen times, always late at night and always by one or at most two people. No-one had dared to approach it, though the feeling which it engendered was a mistrust and abhorrence of the bizarre rather than fear, as in every case the creature had been seen moving away and never stalking a victim. This fact and its predilection for the night were perhaps, Hale surmised, the consequence of fear on its part, and the fact that it never appeared to groups suggested that it hid away when it heard or sensed the approach of humans; that an individual could surprise it was perhaps a consequence of limited senses, it probably being nocturnal from choice rather than by design. Hale inquired of the room, and three of those present admitted, somewhat reluctantly, to a sighting, one never having revealed this before. Details varied – one had heard it grunting, one saw it squirm under a fence – but the essentials were concordant. One of the three sightings had been in Holly Lane, one on the path that runs along the brook at the bottom of the bank behind St. Thomas' churchyard and vicarage, and one at the edge of a field on Stanton's Farm.

By this time, it was dark and the men were anxious to be gone. Unable to supply a ready answer to their questions, when they knew far more about it than he did and were clearly not going to accept such commonplace explanations as stray animals, which they had already considered and rejected, Reverend Hale promised to give the matter some thought before he returned and reminded them than they had plenty of proof that whatever it was it was harmless. He also suggested that it would not help matters if they approached their other temporary clergy in the same manner. As he bade them a good night, he was amused to note that they resolutely stayed together to the bottom of Church Lane and then split into two solid groups, one going left and one right. There being no servant resident in the vicarage, he then went around shutting up the house, noting that the heavy locks on the windows and external doors suggested that Simmonds, for all his dismissive attitude, had been affected to some extent by the anxieties of his flock. When Simmonds had briefly shown him and the Reverend Tall around the house together before his departure, he had said that he would leave everything open for the comfort of his substitutes, except for one or two drawers of private papers; in fact, Hale had already discovered that the stout door to the cellar and several cupboards and drawers in the well-furnished library were locked and answered to none of the keys.

Thinking of the library, Hale decided to amuse himself for an hour or two there before retiring. Inspecting the shelves with the help of a candelabrum, he noted the preponderance of books with Hebrew characters on the spine, together with some in Arabic and some he did not recognize. One or two he pulled out and examined as artefacts, being unable to read them: they were very ancient, being made of parchment with boards of cracked wood or cork, thickly sewn or almost corded together. Hale supposed they must have been brought back from the Holy Land in Simmonds' youth. However, the thing which most attracted his attention was not a book, but a parish map on the wall, crudely but clearly executed, showing the names of all the ways and features, with simple but recognisable sketches of the main buildings in situ – the church, The Green Man, the vicarage. What he noted, and what sent him to bed a thoughtful man, was the location of four places: the path along the brook south of the churchyard; Holly Lane, west of the church and crossing the brook by Grey's bridge; Stanton's Farm, to the east of the church beyond the green; Deep Lane, to the north and parallel to Church Lane. Together, the paths where the creature had been seen formed a rough square, with the vicarage at its centre.

He slept poorly that night, shaken once from a dream of standing in the dark in a lane so sunken as to be virtually a pit; he was turning to face whatever shuffled and grunted behind him, when a sudden act of instinctive self-preservation protected him from facing his inner demons and cast him up into the waking world. Again, he was roused by the sound of his horse stamping and whinnying in the small stable below his bedroom window, ajar for the heat, a little before sunrise. Seeing nothing from the window, he put on his dressing gown and went down with a lantern, taking care to put on as many lights on the way as he could , so as to cast the strongest light possible out of the back door as he stepped into the darkness; he found nothing amiss in the shed, and soon calmed the spooked animal. Emboldened by this and by the first rays of the sun, he took a quick turn around the outside of the house to ensure that all was secure. He examined all the ground floor windows and the doors, looked into the summer house, briefly ran his eye over the hedges, walls and gates of the garden. The only thing he noted which was at all odd and had eluded him earlier was the exterior opening of the cellar at the back of the house, partially masked by shrubs, which was unusual in lacking a door or cover. It was the top of a short chute, and took the form of a semicircle of bricks no more than a foot and a half high and wide. It might once have been used to drop fuel into the cellar, but that was now kept in a large brick box outside the kitchen door. Nevertheless, the cellar was plainly still used for storing something, as there were drag marks leading up to the opening, making a fan-shaped patch of grass thread-bare and muddy – and the interior cellar door was kept firmly locked, as he had discovered.

The rector departed the next morning, still tired from his nocturnal activity, to return to his own parish. He gave only passing thought to the reported phenomenon at Oakbank during the following month and more, when he was not conducting services there: from his study of natural history, he knew that nothing answering in detail to the thing that had been described to him existed in the English countryside, and that if it were some alien species released alone into the wild or some deformed sport of nature, its life would not be a long one – indeed, its laboured grunting and crawling suggested that it was already succumbing. He was therefore, on his return to St. Thomas', somewhat taken aback and even disappointed to be met by Harry Turnbull with the tale of its latest sighting, as close as the crossroads at the bottom of Church Lane. The verger seemed equally downcast that the clergyman did not come with a full explanation of the creature, and a lecture ready to deliver to the whole village after the Eucharist. Mr. Hale was unaccustomedly uncomfortable during the service: he sensed that he was being watched by the congregation for some sign, that they were waiting for him to stray from his text onto the subject on all their minds, that there was an anxiety to get the matter of religious observance out of the way so that they could discuss the nightmare thing. For the sacred revealed truth in the form of words alone must always seem pallid and overfamiliar compared to a truth which, however awful or even profane, stalks in the darkness at the edge of actual perception.

No matter how uncomfortable he felt during the service, he began to feel even more uneasy as it drew to an end; he knew he was going to be questioned and forced to listen to the parishioners' unsolicited opinions again, would have to face a delegation again and would once more have nothing to say to them beyond the easy platitudes of one who did not have to live with the creeping thing outside his door every night. Indeed, although they were not so tactless as to accost him as he shook their hands and patted their children's heads at the church door, there was a small group waiting to intercept him outside as he left the vestry after disrobing. He winked broadly to his conscience as he explained to them that he had considered the phenomenon and had consulted reputable works in his library, and was of the opinion that the creature was either a foreign animal struggling to make a living in a hostile environment or was the deformed progeny of a deer or one of their own beasts; in either case, it was barely managing to survive, as they could see, and would not last much longer. It was incapable of harming them and was certainly not anything of unearthly origin. They themselves knew what kind of bizarre offspring ordinary farm animals, and even humans, could occasionally produce through one accident or another, though such were usually born dead; this was merely one such monstrosity which had actually reached birth but had then been rejected by its kind.

The villagers seemed unimpressed, certainly unconvinced, but were satisfied that he had made some sort of effort on their behalf and so left him, without much comment. Relieved, he continued on his way to the vicarage, and let himself in, first checking that his horse was safe in the stable, where he had left it earlier. Harry had left him some provisions, as arranged, it was warm and sunny and he resolved to make the most of what was effectively a free day, an unusual thing for a Sunday for a man in his profession. He spent what remained of the morning browsing in the incumbent's library, and after a light repast he took several selected volumes into the garden, where he made a neglected bench comfortable with a couple of cushions. He read with the singlemindedness of a man who knows that he might never come upon this interesting text again in his life, and had not Harry arrived to help him prepare for the vespers it might have slipped his mind altogether. After the short service, the verger invited him to a simple but wholesome supper prepared by Mrs. Turnbull; during the meal, they were largely silent, each knowing what preoccupied the other but being unwilling to bring up what had swiftly acquired the status of a virtually forbidden subject. Such nonsense to occupy men's brains – especially men whose trade was the service of God – thought Hale angrily, returning to the vicarage as the sun set. He had promised himself that he would complete the chapter of Simmonds' book which he had been reading, before the short ride home; the writer's whole argument would have gone from his mind were he to leave it until his Wednesday visit. So he lit candles and sat down in the library to skim the remaining pages.

Whether it was the afternoon spent in the sun, Mrs. Turnbull's good hotpot or Mr. Turnbull's strong porter, the Reverend Hale assuredly soon dozed over his book, for he was only a couple of pages further on when the swaying of his head roused him, though from the state of the candles at least an hour had passed. Night lay outside the library window, and, berating himself, he hastily returned the introduction to the Cabbala to its shelf, gathered up the light and made to leave before fully awake. In the passage outside the library, he was forced to pause a moment, if only to work out where the front door lay. As he walked hesitantly past the cellar door, he suddenly became fully sensible: against reason, he thought he heard a noise from within it, as though something had bumped into it gently. He had a sudden vision of a cat trapped behind the locked door, but then bethought himself that there was a way out for it through the chute and that otherwise it would have succumbed a long time before if Simmonds had inadvertently locked it in. Perhaps one of the other substitutes had found the key. He tried the door again, but it was still firmly locked. Then a chill came over him, as not only was there another feeble blow to the other side of the door, as though near the floor, but also a grunting noise which recalled one of the descriptions he had heard on that first Wednesday evening at St. Thomas' vicarage. He briefly fell victim to the unreasoning fear of the unknown or the different, as the idea seized him that the missing key might actually be on the other side of the door, and it not be not his choice whether it should be opened or not. But no – nothing happened; there was a faint sound as of sweeping, perhaps a hint of breathing – but the door was too solid for much to be heard that was not in direct contact with it. As he stood unsure as to what he had heard and what he should do, Hale's gaze paid more attention to this door, which he had taken for granted so far, and he traced its outline with the candelabrum he held. To his astonishment, he realized that there were no fewer than eight keyholes in it, two for bolts into each of the three jambs and two apparently into the floor. Even if one picked several of the locks, and removed the hinges, it would still be unopenable. As with the exterior doors and windows, someone had been very concerned that nothing should be able to get into the vicarage, though why the line of defence had been drawn here in the middle of the house rather than at the mouth of the chute into the cellar eluded him.

Then there was a groan from close behind the door – human and inhuman; pained and desolate. Fear overcame sympathy, and an unthinking instinct drove the rector away from the door in a panic.

Pausing only to lock the front door and struggling into his hat and coat as he hurried to the stable, carefully avoiding looking in the direction of the black conduit of the chute, he saddled his horse with a speed and energy which amazed both of them, and, leaving the verger to work out why the library candelabrum was left out there overnight, he abandoned Oakbank with indecent haste. Had any of the villagers been about at that hour, he himself, as the figure of the dark horseman with the black cloak and broad hat galloping frantically through the village at dead of night, would probably have joined the creeping thing in the roll of Oakbank mysteries. As it was, the sound of swift hooves made several dwellers in cottages cross themselves on their way to bed – as profoundly felt a Christian response as any clergyman could ask for.

So as not to invite speculation, Reverend Hale restrained his curiosity until his appointed return to St. Thomas' the following Wednesday, though early, and in the company of a locksmith he had engaged from Sherborne. Having explained the arrangements during Simmonds' absence, he went on to stretch the truth a little by claiming to have mislaid the cellar door keys and to need access, and gave the man a free hand to do what he had to do to make the door openable – but instructed him not to go so far as to open it without him being present. The locksmith had no reservations about the legitimacy of the clergyman's actions – he wore the cloth and had the front door key, and the locksmith had heard the name Hale somewhere – but he did have limitations when it came to what was asked of him here. Returning after half an hour, Hale found the man staring at the door red-faced, clutching some tools, but with nothing else changed.

"Begging your pardon, sir, but we could be working on this door for weeks and still be where we are now. These locks are very complicated, and the keys that fit them cannot be the same shape as our English locks; and I can't remove them because they are fitted in on the far side."

Hale made a joke – only half a joke – about chopping the door down as the only solution. The locksmith did not laugh.

"Not even that, sir. See this." The man scraped with a tool at the edge of one of the keyholes, and bade Hale to look at it closely. At the bottom of the scratch was not white or brown wood but something grey and slightly shiny. "This door is not wooden; it is of iron, with a wood veneer to make it look normal-like. I fancy you would need to blast it in, sir, with gunpowder; it would be a good deal easier to take the surrounding wall down than to get past this door. I can't be thinking why they needed all this, or what there must be in there; the Crown Jewels themselves aren't so guarded."

Hale responded with some comment about the nervous nature of some bachelor clergy, and showed the man out, having paid him for his time, requesting him to say nothing of what had happened; "No doubt I shall find the key in due course, and I would not like Mr. Simmonds to think of me as so careless as to mislay it."

An awful thought had grown in his mind since his scare on Sunday night, through very plausible logic. He had convinced himself that the creature was using the cellar as a kind of den, crawling in and out of it from the garden at sunrise and sunset. It was apparently harmless and avoided human contact, yet here it was trying to get into this house of all others despite knowing of his presence; and here was the fearful part of the argument – what if it did so *because* it knew of his presence? And just as its tendency to elude was reversed in this case, what if its harmlessness were similarly suspended? In short, what if its attitude to clergymen was different to its attitude to others, and it was deliberately besieging the vicarage? Perhaps it really was a thing of evil, seeking to harm goodness through its ministers. Simmonds was plainly afraid of it, as the locks showed; but why did he suffer it to take up residence under his very feet – and why deny its presence when he needed help to deal with it? And what exactly was his connection with the thing that it should be here rather than elsewhere? What part in all this did Reverend Simmonds play, who dissembled before his parishioners while barricading himself in his house?

Despite the obvious conclusions for himself from this line of reasoning, Hale had decided that he would have to face the creature. He now had to learn more of its true nature and origin, even if this put him in mortal danger. He had slipped back into some primeval mode of thought in which knowing one's enemy, especially his name and background, gives one the upper hand, no matter how dangerous he might be. More rationally, he told himself that it was his duty to natural history, and to the villagers of Oakbank, to find out what it really was, and replace mystery and fear with knowledge and truth. As he had already noted, it was unlike most prodigies in being readily detected and fearful of humans, whereas alleged apparitions were both hard to catch and indifferent to humans, and Hale had no doubt that he would be able to dispel the superstitious leanings of the people. He knew of the impositions and self-deceptions which were possible, smiling to himself to think of the visits he made as a young man to a supposedly haunted house in Oxford, with friends investigating the phenomena – which turned out to be caused by uneven floors, the wind whistling through cracked roof tiles and a gang of street-arabs who threw stones into the property for fun.

Perhaps less rationally, he was ashamed of the weakness and lack of faith displayed in his late flight from the vicarage, and was resolved to put his trust in the Lord and face the source of his terror. He knew it was the only way to drive out his dark feelings, and acknowledged the wisdom of the ancient Greeks in ridding themselves of their inner demons by viewing them in action on stage.

And of course, the story was not just about him. Suppose the creature did turn out to be not a monster but a suffering child of God to whom it was his natural and professional duty to bring relief? A host of possible explanations within the natural and normal world presented themselves: a deformed and mentally feeble creature who had escaped from an institution and taken refuge in Oakbank; a mistreated illegitimate who had been kept hidden but now for some reason was turned adrift; a sufferer from some hideous disease such as leprosy. It would have been an extreme case in each of these instances, but some of the details fitted well; perhaps the creature's reticence was the remnant of a sense of shame at its degraded condition.

First, he would attempt to learn something from Mr. Black, the surviving member of the pair which had first encountered it. They would have approached it with less fear and defensiveness than those who encountered it subsequently, and so he might have a fuller picture of it. Of course, if Black's account was significantly different from the others he had heard, it might help to return him to a state of blessed incredulity. Warning him about the man's unpredictability and generally uncouth manner, the landlord of The Green Man gave him directions to Black's home on the edge of the village, sending him down the Deep Lane which was so suggestive already. Arriving at an unmistakable ill-kept cottage, he made his way past weeds to the peeling door and knocked. Sensing movement inside the small building, he knocked again, and was relieved when a face framed by unkempt grey hair and beard appeared at the window, and he heard a loud but muffled "Go away!" from inside. He pressed his own face to the window, and took some encouragement from what he saw in the other man when he recognized the cloth: here was a man who felt alienated from God but had not despaired of Him, who did not attend church but could still feel the comfort it might give. The voice was a little softer as he opened the window a little and inquired as to what he might want in the devil's name.

"Nothing in the devil's name, I hope," replied Hale, "but I had hoped to speak to you just a little about something which you saw a few years ago – I believe you cannot but chose to know of what it is I speak – as I myself intend to search it out in order to attempt to bring some peace to it and to those who have encountered it and have been stricken by fear and incomprehension. Now, sir, will you let me in?"

127

The man softened in expression again to hear for perhaps the first time in years any recognition of what he had borne, but he maintained his stance against the world for a little longer: "What's over is done and I've nothing to say."

"I am sorry to hear that, as I was hoping to learn much from you, and thought that you might in turn be interested to learn what I might discover." It took very little such flattery and concern for the Reverend Hale to gain entry, as the man had grown tired of the loneliness of his self-imposed isolation. Unfortunately, at first Black lived up to the picture the villagers had suggested, being unwilling to speak for himself and largely limiting himself to grunts and gestures in reply to Hale's direct questions, based on the accepted tale as told in the village. But eventually he broke out into a speech which surprised the clergyman and might indeed have been the product of five years' rumination by this simple man.

"Begging your pardon, sir, speaking of God and all before your reverence, but the most important thing is missing from this tale you've heard. You see, sir, when God makes a creature, he finishes it off like, and makes it able to thrive where it is put. The smallest insect and the frailest weed have all they need to get their living and flourish where God puts them. But not so with this creature, sir, which cannot even claim that which the poorest among us can claim as comfort, that God is our maker and preserver. This wretched thing was sent forth cruelly by whoever made it unfinished, with parts not made up, so that it cannot even stand on what legs it has but must crawl in the dust in pain. Oh yes, sir, the creature I saw was in pain, and though I was frighted when I first saw it and loathed it, I have grown to pity it rather. Oftentimes I go down Deep Lane when no-one's about and call out words of comfort, if it should be able to understand them. Sometimes I see it trying to get out of my way, into the hedge, as fast as it can, and then I stand still, or go back, so as not to discomfort it with my approach; perhaps I do so because I still fear it, but also I do not want it to feel any more threatened – though I wish I could bring it some comfort and let it feel some trust in something. That's what's important, isn't it, sir, that we should feel something outside our pitiful selves, have faith in something, not be utterly alone? When I see it, I feel its pain too, its despair and loneliness, and they possess me too. You see, begging your pardon, sir, what you preach isn't the whole of it: there's not only the one loving God who creates and preserves, but there's another twisted one who promotes evil and longs to see his creatures suffer."

Black subsided, and both men were silent and thoughtful for a while.

At the end of the day in the vicarage – and his days at Oakbank were now stressful rather than a pleasant diversion, as always at the back of his mind was the thought of what was, he was convinced, only a few feet away from him; sitting in the garden was impossible unless he sat with his eyes firmly towards the entrance to the cellar – Hale prepared himself for his ordeal with prayer and planning. He believed he was most likely to encounter the creature by sitting at the external entrance to the cellar, but he perceived problems of two different kinds in this plan: firstly, the creature might be dissuaded from following its normal routine if it sensed someone waiting outside for it or saw a sentinel across the garden on its return; secondly, he was unsure if he could stand watching it crawl out of its hole or what its reaction might be if it found its way home blocked. The idea of entering the dark cellar by the chute, even if it were possible, to await its return was of course not even to be thought of. No, better to come across it as others had done, as if by chance, and, as it were, on neutral territory, in the open, where both could withdraw easily without danger. He resolved to follow its circuit around the village, following the darkest lanes. He had set up a little dark lantern, the opening of a door in the brass case of which out sent a narrow but powerful stream of light, and he set out with this in one hand and a good walking stick in the other. It was still summer, and as he set out soon after half-past nine it was only twilight; nevertheless, it was not warm, and he had his hat and coat on.

He decided to see if he could follow its tracks from the cellar. Not approaching the outer wall of the house in case it were still stirring, he scouted along the drag marks away from the vicarage, and soon discovered that they led into and across the orchard – yes, proceeding directly ahead, he soon found a gap at ground level in the copper beech hedge which surrounded the plot. At some point a plant had died and had not been replaced; the foliage to right and left had flourished and soon joined together, but the missing stem left at the bottom of the hedge a hole much like the cellar-chute, which the creature had enlarged by wearing away surrounding bark and twigs and scratching a scoop of earth from the ground. A few yards away stood the garden gate, opening onto a rough set of steps, nothing more than planks enclosing earth and held in place with pegs, descending down the wooded bank to join a footpath along a brook. He recognized this feature from the old map; if he went one way alongside the brook, the path led back up to the far side of the churchyard, and this was the way he chose to go.

He soon regretted his choice: the tall surrounding trees shut out most of the remaining light, and a breeze seemed to run through the little valley making the vegetation sway and sigh in a disconcerting manner. Exposed roots grasping for the water and ancient half-rotted or half-buried trunks made the path difficult to walk on in the dark – especially if one were trying always to look aside or ahead rather then pick one's immediate way. He most profoundly did not wish to meet with anything in this confined space, and although only a couple of hundred yards separated the vicarage garden from the far side of the churchyard, it was with great relief that he scrambled up the next set of improvised steps and emerged at the corner of the churchyard wall, in Holly Lane. For a moment, he seemed back in the real world, rather than the world of decaying wood and shadows; behind him was the bridge, a mundane and useful artefact made by man, and in front of him was the reassuring dark bulk of the church in which he had offered prayers. The moon was still quite low over the trees and the tower and there was a golden glow low in the west, but the last glimmers of blueness were being replaced by blackness overhead. He advanced along Holly Lane, towards the lights of cottages north of the church, but swiftly froze as something scurried across the road almost at his feet; even before he could open the dark lantern, he realized his foolishness – a rabbit was all, nothing like the size or the motion of the thing he both sought and shunned. He feared that his imagination was getting the better of him, and he decided to rest for a moment and settle his mind before continuing. There being nowhere to sit, the lane at this point having the church wall on a low bank along one side and a four-foot bank topped with an overgrown hedge on the other, the border of the land of Fielding's Farm, he contented himself with leaning against the trunk of a stunted holm oak which came out of Fielding's bank almost horizontally before suddenly realizing its mistake and growing straight up.

Yes, it took care not to grunt and draw attention, but it breathed heavily and in a laboured way. Yes, there it was, cowering on the other side of the tree, curled up in the long grass as though to avoid detection. Hale played the same game, straining to see as much as he could in the dying light, without obviously bending or advancing towards it. It was hard to tell from its pose if it were bipedal, but it seemed to be hunched up in a hominid way rather than curled round like a quadruped, and the head seemed to be round rather than elongated. A dark shape, rough but with a leathery rather than hairy covering – though whether this was skin or clothing one could not tell. The size of a large child rather than

131

an adult. More he could not determine, though he was surprised at how calm he felt now that he had obtained his objective and he was finally assured that the thing cowering at his feet could not harm him. But he had to go further, and get the first clear and close sight of the creature that anyone had had; he knew he would only have a moment from throwing the dark lantern open to the creature fleeing from the light and the attention, so he would have to act very carefully. A few slow moments moving the lantern imperceptibly down to about the level of his left knee; carefully propping the stick against the tree and then moving his right hand across his thighs to rest on top of the lantern; bracing himself for a sudden swivelling to the left and downwards while flicking open the catch and directing the beam.

It happened, and immediately he regretted it, knowing that forever afterwards a good day would be defined by him as one on which he did not recall that sight and a bad day – many times commoner – as one on which he did. For one second the light fell on the creature's sketch of a face, which chanced to be upturned as if watching what the man would do, before it turned away to scrabble up the bank and flee, as on all fours, and Hale dropped the lamp in his utter astonishment. Hale had so short a time to stare at that death's head, but the impression it made lasted for the rest of his life. Presented with that bare shape as of a skull scarcely covered in skin, that face with its human features abraded away, its dignity and vitality all stripped away, he thought afterwards of the Egyptian mummy he had seen in London, its solid parts alone preserved in a tarry substance but still recognizable. The creature's nose and ears were mere holes, its eyes dark sunken pits into which he could not, fortunately, see, but worst of all was the little mouth – lipless, almost circular, with stumps as of half-formed teeth within. As it turned away, what passed for its feet and legs swung round behind it and made contact with Hale's shins and boots.

The man staggered back, unable to see more, as the lantern was on the ground and out, but knowing that the creature was escaping through the hedge. He fell on his knees, his hands clasped before him and his eyes closed. He prayed and he wept, out of irrational fear or for fears past; out of pity for the creature as well as out of loathing for it; out of his own weakness and lack of faith and in gratitude for his safety; out of emotions which he could not name but could feel in his clenched chest and in his short, painful sobs. The truth of his own mortality and the inevitability of his own demise had been brought home to him by that death's head in a way more powerful than most men ever experience, even when watching parent or child dying; the loneliness and cold of the universe had made contact with his own heart in the expression of that solitary, half-alive wanderer.

After perhaps ten or fifteen minutes, he stood up, with some difficulty because of the pain in his knees, barely remembered to recover his lantern and stick, and made his way slowly back to the vicarage along the lanes. Clearing his mind of shame, fear, compassion and disgust, he tried to make sense of what he had seen: obviously this was the creature of the villagers' tales, unknown to science but living and in some awful way akin to humankind. He had seen nothing to make him doubt his own theory about its den under the vicarage, but the creature clearly meant him no harm, fleeing when he was at its mercy, despite its apparent curiosity at the cellar door, trying to get through despite knowing of his presence. He was still no closer to the answers to his questions about his origins and its predilection for church property; they could perhaps only be answered by one man – Mr. Simmonds, who held the key to the mystery in more ways than one.

Hale had already decided to confront the man at once on his return, when, on his fourth Sunday of duty at St. Thomas', he was informed by Harry that he had heard that the vicar had landed in

England and was expected back in the parish on Thursday. Hale spent the next couple of days visiting the other substitutes, telling them that there was no need to trouble themselves with St. Thomas' further and that he would take care of the parish while the vicar settled back in. None seemed distressed at this offer, though not for fear of a creature; Hale surmised that they had not spent as long at the vicarage as he had and that they had not been taken into the villagers' confidence. At the same time, he did what he could to make himself satisfied that they had no suspicions about the place; for a terrible moment he thought he was going to have to confide in an elderly rector who expressed great interest in what might be in the cellar – but he quickly realized that the man assumed that the plethora of locks implied treasures of a bottled variety behind them. He took the service on Wednesday, and watched the arrival by cart of Simmonds' heavier luggage – two trunks, and a newer, smaller box of great weight, presumably containing books; it was confirmed that the man himself would be coming on in the Bishop's carriage the following morning. He practised the next day's confrontation several times in the sitting room, taking care that Harry was not about, and finally left, bidding the verger to warn the vicar that he would arrive late in the afternoon to discuss the parish, giving him time to unpack some things and settle himself after his journey.

Twenty-four hours later, Harry was shamefacedly trying to fob Hale off with the story that Mr. Simmonds was too tired to be disturbed "for at least a day or two". He brushed the verger aside and entered the house, calling out for the vicar from the corridor. After a while, he appeared, looking unusually haggard from his trip.

"Sir, I thank you for your solicitude, but I must insist that I have had a long and tiring journey and have slept little for several nights and must have some rest before –"

"Indeed, sir; were I in your situation, knowing what you know, I should not have slept this many a year."

Both men caught Harry's gasp of amazement at this, and Simmonds hurriedly guided Hale into the sitting room with excessive apologies; the older man noted how even in that brief time in the hallway, his gaze was largely on the cellar door, running round its edge to check that the locks held. The door of the sitting room was shut and Hale sat down, though the other paced. He seemed even thinner and equally as anxious as he had been at his departure, and his manner remained distracted, though he had been quite bronzed by the sun and seemed to have more energy.

"I am sorry – I have not been used to Christian company for some months and am forgetting my gratitude to you for looking after my little flock here. I shall be much better in a day or two."

Hale rejected his attempt to diffuse the situation by reverting to the commonplace, and insisted on pursuing his subject without any polite evasion.

"It would be much better for everyone if you were to acknowledge that creature which lives under your house, freeing your flock from their fears about it, and yourself from your nightmares, and showing it some pity."

Hale had risked everything on this; suppose Simmonds accused him of foolishness and denied everything? Suppose Simmonds proved to be guiltless of anything beyond a well-stocked cellar and an exploring house cat? Fortunately, he was taken too unawares to be evasive, and even more fortunately he assumed Hale knew more than he really did. He collapsed into an armchair, apparently choking, and gulped down the brandy which Hale swiftly poured out and handed to him. After an extended period of speechlessness and pained writhings, brought to an end with two

135

more measures, the last in the decanter, he eventually became coherent and faced the rector, who stared at him sternly and implacably; "Well, sir, some explanation if you please. Unless you would rather answer to the Bishop." For the next half an hour – speaking quietly lest the verger should be listening, though Hale heard him depart early on – he divested himself as if in the confessional of the knowledge of his sinful actions which he had carried about in his heart.

In the tranquillity of the sitting room of a rural English parsonage, with late summer sunlight streaming through the windows, the young vicar told of the golem, the creature in human shape made by man rather than by God, an artificial life-form – Hale had read something about this in Simmonds' books – and how he had followed the Cabbala and tried to create it, out of dust. How by incantation and ritual he had, after years of study and labour, coaxed a living shape out of lifeless earth. Had he not already seen the results of this experiment, Hale would have deemed his story to be the raving of a madman. As it was, rather than being craziness, it actually served to make good sense of a mystery.

"And, may God have mercy on my soul, just as He breathed life into the first man, so I breathed life into that blasphemy of man, down in that cellar where I made it. It was not as I expected it to be, but a shambling mockery. Indeed, I have since learned that the old masters deliberately left crucial details out of their accounts, lest wicked men should be able to raise up powerful armies of golems. But it lives; how it continues to live, what nourishes it, I know not, unless it be hatred and pain. I assume it gets what it needs while it is out of the house; I have never given it anything, hoping at first it would simply ..... cease. Oh God, my God, what have I done!"

The enormity of what he had done burst upon him, as it must have done often before, thought Hale, who watched him with a stern expression – though inwardly he could not help but feel some compassion for one who was plainly suffering greatly as a result of his misguided actions.

"Did it not occur to you that this whole project was blasphemous? An attempt to usurp the role of the Creator?"

When he had left off sobbing, disregarding Hale's question, Simmonds continued: "I have since learnt that it is for all practical purposes immortal – or rather, in this half-finished state, its existence depends on mine, its breath on mine; whether the reverse is true, I know not, but I do know in my heart that it cares not for its life, which is a burden and a pain to it. And it would do away with me, whether purely out of hatred for my being the author of its misery or perhaps because it senses in some way that its suffering can only end with my death. It has little strength, but several times I had to struggle with it in the dark, finally locking it out of the house – though I had not the heart to banish it from its only home and shelter in the cellar." Finally, he said, grimly, "And now I defy you to say that you believe a single word of what I have said."

After a brief pause, Hale, who had heard not a secretive man hastily inventing lies to cover his being found out but a sincere man who had inwardly wanted for years to share the burden of his story, shook his head. "Nay, sir; I have seen enough of the creature to recognise the basic truth of what you say – though why you chose to bring it into existence I cannot surmise."

"Indeed, I scarcely remember myself, after so many years of regret."

"I have a few questions of detail, but in essence I believe what you say and furthermore intend to help you in untangling what you have brought about, if that be possible."

137

The stern, aloof expression and reserved manner which Hale had associated with Simmonds since he first met him long before had already been severely strained by his emotional outbursts, and now they were replaced by a look of relief, coming with difficulty after such a long period of solitary strain. He earnestly sought to answer every question as fully as he could, including admitting that his real reason for his recent trip had been to try to learn how he might put right what had been done. Some Cabbalists would have nothing to do with him when they knew what he had done; some were unable to make any useful suggestions; but a few offered advice which might have some merit, though untested. He had brought back with him some rare and ancient texts which contained certain procedures and incantations which might have relevance to his situation, and he intended to put them into practice as soon as he might.

Hale urged caution: the vicar's meddling had already produced a tragedy, and he should embark on nothing without being reasonably certain of its outcome, or at least of the worst which could follow from it. Simmonds, willing to do anything to hold on to his new-found ally, readily agreed to do nothing without telling Hale first, and certainly to attempt nothing that night. Reassured, Hale rode off as the sun set, his last sight of the vicar being of him standing before his house, hugging himself as if cold, looking towards the side where the cellar entrance lay.

Sleep was out of the question that night: whatever fearful and fascinating things Hale had heard, experienced or imagined during the past few months, nothing had been quite so disturbing as this tale of life falsely created and misused. Reverend Simmonds clearly regretted what he had done – and not only because he had earned the creature's enmity – but he had described the creation and turning away of life as though he had been describing the casting of an unsuccessful pot and its subsequent rejection. Was creation that easy, that a Reverend Simmonds could at least approach it? How great was his sin in so doing – equal to that of the one who first set himself up as equal to God? Now that it existed, was the creature to be treated as a form of human life, to be protected by law and cared for, rather than eradicated as seemed to be Simmonds' intention? Ideas as large and serious as any he had encountered in his theological training, and now no longer theoretical but impinging on what he would be doing in the next few days, filled his brain as he tried to rest. Once or twice he slipped from the conscious world from behind his closed eyes, but the images of the unconscious world were worse than the ideas of the waking one. The mummy of a dead Egyptian twisted itself to rise with effort from the painted box in which it had been vainly laid, shaking off its threadbare wrappings as it reached out blindly with shrivelled arms like the legs of the creature, the fragility of all flesh compounded by age; a baby's round face and pouting lips grew, blackened and became the bare skull and horrific mouth-hole of the creature, pressing into his face. Eventually, deciding that wished-for sleep was worse than sleeplessness, he rose and prayed a long time before deciding to ride over to Oakbank early to see how Simmonds had fared. He arrived as the vicar was having a lethargic and sketchy breakfast, and joined him. He was clearly pleased to have company in the house, but this could not raise the gloom which enveloped him. He had slept little too, several times going round the house to check the doors and windows, while being careful not to look out of them; he had been drawn to stand outside the cellar door for several lengthy periods, straining to hear. (Hale gathered that this behaviour had become something of an obsession before his trip, and he was upset not to have shaken it off.)

Hale decided that the only way to interrupt this self-absorption was to suggest some way forward, brutal though it might be. He presented Simmonds with several ideas, some more practical than others and some more humane than others, but all intended to break this stalemate which had lasted for some five years. The creature's existence could be admitted to the villagers – its origin need not be revealed – and its capture could be organized. The vicar's fears inside the house at least could be ended by blocking off the cellar in the creature's absence and improving the walls around the property. A service of exorcism could be performed, although whether this would work in the case of a tangible being was doubtful. And so on. None appealed to Simmonds: he was repelled by the idea of increasing its sufferings, or he feared reprisal by it, or he had some other reservation. Hale enquired as to what Simmonds had learnt in Palestine which might assist him; for the first time, he became less open with his colleague, or else it was simply that he was attempting to explain things which he knew the other would find difficult to accept or understand. As far as Hale could understand, there were two main approaches they could follow, one involving a sacrifice of an Old Testament kind to pacify God's possible anger at the blasphemy which had been performed, followed by lengthy prayers and rituals, including fasting and oaths, aimed at begging the Almighty to reverse what had been done. Hale wondered somewhat at what might pass for Christian belief in this vicar's mind, but he kept his peace. The other approach was frankly magical, involving invocations to spirits and mystical symbols, aimed at trapping the golem in a way which prevented it from having any effect on the things of the world and then returning it safely to dust. Hale looked hard at Simmonds in silence for a while before asking him if he thought that such performances were proper for a man in his position; he replied that it was basically exorcism, as countenanced by the Church. even if some of the terms were different. The creature had come into being through exotic oriental practices, and such might be needed to remove it again. Simmonds did not feel that he was being in any way dismissive of the Christian god in utilising other forces for a worthwhile end, much as he might employ the power of clockwork to turn his meat before the fire. Hale felt this was flippant, but saw that nothing was to be gained by angering him; better to let him try it, if it were not dangerous, and then see that it was in vain. He noticed that Simmonds had fallen silent, but not primarily from fatigue: he was straining in every nerve and the focus of all his senses was elsewhere.

"What is it, man?"

"Don't you hear it?" He rose and walked swiftly into the hallway, Hale following. He stood in front of the cellar a moment, then threw himself against the door, his left ear pressed against it and his arms wrapped round his head. "*Don't you hear it?*"

"No, I hear nothing. It is your imagination."

"No, it is my own breathing I hear. My own breath, in and out of that creature's mouth. Do you understand? It has returned, it is here, waiting for me."

Hale stood in astonishment. When he had heard the creature behind the door, it had clearly thought he was Simmonds returned, though it had not made the same mistake on seeing him outside. He shuddered briefly at the thought that it might have come across him in his clerical attire in the dark, might not have noticed the difference, and might not have retreated. His outward mood was other, for Simmonds' benefit.

"But what have you to fear from it, man? It can scarce move, cannot stand upright, can have no strength at all; and I doubt it has more wit to contrive aught than a beast in a byre."

Simmonds remained pressed to the door, sliding up and down it slowly, his arms embracing the wood in sweeping gestures as though expressing his inner torment through physical agitation; for a moment, Hale saw him as a specimen beetle, its legs waving wildly while its pinned body could only undulate. He moaned: "You

141

cannot understand; it saves everything to use against me; it conserves everything for that one chance. It has no strength as we measure strength, in the muscles, but it has survived on nothing for years – that is true strength. And its strength grows, with its pain, and its anger, and its emptiness......" By now he was on his knees in front of the door, sobbing, and the rest of his words were choked. Hale moved forward to grasp his shoulders, but as he did so he was brought up short by a sudden bump or blow to the door – from the other side. Simmonds threw back his head and let out what could only be described as a howl, borne of despair, and slumped to the floor. Hale dragged him up into a slouching posture next to him and, taking his left arm round his neck and holding it with his left hand while supporting him under the right arm with his right hand, he contrived to half-carry, half-drag him up the stairs and deposit him on his bed, as exhausted collapse rather than sleep overcame him.

Returning to the cellar, with the courage engendered by daylight and the eight stout locks, Hale stood before the door and loudly improvised what was in essence a prayer of exorcism; exactly what he said he could not remember afterwards, but he knew that he had called on the creature, as a thing of darkness which had no place on earth, to leave the world alone and cease its machinations against the Lord's anointed priest – yes, it had fine words and Biblical echoes; but then he faltered and stopped, not believing in what he said. If what Simmonds implied was true, that it was indeed planning some kind of criminal revenge on its neglectful creator, was there not reason, if not excuse, for what it did? And it did not seem just to threaten with damnation a creature which suffered already beyond what fully living flesh and nerves could endure, for no fault of its own. He put an ear to the door: he thought he might have heard a sound as of a light sack being bounced down the last couple of steps, but he could not be sure.

When he returned to the bedroom, he found Simmonds in a fevered state close to delirium, muttering incoherently, writhing as though in torment; the tension of years of living with his terrible secret, the disappointment of apparently failing in his frantic quest abroad, the dreadful journey home to confront it again – all had finally burst out and shattered the strength as well as the spirit of the man. He needed something to settle his nerves and deaden the horror. Hale already knew the contents of Simmonds' study and pantry from his recent visits and was aware that the only alcohol in the house had been in the decanter, except for a small reserve of communion wine over in the vestry, so he determined to hasten to The Green Man and obtain some more brandy for the patient. In the doorway, he almost collided with Harry, coming to see if the vicar was feeling any better and whether Evensong was to take place as planned. Feeling somewhat under pressure, Hale briefly informed the verger that the vicar was feverish from his long journey in foreign parts and led him upstairs; asking him to watch over the sick man without paying heed to any of his ravings, he hurried back downstairs with a promise to take the service himself when he returned. He was in such a hurry that he was through the open doorway and half way down the path before he remembered to go back, pick up his key and close the front door carefully behind him.

It was less than fifteen minutes later that, after brusquely cutting his way through the landlord's intendedly jocular comments about the time and the habits of the clergy, he returned, carrying a quarter bottle of brandy. He was surprised to see Harry Turnbull also converging on the vicarage, from the direction of the church, and remonstrated with him for leaving the sick man's side; the verger explained that, as the vicar had suddenly passed into a deep sleep, he had thought it better to leave him for a few minutes in order to inform the gathering congregation that they should wait to hear the service delivered by the substitute. Hale opened the door, and at once detected a musty smell; no, the cellar entrance was still firmly fastened, but yes, the smell was stronger as he mounted the stairs, and he noted small black particles scattered on the carpet. As he vaulted up the steps, the fatal errors registered in his mind in sequence and pointed him to a dreadful conclusion which he prayed was false. The golem had heard the commotion caused by his creator outside the cellar and had retreated from the door under Hale's condemnation; in hopes that his prey was sufficiently deranged to be lax in his precautions, or perhaps sensing that there would be much coming and going as a consequence of his state, it could have crawled out of the cellar and made its way round to the front of the house under cover of the bushes, to await an opportunity to enter. This might, indeed, have been its daily practice for months or even years. The chance had finally been given to it when Hale had collided with Harry in the entrance to the vicarage and the front door had been left open for several minutes while he two went upstairs; it would only have had to haul itself from the shrubs and through the door to hide itself in an obscure corner of the house. Then Harry's absence might have given it the chance to crawl up the stairs.

Even as he pieced this together in his mind, he prayed it might not be so, but as he rushed into the bedroom he saw that he was in essence right; and so was Simmonds right, for in a paroxysm of saved residual energy the creature had dragged itself onto the bed and was astride the vicar's chest, bending down and forward so its awful face was inches away from the man's bulging eyes and gritted teeth. It was making a faint but dreadful growling sound, and beneath it the man was groaning and convulsing fitfully as he clutched at his chest and collar. The creature seemed to know it had no strength to do the man harm, but could afflict him with fear, guilt and loathing which were as deadly. For one awful second Hale was paralysed by the sight, as the creature bent its head back and opened its mouth and eyes as far as it could in its exertion and its triumph. And then it was gone – quite literally gone, as it seemed almost to burst like a bubble, in a cloud of an ash-like substance that settled on the bed and on the floor around. Hale took a step forward, hesitated, then reluctantly approached the bed. The breath of both had ceased; Hale checked Simmonds' pulse; it had not taken much in his reduced state, even though his feeble opponent had clearly been incapable of even leaving any marks of physical damage.

Hale stood and contemplated the body. The premature death of a fellow-clergyman was sad, and to witness his end in that way was shocking, but his predominant feeling was one of relief: his confused fear and pity were dispelled, Simmonds' anguish and guilt were over, the creature's pain and hatred were ended. And perhaps some kind of justice had been served.

The rector intercepted the bemused verger on the stairs and sent him at once for the doctor; the ash had almost all been brushed away by the time he came and no-one noticed the little that remained, so nothing complicated the verdict of death by heart-failure induced by stress and exhaustion in one of a naturally weak constitution, which the trip had exacerbated rather than cured – and indeed this may have been in part the truth of it.

As Mr. Simmonds fortunately had no family close enough to want to involve themselves, Mr. Hale made it his business to supervise the clearing of the vicarage. The eight keys to the cellar door were eventually found – only one would ever be used again – and Hale stoutly made the descent of the steps, with daylight streaming in behind him and from the hatch in front, with a good lantern and a still-mystified Harry Turnbull beside him. Even so, the place was dank and full of decay, and the atmosphere one of tragic neglect and grief. There were heaps of vegetation in the corners, dead leaves on dried leaves on rotten leaves, and although Turnbull was left to conjecture about them blowing in through the small opening, Hale knew that he creature had tried to nest in them, and his pity for it flooded back as he thought of it huddled thus in the dark year after year. Moved, he covered his emotion with feigned coughing at the smell. There were many remains of small animals and birds on the floor, but whether these were things which had come in by chance and perished there or represented attempts by the half-material creature to feed itself they were too decayed to reveal. Hale had the place fired and fumigated, scrubbed out and whitewashed – but still its air remained too noisome for anything other than the storage of fuel.

Keys were found, cupboards unlocked. Certain symbols and instruments of antique Levantine manufacture came to light, and these, along with the oriental books in Simmonds' library were offered to scholars of those languages at Oxford. Their two representatives seemed disturbed by some of the passages they perused, but they hastily boxed the collection up and curiously and contrarily promised to disperse it to corners of college libraries where the volumes would not be found by any casual reader who might be able to read them. Harry thought he had misheard; Hale knew better.

As for the congregation of St. Thomas', Oakbank – they would not have presumed to query the doctor's diagnosis, or to have pried into the Reverend Hale's silence, or to have tried to preserve things as they were at the vicarage, but they were glad to be able to enjoy a pipe as they walked home from The Green Man under the stars, knowing that the thrill of the darkness and the chill of the night were no more than that.

FLIBBERTIGIBBET

When one lives in a period in which the gallows and the gibbet have been absent from public sight for so long that the technical distinction between them is often blurred, it is easy to forget also the awful appearance they presented when in use, or even when merely having the potential for use. The gibbet more so than the gallows, for, even though it threatened violent death whereas the other was merely in the nature of a receptacle, the gallows was commonly in a frequented spot, in a square in front of the courthouse or gaol or even in a marketplace, and its operation was associated with a social gathering which often had a festive atmosphere - a communal witnessing of the triumph of justice, which was in all but name a holiday. Not so the gibbet: this wooden structure of upright and crossbeam was set up after the crowd had lost interest and gone away, without any spectacle, and its operation was a long process of corruption and decay, painful in its message of mortality, rather than a moment of high drama. Sited away from the population but where passers-by would see it at the roadside and take it as a direct warning of the risks in committing felony, it had the greatest impact when encountered by the lone traveller in a remote spot. Disgusting by day, when pecking birds and sucking insects clustered around the pendant iron cage or chains which held the corpse and made it swing and creak on the end of its rope, it was even more disturbing by night, when the attenuated human shape could be seen inside the bars or links and the orb of the moon could be seen through its ribs. With time, the awful vision of the receding flesh, the widening grin, the glimpses of the inner organs of which we are largely composed and by which we live but of which we are only dimly aware, would pass; but then a new horror would start, and still no rest afforded the inmate, for the upright structure of the skeleton without the attaching ligaments would disarticulate and collapse, and bones would fall through the bars or from the chains until only the larger pieces - skull, scapula, pelvis, perhaps larger limb bones - remained. Unless collected by a mourner, the fallen bones would be scattered around by animals or washed into the soil, and it must often have happened that an excited dog out for a walk proudly presented its owner with a stick which turned out to be a fresh human relic. Although the gibbet was intended to shock and deter hardened malefactors, it probably had more effect on nervous innocents, whose sensibilities must have been severely tested by such sights.

In Theophilus Hale's place and time, both gallows and gibbet were in use, though the latter was but rarely employed, to prolong after death the punishment of those deemed by society to be particularly wicked. One hanged for stealing a loaf or a sheep would not merit gibbetting, but a notorious highwayman, pirate or murderer would, until 1834. Colourful characters of the latter sort were not often encountered around Stoke Armitage, though an old gibbet still stood by the crossroads at Lower Easterby, only about five miles away. A younger son of Lower Easterby Hall had gone to sea in an earlier generation and had turned pirate; he had been brought back to Bristol in chains for execution, after which his corpse had been displayed in his native place, on a gibbet allegedly made from a timber from his old vessel. No amount of pleading with the magistrates by his family could recover the body or even have it removed; his mother died of grief and his father killed himself for shame, it was said.

Half a century on, the structure still stood firm, sinisterly black in hue, perhaps supporting the story that it had been a ship's timber, well-seasoned, sealed with pitch and weathered and tested in use. There was no rot in it, and birds did not care to perch there to foul it – except for one memorable occasion, which gave rise to one of the stories which caused it to have a reputation for ill-luck. One day, about twenty years after the gibbet had been in use, a local farmer called Lynch was slowly driving a laden cart along the road towards it, his lad walking alongside the horses with a whip more for show than use, since the beasts knew their way well enough and had their own pace and rhythm. Dusk was drawing on, but Lynch could still see a great black bird on the crossbeam of the grim structure; it was larger and blacker than any crow or rook, with a great beak of jet – presumably a raven. The farmer pulled his cart up so that he was just below it, and he looked up at it while the boy held the horses; it was the boy who later gave the clearer and fuller account of what then happened. At first the man and the bird just regarded each other, then the man cocked his head to one side; the bird followed suit. The man then cocked his head the other way, and the bird at once mirrored him. He shook his head vigorously from side to side, and the bird ruffled its neck feathers. The farmer uttered a profanity and stood up in his seat to take a closer look at the curious creature; for a moment they stared at each other from a yard's distance, each with the head jutting forward, and then suddenly the bird launched itself without warning. It gave a single great croak as it flew into the man's face, then flapped and stabbed for what seemed like many seconds as the man tried in his pain and fury to both strike it away and catch it in his hands, succeeding in neither. Eventually, the boy drove it off with the aid of his whip, or perhaps it merely lost interest after Lynch had fallen between his horses and was no longer easily assailable. It took the boy some time to calm the disturbed animals down enough to be able to drag the man out from under their hooves, from which he had suffered several kicks and stamps. He was moaning and clutching the upper part of his face with his hands, and blood was seeping between his fingers. He could barely stand, one leg being broken, and the boy hauled him onto the cart. The youngster decided that he was so badly injured and losing blood so quickly that he would not survive the plodding cart ride of over an hour to the nearest doctor, in Stoke Armitage, so, having ascertained that the bird was not lurking to make a second attack, he ran all the way there and made so much fuss that the physician set out at once with him on the back of his horse. It was

149

bad, one eye gone completely and the other damaged so as to be almost unusable, but the farmer survived and the feared brain infection did not follow. That the story was not merely a dark tale fashioned around the suggestiveness of the gibbet was proved by the fact that Lynch, blind and lame in one leg, was still living on the charity of the Easterby parish when Hale first came to Stoke Armitage, and his boy was now tenant where once the old man had farmed.

Once a place has acquired a sinister reputation, not even the complete refuting of the tale which gave rise to it will dispel its notoriety or prevent the spreading of new stories to reinforce it; there is a craving for the dark and bizarre which makes for a clinging to any hint of mystery and horror, no matter how far-fetched or ill-founded. And then that hint is filled out with narrative, description and characters, and absorbs details from other stories, and so grows. The Lower Easterby gibbet was a case in point: it was a wooden structure from which a dead body had once been suspended, and it had apparently once been perched on by a vicious carrion-bird. From these ideas had grown macabre fantasies – of an unnervingly thin figure seen by moonlight, rooting for lost bones around its base; of demons cavorting around it as a rendezvous, swinging and leaping from its arm; of witches scavenging for disgusting ingredients for their potions. Magpies, toads, black cats and unnameable creatures like large, sharp-faced rodents had all been reported as gathering around it. There was the unoriginal tale of the man who had taken an axe to it, only to have it skid harmlessly off the timber and take off his leg, and that of the man who tried to set light to it but was thwarted by a sudden downpour from the only small cloud in the sky, which wet nothing which was more than three yards away. If anyone slipped at the crossroads in muddy weather, had a horse cast a shoe there or had a load tumble from a cart while turning, it was ascribed to the baleful influence of the gibbet; if these things chanced to happen a mile, two miles, even three miles away, it was because the person had passed, or was approaching, the gibbet.

Theophilus Hale was well aware of how folktales develop in this way, and so was sceptical when he was told of the adventure which had befallen Jeremiah Fane. Jeremiah was the nearest thing his village of Stoke Armitage had to a banker. A jeweller and watchmaker by trade, he had taken to supplementing the irregular earnings of his business in such a small place by making use of the stock of gold and silver he was obliged to keep, by forwarding loans; from this money-lending had grown granting mortgages, issuing bonds, taking goods as pledges, dealing in property, and other practices which assisted the operation of local business while earning him commissions, interest and profits. He had grown to be the richest man in the area apart from the largest landowners, though it meant that he continued to live above his shop rather than moving into a grand house, since he did not dare to leave it unattended; shutters on the windows, elaborate bolts and locks on every door and casement and a fierce dog completed his security. However, he had to travel the thirteen or fourteen miles to the county town of Dorchester periodically, to visit the bank, do whatever trading he needed to do in precious metals and gems for his stock, and try to sell whatever pieces he had made or acquired for which there was no market in the countryside. On such occasions, leaving his clerk Josiah Hill immured in the shop with a loaded pistol, he would drive his little one-horse carriage as quickly as possible, stopping for nothing, with his apprentice Nathan sitting next to him with a fiercesome-looking flared musket of the kind known popularly as a blunderbuss, filled with a charge of balls and scrap iron which would scatter and tear through a gang of footpads no matter how badly aimed. Between spring and autumn, they would set out at dawn, arrive at town around midday, leave again after two or three hours at most and return at sunset with the horse exhausted. In the winter, if the trip was really unavoidable, it would have to begin and end in the dark, and this is when the event already referred to occurred. One evening in early November, Fane was urging his horse homeward, anxious because of the lateness of the hour; he had a locked iron box behind his seat in which, amongst other things, were a bar of gold, a small bag of pearls, another containing several gemstones – a fiery ruby he saw as a fine ornament to a ring, a long sapphire for a grand brooch – and a new supply of coins. He rattled intently along the road towards Lower Easterby, looking at nothing except the back of his horse's head, trying to keep on the highway in the dark. So it was the apprentice who saw first, as the carriage topped the slope from where the gibbet became visible, and he was unable to do more than paw at his master's arm feebly and make a kind of croaking noise; Fane looked at him sharply and asked him what was the matter, though his language was rather less temperate, as he was on edge and did not need the foolish boy to distract him. The youth began to emit an inarticulate wailing and raised his arm; cursing, Fane looked ahead to where he was pointing, and added a gasp to the sound. Even though it was dark, he could make out against the stars the outline of the gibbet, a few dozen paces ahead of them – and a large shape pendant from its arm where there should by rights have been nothing. It was too late to stop, but as they came up to it they were halted by the horse suddenly slowing, taking fright and backing off as the shape began to move, almost over its head. It was indeed a human figure, clad in black and with a hood over its head, and there were chains around it, which rattled as it began to sway and lift its arms. It made a loud moaning noise, then as if with a great effort it leapt down from its position, and advanced towards the terrified creature, which was still trying to back away. By now, there was no-one to stop it, as Fane and the boy had both vaulted from the carriage and were running as hard as they could, the jeweller back down the road and his apprentice, who had dropped his weapon, out across the fields to the side.

Fane, who was unaccustomed even to walking more than a couple of dozen yards, was struggling for breath and clutching at his pounding heart and the pain in his side when he arrived at Tom Baines' farm more than a mile away and beat at the door, heedless of the dog barking and snapping at him. The farmer, who had checked his stock for the last time and was beginning to think of retiring himself, opened a window before risking the door, and was amazed to see the jeweller in such a state. It took Fane nearly ten minutes, on a kitchen chair and with a glass of brandy, to recover himself sufficiently to attempt even a brief account of what had happened. It was another ten minutes before he could face returning to the spot with the sceptical Baines and his eldest son – the farmer insisting that he had to see for himself that there was no such thing, though really his motive was an unwillingness to spare the notorious moneylender the ordeal of having to face his fear again. There was indeed nothing to be seen – no carriage, no horse, no chains, no phantom; just the bare beams of the gibbet, and the gun still lying in the middle of the road where Nathan had dropped it, as the only slender evidence of what had happened. There was little sympathy from the farmer for Fane, not as the victim of a severe fright and certainly not as one who made his money, and quite a lot of money, as he did; he would not lend him a horse or accompany him home at that hour, but would allow him to sleep on the settle if he was too fearful to walk home in the dark, and would keep the gun safe until he was able to return to collect it. Fane would gladly have slept on the flagstones rather than face that road again by moonlight, and accepted the farmer's grudging hospitality until the following morning, though he slept little; as the night wore on, the fright he had suffered was steadily replaced by a characteristic passion – his desolation and anger at the thought that his gold and jewels were in a box in the abandoned carriage, and by now could be anywhere.

When the footsore Fane reached the outskirts of Stoke Armitage, his low spirits were suddenly raised when he found his carriage abandoned by the roadside – only to be dashed again when he realized that the cashbox, as well as the horse, was gone. Cursing and walking on a short distance, he found his horse at the gate of a field, having its muzzle stroked by Henry Tate, whose land it was. Fane, who had scarcely recovered from the ordeal of the night and whose temper was sorely tried by the unaccustomed long walk he had had, was blunt, even angry, demanding to know what Tate was doing with his horse and what he had done with the contents of his carriage. The farmer was as indignant as the jeweller was aggressive, pointing out that he had discovered the animal still harnessed, clearly distressed at having been left that way for some time, and had merely freed it and put it in the field to feed and drink, until Fane came for it. And if that was the thanks he got for looking after the animal when its owner had abandoned it to fend for itself overnight, then he wished he had not bothered. When Fane saw that he had seriously misjudged the situation, he ceased his attack, but could not stop himself from being demanding and insistent in frantic questioning of Tate about the carriage and the box that had been in it, clinging to his arm as he tried to move away and unconsciously uttering curses between his pleadings. Finally, the exasperated farmer pushed him away so hard that he fell backwards onto the ground; he instinctively moved forward and stooped to help him up, then changed his action to a driving of his fist into his palm and a final outburst before turning and striding away. "I know nothing of any damned box! The cart is just as I found it, except for freeing the poor scared beast from it. I haven't touched anything in it, and I wouldn't want to touch anything belonging to a damned old miser like you. And if you say I have taken anything belonging to you, then you're a damned liar as well, and you will answer to me for your cursed lies!"

When Fane had picked himself up and dusted himself down a little, he thought it prudent to reclaim his horse, though he could not yet face the effort of trying to hitch up the carriage. He led the animal into the village, ignoring passers-by staring at his bedraggled appearance and unusual behaviour, and made his way to his shop. He found it locked up and the windows shuttered, and although he had to make even more of a spectacle of himself by pounding on the door and angrily calling out his name before Josiah would open it, he was actually pleased that his employee had stayed at his post and had not gone home and left the place unguarded. Josiah opened the door a fraction on its chain, and all that could be seen was half of his face and the barrel of his pistol.

"It's me, you damned fool! Put that thing down and open the door before I fall down exhausted and die on my own doorstep – though perhaps that's what you'd like, so you could get your hands on my money!"

Josiah, who was used to being the target of Fane's quick temper and sarcastic moods, hastily opened the door and helped his master in and to a chair. He brought him a cup of water, and then the brandy bottle when he waved that away. He stood without saying a word; Fane eyed him coldly: "Any trouble while I've been gone?"

"No, sir, nothing at all."

"I don't suppose you're bothered where I've been, are you? I could have been dead."

"Well, sir, Nathan came back last night in a terrible state and eventually told me something of what happened to you. He was making such a noise outside that I had to let him in, though I know you said I shouldn't open the door after dark. I did not think you would want me to go out to look for you and leave the shop unattended, sir; Nathan was quite useless to leave on guard, and in any case he would not have let me go out and leave him on his own. It took several hours for him to be able to get to sleep."

"Where is he now?"

155

"In the back room, still sleeping."

"And what did he tell you?"

"Oh, some nonsense – he is quite an impressionable youth. Nothing I would care to repeat outside this room, sir. But I gather the horse got away from you in the dark and you had to take shelter somewhere till daylight."

A grunt, a long pause, and then grudgingly, "Well, you did the right thing in staying over. I was detained on the way, it is true, and the boy took fright in the dark – no doubt he imagines all kinds of things happened."

Little more was said about that night, even between Fane and the apprentice who had shared the experience: there were fear and embarrassment in equal measure to prevent them from repeating or dwelling on those events. The carriage was recovered later that day, and Fane drove out to Lower Easterby to recollect his gun from Farmer Baines, passing under the gibbet as he did so. In daylight he could see it for what it was – a structure of old timbers; but he shivered uncontrollably for some minutes as his mind involuntarily went back to the scene of less than twenty hours before. The missing cashbox, which had his name engraved on it, was returned to him a few days later – empty, the lock having been smashed open with blows from a heavy tool. It had been found by a labourer in a field half way between the gibbet and where Fane had come upon Tate and his horse, and had been handed in to the farmer. It had evidently been tossed over a hedge from the road, and this suggested that the carriage had been driven far enough to be safely away from any pursuer before it was stopped so that the box could be opened and its contents seized – or perhaps there had been more than one occupant and the box had been opened as they drove on. Then the carriage had been left a couple of miles further on, perhaps because the thief lived not far away – or perhaps it had been abandoned simply to prevent detection when the sun came up.

Fane went through the formality of reporting the theft to the magistrate, though leaving out mention of the hooded figure and any reason for losing the carriage, which made the whole tale as unconvincing as the version he had given to Josiah; with such a thin story and no clues the investigation could only be a formality. But Fane's mind went over and over the facts as he knew them and their possible interpretations. Who had driven the carriage and taken the contents of the box? Surely such things were beyond the apparition or whatever it was they had seen – and certainly that could have no need of the gold and jewels. Presumably some footpad or mere passer-by had chanced upon and seized the empty carriage, and then abandoned it when he found the richer prize. Perhaps the horse had actually made its own way home alone, and the box had first been carried there before being seized – in which case the location of the empty box suggested that the thief had been walking or riding away from Stoke Armitage rather than driving to it. Or perhaps the horse had first stopped where the box was found, and had moved on again after being disturbed by an opportunistic thief. There might have been two thieves, one who took and abandoned the carriage and then one who came upon it and found the box. With all the possible scenarios filling his mind, and the overwhelming rage and sickness in the stomach at the thought of his loss, Fane scarcely gave a thought to the thing which had caused him to abandon the treasure in the first place – the encounter at the gibbet; at the time, the hooded figure had even frightened him away from his precious money and jewels, but as he had ruled out a connection between it and the theft it had not featured further in his thinking. For what could a phantom want with gems and cash?

As the days went on, however, the terrifying vision came back to him more frequently, and finally he woke up one night in a panic, having imagined the black figure standing at the foot of his bed. Nathan had been quiet and edgy ever since the fateful evening, sleeping and eating badly and being unable to concentrate on the delicate craft which he was learning. Finally, Fane snapped at him when he botched the setting of a stone in a ring through the shaking of his hands, and the youth burst into tears and howled, which took his master aback and left him not knowing what to say. The young man brokenly explained that he could not get the ghost, as he called it, out of his head; that he dreamt about it every night and woke up terrified in the dark, hiding in the corner under a blanket until daylight; that he had been afraid to say anything since he knew Fane would be angry as he seemed not to have been troubled by it himself. The jeweller was not angered by this, for it struck a chord in him and made him reflect: no, he actually was troubled by the apparition, and increasingly so, as the wound made by his material loss slowly healed with the making of more money, and he feared that belatedly the mental disturbance affecting the apprentice would come to him too. He had encountered something which he could not comprehend: normally, he paid no heed to what he did not know or understand, and certainly metaphysical speculation had so far played no part in his severely practical and materialistic view of the world, but now something outside his understanding had literally come along the road towards him, with who knows what intent – and might do so again. Perhaps he did need to find out exactly what had happened at the gibbet, and why, and whether it meant anything or might happen again. Like the loss of his money earlier, it began to prey on his mind, and, being the sort of man he was, he had no family or friends with whom to discuss it, or lessen the burden by sharing it. There was only one place he could turn for advice on such a matter, though it would represent a remarkable change of habit – his priest.

It must not be casually assumed from Jeremiah Fane's love of money and solitary existence that he had no time for religion, or, at least, for public compliance with the practices of the established

Church; for while part of him avoided society and its calls upon him, another part craved social acceptance and recognition – and in any case, he had an eye for profit, and if there was any truth in Christianity's promises of everlasting life and spiritual riches to enjoy during it, then he was quite willing to make the small investment of time required. In any case, his shop was closed on the Sabbath, so he had no difficulty in filling in the dead time by attending services, in the hopes of eternal gain. So he subscribed to the articles of faith and attended church regularly, though as a kind of payment in advance rather than from any conviction of principle. He attended as though alone, rather than as a member of a congregation, for he spoke to no-one, apart from the briefest of nods to the recently-arrived couple who occupied the other half of his side-aisle pew; he murmured the hymns, recited the prayers under his breath, sat through the readings and sermon with his mind elsewhere, and promptly departed at the end. Oh, and he nodded to and shook the hand of the rector, who seemed a good and sensible man, unlike some of the feeble clergymen he had encountered, who usually seemed to be infected with undue enthusiasm, or optimism, or otherworldliness – none of which accorded with his notion of what a proper view of the world should be like.

So when a reticent Fane presented himself at the rectory, the Reverend Theophilus Hale knew well enough who he was, but was surprised and puzzled, though he concealed it well: the jeweller had never sought his advice before, nor ever confided in him – indeed, had rarely spoken to him. He knew little of what had happened, since Fane was too remote from village life for his loss to be a matter of concern even for gossiping, and even the story of the ghost had not spread, Nathan being too disturbed to speak of it and Josiah Hall having taken his master's hint and being discretion itself. The man looked worried – not only nervous about being in an unfamiliar situation, but, more than that, deeply troubled by something which he had clearly not divulged to anyone. They sat in Hale's study, with a glass of wine to steady Fane's nerves, and the rector gently led him into talking with some general observations about life and its vicissitudes, and the part played by Providence in the drama. Eventually, Fane, by fits and starts – for he was little used to telling stories, and even less to describing how he truly felt about things – recounted the events of the night two weeks before. He could not help dwelling on the cashbox and the puzzle of the theft, but nevertheless he managed to make clear to the rector than he had not come merely to bewail his earthly loss but to seek advice, information even, about the thing he and the lad had seen and how it was affecting them. When he had finished, he sat back and sighed, as though recovering from a great effort, and then leaned forward with almost a kind of eagerness about him, as though Hale was about to expound precisely what manner of thing it was, what its haunts and habits were and how it should be dealt with; in his mind, he imagined the priest as analogous to the doctor, but trained to recognize, diagnose and prescribe for all matters spiritual and supernatural. So he was a little discouraged when Hale did not produce a complete, definite and ready answer.

"What you saw may well have been an hallucination, a trick of the eyes or the light or the shadows, which the mind interpreted appropriately for that sinister context. But I see that you are not impressed by such arguments: you are a practical craftsman and a hard-headed man of business, and you know what you saw and are not given to flights of fancy. Well, it may have been something else. Now, the Church does not really hold with such notions as ghosts, and certainly not with superstitions, but it does acknowledge other forms of existence – its whole basis rests on belief in such ideas as souls, angels, divine intervention, another life elsewhere, so it could not logically deny the possibility of what may be called the supernatural. It may be that sometimes things which are not material make themselves visible to us for a time, perhaps resonances of strong emotions such as anger or grief, or

160

echoes of violent deeds, and it may be that they take a form like that of the human figures involved. However, in my experience, and I have had some experience of such matters, these phantasms are simply that – they have no substance and can do no harm in our world, apart from terrifying those who see them, through their strangeness and their disturbing similarity to ourselves."

"So it might have been the ghost of the dead pirate which stopped me on the road?" asked Fane, having taken the basic idea in Hale's circumspect explanation and made it as blunt and clear as he could.

"I did not say that. The Church would have difficulty reconciling the ideas of a merciful God and the salvation of souls with the notion of unhappy spirits left to wander the earth and plague the living. What I am suggesting is that it is not impossible that you saw some remnant of another time, but that if you did then it was more like a dream or a mirage than a material thing. Then, of course, there is another possibility, a much more commonplace and obvious one, which you seem to have overlooked in dividing the story of your encounter on the road from that of the theft of your box."

"What do you mean?"

"Quite simply, that what sprang down from the gibbet was a man disguised and acting in a manner likely to frighten you off, given where you were and when – a man who subsequently took your carriage and stole your valuables. Surely you had considered this possibility?"

"Well, no, not really. What on earth would anyone be doing there at that time? So few people travel that road at night, it would be an absurd plan to hang there until someone came along who chanced to have valuables which they might have to abandon." But a whole new perspective on the incident had opened up in Fane's mind.

"Perhaps it was merely intended as an elaborate joke in very poor taste, until the prankster discovered the chest." Hale was pursuing his line like a detective. "Or if it was a premeditated robbery, then it argues a robber who knew he could expect you there at that time, with the box. Did anyone know of your movements, apart from the boy with you?"

"No. My clerk, Josiah Hall, knew what I was doing in a general way, for he guarded my premises until I returned, as always. But he is discretion itself, and is as unsociable as I, which is why I employ him, and he would not have told a soul. Those I visited in town would have an idea of which road I would take back and when, and some would have an idea of what I carried, but I cannot think any of them would risk their positions for such a reward, and they would scarcely have had time to set their ambush. And I doubt they would know of the gibbet, its story and how it could be exploited in such a way."

After a little more such discussion, during which Fane became increasingly convinced by the idea that he had been duped and robbed by a mortal man, though by whom he could not guess, he departed, feeling relieved. He was no nearer apprehending the thief, but at least the fear of being persecuted by a supernatural entity had been lifted from his mind, and he slept more easily for it. Over the next few days, he took the unusual step of speaking to his troubled apprentice on this, a matter not directly relating to his work or discipline, and succeeded in reducing his anxiety considerably. Nevertheless, neither of them looked forward to their next night journey through Easterby with anything but trepidation.

This became inevitable a few weeks later: although the earlier nights and worsening weather made traveling any distance even less appealing, with the approach of Christmas it was necessary for the jeweller to visit Dorchester to take advantage of the increased demand for his wares and replenish his own stocks. And so, for the first time since that terrible experience, Fane and his lad set out so as to arrive as soon as possible after dealers and shopkeepers had opened for business. "And you mind now, if anything threatens us, be it at the gibbet or elsewhere else, I want no running away, but you use that gun for what it is meant for. Do you understand? No running away!" It was a dismal morning, dark, blustery and intermittently raining; the little carriage had a tarpaulin pulled across it and Nathan had an old blanket wrapped around the blunderbuss to keep out the damp, though compromising the speed with which he could have brought it to bear on any sudden assailant. As early as they arrived and as swiftly and impatiently as Fane rattled around to get his business completed, the sun was already low in the sky as they set off homewards, and it sank out of sight fully an hour before they reached Easterby. The rain had stopped, and the clouds had lifted to reveal stars shining brightly as though cleansed by the deep chill which had set in and polished by the wind which still blew strongly. The swaying and creaking of branches overhanging the roadside brought vividly to mind something else which had swung and clanked by the highway, and so this time they were less surprised when the gibbet came into view as they ascended the rise and there was indeed an ominous black form hanging from it, over the place where they must pass. The horse saw too, and reacted more swiftly this time, halting and trying to back away, whinnying as the figure began to swing and emit groans, to the accompaniment of rattling chains, heard faintly over the wind. This time Fane did not flee, but stood up and wielded his whip, urging the horse on, though Nathan shrank back in his seat, clutching the wrapped gun like a shield in front of him. The horse steadied and advanced a few paces before halting again.

At this moment, with the carriage almost motionless apart from a slight swaying caused by the wind, one side of the covering was suddenly thrown back and a man stood up, between and behind the other two. He raised a pistol, aimed it over Fane's shoulder at the hooded figure, and fired. The low moaning was sharply replaced by a scream, and immediately Nathan regained his spirit, tore the blanket from his weapon and fired randomly ahead, the unexpected recoil of the huge old piece throwing him backwards so as to knock Ned Blunt down onto the wet tarpaulin. As was revealed later, some of his spray of shot just caught the head and shoulders of the figure as it fell from the gibbet. Ned, a prominent local poacher and former soldier, whom Fane had hired that day while lounging outside the Antelope in South Street, cursed and rolled off the carriage; he pulled out from under the cover an ancient sword taken from his collection, and walked slowly towards the dark hump in the road before them. Fane got down, took up a lantern and followed him; Nathan, nursing a sore shoulder and flexing a bruised back, clambered down and followed even more slowly. Ned poked cautiously at the shape; it groaned softly, but this time in pain and fear rather than in an attempt to frighten. Flesh and blood it clearly was, for the latter was seeping from the tears made in its rough cloak by the fragments of shot. Fane held the lantern high over the scene as Ned rolled the body over, revealing the great hole made in the chest by his bullet. Kneeling, he pulled back the hood and tore off a black-dyed flour bag with eyeholes which covered the face; it was Josiah Hall, his eyes wide and unblinking and his breath coming in short irregular gasps. As the three men stared at him in silence, he died as he lay in the road. Ned looked up at Fane for an explanation, as Nathan peered round his master at the hideous spectacle; all their eyes were drawn upwards to the arm of the gibbet overhead, where hung a kind of trapeze on which Josiah had perched while awaiting his victim, and by it several lengths of chain, for rattling.

164

It was clear what had happened. Exploiting his position above suspicion and his knowledge of his master's movements, the clerk had devised a plan to enrich himself while the ghost took the blame. Under cover of night, he would leave the house where he was supposedly on guard, carrying his costume and equipment, and take up his post at the gibbet shortly before the earliest time when Fane could be expected back. Then he would frighten the two off the road, so abandoning the chest, and take off the hood, so that the horse would recognize him; he would then take possession of the carriage and drive back towards Stoke Armitage, stopping outside the village and forcing the box open. Finally, he would abandon the vehicle, and hurry back with his disguise and his loot to resume his watch before either of them could return. And indeed when his lodgings were searched later, the bulk of his first night's haul was discovered in the bottom of a linen chest, and promptly reclaimed by the jeweller.

No charges were brought against Blunt or Fane in connection with Hall's death. The magistrate could not declare it to be accidental, for the shooting was clearly intentional, as Blunt had been there solely for that purpose; nor could it be self-defence, as Hall was unarmed and at the time of his shooting not posing any threat to anyone. Nevertheless, he declared, it had been an informal kind of justice: the dead man had brought it wholly on himself by his provocative behaviour, and in any case he was a proven thief and his killing had saved the trouble of a hanging. In a wry aside, he pointed out that the sequence of events was probably unique in having the felon displayed on the gibbet before his dispatch rather than after.

Theophilus Hale was not quite so comfortable with what had happened: he had meant well, and had been right, in persuading Fane that the hooded figure and the robber were one and the same, and entirely human, but it was this that had led directly to the jeweller taking the law into his own hands and having Hall killed. And he had failed to end the superstition attaching to the old gibbet, for now to the stories of the phantom pirate and the demon raven was added the tale of the ghost of the jeweller's clerk, in time elevated to the status of a demon which lies in wait for unwary travellers along that road on dark winter nights – the flibbertigibbet.

DISTURBANCES

As Dr. Walter Ashurst looked through the railings which surrounded the churchyard, such was the depth of the shadows at sunset and such the profusion of elaborate and fantastical monuments – these making up one of the most celebrated features of St. Dunstan's – that he scarcely noticed the hideous, squat image amongst the more conventional headstones away to his left in the north-west corner; nor did his returning eye, having scanned the rows of free-standing crucifixes, weeping angels, Celtic crosses and Grecian urns, consciously mark its subsequent absence. He did, however, recall the glimpse he had had of it, as he walked back along the lane to the high street. A strange choice indeed for a funerary monument: something of the gargoyle in its deformity, but lacking the serenity of the silent watcher over Paris that he had seen at Notre Dame the year before; something of the diabolical in its leer, but more like a rustic goblin of English folklore than the creature which St. Dunstan himself famously had by the nose with his pincers. Dr. Ashurst was still chuckling to himself at the old story when he arrived at The Red Bull. Cassington being the furthest point of his summer walking tour, he had decided to take lodging here for the whole week, to allow himself a rest; the inn had been recommended to him in Oxford, as having suitably quiet rooms in an annex and as keeping as good a table and cellar as could be expected in such a remote part of the country. He availed himself fully of these facilities before retiring quite early, having extensively investigated four churches that day, as well as covering the miles between them on foot.

Whereas he had slept soundly on the preceding nights of his tour, after days of walking and investigating, Dr. Ashurst arose next morning feeling little benefit from sleep. Why that should be he did not know: he had had as much exercise as in recent days, and his accommodation was at least as comfortable. Whatever the cause, his sleep had been fitful, vexed by dreams he could not remember beyond a general impression of darkness and something of which to be afraid.

Later in the morning, Dr. Ashurst asked the curate of St. Dunstan's why the churchyard was kept locked.

"Surely in so rural a spot as this there is no need to take precautions against such depredations as might be feared in an ill-favoured quarter of a great city, when the clergyman is absent?"

Francis Trent, pale of complexion, anxious in expression, quick and nervous in his movements, was unable to say more than that it had always been the custom of the previous incumbent, recently retired through ill-health and old age, to lock the churchyard at nightfall or in his absence from the vicarage. The curate, less than six months ordained and only weeks in the parish, did not wish to take responsibility for any changes before the appointment of a new vicar; Dr. Ashurst understood that the inexperienced and insecure young man was frightened of the unexpected and unwelcome burden that had been placed upon him so suddenly, and did not seek to discomfort him further with questions. Accepting a somewhat strained invitation to tea later that day, he took his leave.

The particular project which Dr. Ashurst had appropriated to himself for this summer vacation was an account of the surviving Romanesque architecture in the parish churches of that part of the country. The church at Cassington was indeed a Norman foundation with surviving work of that period, but Dr. Ashurst was somewhat disappointed to find that extensive rebuilding in later periods had left little identifiable; the lower portion of the west tower and the arch into it from the nave yielded some good features, however, and he was busy with notebook and sketch pad for nearly two hours. Emerging into the sunlight, he found it to be a brilliantly sunny and warm day, of which he had been unaware whilst working inside the chilly building. Deciding that it was too hot for much walking and that the generally picturesque appearance of the church merited a temporary desertion of the Romanesque for the Gothic, he resolved to return in the afternoon to sketch the north aspect of the exterior in its entirety, that being the side which afforded a more convenient position from which to view the building, as the churchyard extended further in that direction.

After lunch at the inn, Dr. Ashurst took up his position at the furthest point of the enclosure, so as to enjoy the widest view of the church, which was flanked by splendid yew trees, quite unlike the dark oaks which loomed from beyond the wall behind him. Looking around at this contrast, he noticed that the railings through which he had peered the evening before did not extend all round. Along the east and west sides, all but the last twenty feet or so were bounded by what he assumed was the original wall, three feet or so high, made of rough and irregular stones and capped at some later date with cement in which the iron railings of similar height had been set. The last part of the wall on either side, however, and the whole of the wall along the northern edge, were clearly of more recent date, made of finer masonry blocks and built to the full height, a head higher than a man. At least in the north-west corner, this wall appeared to serve a retaining function as well as marking the boundary, for Dr. Ashurst noted with surprise that there was a grassy hump visible over the top of it and clearly very close to the far side of the wall. He concluded that, since the area enclosed by the new structure was occupied by the three most recent and most orderly rows of graves, compared to the more random scattering of earlier burials, the churchyard must have been extended, the original wall having been demolished and the new one erected further out, probably within the past half-century.

Dr. Ashurst made himself as comfortable as he could on the cushion which he had brought with him, perched on the edge of a table slab, and took up his pad within the crook of his left arm. He sketched in the rectangles made by the lines of the nave and aisle walls and roofs and the tower, and began to work with greater precision on the positions and shapes of the windows. As he paused in his concentration to erase a false line, his thoughts returned to his speculation about the history of the place in which he sat, and into his mind came from nowhere the all but forgotten goblin-figure of the previous evening.

He glanced over to the right, to the spot where he had peered in through the railings, where there was a gap in the brambles and nettles outside the wall, and allowed his eye to trace the direction in which he had looked. Craning round with some difficulty, he searched over his shoulder for the curious monument. He could not see it, but his view of the corner was obscured by a large angel on a plinth, holding out the victor's wreath. He turned back to the rudimentary sketch, but the image kept coming back into his mind, and he repeatedly found himself half-turned to look for it again. At length, he surrendered to this urgent curiosity; shrugging resignedly, he slipped off his perch and walked the two steps necessary for a clear view of the corner.

There was no goblin figure. There were, in fact, no upright monuments beyond the angel of victory, only flat stones and a few crosses: surely he could not have mistaken the very sign of salvation in such a way? He walked over to inspect the monuments: Margaret, beloved wife of Nathaniel Stanton, the said Nathaniel and three infant Stantons; William and Mary Lister, brother and sister; Ezekiel Morton, late of Little Cassington – nothing exceptional. What he had seen had to have been a shadow, perhaps cast by a tree or by the statue of the angel, despite reason telling him that shadows are not that distinct or free-standing, and that the sun had been setting behind him and casting the shadows the wrong way.

Pensively, he returned to his seat and his drawing, and tried to concentrate on detailing the parapet and waterspouts at the top of the tower, but he continued to be unsettled in some undefined way. Twice he caught himself turning his head, as though to catch sight of someone moving behind him, but he could put this down to the slight swaying of the oaks beyond the wall, as a breeze began to blow from the north. He recalled hearing, or more probably reading, of people having the sensation of being watched by an unseen viewer, a notion which had always struck him as absurd, unless one subscribed to a version of the atomists' notion of sight involving collisions of physical particles; but now he understood the conceit, an instinct left perhaps from a distant age when man was the prey of leopard and wolf, and relied for survival on sensing the attentions of the concealed predator. He realised that he had stopped drawing and was gazing vacantly at his sketch. This was absurd. He put the pad on the stone beside him, stood up and turned round. He scanned carefully from left to right and back again, along the rows of monuments, as he walked up to the wall: there was no-one tending a grave, no-one hiding behind a headstone, no-one peeping over the wall or standing on the raised bank behind it. He was completely alone, the only changes since he had first entered the churchyard being the movements of the trees in the wind and the dark clouds now gathering swiftly above them in the northern sky. Satisfied, he resumed his sketching.

The sky clouded behind him, then overhead, and the sudden comparative darkness, and the mounting wind driving it towards him, began to inconvenience him in his work. At the precise moment at which he glanced up to judge whether rain was imminent, the first drop of a summer shower fell onto his face; he swiftly closed his pad and, clutching it and his cushion, hurried to the safety of the church – just in time, for the heaviest downpour he could remember witnessing for several years burst just as he reached the porch on the far side of the building. For some minutes he stood transfixed, watching from his shelter the cascade of water and listening to it rushing through the runnels, pipes and spouts overhead and down the walls. As the initial cloudburst settled into steadier rain likely to last some time, he abandoned his project temporarily and ventured back into the church to await the hour for tea.

Although he now had a perfect knowledge of the western end of the building and an adequate record of it, he had so far paid little attention to the rest, though he knew that the church at Cassington had some interesting features. The zeal of the reformers had been modest in this area, and there were several specimens of medieval glass in the windows; there were two brasses, of the late fourteenth century, in the nave; and, rarest of all, part of the original wall painting (considered to be of the mid-fifteenth century) had survived in the north aisle. As happened everywhere, most of the medieval decoration had been defaced or whitewashed over, but here two sections had been preserved by being covered by woodwork put up shortly before the Reformation. Dr. Ashurst recalled reading, a few years earlier, that when the bookcase at one end of the aisle and the cupboard for church furniture at the other had been taken down, the builders had been astonished to find the first and last sections of what appeared to be an extraordinary frieze on a level with the viewer, depicting the traditional Dance of Death in Cassington itself. Going straight to the north aisle, he examined the final panel, defaced by the holes left by the bolts which had held the old cupboard in place and in its shape recalling the square outline of the cabinet, but with its colours, untouched by light or dust for centuries, still remarkably vivid. It depicted the leader of the Dance, Death in a monkish black habit, hooded and with no face visible but playing a bagpipe, approaching the churchyard: he stood on a grassy bank, with the church recognisable in miniature, as though seen from a distance, a little below and behind him. Dr. Ashurst noted how striking this image of imminent, inescapable mortality must have been for its first viewers, for the church was recognisably the north side of their

172

own parish church, the ground around which would be their own last resting place; a pale band between Death and the church indicated the boundary wall, and the tall west tower, in the corner of the aisle, was a fitting border for the work. Next to Death and following him, just the face, an arm and a leg of a man apparently in clerical garb were visible – presumably a pastor leading his flock; Dr. Ashurst wondered if it was in fact a portrait of the parish priest of the time.

He walked down the aisle to inspect the tail end of the frieze, in the north-east corner. The artist clearly had a Chaucerian view of the fullness of humanity, and a Chaucerian sense of humour, for the man of God at the front of the procession was balanced by rogues at the back: the village drunk, plainly swaying and clutching a flagon, made his unsteady progress behind a partially-visible figure swinging between crutches. Dr. Ashurst speculated whether these were also familiar figures in the village, and whether the drunken man had ever made his way from The Red Bull and into the church to view his likeness. However, his smile faded when he looked down into the bottom corner of the panel, which was all but obliterated by the end of a pew pushed almost against the wall. In that dark space close to the floor, nearly obscured by painted shadows, there was the outline of a squat figure, half the size of the others, which he recognised, or which at least stirred a recent memory in him. A squat goblin peered from behind the cover of a bush, its face twisted into a diabolical grin as it watched the villagers dancing away to their end. The size, shape and general appearance of the imp convinced Dr. Ashurst that he was looking at a creature similar to the vision he had seen in the churchyard the previous evening, and for the first time he was able to study its features closely. The artist had given it long, prominent ears, the slanted eyes of an Oriental, a wide snub nose, a mouth too large for its face and slack jaws; the body was partly obscured, but short, thick limbs were apparent. Dr. Ashurst felt an involuntary shudder as a thrill like coldness momentarily spread from his lower back before fading in his arms and legs.

He had been staring at the image for some time, during which the sound of rain and water in drains must have ceased, when the church clock struck the hour for tea and roused him. Not yet fully focussed on his surroundings, he picked up his pad and slowly made for the door, returning hesitantly to collect his cushion. He hurried down the path outside without looking to left or right, and by the time he had reached the entrance to the vicarage he had recovered himself sufficiently to greet Francis Trent in a normal manner.

Over tea in the drawing room, Dr. Ashurst attempted to discuss with the curate what he had seen in the church and in other churches nearby – without mentioning the thing which had most engaged his attention – but the young man knew little of ecclesiastical architecture or, being new to the area, the surrounding parishes. However, without wishing to embarrass him in this regard, Dr. Ashurst could not refrain from asking him if he knew anything about the rebuilding of the north boundary wall. He was unable to assist, having, he said, heard nothing of it from the previous vicar, and his inability to help made him even more nervous and agitated, and he stumbled over his words of apology. Perhaps to compensate for his inadequacy in the conversation, he offered instead to show his guest a painting of the church done by the incumbent before the last one, some fifty or sixty years earlier, which hung in the dining room. When he saw it, Dr. Ashurst knew his surmise had been correct. It was a view from the north, and clearly showed the original low wall, not yet topped by railings, enclosing the whole churchyard. The view was as from an elevated position to the north-east, and at some distance; in the bottom right hand corner, there was a low but prominent grassy mound, oval in shape and sloping down to stop short of the wall, rather than being cut into by it as at present. This mound had to be the origin of the

174

bank just visible above the present structure; it had been halved by the redrawing of the boundary, the portion inside the church ground being flattened. Excited, he returned to the drawing room to collect his pad, so that he could compare the painting to his sketch, to see if there were any other changes evident. He made an effort not to betray any emotion in front of the nervous curate, but there was obviously a momentary look of fear rather than mere surprise on his face before he could control himself, and the young man enquired if he was unwell. Dr. Ashurst forced a weak smile and shook his head, but he could not quite speak, or trust himself to speak. For the sketch was not as he remembered it, but featured in the bottom right hand corner a depiction of a low slope, covering the ground next to the spot where he had stood. It was clearly executed in his style, and with his instrument, but he had no recollection of having drawn it.

Making his way back towards the village, Dr. Ashurst paused at the gate leading into the field to the north of the church, and looked in. It was used for grazing cattle, and a few oaks around the edges and in a central clump provided some shelter for the animals. As he had deduced, there was a hillock or mound in the near right hand corner of the field, rising to perhaps seven or eight feet, curiously symmetrical in shape but truncated where it met the wall. Walking on, he passed the entrance to the farm, and, despite the events of the day, managed a wry smile at the board bearing its name – "Poxdown Farm"; more like a Restoration oath than agricultural in flavour. He thought of going in to make enquiries, but decided that it would be, to the outside observer, a most eccentric act; instead, he saved his questions for the landlord of The Red Bull, whom he found renewing the supply of bottles in the public bar. He started by mentioning some details of how he had spent the day, and so by degrees came to the subject of the church wall and what lay beyond it.

Harry Paley was florid of face and hearty of manner, and Dr. Ashurst thought it apt that his name should be only a syllable away from Chaucer's host of the Tabard, though he sensed that his manner was purely professional and that there was an emptiness, even a coldness, behind it. Nevertheless, he was polite and helpful towards his guest, who had, he knew, come on a recommendation which he could either contradict or send further around the wealthy city of Oxford and potential future customers. No, he was sorry that he did not remember the extending of the churchyard, or the building of the wall, or the addition of the railings, all of which occurred around the time when he was born; nor would the previous vicar be likely to able to help much, as he remembered him first arriving when he was himself a young boy. However, he could date the events quite precisely – 48 years before – as his father had been accustomed to say to him, when they passed the church, that that wall and he "came into being at the same time, if you'll pardon a plain manner of speaking, sir". He could even introduce him to his old father, who might still remember the event and who now lived in retirement in a small cottage behind the inn, where Harry's wife and daughter could keep an eye on him – "though he is inclined to be muddled, sir, and often not quite in himself these days, if you understand me, and you mightn't be much wiser after you've seen him than before". It seemed to Dr. Ashurst that Harry regretted the offer almost as soon as he had made it, but it had already been accepted and could not be withdrawn in politeness; for his part, Dr. Ashurst was unwilling to forgo this chance to learn more of the mystery just to spare the landlord's feelings, when he could perceive no harm in what was proposed. It was agreed that he would see the old man the following morning, giving Harry time to prepare him for the unaccustomed visit and late morning being "the time o'day when he's least muddled".

Sitting in his room, from the window of which he could see what he now believed to be the old man's small house, Dr. Ashurst put aside the pocket Pliny which he had brought with him for the evenings after dinner, and gave himself up to the thoughts that could not be dismissed. Perhaps the exertions of recent days, walking in the heat, had affected him in ways he had not realised; he was perhaps getting too old to punctuate with impunity – he liked the alliteration – an otherwise sedentary way of life with such bursts of activity. A trick of the twilight and a fancied likeness to a painted image were playing on his mind in a way scarcely sane; that he should have connected the two disparate things at all was evidence of some mental aberration, further attested by the fact that he had forgotten what he had drawn within two hours of the action. Perhaps he should abandon the walking tour and obtain transport back to Oxford immediately, possibly to seek medical advice. But he resolved to wait and see if a few days of rest at The Red Bull and Mrs. Paley's excellent cooking could restore his equilibrium. As he drew the curtains and caught sight of the cottage outside, he wished that he had not arranged to see the old man and so prolong the obsession; but he reminded himself that it would be rude to cancel the visit now that his host had perhaps gone to some trouble to explain to his father who was coming to see him and why.

That night, his sleep was more troubled than it had been the night before, and more than once he half-woke to the empty blackness of an unfamiliar room, before lapsing back into torpor. The memory of that night's experiences which stayed with him longest in the pallor of dawn was of something above him as he lay in his bed, something so light as to be scarcely felt but evident as a shape confronting him, darker than the darkness around it, the slight movements of which could just be discerned against the square of his window, faintly illuminated by the moon, as he lay on his back and looked down towards his feet. It was definitely his own room and his own bed, and his senses seemed to be sharp, so that knew not whether he dreamt or was awake; what was happening seemed so real, and yet surely such things did not happen in the real world. Did being able to question whether it was a dream mean that in fact it was not? Or could one dream that one wondered if one dreamt? In his panic, he fought to stir himself violently, to shake off both his visitor and his sluggishness, so that he could defend himself against whatever threatened him from whatever source; but he could not move. Was he paralysed by fear, under some bewitchment, or in fact asleep? The shape had crawled up the bed to the level of his chest, and suddenly he felt his left wrist seized by a grip far stronger than he would have thought possible from the shade: a steely, icy grip, so powerful as to cause him pain, and he could not even move the hand so trapped. He tried to cry out, but could not; he sensed the thing straddling him and looking down at him, and he closed his eyes in a desperate attempt to block it out. Finally, with one convulsive effort, he succeeded in hurling himself out of his bed.

He found himself sitting upright in bed, sweating, panting and with his heart racing, his own right hand clutching his left wrist fiercely, as though he were tensing himself against some great effort.

Just as Dr. Ashurst had doubted the wisdom of pursuing his quest in this way, so Harry Paley clearly wished he had not tried to ingratiate himself with his Oxford guest by introducing him to his father; but it was too late for either of them to back down. Before ushering him into the parlour of the cottage, the landlord muttered apologies for "the state o'the place" and for the old man's condition, "not being one o'his best days, sir, if you see what I mean; he ain't always as bad". Dr. Ashurst scarcely noticed the state of the place, being concerned only to avoid prolonging the interview to the general embarrassment and to obtain what information he could as quickly and painlessly as possible. Harry clearly had the same aim, and had prepared the way as much as he could: "This is the gentleman as wants to know about the churchyard. You recall, father, what we spoke of: when they made the churchyard bigger.

Do you remember? We went over what you were going to tell him, earlier on."

Neither Paley suggested Dr. Ashurst should join the old man in sitting, but with some prompting from his son the father began to look a little animated and stirred in his seat. "Ah, you and that wall came into being at the same time!" The old man's laugh passed into a cough as Harry smiled an apology across at the visitor. "That's right! He's a good boy, is my Harry. Do you know my Harry, sir? One day he'll be landlord of this inn after me, but he'll have to work a sight 'arder than he does now. Oh yes. That he will!" This time the younger Paley made his apology a verbal one, and he prompted the older one again.

"That's right, father, tell about the church and the new wall." The old man returned to the theme in a rambling fashion, speaking more to himself and not looking at his companions, who occasionally exchanged words above his monologue, unheeded.

"Th'old vicar needed more ground for burying, like; the church field was near full and they needed more room for burying folk what had died from the fever. That were a terrible year for the fever, that'un. Well, the lane is one side of the field and th'other lane is on one side, and Selwyn's cottages are on another side, so he can only go to th'other side that's left. So he goes to old Hatch at Pox Farm –"

"I thought it was called Poxdown Farm?"

"He always calls it so; the old folk in the village often did, but you don't hear it much these days."

"– though there were no love lost between 'em, Hatch and the vicar, and the vicar, he says to 'im, the church needs more ground for burying and I will give you a good price for a strip of your land

179

next to the church field. I doesn't ask for charity; you put aside all our quarrels and make a fair bargain. And old Hatch, he says to the vicar, I will sell you a strip of my land if you pay me enough, and much good may you 'ave of it. He demanded twice what the land were worth, a poor piece of grazing, but th'old vicar, he had no choice, as they needed more ground for burying, you see. Much good may you 'ave of it, says old Hatch. So they pulled down th'old wall and put up the new one, round Hatch's land. But they 'ad to cut through the mound first, and flatten the church's 'alf of it, like, to make the burying ground. It were 'alf in and 'alf out of the land what 'ad been bought and sold, you see, that mound. My Harry and that wall, they came into being at the same time...."

The old man, who perhaps had not spoken so much for some time, appeared to be overcome by tiredness and ended by closing his eyes and nodding forward.

"Well done, father. See, he did all right after all, sir, didn't he?"

"Yes, thank you, and do thank him for me. His story confirms what I had suspected."

They both began to move towards the door, glad that the interview was over, when the old man awoke again with a sudden jerk of his head, as though a brief rest had reinvigorated him. "They should never a'done that, disturbing things what they 'ad no call to disturb! They soon found they 'ad to make that wall higher, and they put railings up, but that were no use! Walls and railings were no good for that. Old Hatch knew what he were about all right, and made himself a pretty penny into the bargain. Much good may you 'ave of it, he said! He always were a crafty old sinner, old Hatch. Not like my Harry; he's a good boy, is my Harry. Do you know my Harry, sir? One day he'll be landlord here, if he shapes 'isself." He subsided again, and within moments was snoring.

180

"I'm sorry, sir. You see, it comes and goes. Sometimes he makes no sense. We must leave him now."

But the second part of the old man's story, though less coherent, had given Dr. Ashurst more to think about than the first, and he would have questioned him further had not Harry insisted that he was merely raving and now needed rest.

Dr. Ashurst apologised for getting him so agitated, and they left the old man in peace. He had hinted at something unpleasant resulting from the building of the wall, and in Dr. Ashurst's mind – or rather in the sensations he felt in the churchyard and in his imagination – there was some link between that and the sinister vision he had had in its vicinity. Indeed, its origins seemed to be even older, much older, being replicated in paint inside the church. He had not invited ridicule by mentioning, to the curate and the Paleys, what he thought he had seen, but had hoped that his questions might lead one of them to volunteer knowledge of it.

In his reverie, he found himself drawn unconsciously down the lane towards St. Dunstan's church again. Surely, if anyone could answer his questions, it would be those on whose land the troublesome mound stood, the descendants of "old Hatch", of whom Mr. Paley had spoken. Turning off the lane, he went through the gate by the sign "Poxdown Farm" and down a short track into a farmyard, at the back of which was a substantial house. A florid man in a shirt and a waistcoat open for the heat was giving instructions to a labourer; Dr. Ashurst approached him as the worker moved off.

"Can I help you, sir?"

"Pardon me for this intrusion, but have I the honour of addressing Mr. Hatch?"

"My name is Jenkins."

"My apologies, but could you tell me if it would be possible for me to speak briefly to Mr. Hatch?"

"There is no-one of that name here, sir."

"But, if it is not impertinent, do you not own this farm?"

"I am not the owner, but I have farmed here as tenant for some twenty years. I could not tell you who is the owner, whether his name be Hatch or not, as I pay my rent to the solicitors who administer the trust." (So that was it: Hatch had died with no direct descendants and the property had been left in trust.)

"I am sorry to have troubled you; I have evidently misunderstood the situation. My apologies again."

"That is quite all right, sir. I am sorry that I have not been able to assist you."

As he turned to leave, Dr. Ashurst could not resist asking, "Do you know of this place being called Pox Farm by the local people, the older ones at least?"

The man's attitude changed briefly: "I do indeed, and I would thank you not to name it so. My apologies, but when I first came here to Church Lane Farm, as the trustees named it, and I heard people calling it by that other name, I wrongly believed they were using it as an offensive term and I was often angered by it. In time, I came to call it Poxdown, not too remote from what people were used to but less brutal in its sound. Poxdown, I would explain, is a name I learnt from the plan which came with the lease; it is, properly, the name of a mound in a field at the edge of the property."

"The mound by the wall? I have seen it, from the churchyard. Have you never thought of reducing it, to improve the use of the field?"

"I have considered such on several occasions, but have never put the design into practice for fear of bringing down the churchyard wall which seems to rest against it. My workers have warned me that such would be likely to happen, and I would not want the trouble and expense of repairing the damage."

"Quite so. Very wise, I am sure."

After taking his leave, Dr. Ashurst went straight into the shelter of the church, not wishing to linger outside. He sat at the front of the south aisle, as far as he could from the painted image of his fear, and pondered how he could now further his inquiries – though part of his mind told him that he was slipping into an unhealthy obsession with the history of a place of which he had known nothing two days earlier. It was evident from the unstrained way in which he spoke of it that Mr. Jenkins was not aware of anything untoward about his land; he did not wish to vex Mr. Paley again, and it was in any case unlikely that his son would allow it; the retired vicar might know something of the history of the site, but had not been actually present until some years after the crucial time. The one source of information which he had not tried yet was the builder of the wall, who, presumably, was also involved in the digging up of the Pox Down itself. Who would be likely to know to know the identity of the builder, and would any record of those times still survive? He would try again at the vicarage – even though he had no clear idea of what information he sought or what use he could make of it.

A housekeeper or maid answered the door, and curtly informed him that Mr. Trent was out visiting a sick parishioner, but would be back soon after noon, at most an hour off. As she was less than welcoming and he was unknown to her, Dr. Ashurst did not wish to press her into giving him entrance to await her master's return, so left her his name and promised to return shortly. While he waited, he walked slowly around the nearer part of the churchyard. To prevent his thoughts from drifting too deeply into that dark area of his mind which he wished to avoid, he diverted himself by studying the external features of the building, to the south side of which he had given little heed during his time in Cassington. Staying on that side of the churchyard had the added advantage of blocking his view of the troubling north wall. The windows of the north aisle were in a simple early version of the Decorated style; the south porch sheltered a tympanum depicting our Saviour seated centrally, hand raised in blessing, flanked by the signs of the four evangelists; the edge of the roof was decorated with grotesque carved faces, some being actual gargoyles with waterspouts issuing from their mouths and some being simply masks and smaller in size. Humour was evident in some – one had a hand to a swollen cheek, as though suffering toothache; another winked lasciviously – though others were plainly horned devils. They were generally regularly spaced, but Dr. Ashurst's sensitivity to asymmetry was disturbed by a break towards the east end, where one very small face seemed to be too close to the larger ones on either side. However, this disturbance of his feelings was nothing compared to the horror which seized him as he peered up at the offender, the tingling cold which spread from his back to his upper limbs accompanying the recognition of the goblin features leering back at him. The hideous creature had been as familiar to the fourteenth-century carver as it had been to the fifteenth-century painter, and as it now was to him. But worse was to follow: as he looked, he thought the face moved, the eyes matching his stare, though the cold and giddiness which now took hold of his whole body caused him to stagger and fall flat against the wall for support before he could see the creature stand fully upright from its prone position on the roof. When he had recovered himself enough to look up again, it had gone, leaving the expected space between two carvings where it had hung its head down over the edge.

He looked around, in extreme agitation, wishing he had not lost sight of it. Had it come down from the roof? What did it intend to do? Could it in fact do anything? It seemed corporeal, and if its intentions could be gleaned from its expression, its feelings towards him were certainly not benign. Was it a rational being, or did it act purely on animal instincts? In despair, Dr. Ashurst fell back on superstition, and, convincing himself that if it really was a creature of evil it could not enter the house of God, he rushed inside the building; he tried not to think of the contrary argument, that the goblin was clearly at home in the consecrated ground of the churchyard. He hurried into the chancel, and knelt before the altar – only momentarily, as he could not bear to stay with his back to the body of the building, and he pressed himself into the corner between the altar and the wall, sinking as low as he could while still being able to see over the top of the communion rail, should anything follow him through the porch.

How long he stayed thus he did not know, but it seemed like hours, during which he dared not move in case the creature was at hand and should be attracted to him. Then the feared horror started; he heard the lifting of the latch of the door down the south aisle, to his left; it was pushed open, and a dark figure entered the church. The pounding of Dr. Ashurst's heart filled his head and the sickness in his stomach rose up and unfocussed his eyes, and for a moment he could not see clearly what it was; but then he recognised the curate, looking around the nave and aisles. Though he was too tense and now too stiff in the muscles to get up from his crouching position and his voice lodged in his dry throat, he was able to croak the clergyman's name and wave a hand feebly.

"Ah, Betty said you had just called and I thought you might be in here, as I did not pass you in the lane. But what are you doing there? Are you all right?" The young man hurried forward solicitously, and helped Dr. Ashurst to his feet.

"I felt giddy, and had to rest."

The curate looked at him quizzically, as if to doubt that, in a building filled with benches which could conveniently be sat or lain on, he had chosen to rest by crouching in a corner which he must have gone out of his way to reach. He now sat him on such a bench, and placed himself there too, half-turned towards him. "Dr. Ashurst, I should tell you that I have just come from William Paley, whom I visited shortly after you did; he is unwell, and I call in often to see him. He was speaking of the churchyard in sinister terms, difficult to comprehend, and I understand from his son that you had been asking him questions about it. Is this so?" The other nodded. The clergyman was speaking far more clearly and more forcefully than he had at their first meeting, but Dr. Ashurst noted that his speed was itself a sign of his extreme nervousness, which also expressed itself in his repeated glancing round. "I apologise for the bluntness and, if you judge it so, absurdity of this question, but it admits of no comfortable compromises: have you seen something untoward in or around this church?"

Dr. Ashurst was surprised and confused. Could it be that Trent knew of the thing which had so disturbed him, or was he merely trying to account for his strange behaviour by asking a very general question? He merely nodded his head again, more vigorously and for longer, his lips tight and his cheeks filled as though by the words he could not bring himself to speak. "Come," said the young man, "we must not talk of this here." He led him back to the vicarage, hurrying him through to the drawing room and a chair in which he could relax and compose himself, before summoning Betty and briskly ordering tea. They sat in silence until it had been brought and they had drunk a little.

"What is it that you have seen, if it is not impolite of me to ask?" Dr. Ashurst hesitated before answering, unwilling to commit himself in case he was misreading the curate's understanding. "Pardon me, if I am intruding, but might you have seen a strange creature, perhaps?" He nodded. "A small, deformed being?" Dr. Ashurst, now convinced that his host shared what he knew, in a rush unburdened himself of the events of the past two days; the curate listened carefully in silence, and when he had finished his story he added his own experience.

"Rest assured that I do not believe you to be falling into a madness, as you fear. I have myself seen it on several occasions, usually at the north side of the churchyard, which I now avoid as much as I can for that reason. The first time was at the end of a funeral service I was conducting after some two weeks in the parish. It was standing against the back wall and clearly visible, and I was taken aback, as you can understand; quite apart from its grotesque appearance, it was grinning in a most diabolical way at the sad proceedings. But I swiftly realised that no-one else present was aware of it, and I said nothing; in fact, I have not spoken of it until now. The vicar may have been aware of its existence, but he never mentioned it, and I did not think it appropriate to raise the subject. I think that may have been the origin of his concern to lock the churchyard."

"A vain undertaking! The creature seems to be able to enter the grounds at will, locks or no."

"I fear you misunderstand me. It is my belief that the wall, railings and locked gate were intended rather to keep the creature from leaving the churchyard, which seems to be its habitual abode, and wandering into the village. But, as you say, if its nature is not, as it were, of the same order as ours, then mere locks will not contain it. However, I have not seen it outside the bounds of the churchyard, and believe it to be locally confined in its movements. It is also my belief that William Paley has seen it as well as ourselves, but his speech is regarded as raving; however, it was

187

that knowledge which saved me, after weeks of anguish thinking myself mad, from believing that I was alone in a delusion, and imagining in daylight what I had already seen painted in the church. I take it that, in your study of it, you have seen the last figure in our famous wall painting?" The curate gestured towards the far wall.

"Yes, and I saw the creature before I saw the frieze, so could not simply be remembering the image. But why should it be visible to so few people? Why should you and I, and poor Mr. Paley, see it and not many who live hard by? For I have spoken to the tenant behind the church, and he does not seem to be aware of anything untoward so close to his property."

The curate paused before making his suggestion. "This may be presumptuous, but it seems to me that only those of a certain sensitivity are able to see it...." His voice trailed away in embarrassment. "The artist of the frieze must have seen it, though who can say if any of his fellows realised that it was taken from the life? It may be that more see it than we know, but are too fearful of being taken for mad to speak of it, as I was, and, as I gather, you have been for the past two days."

Dr. Ashurst nodded his agreement. "Do you think that Harry Paley sees it, as his father did? Is that why he is so unwilling to let the old man speak of it?"

"I doubt it; he is not exactly a sensitive soul, if I might say so. I think he considers what his father says about the churchyard to be meaningless raving, and he does not want others to hear it in case the old man is taken for a lunatic; he is simply protecting him, in his view."

"But what do you believe the creature to be, and what does it intend? You must have speculated on these things."

188

"I fear that it is beyond my conjecture as to what manner of being it is, but I doubt it to be of the same order of nature as any other creature with which we are familiar. It has no evident means of sustenance or shelter – I have not seen it indoors; it appears – though only to some – and disappears; and it may have a very long span of life, perhaps even immortality: for I have only seen one, and that exactly the same as the one depicted by the old artist, so it may be that there is, and always has been, only one of its kind, over many of our generations. But this is mere surmise. As to what it intends, it has to my knowledge done nothing so far, except frighten those who see it, with shows of malevolence. Perhaps it can accomplish nothing in our world."

"Let us pray that it be so," said Dr. Ashurst, "for if it could do the evil its expression betrays, we could expect little mercy. I wonder that such a thing of evil would be allowed free rein on holy ground."

"It has never to my knowledge tried to enter the church itself."

They lapsed into a ruminative silence for a while. Ascertaining that his guest would stay to eat with him, the curate rang for Betty to take the tea things away and asked her to put out some food for them in the dining room. They sat at the table, eating little but both looking at the painting of St. Dunstan's which hung on the wall between them. Dr. Ashurst conjectured that, although the creature had clearly been known in the area for centuries, as the medieval painting attested, it seemed to be in some way connected specifically with the north end of the churchyard and the wall; both of them had felt that. He recalled also William Paley's words about something being disturbed when it was built there.

They reflected a moment, and then ideas, thought on in one case for months and in the other for only hours, seemed to come together meaningfully, as each spoke briefly in turn, with long silences in between as they picked at the cold beef.

189

"The mound on Jenkins' land must have something to do with it; it was clearly cut in half when they extended the churchyard, and the part on this side was flattened. You can see the original extent of it on the painting."

"The mound seems to have a curious fascination –" and here Dr. Ashurst admitted the true cause of his upset the previous day, when he had found that he had unconsciously added it to his sketch.

"Indeed. You may also have noticed that the painting in the north aisle clearly shows Death standing on the brink of a hillock overlooking the church from that side. It is my belief that the whole painting showed the villagers assembled behind him on that very mound, about to go down to their graves while the creature looked on gleefully – just as I first saw him at the graveside."

"Mr. Paley said something about the churchyard being extended during a particularly grievous outbreak of a fever." Dr. Ashurst went on. "I understand that such mounds are reckoned to be ancient burial places themselves, and that superstitions accrue to them amongst rustic folk. I have often observed them on my walks around the country, left avoided and unploughed in the fields."

"Just so..... Spirits or monstrous beings are often believed to inhabit them, even as guardians."

The implications of their line of reasoning here left them silent for a while. Then Dr. Ashurst, whose notion of what he was seeking to find out was becoming clearer, mentioned his plan of trying to contact the builders, with a view to seeing whether any memories or records remained of what happened when the disturbance of the mound took place. Mr. Trent swiftly concurred with this in principle, though doubting whether this could in fact be pursued;

they could inspect what records from that far back remained in the vicarage and in the sacristy, but, apart from the parish registers, which he had already thoroughly perused, they were very scant. When they had hastily finished their desultory meal, they retired to the study and went through the drawers of the vicar's desk before, with some nervousness, going over to the church and turning over the papers in the sacristy, primarily in search of a note of the name of the builders engaged to construct the wall. Mr. Trent had done much of this already, since the departure of the vicar, with a less defined objective; success in finding anything relevant on this occasion was just as lacking. However, he knew that a box had been sent to another local clergyman by the vicar shortly before he left, containing, he had said, papers of a legal nature concerning the church property, which should be kept for the new vicar; he had been unwilling to leave them with a new curate, he had said by way of apology, as he knew that curates sometimes moved on suddenly and swiftly and the box might be overlooked. Mr. Trent immediately resolved to send a message to Reverend Hale at Stoke Armitage, asking for return of the box, or, if his promise to the old vicar prevented it, permission to view its contents; he did not give his reasons, beyond saying that he wished to ascertain whether certain information was contained in the documents.

By now, the sun was sinking and Dr. Ashurst was anxious to be gone and safely in his room at the inn. Taking his leave of the curate until the morrow, he made his way swiftly past the churchyard, upset that it was already darker than he would have wanted and trying to think of anything but that which had grown to obsess him in so short a time – but it was no use; he had to turn a little to glance inside, and being slightly off-balance and moving too quickly he was badly affected when a dark shape leapt up from its hiding place behind the solid part of the wall and hurled itself at the railings next to him; he was shocked to an unsteady, swaying halt, then staggered out into the lane backwards as he fought to stay upright. Whether any noise were made by the creature's action, he could not later be sure, but he thought the whole episode was conducted in an eerie silence, apart from his own incoherent cry. It took a moment for him to realise that the shape was truly on the far side of the barrier, standing on top of the wall and holding a rail with one hand, and was making no move to surmount the fence; but it stretched its free arm towards him between the bars and made swift slashing motions in his direction with its curled, claw-like hand, the gnarled fingers of which ended in sturdy black nails, overgrown and curving inwards. Though far out of its feeble reach, Dr. Ashurst took several involuntary steps back, and, before he swooned through inability to breathe, despite the gloom he was able to take in a few details of its appearance, this being his first close look at the creature of his nightmares. Later, he could recall – though he tried not to do so – its dark and wrinkled skin, like that of mummified Egyptians he had seen, the curled black hair covering its nether parts thickly and the sharp, yellowed teeth visible between the open lips of its disproportionately large mouth.

Dr. Ashurst was conscious of some of what happened over the next few days – of being carried to The Red Bull; later, of being moved from his room there to a spare room in the vicarage; then of telling Mr. Trent of his last experience – but of most he was unaware: of being found in the lane by Mr. Jenkins' workers, in a dead faint; of frightening Harry Paley by raving worse than his father in his fever; of being rescued by the curate and carried off before he could be pronounced insane. Thankfully, there were other episodes of which he was too much aware at the time but of which he retained only the most vague and general memory: the terrible nightmares in which iron railings melted at the touch of dark shapes which swarmed through to seize him, pressing their leering and slavering faces close to his, taking his breath, and clutching his throat in a hard, tight grip.

It was the third day before he was fully recovered. Mr. Trent filled the gaps in his knowledge of his own recent past, and told him that he had sent word to Reverend Hale, asking to inspect the box of papers, in case it should contain anything relevant to their inquiries. However, before a reply was received, he was on a coach bound for Oxford, being too anxious to leave Cassington for safe and familiar surroundings to wait even for a possible solution to the mystery – which was still in his thoughts for much of his days and for some troubled parts of his nights when, three weeks later, he received a letter from the curate:

THE VICARAGE, CASSINGTON

My dear Dr. Ashurst,

I hope I find you in better health than when we last met and fully recovered from your late disturbance of spirit. I trust it will not disconcert you further to hear of what I have chanced to learn in connection with the cause of your distemperature.

The Reverend Hale himself rode over with the contents of the parish box safely in his saddlebags, shortly after your departure. Having heard something, from the local gossip, of what had happened to a distinguished visitor to Cassington and construing that my request was not unrelated, he was concerned to offer his support and experience to the parish novice he knew me to be. He is a wise and learned man, and I have since learned that he has some reputation in the county, and in his uncompromising way he questioned me closely as to what had occurred; unexpectedly, but fortunately, he was prepared to give credence to the things of which he had already heard, and I found it easy to confess all to him plainly, showing him also the paintings in the church and in the dining room, and the north boundary wall of the churchyard. He left me to start looking through the papers, while he went over to Mr. Jenkins' farm for permission to examine the mound on his side.

When he returned, he joined me in sorting through the documents, on the dining table. They included the deeds to the strip of Poxdown land, and a number of bills, pinned together, from a builder's firm in Dorchester (which I have since discovered closed down some years ago, the proprietor having died). One was for demolition of the old wall and what was described as "clearance work", including "spreading the excess earth over the church ground"; another, dated a fortnight later, was for building the wall itself, but a third, another three months on, was for raising the new wall from one yard to two yards high and topping the remaining lengths of old wall with cement and rails. In themselves, these documents added nothing to what we had surmised, but there were notes scribbled on the back of the last one which caught our attention.

First, in a hand identical to that on the face of the bill and presumably a communication from the builder to its recipient, the vicar of the day: "Reverend Sir: I trust this further work, with whatever devisings of a spiritual nature you are better fitted to perform, will repair the mischief which has troubled you." Beneath, in another hand, perhaps as a memorandum by the vicar: "What was uncovered has been buried in the corner. I have decided not to attempt a repetition of the consecration of the new ground, in case further disturbance results, and trust that the sacred nature of the wider church land will suffice for the souls to be buried there. God grant that this will suffice to placate it."

When I exclaimed that we should dig in the corner of the churchyard to see what might have been buried there, the Reverend Hale cautioned me in the strongest terms consistent with his office that on no account should I attempt such a thing, and that I should never give the slightest hint to anyone that anything might be concealed there. To prevent such a thing from happening, he took away that bill, and I believe he has since destroyed it. Furthermore, he went straight to the north side of the

194

churchyard, to ascertain that there is a strip perhaps four feet wide, nearest the wall, not yet used for burial; he gave instructions that the earth in the western corner should be lightly turned over, without digging, and that hardy shrubs should be planted there to deter disturbance in the future. This work has now been undertaken. He also performed there a service as though of exorcism, none else being present, in the open air and in daylight, such a thing as I have not seen before, and persevered in it despite the strong wind and downpour which came suddenly upon us. Although we believe, from what was written by, I presume, the penultimate vicar, that the added ground was never formally consecrated, he determined against attempting this further action.

As to what the creature itself might be, if it is indeed a thing created by God, Reverend Hale did not speak his mind fully to me, I fear, but he seems to agree with us in associating it with the mound, which he calls a barrow, even to believing that the range of the creature may be restricted by the extent to which its unconsecrated soil was spread over the churchyard. I would conjecture that when you saw it on the roof, it had reached its furthest limit, following the spread earth to the north side of the church and then having freedom to climb its walls upward and seemingly to cross its roof, as not being on the ground. In any case, Mr. Hale is very much of the conviction that the creature, being seemingly unique, immortal and bound in ways which do not occur to us, is not material to any great degree and so is unable to accomplish much in our world. He recommends ignoring it in the hope that eventually it will lose interest in terrorising those who can see it and perhaps pass back to a more suitable world, or at least stay in the remaining portion of the mound.

Exactly what all this may mean I know not, but I pass on the rector's words as I remember them. He appears to speak with knowledge and confidence, and it may be that in Oxford you will be able to

195

make further inquiries of those who might know more of such matters.

I hope that you are recovering and will be able to visit us here again, if you feel inclined to do so.

Your Obedient Servant,

Francis Trent

But Walter Ashurst took Mr. Hale's advice very much to heart, and avoided Cassington for the rest of his life.

OUTPOST OF EDEN

Given the amount of his waking time which the Reverend Thomas Pointer spent in his beloved garden, it was perhaps almost inevitable that it should happen to him there; but it was also ironic that the place wherein he took so much solace and renewed himself after the pursuit of his pastoral duties was the site of his total downfall. Indeed, it was the very cause, for as he contemplated nostalgically the last of his spring flowers and directed his gardener in the tending of the first buds of summer, with the late May breeze waving the tops of the orchard trees and blowing apple blossom in a gentle snow shower across the lawns, the scene before him flew into thirteen distinct pieces, like a looking-glass smashing and scattering a rainbow. Each shard pulsed and beat about his head as though made of monstrous wings, then soared and spun as though chasing and evading its fellows in a kaleidoscope of shapes and shades: the stiffly bending garden wall, its ancient faded bricks now suddenly as red as blood; the acrid green of a billowing sea of grass; the shocking mosaic of a cavorting flowerbed; the mad dance of the liberated chestnut tree – all contrived to batter at his senses with their flaming colours and swirling arabesques and confuse his brain with the sheer impossibility of what he was witnessing. The Reverend Pointer clutched his temples as he swayed in despair and dizziness; he felt nausea, a motion sickness rising from his stomach, choking off his scream, and he fell to the ground, rolling himself into a ball with his arms over his head in an attempt to ward off the circling harpies which dived at his mind with claws extended. It was in vain, for no matter how tightly he squeezed closed his eyes screened by his hands he could still see the sharp and gaudy fragments of the shattered prospect lunging and taunting him. In that moment he knew his garden to have been possessed by devils, his personal Eden to have been conquered by the serpent, with no hope of divine redemption; and now the evil was forcing its way into the

197

bastion of his own skull, so that unclean spirits might take possession of his soul. As he lay on his bed when they had carried him into the vicarage, writhing in the fiery grip of the demons and trying vainly to throw them off but being hindered by the ropes holding him down, he cried out the names of his assailants as he knew them – Flibbertigibbet, which seemed familiar to his hearers, Modu, which did not, and the rest.

It was this which gave Theophilus Hale the vital clue. Summoned by the Bishop to attend what appeared to be a severe case of demoniac possession – of which, it was rumoured, he had had some experience – he soon realized that the names which Pointer was crying out were the five demons listed by Edgar in his disguise as the madman Poor Tom in Shakespeare's *King Lear.* Of course, he did not conclude that the distressed clergyman was pretending, as Edgar was, but realised that some illness or disturbance of his faculties had thrown the man into a nightmare world in which remembered fictitious horrors had become as realities. A few inquiries revealed that Pointer had indeed played Edgar in a performance of the tragedy when he had been at St. Jerome's College; the Bishop's secretary had been a fellow student and recalled vividly the way in which his old friend had thrown himself into the part, both as the noble Edgar who transformed himself from a gullible fool into a gallant hero and as the madman whose identity he assumed on the way. His simulated ravings on that occasion had caused almost as much consternation as his real ones now, so lifelike and heartfelt they seemed.

Although Hale was deeply saddened by the circumstances, for his own earliest happy memories were of childhood play in the garden paradise of his father's vicarage, he was relieved to be able to report that the afflicted man needed soothing care rather than the rigours of a hard-fought exorcism, and Pointer was conveyed to St. Faith's Hospital for a treatment of drugged sleep in a darkened room. He did indeed benefit from this: within two weeks he was able to stay conscious without screaming and throwing himself around the room, within a month he was speaking coherently if briefly, and by the end of the summer he was regularly leaving his room to go to the refectory or the chapel. Venturing outside took much, much longer, as terrors associated with plants and lawns continued to haunt his dreams for years after, but in later life he made sufficient progress in controlling his fear to be able to walk around the hospital grounds, and even help tend the herbs and vegetables in the cottage garden. Trees, though, he never did learn to endure, and to the end the merest glimpse of dark branches waving towards him over the boundary wall would cause him to swoon or run screaming to the shelter of his room.

Sad and protracted as the Reverend Pointer's affliction was, Hale found some consolation in the fact that he was not the victim of an assault by the forces of evil and that he was eventually able to regain some innocent pleasure in the simple workings of nature. Indeed, visiting him some years later, Hale almost envied his condition, intellectually limited as it now was, for being free of most of the constraints, anxieties and responsibilities of normal adult life: he seemed to Hale not so much as to have regressed as to have regained a childish wonder and trust, as he watched the seeds sending living shoots out of the earth and accepted in a literal fashion the simplistic religious teaching in which he was re-educated. For Pointer, it seemed, each leaf unfurled, each bud opened, because an unseen white-bearded God had touched it individually; the same God painted the sky blue and threw the sun across it daily, and there was no need to worry about anything as long as He was in charge, like an omnipotent Headmaster ever-mindful of those in His care. Hale wished his own faith could be as simple and hence as strong; and yet those occasions when the power of evil and the realization of the potential for misery in human life had been most brought home to him had also often led to conclusions reaffirming his belief in goodness and its intervention in the world. One such occasion had also taken place in a garden, and it had all but destroyed Hale's reason before its resolution.

Dr. Thomas Findlesham, Dean of the cathedral of Hale's diocese (at that period being Bristol, before Dorset was annexed to Salisbury), was well-travelled and well-connected, and the main consequence of his travels and connections was the acquisition of plants for his garden – not the modest garden and orchard of the deanery which was his occasional place of residence in connection with his duties, but the far larger grounds of Findlesham Hall, the Dorset house left to him as the only surviving son of Rear-Admiral Sir Henry Findlesham; notwithstanding that he was to be the last of the Findleshams after eight generations at the Hall, and that on his demise the unentailed estate would probably be divided between his sister and four cousins, he was determined that the garden would be a thing of wonder that none would dare destroy after his death and which would serve as a lasting memorial to his endeavours. For it was not, as other fine gardens were, simply a remarkable collection of exotic plants or an intricate design of flowerbeds, lawns and paths, or even a romantic landscape filled with lakes, streams, ruins, follies, pastures and woodlands, but a living reflection of human culture, with themed sections bringing together plants associated in different ways. For example, there was a Shakespearean garden, which sought to exhibit every shrub, flower and herb mentioned in the bard's works and also to recreate some of the settings described therein: there was a miniature Forest of Arden, complete with rocks and running brooks, Oberon's bank of wild thyme and Prospero's cave by a pool and sand bar to represent the shore. Another area was a Biblical garden, basically an orchard, dominated by a young cedar of Lebanon already substantial and destined to grow into a mighty tree; here one could find the source of the gopher-wood of Noah's ark (which he took to be cypress, whether or not coated with kopher, or pitch), the hyssop shrub of the Passion story, and of course the vine and the figtree, admittedly in a greenhouse. Dr.

Findlesham would dearly have loved to have known for certain the identity of the fruit which tempted Eve, but had to content himself with following Milton and including a token apple tree.

Such horticultural projects were not without precedent, but the unique feature of the Dean's garden was that it did not merely include generic specimens of the plants mentioned in the texts but as far as possible it incorporated possible descendants of the originals – a curious notion, but one which he saw as exactly parallel to the idea of family descent amongst people. He reasoned that a plant growing where an ancient writer had described it could well be a direct descendant of the one originally seen and as nearly identical to it as possible. Thus, the hyssop plant which he had himself taken from a hill outside Jerusalem and carefully tended on the journey back to England could well have been, in his view, a descendent of that hyssop which provided a stick with which to lift the sponge to the lips of the crucified Christ. His travels focused on the collecting of such specimens. In England, he went to Glastonbury to take a cutting from the Holy Thorn, sprung from the staff of Joseph of Arimathea; to Dover to collect a samphire plant from the cliffs, as described by Edgar to his father Gloucester; to Edwinstowe in Nottinghamshire, to collect acorns from which to grow the offspring of Robin Hood's Major Oak; and many other places known from history, literature and legend. Abroad, he acquired a young olive plant from the stock which first brought wealth to Athens, another from Olympia from which athletic victors' wreaths might have been fashioned and, in place of common daffodils, bulbs of asphodel from the threshold of the underworld at Enna in Sicily.

What he could not gather himself he had others send him. The British Consul in Constantinople had supplied a tamarisk from the alleged plain of Troy, perhaps descended from that in which the chariot of the hapless Adrestos had become entangled before his death at the hands of Menelaos, according to Homer's Iliad. A

Lutheran pastor in Norway with an interest in antiquities sent a sprig of that mistletoe which had allegedly slain the Norse god Baldur, even though it was probably a quite different plant that had been meant.

Nevertheless, his project gained immeasurably greater depth after a visit to Pisa to see the fairly-named Campo dei Miracoli, the green lawn from which arise in succession the famous leaning tower, the magnificent cathedral and the glorious baptistery; however, impressed as he was by these marvels, it was another structure nearby which inflamed Findlesham's imagination. Within the fresco'd marble walls of the Camposanto he saw the rectangle of the most beautiful cemetery in the world, and heard how in crusading times earth had been shipped there from Golgotha to recreate a corner of the Holy Land as a sacred resting place for the pious dead. Immediately, he regretted all the opportunities he had missed to take the soil with the roots, and what he had achieved suddenly seemed only a half of what he had intended it to be. Henceforth, all his schemes included not only the plant but also its native earth. When saplings from Macbeth's Birnam Wood were transported down from northern Scotland to form a windbreak for the Shakespearean garden, a half a ton of local soil was carted with each young tree; a barrel of Dardanian soil was begged from the Consul at Constantinople, to dig in around the Trojan tamarisk.

It was after this that the final great project at Findlesham was undertaken. The Dean had sold the last family asset of which he could legally dispose – an outlying tenancy – and paid the proceeds to a Dutch merchant from the East Indies for space in his hold and the collection of specimens from his ports of call, for what he called the Marco Polo garden. Some months of anxious waiting later, the Dean's growing fear that he would never see the plants or his money again was dispelled by news that he was required to take delivery of part of the cargo of an East Indiaman that was

202

docking at Bristol. His sudden and unexplained absence from Cathedral services did not go unremarked as he hurried to summon the various carters whom he had provisionally engaged against this day, and there was much shaking of heads local and ecclesiastical throughout the shire and the diocese as an intermittent convoy of carts, farm wagons, drays and packhorses made its slow progress from the coast to Findlesham, carrying for the most part barrels and sacks of earth of various shades and textures, all carefully labelled so that they could be reunited with the shrubs and saplings which stuck out from amongst them in pots and tubs. The Dean himself was the target of most of the murmured censure, as he rode day and night up and down the far-spaced column, like a demented general encouraging a ragtag army. He leapt onto a rickety wagon to pack bags of earth around a mulberry from China, to prevent its tall pot from rocking dangerously; he forced several surly Somerset carters to stop by rivers or village pumps so that he could water the drying plants; he took off his coat and spread it between two broomsticks stuck in gaps between the planks of the floor of a cart, as a makeshift windbreak to protect a delicate bloom from the Spice Islands.

At length the last wagon had been emptied at the Hall, amid much inappropriate language from the Dean as he cursed any workman who threw down his burden roughly or tipped his load to save time. Coins from a dwindling supply were doled out to the conscripts, who retreated northward as swiftly as their vehicles and horses would allow, to be replaced at once by another dishevelled battalion, this time of local labourers, sappers whose task was to dig and fill as the Dean directed the planting of his new specimens. Most of these were placed together in the Marco Polo area, where an ornate greenhouse in vaguely Oriental style was to house the delicate plants which were to be raised from seeds in their native soils; the larger and more robust imports were positioned by a lake, in an adjacent marsh or on a raised terrace overlooking them, intended to replicate locations in Java, India or Ceylon, or on an artificial hillside copied from Chinese paintings, which would have been surmounted by a pagoda had funds allowed. A few of the plants were taken to other parts of the grounds, such as the Biblical garden or the Shakespearean garden, where Iago's coloquintida found a home.

The great effort of this task, and the muted displeasure of the Bishop and the Chapter at his long absence from his post, led to the Dean retiring on the grounds of ill health soon afterwards. He did not object much to having this urged on him, as his thoughts and desires were now wholly, rather than merely largely, directed towards his garden, and being obliged to spend even a little time in traveling to the Cathedral and carrying out the barest of his duties seemed no more than an irritating irrelevance. The fact that the diocese was prepared to compensate him for the premature loss of his stipend with a generous pension encouraged him further, for the last project had left him actually in debt. He retired to Findlesham Hall, or at least to the handful of rooms still furnished and kept warm, with the smallest of staffs – a cook of indifferent skill but prepared because of that to undertake washing and cleaning also, and an elderly footman who played the part of a butler but for a smaller wage. However, savings here were dissipated by the size of the outdoor staff: a resident head gardener, another plantsman and a forester, and two men permanently employed in mowing and weeding in the summer and gathering leaves and carrying out maintenance work in the winter. Despite the protests from afar of his sister's husband and his cousins, he allowed gaps to appear in the roof of the Hall, rot to creep into window frames and doorframes, and paintwork and plaster to crack and peel in damp and unheated rooms; every penny was spent on the upkeep of the garden, until the house began to look like an artistically semi-ruinous folly decorating the grounds – not that many were able to appreciate the effect, for the master of Findlesham was practically a hermit, partly from the inability to afford to entertain guests but much more from a growing indifference to the world outside his garden. He had never been particularly gregarious or outgoing, but he had once been sufficiently sociable to make progress within the Church hierarchy and he had travelled to Italy, Greece and the Holy Land; now his horizons were defined by his own boundary walls and his society was entirely leafy and flowering.

It was three years after the former Dean's permanent removal to the Hall, by which time he was well over sixty years of age, that the talk began. Of course, the eccentric and the prominent always excite some rumour and speculation, and Dr. Findlesham could be considered to belong to both groups; however, he impinged so little on the consciousness of his neighbours that whatever gossip there once been about him had long since faded. Instead, the talk was actually about the Hall, itself, or rather the grounds, and it originated with Ned Hurst and Joshua Bonner, the two undergardeners. Both men were little given to socializing, out of a natural disposition to taciturn solitude and also because of limited means, factors which had caused them to take up their jobs, ill-paid and secluded, which no-one else had wanted. When they were not working at the Hall, their usual recreation was to share a small table in an alcove in a corner of The Jack in the Green in Edgely, one of them sitting with his back to the bar so as to shut out the rest of the world; there they would sit for two or three hours over one or two pints each, in near-silence. Nevertheless, when Ned was laid up for a few days with a sprained ankle, Joshua eventually appeared in the pub on his own, out of habit. In their absence, two travellers had occupied the alcove, and the gardener was left standing at the bar; questions were asked about his colleague, he was bought a drink more than his usual allowance, and so he was led to talk more than he had ever said to his neighbours before – until he seemed to realize he was saying what he should not and promptly left, walking with an unaccustomed swaying motion.

What he said about the grounds stayed in the minds of many of his listeners and fired the imaginations of a few. Hardly any of them had ever been within the boundary wall, and most knew only the scene glimpsed through the main gates and the view of a part of it behind the house as seen from the road coming down Edgend Hill. Despite his limited experience of using language expressively, he found words to convey the grandeur and strangeness of his employer's vision and described vividly what it was like to work inside the grounds – how one could seem miles from human habitation when screened by dense shrubs and trees with no sounds except for birds and insects. And yet it was not idyllic. It was fine when the two of them were working together or when one was working under the direction of the head gardener or the master himself, but when he was alone in a remote corner of the grounds he often felt uneasy, almost as though he felt himself watched, stalked almost, by something down in the undergrowth or overhead on a bough. Then sometimes there were noises, but not just the pleasant sounds of nature; the rustling of leaves and the rubbing of reeds in a gentle breeze became as whisperings between giants. "It's not the being alone that's so bad," he said, not really aware of his audience; "I don't mind the being alone, not one bit; in fact, I would rather be alone than with most folks. It's the being alone and not on your own that's not right, not right at all." When pressed for an explanation, he drank more deeply and forgot the question and the questioner.

Joshua was unused to having an audience and the influence of the alcohol acted as a further barrier between him and those around him, while loosening his tongue; he was in effect speaking aloud to himself. Without consciously realizing it, the crowd in the bar sensed that this was an opportunity not to be repeated, that having slipped into this state once the man would never do it again, and indeed that the present circumstances were unlikely to recur. They continued to question him, not expecting direct answers but hoping to prompt his ramblings to take certain directions.

206

The worst part of the grounds to work in was the Biblical garden, God help him; there was nothing holy about it, and neither of them liked to have to be there alone for any length of time. It occupied one side of the main ornamental lake, which on this shore served as the Sea of Galilee and was fed by a stream harbouring the bulrushes of Moses' Nile; there was a deliberately arid strip for the desert, featuring a domed and minareted greenhouse, and beyond this a version of a flowering Eden. In between lay the garden of Gethsemane and that which most disturbed the men, the recreation of Golgotha, the place of the skull. The Dean had taken this at its most literal, and had created from boulders a rocky hill which took the shape of a death's head, with on one slope a rudimentary face with hollows for eye sockets, nose cavity and mouth. To one side was a garden planted with herbs and spices suitable for preserving and embalming, in which was a great rock which had been hollowed out to form a narrow room with a ledge inside; the main slab which had been cut out stood at the side of the entrance like a door standing ajar. This was the tomb of Jesus. When the sun was setting, the shadows moved across the scene, making the door of the tomb and the eyes of the skull seem to move, and when the sun went down behind Golgotha, it was suddenly cold in the shadow of the rocks. Then sparkling Galilee turned grey and a chill breeze came off its water, changing the delights of Eden into menace by stirring up the trees and making them moan. God help him, it was not right for the Dean to mock the Almighty by copying his work, and what if he had once been a holy man? It just meant it was even more reprehensible – though Joshua actually said "even wronger".

The gardener had started trembling when describing Golgotha, and now he gave a convulsive shake; this seemed to clear his head for a moment, as he focused and looked about him in a shocked or embarrassed manner. He slammed down his still half-full tankard and lurched purposefully towards the exit, as though angry. He wrestled briefly with the door and left it open as he strode out into the night. A few days later he reappeared with Ned; they re-occupied their alcove in silence, and never again did either of them say more than a dozen words together to anyone else.

That was in the spring; in the autumn, Joshua's misgivings about his place of work seemed to come to fruition, when Ned went missing. On Friday morning, Joshua had been instructed to take a scythe to the lawns around the house, while Ned had been detailed to tidy up and attend to watering in all the greenhouses in the grounds. He had been checked on by the head gardener in the East Indian greenhouse in the middle of the morning, but he had failed to reappear for his midday break. In the afternoon, the head gardener visited all the greenhouses in turn, without finding him, and informed his employer. By the end of the day, there was general concern about his whereabouts, and a search was organized, with the master and Joshua taking one section of the estate, the other gardeners a second one and the forester and the butler the third. Ned, like Joshua, lived alone and had no known family, so there was no-one else to inform, and it would never have occurred to Dr. Findlesham to ask for help from outside. Night fell, and the forester recalled them to the house with a shot from his gun. After a frugal bite to eat, they resumed their search with torches, until all heard the signal from one of the pairs; they hurried to the Biblical garden, where the Dean was struggling to sound an old hunting horn.

It had been Joshua who had found him, hanging from a branch of an English oak, centuries older than the imported saplings around it in the garden of Eden. He had been staying close to the Dean in the dark, but then had wandered off to investigate a strange repeated noise; soon, by the light of his torch, he could see a large shape swinging very slightly in what was now a noticeable breeze, the harsh creaking of wood and of belt-leather being clearly audible above the whispering and whistling of the trees. There was no question of it being other than suicide, as none of the men on the estate had any motive whatsoever for killing Ned, though none had an alibi to cover anything like the whole day. It was clear to see how he had accomplished it. Climbing up the tree to sit on one branch, he had fastened his belt round another branch a few feet above and to the side of his seat. He had then threaded through the loop of the belt several lengths of stout twine, which he had twisted together and tied in a knot around his neck, before launching himself off his branch. The twine, which might have split if rubbing on the bark, took his weight despite his involuntary struggles, and the belt held fast. Next day, the local Justice declared him to have died by his own hand and no-one protested or thought to inquire further as to the reason, as though the joylessness of Ned's existence were a self-evident cause and it had only been a matter of time before he took steps to end it.

Only Joshua was moved, and even in his case it was a matter of being fearful for himself rather than sorrowful at the death of the nearest thing he had to a friend. He had been right in thinking this a place of ill-omen; it had claimed Ned and now it would come for him. The idea of working entirely alone now on the estate, and, even worse, of having to work in the place where he had seen that sight – not truly alone, for he would never get out of his mind the image of Ned's twisted and blackened face and stretched neck as seen by the light of a flickering torch – terrified him. He was destined to be the next, inevitable victim of something nameless and unseen which dwelt in rocks and trees, in wind and water.

He had been sent home after the discovery, so that he could have until Monday to recover himself; that Sunday, he was seen for the first time in many years in the churchyard in Edgely, standing just inside and to the side of the lychgate as the congregation departed after the Eucharist service. They tried not to stare at him as they walked past and he looked intently at the ground before him; he was wringing his poor hat in his hands and kept making a strange

209

jerking motion to his side, as though feeling impelled to rush out of the gate and just holding back from doing it. The vicar, who knew what had happened and was turning over in his mind whether he could countenance the pauper's burial being in consecrated ground, given the circumstances, approached him as the last of his flock departed, somewhat more hurriedly than usual. He assumed that Joshua had come about the funeral, and that his mood was one of sadness, and so he prepared himself to be comforting and conciliatory about the burial. In fact, his mood was of terror, not sorrow, and he appeared completely indifferent as to what might happen to the mortal remains of Ned Hurst, as the Reverend Brownlow discovered as he tried to coax some sustained response from the distraught man. Eventually, he led him, virtually by the hand, from his post by the churchyard wall and into the privacy of the porch of St. Andrew's church, where they sat opposite each other on the stone benches which lined it; one could not say "facing each other", as Joshua scarcely raised his head for some minutes but stared at the hat which he continued to screw up in his hands.

"I know that he be one of you, like, and that ye'll stick together, but I thinks as 'ow he 'as not done right up there."

In fact, the Reverend Brownlow had never even met Dr. Findlesham; his predecessor had known the family, but he had been at Edgely for only five years and the former Dean had never attended services at St. Andrew's. It had not seemed odd when he was at the Cathedral most Sundays, but since his retirement it had often crossed the vicar's mind as strange that there could be such a prominent clergyman in the parish who never came to church. He tended to shrug the idea off by assuming that he conducted a service of his own: the Hall allegedly had a chapel, though no-one living had ever seen it.

The vicar employed his usual fomulae to try to give Joshua some general comfort in his loss and his anxiety, without apparent effect; his promise that he would try to see the former Dean that very day did, however, affect the man very obviously, as he stopped racking his hat and produced a toothy and wide-eyed expression which was perhaps an inexperienced face's attempt at a smile. Brownlow did not spoil or complicate the moment by explaining that he was going on a routine visit to console the bereaved and not to confront the Dean in some way; and at least one half of his motive for going, he admitted to himself, was curiosity to see the hermit and his garden at last, since he was himself quite interested in plants.

Hoping that the tragic circumstances and the apparent unconventionality of life at the Hall would excuse his lack of an invitation or even an announcement of his coming, he took horse for the estate after an early lunch in order to be back for the evening service; on the way, he began to wonder what he would do if he could not gain admittance, for the gates were kept closed and probably locked except for the arrival and departure of the non-resident staff, who brought with them whatever purchases were needed from the village, and there was no means of communicating with the house, which was a quarter of a mile beyond. However, although the gates were indeed locked, the old lodge, decrepit as it looked, proved not to be empty; despite the odd missing slate and cracked pane and what appeared to be old sheets up at the windows, the front door was ajar, and repeated calls to attract attention eventually brought out the forester, Birch. The right to occupy this damp and sparsely-furnished three-roomed lodge and to eat whatever was available in the kitchen at the Hall now made up almost all of his remuneration; it had not always been so, and the change had not improved his attitude. He stood squarely in his doorway and looked across through the bars at the impatient horseman outside.

"Who are ye and what d'ye want?"

Brownlow was not impressed: even to one who stayed outside his flock, it was surely obvious in a general sense who he was, and that should have answered the second question in large measure.

"I am the Reverend Brownlow, vicar of Edgely, and I have come to see Dr. Findlesham. Now please be so good as to let me in."

"Don't know about that. Nothing been said to me about you coming in. The Dean don't regularly see folk much."

"Be that as it may, I have come here in order to carry out my duties as vicar of this parish following the recent tragedy here."

"You be meaning that business with Ned. Now, it seems to me Dean's more than a vicar, if it comes to that. If there's any duties of that sort need doing, seems to me he's the one to do them."

"I do not have time to stand here arguing in this nonsensical way. I demand that you either let me in or go to the Hall and find out if your master wishes to see me."

Something in the vicar's manner made Birch stop halfway through his cursing if he would be spoken to like that, and instead he contented himself by spitting as he strolled as slowly as he could manage up the drive. It was a full quarter of an hour before he returned, still slouching along; he took a small bunch of large keys from his belt and unlocked the gates as the vicar, who had dismounted and was sitting on a grassy bank, got up and retrieved his grazing horse. "Master'll see thee at the 'ouse," was all he said as the visitor passed him.

Brownlow was relieved to find that Findlesham was by no means as aggressive or rude as his servant: eccentric, as might have been expected after his living nearly cut off from the world for so long, but not ill-mannered. One who knew his story could still just picture him as a leading dignitary of the Church, though one in severe decline. He wore old-fashioned ecclesiastical costume apparently as his everyday attire, with tights and bands and gaiters, though his black was rusty in places and some seams had been badly mended and remended where bending and kneeling at his weeding had put unplanned stress on them. His white hair, which had not yet receded far, had been left to grow long, hanging straight and thin to his shoulders. His eyes were bright, and stood out the more from a complexion unfashionably marked by the sun and wind; however, they were not lively, and tended to appear fixed on some distant object. He had come out of his house on hearing of his visitor and was standing at the foot of the sweep of stone steps which led to his front door; he appeared somewhat agitated, rubbing his hands and swaying slightly, which Brownlow put down to recent events, though he soon realized that this was his natural demeanour, as though always anxious at having his plans delayed and his time taken up. The vicar shook hands with him and introduced himself, with some expressions of regret at their not having become better acquainted in the past, and then made some silent play with the reins in his hands and nodded towards the horse which he had led in, but without provoking any response about what he might do with it. The former Dean was not ungracious but came quite swiftly to the point, asking what the immediate purpose of the call was; clearly, the idea of purely social visiting had faded from his memory.

Despite his bravado with the gatekeeper, the vicar was not clear even in his own mind what his exact purpose was and for a couple of rather awkward minutes he spoke somewhat disjointedly of his sympathy for the bereaved and the arrangements for the funeral, without, he hoped subconsciously, allowing simple curiosity to be evident as a motive for his presence. Eventually, as Findlesham spoke hardly a word to help him out and there appeared little hope that he might be invited into the house, he asked bluntly if he might see where the tragedy had taken place. The Dean seemed hesitant rather than openly reluctant, the main impression which he was giving off being one of controlled irritation at having his peace disturbed and his time taken up needlessly, but he agreed briefly and, turning abruptly, he began to walk quite quickly along one of the paths leading into the grounds. Clearly, if he wished to see the spot, he had only the option of going immediately, so Brownlow followed, after tying his horse hurriedly to a ring set in the wall at the foot of the steps for the purpose. Catching his host, he tried to engage him in conversation about the gardens, but Findlesham gave only the shortest of replies to his direct questions and volunteered nothing, evidently desiring only to dispatch his visitor as soon as he could without too much rudeness. The vicar gave up the attempt at conversation and instead concentrated on looking around him as they walked at what was probably the fastest pace the older man could sustain.

What he saw amazed him: on every hand, plants which he could not name in profusion, artificial vistas cunningly contrived in small spaces, exotic tableaux of vegetation and natural features. Their path led through a small, watered meadow filled with asphodel, then went up a gentle slope. Here the grass ended abruptly, to be replaced by bare earth and whitened rocks amongst which broom plants burst forth. At the top of the rise, two columns of fluted marble drums supported a fragment of pediment above a statue of Athene on a pedestal; parts of broken columns lay by them, and beyond were stunted olive plants, struggling to survive on the hillside at this latitude. The whole scene was ringed by bushes of laurel and myrtle which were coping much more successfully. Passing down through these, they came in sight of a small lake, roughly round in shape. The ground became sandy as they approached the water, and plants of the desert succeeded; they veered away before reaching a simple-looking boat hauled up on the strand, with nets hung up to dry between it and a white-washed thatched hut. The path led them to a green, wooded area around a dip caused by a stream flowing into the lake; walking back up this a short way led them into a stand of ancient trees ringing and screening a glade spacious enough to allow enough light for the growing of a kind of semi-cultivated, semi-wild cottage garden. There were neglected but fruiting apple, pear and plum trees, bushes of soft fruit and berries too luxuriant for most of their crop to be gathered, clumps of wild onion, garlic and herbs. The soothing cooing of wood doves came from the trees, the slight splash of water running over rocks from the stream. Odd stakes and some shallow channels scraped in the earth to spread the brook in a rudimentary irrigation pattern served to demonstrate that this was not intended to be a purely natural scene of abundance but one lightly touched by human hand, though without fire and tools. Brownlow stood for a moment, reading the scene. "Eden," he said; Findlesham nodded, but continued walking across the clearing to a large oak tree near its edge, a little aloof from the other trees around. He stopped under a low bough and, without raising his eyes, pointed upwards. The vicar understood what was meant, from what he knew already: this was the spot where the unfortunate gardener had hanged himself.

For a short while, the two clergymen stood in silence under the spreading branches, one looking up and one looking down; then Brownlow, mindful of the fact that he was not supposed to be a mere sight-seer, crossed himself and commenced a short series of somewhat randomly-chosen prayers and pious observations. The old Dean's inclinations were of a similarly High Church cast and he did not object at all to the vicar coming close to praying for the dead in Popish fashion: in fact, he said nothing beyond the occasional "Amen" throughout the impromptu service. They finished by crossing themselves, and Brownlow expected to be hurried off the estate: however, Findlesham was distracted by some unwanted weeds and knelt to uproot them, seeming to forget about the presence of his guest.

As he stood waiting, Brownlow noticed a curious tree, of a species he did not recognize, perhaps thirty yards down a gentle slope from the great oak, towards the stream. It was clearly one of the recent exotic imports into the garden, as it was only a sapling and, quite out of keeping with the rest of Eden, was protected by a wooden fence, presumably intended to keep off any grazing creatures; however, it did occur to the vicar in retrospect that no such precaution had been taken with any other plant he saw in the grounds and there were in fact there no creatures like deer which might have harmed it. He walked down towards it, and as he approached it he became unable to see anything except its top, peeping out above the masking fence. This enclosure was of rough but substantial split logs bolted closely together to stout uprights two yards high at the corners of a six-foot square – sufficient to prevent one from touching the trunk without climbing over. As far as Brownlow could see, the thin, branchless stem was covered with a very smooth, dark-brown bark which seemed almost shiny, more like a metal than wood; about eight feet from the ground a handful of large, palm-like leaves sprouted from a bulbous structure at the top of the trunk. These fronds were a yard or more long, bright green above and yellowy on the underside; initially they stood upright, but after about eight or nine inches they bent gently downwards and then outwards, thickening as they did so. As he stared, Brownlow thought he could see what might have been a fruit or a seedcase, in the shape of a small yellow candle, hanging down from the point at which a couple of the great leaves, or perhaps slender branches, bent. He reached up; the end of the nearest branch was just a foot or so out of reach above the top of the fence; he strained up on tiptoe; just a few inches more; he put a foot on the top of a split log where there was a small gap between planks and grasped the top of the fence and tried to swing himself upwards with a great effort, flailing at the overhanging foliage with his free hand –

A hideous screeching cry made him fall back heavily to the ground and he stood silent and motionless in his embarrassment as the old Dean hurried up to him, more agitated than ever – in fact, he was clearly angry, though unused to expressing it.

"What are you doing? What are you doing? This tree – this tree is the only one of its kind in England. In Europe. It is priceless. Do you understand? Priceless, unique. I cannot risk anyone touching it – no-one. Why do you think I have gone to such lengths to protect it with a fence? And here you are trying to pull it to pieces. What do you think you are doing?"

"I am sorry. I don't know why I was trying to touch it. I just felt I had to feel it. I am very sorry: it is obvious that you do not wish it to be interfered with and that it is still delicate."

Brownlow genuinely felt very foolish and in the wrong – and why he had acted so he really did not know. It was completely out of character for him to have committed what was in fact a serious breach of the social code in blatantly ignoring his host's obvious wishes, as symbolized by the fence. He felt like a naughty schoolboy caught stealing apples despite the warning notices. And yet, Findlesham's reaction was excessive, and he might have been deemed to have gone too far in his berating of a guest: only gradually did he stop stamping and waving his hands violently in front of the hapless vicar, almost as though he was struggling to prevent himself from striking him. At length, a kind of snort ended his tirade, and he turned abruptly; "Come along," he said without looking round, and Brownlow followed him, rather than walked with him, back to the house in silence – though he felt strangely compelled to cast the occasional glance over his shoulder until the curious tree was out of sight. When they arrived, the older man simply pointed to the horse to express his wish for the other to leave, and began to mount the steps to his front door. Sadly, muttering another apology, Brownlow released the horse and led

217

it back towards the gate; as he passed under Findlesham, he looked up and asked a question which struck even him as somewhat impertinent in the circumstances – and why he asked it he did not really know:

"One last thing, sir: that tree that I was looking at too closely, whence did it come? I have indeed not seen its like in this country."

Findlesham paused at the top of his steps and answered briefly: "From the east, from an island near India called Serendip, or as some have it Ceylon, or Taprobana". In some obscure way this seemed to Brownlow to be important information, though in reality it meant nothing to him.

As far as he was aware, the Reverend Brownlow slept well enough that night, though he felt less refreshed than usual when he awoke on Monday morning, which he ascribed to the change in the weather and the depressing prospect of Ned Hurst's interment. He had decided that, despite the apparent circumstances of the death, he could not refuse to bury him in consecrated ground, after making such a show of concern with Joshua and then at the Hall. In the event, there was no-one to find fault, as no-one attended: the vicar, the verger and the sexton were alone under a grey sky in accompanying Ned to his pauper's grave in the back corner of the churchyard, against the vicarage wall. As Brownlow pronounced the words, the other two sufficed to carry the bier and drop the sheeted body in; it crossed all their minds that Dean Findlesham might have paid for a simple coffin if not a headstone, but no such offer had been made. As the vicar returned briskly to the church, leaving the others to fill in the grave, he noticed Joshua Bonner hovering by the lychgate, just outside the churchyard, watching him and screwing up his hat nervously. He realized that the gardener had come to see him rather than to attend his colleague's funeral, to ask what had happened at the Hall, and he hurried on, trying to give the impression of not having seen him,

218

rather than face awkward questions to which there was no possible answer. It was feeling decidedly chilly for so early in the autumn and there were the first spots of rain, so his behaviour did not appear odd.

After an hour or so, the vicar began to relax, as the threat of Bonner knocking on his door receded, and the rest of the day passed quietly enough, the rain having set in and precluded any activity. However, his thoughts did frequently stray to the fate of Ned and the image of the tree where he had met his end, and from there, curiously, to the memory of the strange plant which had caused him to behave in such an undignified fashion. As he prepared for bed, he wished that he could not see the edge of the new grave, just beyond the garden wall, from the corner of his window, and he drew his curtains quickly.

Now, there are those who speak with animation about a particular dream which they have had as though it were an unusual and interesting occurrence, and even those who claim never to dream at all; on the other hand, those who know about such things assure us that we all dream a great deal every night, varying only in our capacity to recall something of the experience on waking. Exactly what a dream is and what significance should be attached to it have been debated for as long as civilization has existed, and probably for much longer; after fallen man had solved the basic problems of feeding, sheltering, defending and warming himself, perhaps the first question of a non-practical nature which he addressed was the nature of the strange other world which he entered when unconscious of this one. Visions of the future, memories of the long past, the clearing out of superfluous sensations and ideas, glimpses of other lives, warnings from another level of existence, eruptions of subconscious desires have all been suggested as the causes of dreams, and reactions to them have varied from total indifference to religious awe. The Reverend Brownlow was one who "did not dream", and thought of dreams, if he thought of them at all, as the idle doodlings of a mind unoccupied – until this night: on the night following Ned Hurst's burial, he knew what it was to wake up suddenly and violently from a terrible vision in a cold dark room, with the knowledge that the new corpse of one unnaturally dead lay even colder and in an even darker hole just a few yards away below his window. He knew, or thought, that he had screamed himself awake, and for the briefest second the vision that had provoked this stayed with him; then it faded, leaving him mortally afraid of something which he could not quite identify. He wanted to screw up his eyes so as to see nothing, but fear of the darkness around him and what it might conceal kept them open as the blackness solidified into the familiar shapes of his window, palely lit by starlight, his heavy furniture, his door. The tension with which he clutched his bedclothes and kept his body still and rigid began to ease, and he sank back into his pillow – but as he did so a faint memory of the dreadful vision came to him and made him tremble again.

It had begun with the ill-omened oak tree at Findlesham Hall: he was standing under it again, but this time the sky was dark and a wind was threshing the woods, which hemmed him in closely, and making the branches of the great oak sway ponderously and creak like the timbers of a ship in a storm. He looked up, and there was a hideous sheeted figure – he did not really know Ned well enough to picture him in any other way – sitting upright on a bough; as he rocked to and fro on the branch, he leapt off, and the vicar fell to the ground in terror that the dead man was jumping onto him. After a moment he risked looking up, sideways, from his prone position, and saw the figure swinging slowly above him from a rope round another branch. He scrambled to his feet and stared at it, unsure what to do or even what to feel, and then cast about him in case there was anyone near who could help. Then he saw the tree from Serendip, being blown in the wind and bending towards him, straining as though almost being uprooted; the fence was gone from around it, and he walked into the teeth of the gale towards it.

220

As he did so, the wind died down and the sky brightened; it grew much warmer, birdsong commenced, and he was standing in the middle of a great sunlit clearing, ten times and more the size of the glade at Findlesham, ringed by distant trees and with a great mountain rearing up above them miles away. The strange palm was before him, perhaps four times taller than it had been; then he noticed that there were several smaller versions, of different heights, scattered around it at varying distances, as though the offspring of its seed. But it was the parent which fascinated him: its trunk was perhaps a yard and a half in diameter, and covered with the smoothest, shiniest bark he had ever seen, more like metal or mineral than vegetation; it had about twenty fronds coming from its crown, from each of which hung a fruit, pale yellow and like a thin pear, five or six inches long, waxy-looking. There was a heavy scent in the air which seemed to come from the fruit, which began to glisten as the heat made Brownlow feel thirsty. He reached out for the fruit, though it was far above him; to his delight, the tree began to stoop down, as though to put the desired fruit into his hand; the trunk bent stiffly, and the crown was lowered towards him. But he did not grasp the fruit: instead, the fronds were drawn back and the crown was exposed above his head before suddenly splitting apart like a gigantic mouth opening. It came down, drawing him into its interior, vividly red, viscous, like bloody raw meat, sealing him in a tight sticky tube, choking him in the darkness where it was all he could do to catch his breath – and scream himself awake.

If he closed his eyes, he slipped back into that suffocating hole, like the maw of a great beast, though it was a plant – although it was only a dream, which should have ceased on his waking. He had to keep his eyes open and brave the real darkness, trying not to think of the gaping mouth, of that thing which had been Ned Hurst sitting on the garden wall in his shroud. The two hours which preceded that Tuesday's sunrise were easily the worst of Reverend Brownlow's life so far, and when the dim shape of his window became a pale square of curtained dawn he staggered from his bed and threw it open. He looked down, determined to face whatever might be below in the softening shadows – nothing. He went back to his bed and lay motionless, looking up at the ceiling for another hour before finally rising, dressing, and taking an early turn around his garden.

He took a stake from his potting shed and carefully positioned it by the wall adjoining the churchyard; it was exactly where he reckoned a sapling could be planted to break the line of sight from his bedroom window to Ned's resting place; it would be two or three years before it grew to do the job effectively, so he could not make a start soon enough: he would talk to his gardener about it that very day – perhaps another fruit tree would be suitable. The thought of that made him feel suddenly hungry, and he looked over to his apple trees; no, he was more thirsty, and something more juicy, like a pear, appealed. But his pears were small, hard things, scarcely fit for eating, and would not do; nothing in his garden would, now that the strawberries were done. He put it from his mind, and went in to prepare for the morning service. It was not until a good way into the Eucharist that the thirst returned, and then he was hardly aware of it until, to his horror, he realised that he had drained the cup of wine and had none to distribute with the wafers; a bemused verger was hastily dispatched to the vestry for more wine while the small congregation looked on and wondered. No-one mentioned the incident, but he noticed that they left the church more quickly than usual and with hardly a word to him. He sat alone in his study for some time afterwards, troubled, turning over in his mind his bizarre behaviour at the Hall, this business with the wine and his awful dream, the essence of which he could still recall; was he losing his grip in some way? He was not aware of any physical ailment, but that in a way made it worse: yet his memory was perfect, he read a few pages of Sophocles or Homer every night and he could recite the Third Book of the Odes of Horace without hesitation – surely his mind could not be failing?

Although anxiety itself might have kept him awake, the lack of sleep from the night before overtook him as he sat unmoving, and he dozed off.

He was back in front of the Serendip tree, the tall one in the great clearing of his dream, not Dr. Findlesham's sapling. It was not threatening him this time, but simply standing in the manner of trees, its light fronds tossing in a gentle breeze, shaking their shiny yellow fruits, which glistened as though moist. As he looked at them, his thirst returned fivefold, and his gesture of straining out towards them woke him in his chair. He really was thirsty: he went to the pump in the scullery and filled a flagon, which he promptly drained. He felt bloated and slightly chilled, but the underlying thirst was still there. He found a bottle of beer in a cupboard and drank that in the same way: better, but still not satisfied. He contemplated a bottle of claret: no, to start drinking in such a way, alone, early in the day, was the way to ruin, and he put the wine bottle back. In any case, he could already imagine the taste and effect of the Bordeaux, and knew that it would still not meet the case.

He continued to feel restless and uncomfortable throughout the day, unable to settle to the reading and sermon-writing which he had planned, and in the afternoon he decided to take some air by going for a ride, in the hope that it might clear his head; he had no particular route or destination in mind. He was not a great horseman, and when he followed the hunt he did just that, a considerable way behind. His usual recreational rides were just along the bridlepath through Edgely Wood or along the riverbank to Chormond; if he wanted a longer ride, he might take the Bristol road, passing Findlesham Lane, and go up Edgend Hill. On this occasion, he all but left the choice to his horse, and they made their way westwards out of the village along the road. Now the horse had been this way at least fifty times before, and knew well enough that it had to keep to the highway until it reached the White Hart at Edgely Parva, where it turned off to the left onto a green lane to climb the slope into the trees: so it cannot have been without some unconscious guidance from its rider that it turned right down Findlesham Lane instead, which it had done only three or four times in its life, though it was another mile before the preoccupied vicar realized where they were. He was passing the handful of small cottages that made up the hamlet and approaching the boundary wall of the estate, which edged the lane. He had no reason to be there: in fact, after the episode of the day before, he really did not wish to risk meeting the Dean, whom he had angered, or the antagonistic forester Birch, who clearly mistrusted him, or the troubled gardener Bonner, who was probably very disappointed in him for not taking some unspecified and inconceivable action about Ned. Yet he did not turn back: he felt an urge to look in through the gates, which he did for some minutes, with his horse pulled up right against them, risking the wrath of the gatekeeper. Had they not been locked – and he actually put out a hand to try them – he would probably even have ridden in, though for what purpose he could not have said. Fortunately, they were locked, and there was no-one about, and he turned his horse back down the lane, though with a strangely dejected feeling, as though he had actually had an objective which had been thwarted.

Why he had made his way there without thinking of it was added to the unanswered questions which harried him. It was not to do with Ned Hurst, either sorrow at the tragedy or morbid curiosity about it, for, although he kept thinking about and even being drawn to the place where Ned had died, it was not Ned's death which fascinated him, and even less Ned himself. It was about his own response to the strange place, epitomized in that exotic palm – though why a mere plant should affect him so was a mystery. He was in a pensive mood for the rest of the day – the congregation for evening prayers thought him upset in some way – and he was unusually reluctant to retire that night, lying awake for a long time partly through an overactive brain and partly through fear of what he might dream. Eventually, he slept, and his fall into unconsciousness was broken by a landing on a great yellow mattress – though it was not a mattress, for it was far softer, and moist with a cooling dewiness which seemed to ooze from it as his elbows and hips and the back of his head struck it. It was like nothing so much as landing on a gigantic slice of soft fruit, perhaps very ripe melon or more closely, had he known of it, mango. He could not rise from it, but thrashed about trying to get purchase on it: the more he struggled, the more yielding it became and the more juice was squeezed onto the surface, so that soon it was like trying to escape from a quicksand with the tide closing in. He felt himself slipping deeper into it – or was it sucking him in? – and although its liquor chilled and refreshed yet he knew that it would soon drown him. As he fought to get up, the juice came over his head and then the fibres of the fruit: with one last kick, he pulled the sheet and blanket from over his face and jerked himself into a sitting position. He was facing a completely black wall, and as soon as his nerves had settled and his breathing and pulse had slowed down he felt suddenly afraid: he was again worried about his own mental state and, if he were to be honest with himself, he did not like the dark, not now. He felt thirsty – was it from his dream? but there he had been drowning – and climbed out of bed laboriously to get a drink of water. He was drowsy and unsteady, and already out of the door of his bedroom and negotiating the landing by flailing around with his outstretched arms before he thought of the tinderbox and candles by his bed. He began to panic – nothing seemed to be where he expected it – the darkness enfolded him – he bumped into the balustrade – anything could be there – he collided with a door post, hitting his nose and bringing tears to his eyes; then he was falling again, but more swiftly, and this time it was punctuated by sharp blows to his back and rear. He lay at the foot of his stairs, his eyes closed as he analysed the pain and moved each limb in turn. Soon he was sure that he had not hurt himself seriously – though that would be proved when he actually stood up. Better not to risk it. And somehow, he actually felt more

225

comfortable like this, in this low, hidden place, so much so that he finally slept there, lying like a broken mannequin. Only when black had turned to grey and then to muted light did he stir and slowly drag his limbs together before pushing upwards. He was bruised from the fall, stiff from sleeping on the floor in a draught and still weary from an interrupted night, but he made his way painfully upstairs to dress and prepare for the day.

It was now Wednesday morning, little more than a hundred hours since Ned Hurst had launched himself out of this life from the branch of an oak tree, alone on a dark night, but the Reverend Brownlow could already scarcely remember a time when his thoughts had not been filled with Hurst's death, the reclusive dean, and above all a rare tree with strange bark and unknown fruit. He stared at his haggard face in the mirror, and remembered that he had not had the drink which had been the cause of his literal downfall; he realized gradually that he was still very thirsty, to the point of an ache in his dry throat, and that plain water was not enough. When he had dressed, he went to the pantry. The remains of yesterday's milk: warm, not good. No beer left, only wine: tempting, but too dangerous this early in the day, and he knew he would not be able to stop until the bottle was empty in mighty swallows. Then something much more promising, pears: a half a dozen ripe pears, pale green and speckled. He picked one up, gave it a perfunctory rub and bit into it deeply and widely. That was what he needed; he tore at it hungrily, sucking out the juice, straining the fibres between his teeth, and then it was gone, apart from the stalk and the stringy centre around the stony seeds. He took another, without any pretence at cleaning it; then he had one in each hand, ripping at them alternately; then there were none left, and he heard Mrs. Radley, his cook and housekeeper, letting herself in. He hastily wiped his face, scooped up the stalks and walked into the kitchen, where he greeted her as though nothing had happened and left her to prepare a breakfast he no longer wanted.

Despite his fatigue, he got through the morning service with something approaching a smile, as he resisted the urge to finish the wine and so prevented a recurrence of Tuesday's scandalous behaviour. He was feeling so pleased with himself, indeed, that he failed to notice Joshua Bonner waiting for him outside the vicarage and did not take evasive action in time.

"What do you want of me, man?"

"Begging your pardon, sir, but I was wondering if you 'ad 'ad any more thoughts about what we was discussing a'Sunday. I know as 'ow you went up to talk to the Dean straightaway, and I was wondering what was said and what might 'appen now."

"If you must know the details of a private conversation, we spoke about Ned's tragic death and we prayed on the spot where he died. What else do you expect me to do?"

"I was 'oping you might make 'im see as 'ow things aren't right there, begging your pardon, sir, and what 'arm there might be in copying 'oly things like that. Blastphemery is the word, isn't it, sir?"

"As far as I can see, there is nothing amiss at Findlesham Hall. Many wealthy men like to build elaborate gardens which remind them of places where they have been; there is no harm in that."

"But he don't go to church, and his people don't either."

"I understand that the Dean makes his own arrangements up there." A mixture of his own supposition and something the gatekeeper had said lay behind this claim and prevented it from being a downright lie. "As I say, as far as I can see, he is a quiet, respectable gentleman who keeps himself to himself and indulges a harmless hobby."

227

"'Tis no use talking to thee, then. You and he be the same sort and that's that. But I don't mind saying as 'ow I don't feel right working up there, not with none to 'elp me, nor even the vicar listening to me."

With a tone of disillusion and disgust and a shrug of disappointed resignation, Joshua stopped twisting his hat and turned away determinedly. He had recently overcome with reluctance a lifetime's mistrust of the clergy and organized religion to approach the vicar appointed to aid him, only to find that he had been right about them all along: he and his concerns did not matter to them, and he resolved not to be so foolish as to demean himself before them again.

It would be harsh to say that the Reverend Brownlow did not care about Joshua's well-being: if he had been a churchgoer, a regular member of his flock, and if his problems had been of a more conventional and tractable sort, he would have found the vicar to be as sympathetic and as helpful as he could wish. But he had not come to ask for an exegesis of a Biblical parable or to arrange a baptism or to seek advice about doubts concerning the Thirty-Nine Articles: he had come to make vague complaints about a major local landowner with ecclesiastical connections at the very highest level. Despite the simple fact that he was being put in an impossible position, Brownlow did have the conscience to feel impotent, unable to do his duty by a parishioner, and it was his frustration and embarrassment, rather than disdain, which came out in his harsh words to Bonner.

He sat in his study feeling deflated and drained, physically by his tiredness and spiritually and mentally by his confrontation with Joshua, his worries about his own state of mind and his recent lapses, and his concerns about Findlesham Hall. Despite what he had said to the gardener, he too felt that all was not right there, although exactly what was wrong he could not begin to identify. His decline into his present condition had started, he realized, with the first mention of the place on Sunday morning, and each step down had been connected with it – the death of Hurst, his visit to the Hall, his memory of the visit, his dreams about the place. For some reason, the palm tree close to the suicide tree seemed to encapsulate for him all that was intriguing, threatening and fascinating about the place, and it had dominated his thoughts and feelings on the subject. There was only one thing to be done – he had to go and confront the problem.

It was only when his horse was once again making its comparatively unfamiliar way down Findlesham Lane that he tried, unsuccessfully, to explain to himself what this meant and what it might involve. Did he intend to confront the Dean? About what? About failing to attend church, planting alien shrubs in his garden and having unstable characters on his staff? He would be laughed at. Did he intend to take up a mattock and dismantle Golgotha, Eden and Galilee as being profanations of Scripture? He would be arrested and charged. Perhaps it would be enough for him to face seeing that fateful place again.

The wall around the grounds of Findlesham Hall were of stone and high enough to be a serious deterrent to a potential intruder and to prevent casual spying by even a man on horseback. As Brownlow rode alongside it, he suddenly felt a strong desire to see over into the garden and desperate frustration gripped him: if his horse were a hand or so taller he might just see over; when he stopped and strained upright in the stirrups he was tantalizingly close to viewing beyond the wall. He drew the horse up as close to the wall as he could, made it stand still and took his feet out of the stirrups; with some difficulty he manoeuvred his offside leg over the horse's neck so that he was sitting sideways, facing the wall, his knees practically touching it. He reckoned that, if he shortened the stirrup as far as it would go and put a heel in it, and reached up to grasp the top of the wall with both hands, he could boost himself up sufficiently to be able to put the other foot on the saddle and so vault onto the wall. From there he could jump down into the grounds, if he did not roll off at once. He was reaching up for the top of the wall before he realized what he was doing, how ridiculous his actions were. If he did get over the wall without injuring himself in the fall – and there was no telling what might be on the far side – what purpose would it actually serve, and how would he get out again without revealing himself to the inhabitants? Suppose he ran into one of the staff; suppose that man was armed and saw him only as a distant intruder who might be a thief, or worse. And even before any of those practical issues, what stopped him was the thought that someone might come along the road at any minute and see the Reverend Francis Brownlow, MA, vicar of Edgely, in the absurd act of trying to stand on a horse and vault a high wall into private property, an action not only illegal but also unbecoming his professional status and his lack of athleticism. Again, the thing that overcame him and on this occasion saved him was that more worldly brother of conscience known as shame. He resumed a more dignified position on his horse and rode on.

The day passed again in a listless round of self-doubt, restlessness and frustration; he drank water copiously but periodically still felt thirsty, which he ascribed to the warm weather and tried to counter with a bottle of claret. At dinner, he asked Mrs. Radley to buy some more ripe pears the next time she did his shopping, and waved aside her query irritably when she looked in the pantry for the last bagful. A second bottle accompanied his game pasty, and then he ate the whole spotted dick to counter the giddying effects of the alcohol. When he finally fell asleep that night, after lying awake a long time with the same stale ideas presenting themselves over and over and with an uncomfortable feeling of fullness, he was back in front of the tall palm, on a dark night, with a wind howling through the surrounding trees; the same gale against which he strove to stand upright was bending the trunk down towards him, and again the crown opened up to swallow him – but then it was a huge serpent, the type of great Amazonian snake of which he had read, which swallowed its prey whole with its tremendous gaping jaws. Coiled on the ground, it reared up the front of its body in front of him to a height of nearly twenty feet, considerably wider than a barrel, then opened its mouth wide, wider, like a dark archway through which one might drive a small cart. The scythe-like teeth were too far out and separated for him to be in any danger of a bite, but the dark cave descended over his head, his shoulders, his knees, then closed round his feet, shutting out all light, and drew him up. Suddenly he was compressed and thrown upside down as the serpent straightened up and began to work him down its throat. There was great pressure on him all over, except on the soles of his feet, and he could feel the hard ribs and firm muscles of the creature which were tightening around him, especially around his chest. Every few seconds a relentless peristalsis pushed him another foot or so further down the slightly narrowing tube. He was now struggling for breath, his own body being the stopper which prevented fresh air from reaching his mouth and nostrils, and he knew that in a very short time he would start to be ground up and digested. He could already taste the bitter juices which would dissolve his flesh, and he woke up choking on a reflux of digestive acid. He choked, then deliberately coughed and wheezed to force some air into his heaving lungs, thumping himself on the chest. When a normal pattern of breathing had been resumed, he lay back exhausted, his once dry throat now burning with the acid. Too much rich food and red wine had affected him this way before, but on this occasion he could not help but see the episode as part of a wider and more sinister pattern.

By Thursday, his congregation were thoroughly bewildered by his changes of mood: they had been pleased the day before to see a return of their usual cheerful pastor, in place of the withdrawn character who had swilled down Tuesday's wine, but now they were disappointed by the slow, grim-faced individual who presided irritably over their service. Brownlow knew it, and knew himself to be at fault, but with the weight of anxiety that was bearing down on him he could not shake off the visible signs of his inner confusion and worry. His thirst had also returned, in the wake of the burning of the back of his mouth, though he restrained himself with the altar wine. In the vicarage, he waited all morning for the grocer's boy to call, literally praying that Mrs. Radley had remembered to order the pears and bottled beer he had asked for; when the lad came, the vicar sent him away without waiting for the change and hurried into the pantry with the parcels he had delivered: she had ordered only two bottles of beer, in place of the "some" he had discreetly requested, but there was indeed a paper bag of rounded shapes, which he tore open. Stunned and disappointed. They were indeed pears, but small, hard things, a week off ripening, and even then they would be so much thinner and harsher than the plump, yielding fruit, with juice bursting out at the bite, for which he longed. Disconsolately, he opened and drained one of the bottles, dregs and all, without even pouring it into a glass. He hardly spoke to the cook when she came to prepare and serve his dinner, inwardly blaming her for the state of the pears and hence his condition. After she had gone, he drank the other bottle, and fell asleep in his armchair.

This time, his dream soothed him, for it provided the cooling balm he sought: he was back at Findlesham, but the little brook that was its Jordan, flowing through Eden to Galilee, had become a tropical river plunging over a waterfall. He was standing in the basin at its foot, his head thrown back and his mouth open so that the cool stream poured straight into him, washing out the acid and the dryness and directly revitalizing his blood and nerves. And the Serendip tree leaned over him from the bank like an exotic willow, but did not eat him: instead, it let him pluck its fruit, so much richer than the hard pears, and he bit into the yellowness, which tasted of butter and sunlight and sea air and flowers as he lay down in

232

the pool and let the pure water seep through his translucent skin. But suddenly, drumming sounded through the forest: gaudy parrots and busy monkeys squawked and flapped in alarm, and Brownlow looked around him anxiously, though without rising.

Arise he did eventually, awoken by the verger beating on his front door: he was late for evening prayers, having slept for hours. The mutterings in the small congregation ceased as he entered, hurriedly, still arranging his surplice, but he sensed that eyes were on him more than usual during the service, instead of being on prayer-books and hymnals.

Sleep hardly came at all that night, and certainly not enough to support sustained dreams, partly because of the anxiety that precluded rest, partly because he had already slept during the day, and partly because of a return of the thirst which large draughts of water barely assuaged. Thursday night passed into Friday as Thursday had passed into Thursday night, and the Reverend Brownlow took services hardly knowing which of the day they were or even which day it was, though on Friday night he went to bed at an early hour, having convinced himself that the thirstiness was a symptom of a strange fever for which he would forthwith seek medical attention – an idea which went some way to calming him and allowing him to see things more clearly again. It even occurred to him that it was just a week since Ned's death, and he fell asleep in the hope that the period of confusion which he had suffered since was now passing and that he would soon be himself again.

This time, it was not merely the act of turning his horse down Findlesham Lane which he must have performed without realizing it: he had to have risen from his bed, put his boots and his coat on over his nightshirt, descended, saddled and mounted his horse and ridden to the Hall, all without waking up. It was only the fall onto the top of the boundary wall, having boosted himself up from the back of his horse as he had contemplated before, which brought him to his full senses. He found himself hanging across the wall, his head and arms hanging down on the estate side and his legs dangling on the lane side; in between, his ribs and stomach ached from the effort of forcing himself up and then falling down onto the stones. He was kicking and struggling, not really bothered which side he fell on but acutely aware of what an absurd picture he would present if seen by some later wanderer – when he lifted his head with some effort he could just see the half-moon rising above the treetops – in this undignified position and in a state of half-undress, doing something which was inexplicable even to himself. He could hear his horse moving slowly away down the lane. He made several convulsive heavings, and found himself slipping forwards, or rather downwards, into, as far as he could judge from his inverted position and the darkness, a flowerbed. He passed out.

He must have continued to function unconsciously, for the next time he was aware of where he was and what he was doing, he was scrabbling at the fence around the Serendip tree, as though trying to climb it in great coat and riding boots without a method for scaling its planks. It was some time later than his arrival at the Hall, as the moon and stars had moved on some distance. He was now conscious, but still he did not understand – all he felt was a desire to get over the barrier; then it came to him that it was the fruit that he craved, the fruit that would soak his parched throat. At the same moment, he realized or remembered – the thought shared features of both ideas – that what had awoken him from his walking sleep had been a gunshot, not far away. Then he heard a horn. There was a hunt in progress; the terrifying thought came to him that he, the intruder, might be its intended victim. The signals were succeeded by lights from several lanterns, perceived moving in on him through the surrounding woods; finally, they were close enough for him to hear voices. He began to run, away from the approaching lights but to where he did not much care; he was going up a slope towards a great dark shape standing out blackly against the backdrop of the stars – a great tree which might shelter him. He was running awkwardly in his riding boots, with the coat and nightshirt flapping around him, and he could not see much ahead of him in the dark, but as he approached the tree something struck him on the forehead, something which was part of the tree into which he had run rather than something dropped or thrown at him. He stopped and raised a hand: it touched a boot, moving to and fro slightly.

He began to run again, this time not from the hunters but from what was hanging from the tree; perhaps not even so much from that as from something nameless which might have been inside himself. He knew that it was Joshua up there, although in the darkness he could not really make out anything past the knees except a shape; even if he had been able to see the face, he would have been hard-pressed to identify it, so distorted and blackened had it become already. The darkness deeper than night which pursued him on relentless wings but never overtook him, beating always at his back, was born of many things: the terrible image of death; the inexplicable, seemingly inevitable replication of events; the feeling that he might be the next to be infected by the doom on the place; the guilt of having turned Joshua away to face the ultimate despair; the fear of being caught in this compromising situation. When they finally caught up with him, he was scrabbling frantically at the boundary wall as though trying to climb it, breaking his nails and bleeding from his torn hands and grazed knees, leaping up desperately and vainly in an attempt to clear its height, hammering at the stones with feeble fists as though wanting to break through. He crumpled up and wept unstoppably when the Dean and his forester laid hands on him and led him away to the house. They had missed Joshua at the end of the day's work, and had been seeking him as they had done with Ned the week before, though not visiting the oak first, from a shared if unspoken feeling that this might in itself have brought about the fulfilment of their great fear. When they finally converged on the grove, they were astonished to see first a figure in coat and hat running off into the gloom, and only then the missing gardener, as they drew nearer. The Dean and Birch, the man with the gun, gave chase, as fast as Findlesham could hobble, leaving the younger, stronger men to get the body down as quickly as they could, though it was clear that it was too late for any good to be done. Whether Dr. Findlesham would have allowed the forester actually to fire on the fugitive, as he wished, was never put to the test, for, having lost him in the darkness, they found him again only by following the sound of his grunts and of boots kicking at stone; what they discovered was the pathetic figure of a man broken by terror and frustration, locked into a hopeless task which he continued from lack of any alternative. The magistrate later saw nothing in the case beyond two suicides by men who were known to be morose and unsociable and a mental breakdown on the part of a vicar who may have been affected by the, to him, unfamiliar sight of a hanging corpse seen in the dark, and he declined to investigate further, leaving unanswered the question of why a respectable clergyman should be wandering the grounds at night, uninvited, in his nightshirt.

So much was Theophilus Hale able to piece together from his interviews with the scarce-lucid Reverend Brownlow, with the evasive Dr. Findlesham and his taciturn remaining staff, and with the verger, the vicarage cook and some of the parishioners of St. Andrew's, filled out with some surmises and links of his invention. The people of Edgely were more than willing to contribute theories and opinions of their own, and Hale felt obliged to waste a certain amount of time listening to individual versions of the events which varied in their bizarreness; he had to listen with feigned sympathy to explanations which included witchcraft, Popish conspiracy and the malign influence of foreign soils. The co-operation of those at Findlesham Hall was harder to secure, and then only with pressure from the Bishop, who was worried about the way the matter might reflect upon the diocese, because of the involvement of the former

236

Dean. Suggestions that his pension might be reviewed and even that an ecclesiastical court might be convened to investigate his part in the events, even if the civil authorities saw no reason to act, were needed to bring Dr. Findlesham to heel and make him agree to be questioned and allow his premises to be inspected. Hale was chosen as the Bishop's representative and investigator because of, amongst other things, his success with the Reverend Pointer in somewhat similar circumstances, and he arrived in Edgely to conduct a diocesan inquiry into, at least nominally, the behaviour of Reverend Brownlow and the circumstances surrounding his sudden partial loss of reason. He found Dr. Findlesham coldly polite, answering his questions briefly and precisely without volunteering more. The former Dean was unable to help much, professing ignorance of what might have driven two employees to suicide on his estate and having knowledge of Brownlow extending only to his two recent visits; his account of the latter did not reflect well on the vicar, as the main feature recalled from the first visit was the bizarre incident involving his attempt to climb over a fence protecting a rare plant and the second episode was the wholly extraordinary one of the night visit. Without losing his reserve or composure, Dr. Findlesham drew attention to such unseemly features as the trespass and the nightshirt, and his presentation of the whole incident posed the question as to why the vicar should be standing beneath a newly-hanged man. But of course, there was nothing to connect Brownlow with Ned or even Findlesham before Hurst's death – though on his daytime visit he had seemed curiously interested in a man whom he had, presumably, never met, and almost morbidly fascinated by the means and place of his end.

Hale knew enough about Brownlow, at least by reputation in the diocese, to discount Findlesham's insinuations; any eccentricity in his behaviour, as his verger confirmed, had been observed only in the few days before his breakdown, and well after Hurst's death. However, there was truth in what the Dean had said about his obsessions, for when Hale spoke to him at St. Faith's hospital it was as if his whole existence had been within the confines of the Findlesham estate, though he had spent probably no more than two hours of his life there. It was as though the five years as pastor of Edgely, the similar period before as curate at St. Sebastian's, the time as a student at Oxford, his childhood near Bath, all had passed completely from his mind, and all he could talk about were such things as his guilt at not helping Joshua, his desire for ripe pears, his fear of Birch catching him, his cunning at getting over the wall, the sight of Ned's grave from his window, the terrible thirst which afflicted him, the creaking of the great oak branches, and, most frequently, the thing which he called the Serendip tree, and its yellow fruit. He repeatedly expressed an urgent need to return to it, and it was clear to Hale that this, whatever it meant, was the motive for the trespass. Unlike Pointer, he was confined to his room most of the time, since he had made several attempts to escape within the first two days; twice he had got out of the grounds and had been picked up hurrying instinctively in the direction of Edgely – or, as Hale now believed, more precisely in the direction of the garden of Findlesham Hall.

When Hale returned to the Hall, it was clear that the owner had not expected to see him again, and he was at first reluctant to comply with Hale's request to see the tree where the men had died; he even commented that this was exactly how Brownlow's collapse had started. It needed mention of the Bishop before the former Dean escorted Hale up the slope to the Greek folly and then through the desert to Galilee and so into Eden. Hale looked carefully at the oak, while the Dean stood and watched, exuding impatience. Though no longer a young man, the rector climbed up somewhat awkwardly and sat on the fatal branch; the deceased gardeners would certainly have had no difficulty in getting up to this point unaided. He looked around, and noted a fenced sapling some distance away; he recalled that the vicar had confusingly described the Serendip tree as being fenced in, necessitating a climb to get at it. He slipped down, and asked Dr. Findlesham to show him next the Serendip tree. After the briefest of pauses, less than two heartbeats, he replied that he knew of no such tree; Hale pointed out that Brownlow had told him of it, that it was close to the suicide-oak, and that it was a rare specimen. Ah yes, he knew which tree Brownlow meant; it had no name yet, but it had come from the island of Serendip. He led Hale a dozen yards, down to the water's edge, and pointed to a young mountain ash heavy with red berries.

"Indeed, I fear you are strangely mistaken, Dr. Findlesham, for that is a common rowan or mountain ash, and I need go no further than to my own garden for such a specimen, without the expense of a voyage to Serendip. Now the real Serendip tree if you please, and before you try to deceive the Bishop's representative again I would point out that I know it to be the one inside the fence over yonder."

They walked across in silence, the Dean with his head bowed in shame. For a few moments, Hale contemplated as much of the tree as he could see through and over the slats. It was certainly curious: he had seen nothing like it before, even in illustrations of palm trees and the like, and the bark, if bark it were, was unlike any plant material with which he was familiar. Why did this tree figure so prominently in the ravings of the Reverend Brownlow, and had it any connection with the deaths close by? He questioned Dr. Findlesham as to its name, its place of origin, its native habitat, its lifecycle, only to be told that it had come onboard an East Indiaman, having been collected by a Dutch sea captain from the island of Serendip, south of India; that was all he knew. As far as he knew, it had no name, not yet being described in any of the standard books. Hale requested that he should have as much of the fence taken down as would allow him to examine it more closely; the Dean protested that it was outside Hale's brief to examine plants, that it was a rare and expensive specimen which would easily be damaged now that it was exposed to the English climate, that the men were all over the estate working and could not be called back immediately. Hale flatly stated that he would wait while a workman could be summoned, that he had no intention of harming the tree and that it was not up to the Dean to decide what was relevant to his investigation.

Reluctantly, Dr. Findlesham went off to find a man and tools, shaking his head as he went. Hale went back to looking at the Serendip tree while he waited, pressing his face to the planks to peer between. For the first time, he noticed a heavily sweet smell in the air around it, which he could not quite describe, so unfamiliar was it. As he moved, he noted that It was stronger towards the top of the tree, and then he noticed the yellow fruit for the first time. Its shiny, waxy quality was as uncharacteristic of fruit as the shiny, metallic stem was of ordinary tree bark. He reached out to seize the nearest fruit, and then suddenly realized that he had one toecap squeezed into a gap in the fence and was balancing precariously on one foot with one hand on top of the barrier and the other extended and grasping. He jumped backwards and to the ground in embarrassment and fear, for he had no recollection of getting into that position or even of having decided to do so. He stepped backwards several paces, until the scent had left him. The former Dean appeared a few moments later, having met with Birch nearby.

"If you are sure it is what you want, Birch will assist."

"No, on second thoughts there is no point in my examining the tree, as I know little of such things. I am sorry to have troubled your man. But I would like an expert to look at the tree – an expert who would know it from a rowan – so I would be obliged if you would extend the same courtesy to such a one when he should arrive."

Dr. Findlesham started muttering again and instead instructed Birch to show Hale back to his horse – evidently, the interview was finished for the present. Hale was not simply fearful of the tree and what appeared to be its strange attraction: he had in mind that Quintus Althorpe was a fellow of the Bishop's old college, Allhallows, though now almost wholly engaged in work at the Botanical Gardens. He had indeed visited the cathedral two years before, to plan and supervise the construction of the new herb garden – as a favour to the Bishop, for the well-known collector of Asian flora and respected author of the standard *Flowering Shrubs of Hindustan* would not normally have concerned himself with anything quite so mundane. Hale called home only briefly to check on his locum before travelling on to the Bishop's Palace, where he was seen almost at once, so great was the concern to avoid a scandal at Edgely. Without going into details which might have undermined his own credibility, he explained that he believed that the exact similarity between the two deaths pointed to a single powerful motive and that the Reverend Brownlow had apparently been drawn into the same pattern through concerning himself with them, though in his case the resolution had been prevented. He suggested that the effect of a strong herb or drug to be found in some part of one of the exotic plants in the garden at Findlesham Hall, as curare and quinine are found in tree barks, might be involved, and requested that an expert in oriental plants be engaged to carry out an investigation. He rejoiced inwardly when the Bishop at once named Quintus Althorpe, and a letter was sent to Oxford the following day. Less than a week later, a messenger from the Palace arrived at Hale's rectory at Stoke Armitage with the news that Dr. Althorpe had acquiesced to his old friend's request and would be at Edgely in five days' time: he would be staying in the vicarage, at present occupied only by a young curate covering for the absent Brownlow. The Bishop was dispatching a valet to Edgely to prepare for his arrival and a letter to Dr. Findlesham demanding full co-operation.

And so it was that after less than two weeks' absence Hale was back at the Hall, this time with the great expert in botany. A side of the fence around the Serendip tree was taken down, and Dr. Althorpe approached the tree, visibly trembling with excitement, since, as he exclaimed several times, he had never seen such a thing before and it was almost certainly new to science. He stepped inside the barrier, exchanged his ordinary spectacles for those he used for reading, and began to examine the bark, touching it, scratching it, peering at it through a hand-lens he produced. He walked round the tree, and began to write in a small notebook. Hale was watching from a distance of ten or twelve paces, not wishing to get too close to what he thought of as the tree's influence. Birch, who had taken the fence apart, had retired with his bag of tools back towards the surrounding trees, waiting for the performance to be over so that he could rebuild it; there at the edge of the clearing stood also the head gardener, who had been given the task of supervising the visitors: Dr. Findlesham had not deigned to attend, or even to meet his illustrious guest, but remained aloof in the house.

Dr. Althorpe was peering up at the fronds, apparently sketching, occasionally reaching up to touch the one which hung down closest to him, feeling its texture or dragging it down so that he could inspect its detail. Hale looked around: the two others were talking together in what seemed a serious manner; dark clouds were appearing over the trees in what Hale reckoned was probably the west; some magpies were fighting over something down by the stream. Suddenly, the head gardener let out an inarticulate cry, drawing Hale's attention: the two men were running towards him – no, they were running towards the tree, and Hale immediately saw why. The botanist had apparently taken one of the loose planks and had jammed the ends of it into gaps in the fence so that it spanned a corner of the little enclosure. He was using this as a step so that, steadying himself with one hand on the trunk, he could reach right up into the crown of the tree; he was in the act of picking one of the fruits. Although this would be, at least in Dr. Findlesham's eyes, a serious abuse of his reluctant hospitality, a casual onlooker might have thought it merely a part of the examination – until such a one noted Dr. Althorpe's manner: quite out of character, he leapt onto the unsafe perch, his hat flying off and his spectacles hanging from one ear as he swayed precariously, and he clutched at the tree like a desperate man.

Hale darted forward, shouting at the man to stop, and stepped through the gap; he grabbed the arm which was against the tree and pulled him down from the step, but it was too late – he had already taken a great bite which had consumed the greater part of the fruit, and was chewing and swallowing frantically. Hale was shocked at the desperate way he ate, his eyes fixedly staring wide, his mouth drooling and his jaws working in a way which belied fifty years of living in polite society and even many centuries of civilized behaviour. He did not care that his hat was off and his spectacles were dangling, did not seem to notice that the vicar had manhandled him, ignored the group of people around him variously begging and cursing him to stop. He slumped on the step, his back to the trunk, having devoured the whole thing, and his maniacal face collapsed: his eyes were closed, his mouth was hanging open.

The others stood at the opening in the fence for a minute or two, unsure what to do. Suddenly, the botanist jerked upright and his eyes snapped open; he looked about him aghast, but seemingly not noticing the men around him, and sprang to his feet, finally losing his spectacles. He threw himself at the gap, not heeding the arms spread to catch him, and tried to kick and punch his way past his companions. His fist connected with Hale's jaw, and the rector staggered aside as the others wrestled him to the ground and held him down as he struggled frantically. He was shouting "No, no!" repeatedly, in a voice close to a howl of despair, and then, "Sickness, the evil, everywhere; the filth, the wickedness, and death, death everywhere!" He sagged after the effort, and began to weep pitifully. Birch knelt up, releasing his hold on his shoulders, but immediately Dr. Althorpe jerked forward and tried to lever himself up, his tears forgotten; Birch threw himself across his back and knocked him to the ground again, winding him, while the gardener sat on his legs. Hale, almost recovered from the blow, returned to them somewhat unsteadily, rubbing his jaw; he stood for a moment, and then, unable to decide on a course of action, lamely announced that he would go for help. Birch shook his head, and pointed over to the trees: "Fetch that," he said, and Hale, following his finger, noticed for the first time the gun leaning against a trunk. He staggered over to it, picked it up and carried it back. As he approached the forester, he hesitated, for it suddenly came into his mind that he meant to shoot the madman, but Birch swore and gestured angrily and shouted, "Fire it, man, into the air! It will bring the others." Hale, who was unused to firearms and had never actually owned one, put it to his shoulder and aimed back over the tops of the trees. He pulled the trigger, there was a flash and a crash, and he felt as though his arm had been broken to match his jaw. The gun dropped from his hands as he clutched at his shoulder; Birch swore again, and the gardener said, "You'll be all right, sir, it's just that you don't hold it quite right, and it gives a terrible kick."

A short time passed, during which Hale sat on the grass and watched in case Dr. Althorpe should succeed in his periodic struggles to throw off the other two, who kept a grim hold on him as he alternated between exhausted silence, hideous cursing and fearful lamentation, prominent in which were words to do with corrupt morality and mortality – evil, filth, decay, death. He was also able to contemplate the Serendip tree, which seemed intimately bound up with the botanist's terrible collapse, which reminded him of the Reverend Pointer's equally sudden fall. It gave him a few minutes in which to consider the possible connections and causes in this story. Perhaps Hurst and Bonner had done as Dr. Althorpe had done, and perhaps he too would have ended his apparent torment as they had done if he had not been stopped;

244

Brownlow too, though the account he had had of his being discovered by the oak tree by the hunters perhaps indicated that he had been interrupted before reaching this extreme and desperate stage. But interrupted in what? It surely had something to do with the Serendip tree: he recalled how he had been strangely fascinated when he first saw it, and had almost forgotten himself so far as to try to pick the fruit, despite the fence, which he suddenly realized was the only barrier, apart from growing ones, inside the whole estate. Forbidden fruit. A curious idea came to him as Dr. Findlesham and the remaining gardener, followed by the aged butler, hurried into the grove; they were clearly heading for the oak, fearing that they were being summoned to another fatality discovered there, but then saw the group further off. Before Dr. Findlesham could remonstrate with him, Hale stood up and briskly took command of the situation.

"Dr. Althorpe has suffered a severe fit which continues in violence and, despite the indignity, I recommend that he be bound and escorted to a suitable place for his recovery. I would be obliged if your people could organize transport to St. Faith's hospital; the diocese will, of course, cover any expenditure. In the meantime, Dr. Findlesham, I am afraid that I must again tax you with some serious questions, to which I shall require equally serious answers." The former Dean began to protest, but Hale cut him off. "I should warn you that I shall be reporting fully to the Bishop immediately on my return to the Palace, and that in the absence of sufficient information supplied by you I shall be including my own opinions as to what has been going on here, which will, I am sure, result in a much more thorough investigation by not only the ecclesiastical but also the judicial authorities, with resulting disruption to the estate, of a physical nature as well as regards its routine, and to the lives of its inhabitants. If, on the other hand, you co-operate fully with me now, I shall report in as fair a manner as I can so as to bring this matter to an end with the minimum of trouble, and shall present your willingness to assist in this as clearly as I can."

Dr. Findlesham stopped, muttered words inappropriate to his position, considered a moment, and finally said impatiently, "Oh, very well, as long as this matter ends here. But can we please retire somewhere private?" Hale consented, and the others, who had been hanging on the exchange so as almost to forget Dr. Althorpe, were plainly disappointed. Leaving them to secure the botanist and bring him after, while the doctor and his carriage were being summoned, the two clergymen walked back to the house in silence, until Dr. Findlesham finally asked, "What do you understand of this matter?", to which Hale, taking a chance, replied, "That it concerns the baleful influence exercised by the fruit of the Serendip tree," which elicited a grim nod. In his study, the Dean, whose taciturn and aggressive manner had been replaced by apparent relief that the matter had ceased to be a dark and guilty secret, began, in almost sermonising mode: "First, you must understand that the location of the first place on this earth which the Bible mentions is still known to some. The site of the garden of Eden is, as I understand, actually in a remote place near a great mountain in the middle of an island in the Indies called Serendip or Ceylon. I say site, because, as I understand it, the idyllic qualities of the place ceased when man transgressed and was driven out, and today it is covered with tropical forest such as is found across the whole of the island."

"I take it from what you say that you have not been there. How do you know all this?"

"I learnt of it from a Dutch sea captain, who had been recommended to me as a supplier of exotic plants from scarcely-visited places. He had only recently heard of it from some converted natives, who had realized the connection between the Bible story they had just been told and their own traditions about

246

the heavenly garden, but he had also acquired an ancient map showing it and was planning an expedition to find it. He showed me the map, and a dried frond from a Serendip tree which had come into his possession. I examined the frond, realized that it was from a completely new species, and gave him a large sum for exclusive rights to whatever plants he brought back, with more to come on delivery. He was honest enough at least in that regard, and returned with a large number of rare and unique specimens."

"Including the Serendip tree."

"Quite so." The Dean paused a little before resuming. "When I said that the jungle has taken over Eden, I meant that the fruit trees and vegetable plots which first sustained Adam and Eve and the flower beds which delighted them have long since disappeared under lush wilderness: there are, however, survivals of the original plants here and there in the vegetation." Another nervous pause. "One such plant is the one referred to in the Old Testament as the Tree of the Knowledge of Good and Evil, the fruit of which tempted and ruined our first ancestors. Examples of the species are still occasionally found by the local people, who fear them as inducing madness." Again he paused and looked even more nervous, or embarrassed; Hale nodded to encourage him. "I believe that it is a direct descendant of that tree which stands fenced in the park outside and which, I must now confess, is probably responsible for the deaths of poor Hurst and Bonner and for the madness of the Reverend Brownlow and Dr. Althorpe." He fell silent and looked down.

Hale was equally speechless for a brief space; then, shaking his head in disbelief at himself rather than at his companion, "What you say might well itself be taken for madness in any other setting, but given what I know to have happened here, and especially what I have experienced myself, I am inclined to give some credence to what you say. Certainly, that tree exerts some baleful influence of great power. Why did you not speak out when the first death occurred?"

The defensive reserve with which Dr. Findlesham had covered his anxieties in recent days was replaced by an unaccustomed willingness to speak, to share and so dissipate his feelings of guilt.

"For fear of what is now I suppose inevitable, the destruction of a unique tree. You must believe me when I say that I did not know the extent of the power of the tree, or perhaps rather its fruit, and I certainly had no idea that it could drive men to such extremes. In the case of our first ancestors, innocent and in a simple world, giving in to the temptation and eating the fruit awakened carnal thoughts and a sense of shame; it seems that modern man, already fallen, is seized by greedy desire for the fruit and then is cursed with knowledge of all the evils and pain of the fallen world – a burden too terrible to be borne and so leading to self-destruction."

"It seems sad that Knowledge of Evil so outweighs Knowledge of Good."

"The Dutchman warned me about the power of the tree, but I chose to treat it lightly," continued Findlesham. "He said that the local people in Serendip give it a wide berth when they find it in the forest; they will always try to destroy it, which is why it has not spread far, but its bark is very resilient to fire and they will not approach it closely enough to try to chop it down. He said that digging my specimen up had cost the sanity of two natives and that he had kept it, and a few poisonous plants, in a boat lowered over the side of his ship during the voyage back, to prevent the crew from coming into contact with it. It was brought here in a covered wagon and planted swiftly by night, though even then, I must confess to my shame, I sensed its influence working on me and saw it in others, but put aside my better judgement. I merely had it fenced in and ordered my people not to approach it, but, it seems, to no avail."

He paused, and Hale awaited the resumption silently, fearing to make his presence more apparent and hence threatening. His eyes fixed on the far wall, the Dean went on in thoughtful vein.

"It seems to me that the tree affects people to different degrees, according to their temperaments. The poor vicar and your botanist succumbed violently and almost at once, whereas my man Birch seems virtually immune to it: he spent most of a morning by it erecting the fence, without effect. It seems to have greatest potency at short range, but it can work on a man at a distance, over a long period of time, as I fear happened with Bonner and Hurst. A man alone and little occupied, or occupied with something tedious, is also at greater risk of attending to it and becoming fascinated than a group of people or an individual concentrating on something else. So what is to be done now?" Dr. Findlesham finally focused on his visitor. "Obviously, I will abide by whatever the Bishop decides; please convey this to him."

"I fear we do not have time to await advice from the Palace: the tree has already wrecked several lives, and there may be others falling under its influence. I have come with the Bishop's authority to do my best to amend things here, and my decision is that the tree must be destroyed at once. Are you prepared to abide by this?" The Dean pulled a somewhat sour face but nodded. "Now what did the Dutch captain say about destroying the tree?"

"He said that burning the tree is the only way to end its power, but that simply trying to light it, even in a great bonfire, will end in failure, as the bark resists fire. The tree must be cut open so that the flames enter it, but no man can stand close enough to the tree to cut it down."

249

"Please summon your people, and tell them to bring kindling and an axe."

Hale had so far controlled his anger at the Dean's reckless conduct only by telling himself that the old man must have been as much under the influence of the malignant tree as the others had been, including himself, and now his anger was safely directed at the tree itself. He was loath to let his guest Dr. Althorpe be carried off by strangers, but the botanist, whose actual eating of the fruit had clearly induced the most intense insanity, went in the doctor's carriage with the butler, who was to collect his possessions from the vicarage on the way to St. Faith's and to arrange the dispatch of urgent letters to Oxford and to the Bishop's Palace explaining events in outline. Firmly trussed for everyone's protection, including his own, Althorpe was still raving about the iniquity of man and the sordid nature of the world as the coach pulled away, and Hale wondered if he, and indeed Brownlow, would ever fully recover from this experience.

Hale led the remaining group back to the Eden garden. He and Dr. Findlesham carried kindling, dry leaves and sticks, while bundles of small logs were borne by the gardeners and Birch, who also carried a large axe. When they approached the fatal tree, Birch was sent ahead to smash away one side of the fence and two corners entirely, so that a clean swing at the trunk was possible. The kindling was spread around the base and the logs put on top; this was performed gingerly and as swiftly as could be done without scattering the wood randomly. Hale then applied a light from his tinderbox to three clusters of leaves and backed away at once; as the kindling flared and sticks began to char and then catch flame, he instructed Birch to go forward and strike the tree so as to open it.

"Not I."

Hale gestured, and Dr. Findlesham repeated the order more forcefully, assuming that Birch was simply refusing to obey the outsider.

"No, begging your pardon, Dean, but I have seen what that tree can do to a man for no reason, and I am not giving it just cause to take agin me."

He was standing stiffly with the axe diagonally across his chest, right hand low on the end of the handle and the other just below the blade, as though on guard; his face was grim-set as usual and his eyes reflected redness from the fire so that one might almost fancy that he had fallen victim to the tree's fascination and sought to preserve it The flames were beginning to take hold, and soon the heat would make it difficult for a man to stand close enough to the tree to deal it a stroke. Hale resolved to finish what he had started. He walked over and grasped the haft; Birch seemed at first preoccupied and hardly noticed, but when Hale tugged he pulled it back out of the clergyman's hands and stared at him with a fierce expression.

"Let him take it!" cried Dr. Findlesham, with reluctance both to lose the tree and to lose the chance to destroy it in his voice. Hale prised the axe from Birch's loosened fingers and made his way to the tree. He stood in front of it, the flames now almost licking his coat tails, and swung the axe back over his shoulder; he struck the sapling with as much strength as he could muster, and was horrified by the juddering shock which he suffered when the blade was stopped and bounced back with even greater force. His arms and sides were wrenched much more than they had been by the recoil of the gun, and he could not hold the axe, which flew across the clearing, narrowly missing the former Dean.

"What did I tell 'ee!" cried Birch, with a mixture of horror and triumph.

251

The blow should have shaken or bent a normal springy sapling, or snapped one which stood stiffly. The bark of this tree was unscratched, and there was no sign of charring. Hale recovered the axe and returned to his position. This time he paused to pray, and swung a second blow, this time downwards rather than across, aiming to graze the bark rather than cut into it. The axehead buried itself in the kindling and had to be pulled out amidst ash and sparks which burnt small dark spots in Hale's clothes, but this time there was a result – a thin sliver of the bark was seen to hang down the trunk and a spot of sap appeared, which was licked by a flame and began to fizz and bubble. Soon there was a small patch of burning sap clinging to the spot where the axe had wounded the tree, and Hale risked another blow, which opened a second lesion. Hale was now choking on the smoke from the fire in which he was almost standing, and the heat on his legs was becoming intolerable; then it happened – the tree fought back. The trunk began to shiver, and the motion increased up the tree so that the crown and the fronds danced about; they swayed over and down towards him so that he could see the fruit clearly – more than a dozen yellow pears at various stages of development and three bare stalks where presumably Bonner, Hurst and Althorpe had succumbed. He was so thirsty from the effects of the fire, so tired by his exertions with the axe, and the fruit looked so lush and juicy. The axe slipped from his grasp, and he reached up to pluck the largest and ripest, even as the bottom edge of his coat caught fire.

It was Dr. Findlesham himself who pulled Hale away, beat out the infant flames and struck him to wake him from his trance-like state. When the rector had recovered himself, they all stood and watched as the burning wound on the side of the tree flared up and spread; it must have spread even more quickly through the sap or whatever it had as heartwood, for flame began to burst out of the trunk from within, up and down its length, and it became first one with the bonfire around its foot and then as a torch glowing more redly and more brightly than the surrounding blaze. And then the most extraordinary thing of all was seen, for as the fronds began to shrivel from the great heat which the tree itself seemed to be generating and the yellow fruit turned into brown husks, a long, thin black shape appeared out of the top of the tree, writhing and whipping about amongst the branches as if in desperation. There was a tremendous cracking sound as the trunk split open from top to bottom and a great flame shot up from within, then an inhuman scream as the rearing black shape toppled into the gap. For a small sapling, the tree burnt with incredible ferocity, with heat of an intensity to match the hardness of its bark, then collapsed in a pile of embers mingling with those below. It was over.

No-one was inclined to speak, or even to move. Hale could only feel his own shame at almost succumbing to the temptation of the tree even at the moment of victory over it, which he saw as a failure of faith; Dr. Findlesham was still torn between mourning the loss of his unique specimen and feeling guilty about the destruction it had caused; both men sensed that to some extent they had fallen short of the standards expected of them in their calling. The head gardener and his assistant watched them expectantly and in wonder, ready to follow the clergymen's lead in behaviour and expression, and Birch – well, Birch looked on grimly as ever, and one would have been hard-pressed to detect any change at all in him as a result of the whole series of dramatic events.

Eventually, they made their way back to the house; thence Hale returned to the vicarage at Edgely, to prepare his report to the Bishop, which, as promised, drew attention to Dr. Findlesham's co-operation and his swift action to remedy the evil on his estate when its nature was known. Exactly what that was Hale was less than clear about: he was truthful as to its origins in an oriental tree and, as far as it went, its effect of driving men to suicide, but the exact mechanism he did not describe, suggesting only that it produced a kind of madness and making imprecise comparisons with quite recently-discovered trees which yielded such drugs as quinine and curare. It would not, he decided, help to put the Bishop's mind at rest to tell him that the Evil One himself, the tempting serpent, had for a little while been in residence in his diocese as the unseen guest of his former Dean.

LIMITS

The Reverend Hale, usually observant and quite precise on matters of detail, could not be sure whether or not Lost Man's Bog lay within his own parish – but this was hardly surprising, given that this twenty acres of low-lying swamp, punctuated with gigantic rocks and deep, stagnant pools, was one of the oddest pieces of ground in the entire kingdom; if, indeed, it could be said to be in the kingdom at all, since no authority, civil or ecclesiastical, claimed it and it stood outside the recognition of the law. No-one had ever really known whether it was part of Stanhope's Farm, which lay to the north in the parish of St. Alban's, Armitage Cross, and included the field immediately to the west of the bog, or of Buckley's Farm, now properly Hyde's Farm, to the south and east, in Hale's parish of Stoke Armitage. In that it was entirely enclosed by the two properties, there was no question of it being common land, but such was the low opinion held of the place that for generations neither side had shown any interest in taking it over. That had changed radically about fifty years before Hale's arrival in the area, when the bog became briefly the focus of the long and bitter feud between Thomas Stanhope and William Buckley.

They were the worst of neighbours, though some claimed that they had actually played together as small boys as often as the jealousy of their protective families had allowed. Then their fathers had fallen out savagely – the cause being less interesting than the consequences, and so forgotten. Barriers of hatred and suspicion descended between the farms, and in time each of the heirs devoted the rest of his circumscribed life to doing down the other, and in particular to an obsessive defence of his property against the real or supposed incursions of his former friend. Such an incident occurred when they had been masters in their own homes for perhaps five years. Very early one late spring morning, following an episode concerning a ewe strayed from the north and

255

allegedly carried off from the swamp by the southern neighbours, Stanhope and his men crossed the tricky ground with some difficulty, carrying tools and hurdles of their own with which to replace the decaying fencing put up by Buckley to keep his sheep in, and thereby establish the southern limit of the Stanhope territory. Within the hour, this project had stalled, the inhabitants, workers and supporters of each farm facing each other over a gap in the fence while sheep looked on uncomprehending; the men had pitchforks, rakes, scythes and in a few cases old muskets left over from the Great Rebellion, should the quarrel get out of hand, which only the timely arrival of prominent villagers from either side prevented. But this interruption only allowed a sickness to fester in the mind of each of the farmers, an overwhelming need to seize that worthless marshland which each wanted only because the other seemed to want it for himself.

A lengthy and, as they tend to be, expensive legal case ensued, each man desperately flinging together whatever arguments he could from family tradition, from village opinion, from geography, geology and botany, in order to present some sort of case in the absence of title deeds, plans and legal records. They employed lawyers, surveyors and land agents to search for clues, but not a mention could be found of their boundary or of the ownership of the bog in any register, note or journal in parish, hundred or county; no map ever published had shown it, no traveller had ever described it, no-one had ever bought it, sold it, bequeathed it, tilled it – and both sides had made similar efforts to fence it. The case passed from local to county level, consuming on the way costs many times greater than the value of the land involved, and upwards until it reached London itself, where, it is said a despairing judge declared himself ready to award it to whichever claimant could produce a map, sketch or painting including the bog which was clearly the work of a neutral artist standing on his property and which predated their quarrel. There was none such.

By this point, Buckley had fallen so deeply into debt that he had to sell the farm to Hyde and leave the area, by defaulting perhaps losing the argument; but Stanhope, himself almost bankrupt, was too far entered into his rage and bitterness to rejoice, distraught that his enemy had so eluded a public defeat. He took to wandering in all weathers along the boundary between the farms and across the disputed swamp – which Hyde was quite content to leave to him – shaking his fist towards the south and upwards towards God, until the cold and the damp took him. Some said it was an accidental soaking in one of the icy pools of Lost Man's Bog which finished him off; perhaps a similar occurrence had been the origin of the name of the place – though others with a turn for romance and fancy maintained that the Lost Man was merely a generic representative of an extinct race of men who had in ancient times built cyclopean walls, before being overthrown by God for their arrogance and covered by the swamp.

(Reverend Hale often smiled at the vivid folk-imagination which could reconstruct a city from those great boulders whose heads showed, iceberg-like, above the stagnant fen and whose bottoms rested on the cup of hard rock into which all the water from the surrounding fields poured. He smiled too at the confusion of details from Biblical stories – Jericho, the Cities of the Plain, the Flood – from which they had made their tale, and promised to sort at least that much out for them one day in a sermon.)

The Stanhopes fared little better than the Buckleys in later years, Thomas' son and grandson being in their turns prematurely crushed by the burden of inherited debt and the opprobrium of two villages. By the time Hale became rector at Stoke Armitage, their farm was being worked by an unmarried tenant called Morton and its rent being shared out by lawyers in tiny parcels between numerous Stanhope descendants.

And so we move forward, though only to a time long before the episodes recounted in the rest of these chronicles. The Reverend Hale, then the recently-appointed rector, had had scarcely six months in which to settle into his parish before a new story about Lost Man's Bog began to circulate in the village and came to his notice; it was in fact the first time that he had heard of the spot and its sad history. Those who favoured the "single lost man" theory of the origin of the name cast the ghost of Thomas Stanhope as the central figure in this new tale, whereas those who subscribed to the more fanciful "lost civilisation" idea had to make the protagonist a representative spirit, or perhaps several ghosts seen separately. Neither version could account for the sudden appearance of the shade at this particular time. Whichever story one supported, the alleged facts of the current phenomenon were the same: a figure wrapped tightly in a long black cloak was often to be seen moving along the northern edge of the swamp, or sometimes flitting lightly between stones and pools in order to gaze briefly at the great rocks. The figure was always seen shortly after dawn or at dusk, first by Hyde's shepherd, then by others of Hyde's household and followers, and finally by small groups of villagers who bribed the workers to let them in, or else illicit spectators who dodged the labourers and servants – on the understanding that they would not be turned out but forced to hand over a few coins to avoid the embarrassment of trespass. It was in fact only a very few days before the truth came out, almost as soon as Hale had first heard of the alleged ghost and well before he could approach Hyde to ask to be allowed to watch for it; nevertheless, there were just enough ignorant tellings of the tale for the idea that the bog was haunted by a figure in a black shroud to become permanently fixed in village lore.

The reality of the situation was made known to some in Stoke Armitage by friends in Armitage Cross when the latter heard what was being said next door; the mysterious figure was actually the widow of Farmer Morton's younger brother, a Royal Navy

258

lieutenant who had died of fever in the West Indies some three years earlier. She had come from Ireland, they said, to stay on the farm with her brother-in-law and his elderly mother, though for how long and under what terms they did not know; the cloak was explained by her maintenance of her widow's black, and her twilight walks by a routine of "constitutionals" informed by a romantic disposition.

When he had heard this, the mind of Reverend Hale ceased to be exercised by the mystery, but the details came back to him a few days later, at the end of August, when he encountered a female figure in black descending Lone Stone Hill briskly on foot as he was skirting its base at walking pace on horseback. As their paths were inevitably going to cross within a few yards of each other, he decided that even in the absence of a formal introduction it would be churlish not to acknowledge the existence of a newcomer to the area, and his clerical garb would prevent any misinterpretation of his actions. He stopped his horse and dismounted when the figure was still about a dozen paces away; holding his bridle with one hand, he removed his hat with the other and called out a suitably bland greeting. He had expected her to make a conventional response or gesture and continue on her way in front of his horse, but in fact she slowed and stopped, though further away than would be the norm in polite conversation. She had on a black cloak, pulled over her head and then wrapped around her down to her knees and held in place by the one visible hand. A straight black fustian skirt and incongruously stout but very sensible black brogues completed her outfit. Hale did not want to stare at her, but noted stray wisps of red hair, large dark eyes and pale complexion; he felt obliged to speak again, but was unsure what to say, and wished he had not begun this encounter.

"Have I the honour of addressing Mrs. Morton, sister-in-law of Mr. Henry Morton of Stanhope's Farm? I presume to ask as I have heard something of you despite our not being introduced. You see, a large number of my parishioners have believed you to be a ghost."

He winced inwardly even as he made the ill-judged remark, but in reply came that interruption of breath and sudden smile which do not make up a laugh but indicate sympathy and good will. A gentle but firm Anglo-Irish voice, more refined than one might have expected from the plain dress and boots and clearly educated, responded in a warm and easy tone at odds with his hesitant manner.

"That Mistress Morton I am indeed, sir, though far from a ghost, as I hope you will agree. And if you are as you appear, sir, I judge you to be vicar of one of the parishes adjoining that of St. Alban's. Stoke Armitage would be the nearest," Hale's nodding led her, "in which case I think your name may be Hale. I have visited your church of St. Mark's already, and it is indeed most charming."

"Thank you for that, and Theophilus Hale is indeed my name." After a moment's awkward silence, the lady bowed slightly and pulled her cloak more tightly about her, as though to proceed. Hale added, "I hope to see you again while you are in these parts," and bowed too.

"I expect you shall, as I may be here for some time," she replied as she passed in front of him and continued over the common towards Armitage Cross. Hale watched her progress, as nimble and purposeful as her speech, for a moment, before remounting and carrying on, and he again put the matter out of his mind until about a week later, when he was surprised to receive an invitation to visit the Mortons – "at home to their acquaintances in Stoke Armitage" – the following Sunday afternoon. The rector was intrigued, and resolved to accept insofar as he was able to find time between his Sabbath duties – as a result of which he arrived a little late, to find the widow entertaining the gathering with a recital of Irish songs in a mezzo-soprano by turns playful and wistful, accompanied by Baines the schoolmaster, playing somewhat inadequately at sight. The fustian dress and thick woollen cloak had been replaced by a semi-formal dress of black satin, set off by a silver brooch of Celtic design, and this time the deep red tresses were on show scarcely compromised by a kind of flimsy black cap in their centre.

Stanhope's Farm had once been very prosperous, and despite decades of decline and neglect the house was still comfortable as well as substantial. Morton was clearly investing heavily in both the building and the farming operations, with a view to settling permanently and making himself prominent in his recently-adopted community by bringing it back into full and increased production and in time, as he admitted, making the owners an offer for the freehold which would be irresistible compared to the small return their rental income offered. The "at homes" which the Mortons were holding, ostensibly to get to know their neighbours and particularly to introduce the widowed Mrs. Morton, appeared to Hale to be aimed at developing Mr. Morton's useful connections in the area: his guests from Stoke Armitage were Butler, a freeholder, and Hamilton, a bachelor tenant in a similar situation to himself, both of whom he had met at market, and Richardson the local builder, whom he was consulting about work to be done on the house. The rector and Baines the schoolmaster had apparently been invited to keep the ladies entertained while the businessmen conversed on serious matters.

Mrs. Richardson and Mrs. Butler were both anxious to take advantage of access to the schoolmaster to discuss the progress of their – and other people's – children, and the older Mrs. Morton, being infirm, had retired to bed already, and so it was that Hale found himself mainly responsible for entertaining the young widow. He swiftly obtained the image if not the detail of his hostess's origins, as the youngest of seven siblings in a barely middle-class

Anglo-Irish family maintaining respectability on the edge of Dublin society; one brother was now a solicitor's clerk there, one a soldier in Canada and one a country schoolmaster in County Down; two sisters were married to farmers and the third to a bank clerk. He learned much more thoroughly about the more recent background and situation of Maeve Morton, née Healy: about HMS Circe being damaged in a storm in the Irish Sea and putting in for repairs, with Lieutenant Morton being seconded to the Customs service in Dublin while his injuries from a falling mast healed; about their meeting at a concert and his six months' courtship of her; about his being recalled to the Fleet six months after their wedding and dispatched to the West Indies as second officer aboard HMS Calypso, only to die of the fever at Kingston, Jamaica. Since then, she continued over tea, she had struggled for three years to keep herself and a maid, and then just herself, in the little cottage they had rented on the coast just outside the city of Dublin, on the proceeds of a small pension and some music lessons. Her brother-in-law had helped as far as he could, and now that he had a large enough establishment and needed someone to run the domestic side of it for him, it had seemed to both of them an ideal arrangement if she were to give up her struggle in Ireland and move to Armitage Cross as housekeeper and, as she put it, "acting lady of the house". Ideal, but surely temporary, suggested Hale, becoming naturally drawn into the line of argument; what if Henry were to marry? Did she have a long-term strategy for living in England? He apologized for having strayed into a somewhat confidential area, and excused her from answering, but she laughed his embarrassment off and said that she was not adverse to taking up the traditional vocation of the modestly educated and even more modestly fortuned woman, that of schoolmistress or governess. To that end, she hoped Mr. Baines would give her some pointers and advice, and she would be willing to benefit from the instruction of any of her acquaintance generous enough to help her in the matter of furthering her own education. Hale felt that he was being steered into making some kind of ridiculous offer, and fortunately at this point the conclusion of tea came with the latest moment for his departure for his next service. He voiced his somewhat hurried thanks and apologies to his host and hostess and mounted his horse for the short ride back to his parish.

He found himself to be strangely ill at ease. He had found his talk with Mrs. Morton – for the "at home" had amounted to little else in his case – most agreeable: her manner, her voice and her singing were delightful, and her conversation was lively and witty even if her range had so far been limited. And yet it was not satisfactory: it had been almost entirely about her, as if she had been instructing him, and her final comments had been clearly intended to push him into making some kind of binding arrangement – he was sure he was not deceiving himself about that. There had been something a little forced, even building into something slightly desperate towards the end, which put him on his guard.

Nevertheless, when he saw the Mortons in his congregation at Eucharist on the third Sunday in September, he felt a sudden elation. He had thought of her more than once during the intervening days – the deep red tresses, the wide dark eyes, the lilt of her mildly Irish accent – and to see it all come together in his own place pleased him in a way which was beyond the rational. He steadied himself, made sure that he acknowledged her brother-in-law with a nod first, reminded himself that the sermon was not a public display of oratory, and did his best not to return her smile when he gave her the wafer and the chalice. The effort was considerable, and he was nervous and inarticulate when he came to shake their hands at the church door. Mr. Morton explained briefly amidst the press that Maeve had wanted to see the church again, preferably in use, and so they had deserted St. Alban's for once; in any case, he had arranged to see Butler briefly, and as his farm was just past the church it seemed an ideal arrangement. As so many people needed to shake Hale's hand and exchange a snippet of gossip on the way out, the rector could not follow or maintain a coherent conversation for more than two lines, and so he did not quite know how it came about that Maeve was left behind as Henry went to Butler's "for an hour at most"; something about her not being interested in ploughs but being interested in old buildings, something about him being pleased to show her round while she waited, something about the need for tea – he could not remember who had said what and so who was responsible for them being alone together, but his elation had passed once again into unease. "Ideal arrangements" seemed to be presenting themselves too easily.

He thought it best to keep their meeting as public as possible, and to delay and so shorten the intimacy of tea in his sitting room. There were a few small knots of people talking around the porch and in the churchyard outside, and Reverend Hale took it upon himself to break into as many as he could in order to introduce Mrs. Morton and tell them just as much of her story as he thought not improper and they would listen to. When this subterfuge was exhausted, still in his vestments, he took her back into the church, where Williamson, the verger he had inherited, had finished collecting and stacking service books and hymnals. After every service, verger and rector would engage in an unofficial ritual of their own: the verger would ask if there was anything else the rector wanted him to do, to which the almost invariable response was negative, except, rarely, if there was something specific they had discussed already. Today, however, the rite was reformed, as Hale had noticed a pair of large candlesticks that were starting to tarnish and needed polishing – preferably now, so that the church would look its best at vespers. The old man was thus busy at one end of the building as Hale showed Maeve around – the font, the windows, the glass, the embroidery, the organ; knowing she was interested in music, he spoke for some time on that theme, while she listened with an amused smile.

"I fear I know little of the Church of Ireland, Mrs. Morton, but would I be correct in assuming that its practices are similar to those of the Church of England?"

The widow laughed aloud; Hale glanced up the building long enough to see that the verger had stopped polishing and was staring at them.

"I am afraid that I cannot enlighten you about that, Mr. Hale. You see, I have never been a member of the Church of Ireland. I was brought up in the Roman religion of my family. Does that shock you?"

"No, no, not at all. Not at all. But you attended here today."

"When I married Lieutenant Morton, I accompanied him to his church as his wife."

"I see. It must have been a great wrench to change your faith in that way."

"It was not such a wrench."

At last, the verger was approaching them, to be promptly offered tea, which he, having already taken the hint, accepted. They all made their way over to the rectory, after Hale had hurriedly disrobed. At length, even the loyal Williamson had to be elsewhere, and Hale sat uneasily facing Mrs. Morton over the china, his mind largely occupied in calculating the acceptability of the number of times he looked at the clock and his nerves mainly exercised in lengthening the gaps between; Morton's hour had already stretched to ninety minutes.

"Am I that terrifying, Mr. Hale?"

265

"Madam?"

"That you cannot face me without other people being present, behind whom you might hide or who might rescue you. No, do not protest; I am not such a fool that I believe candlesticks need polishing immediately after the Eucharist, and I can see now that you are desperate for Morton to return. I also understand enough to know that it is not that you do not like me – you were pleased enough to see me in the crowd of your congregation earlier; and it does not seem that you are fearful of being corrupted by contact with a former Papist. So I must conclude that you are simply frightened of being alone with me," he made to speak but she carried on, "at least in silence. I must admit that I did contribute far too much of the conversation at home the other night, but today you have more than made up for it with your talking about everything under the sun, as if to avoid a space in which something significant might be said. You have today told me everything I knew about music when I was ten, everything I knew about churches when I was twelve, and nothing about yourself. But there is more to you than meets the eye, Mr. Hale. Do you know what they say about the seventh child of a seventh child? Especially a Celtic one; and that is I."

At this dramatic moment, Mr. Morton knocked at the front door. A confused few minutes of greeting, tea declined, shawl, some words about Butler which Hale did not really hear, and gone.

Hale was half-inclined to find an excuse to absent himself from the next occasion at Stanhope's Farm to which he was invited, but as his consent to being a performer was almost being assumed by the younger Mrs. Morton it was doubly difficult to refuse. Maeve, as she signed her personal note on the card, was having a musical entertainment in three weeks' time, in the middle of October; most of those invited were expected to contribute, but there were to be a few worthies of the area present just as audience (this perhaps being what Mr. Morton saw as valuable in the exercise). She herself would be singing and playing the harp, Mr. Baines was being invited to play the fortepiano, Mr. Hale was being invited to play the flute (a hobby which he had mentioned to her), Miss Price of Cross House would be singing to her own accompaniment, and so on.

He did not have to wait the three weeks before seeing the widow again; indeed, even before he had finally committed himself to acceptance of the second invitation, just a few days later, their paths crossed again, this time at the western edge of Morton's property, where it pushed against Stoke Armitage territory as though trying to outflank Hyde's fields in a revival of the ancient feud. She was rambling round the edge of the field in her characteristic black cloak; he was cantering along the bridlepath parallel to her and, having from his elevated position spotted her on the other side of the hedge, he slowed and made to speak – though she had already turned in her walk and was smiling at him. For a moment, he could not recall what he intended to say.

"Mr. Hale, how fortunate we are met! It seems to me that we both have apologies to make, which is easiest done face to face, and hopefully amended."

Her challenging attitude made any pleasantries irrelevant. "Indeed, madam," this in curiosity rather than stiffly, "what apologies are owing between us?" Both had now stopped.

"From you to me, an apology for not replying at once to my – brother-in-law Morton's and my invitation to our little musical gathering. And it is easily amended, and forgiven, by your acceptance here and now."

"Well, I am honoured – but would feel more honoured and more confident if your invitation were the result of hearing me play; it is some time since I played in public and I am quite out of practice."

"That will not do, Mr. Hale! You have weeks in which to rehearse something brief and entertaining. And in any case, the whole idea of a musical gathering came from you."

"From me?"

"Indeed yes – it was your talking about music and about your flute that started me thinking about giving our neighbours a chance to display musical talents which too often lie hidden, as under a bushel! But that leads me to the apology due from me to you," her tone became more businesslike and less gay, "which I fear I cannot make speaking to you like this, stretching into the air up a hedge! But do say you'll come." At the end, a note of pleading.

The rector could not but smile and nod his consent as he dismounted and entered the field by the gate onto the bridlepath, to which, at Maeve's bidding he tied his horse. She was crossing the field to look down at what she called "the ruins", which Hale took to be the great rocks of Lost Man's Bog, and seemed to assume that Hale would accompany her, which he did without thinking.

"I wanted to apologise for my words last time we met. On reflection – "

"My dear lady – "

"No, please let me finish. It was very wrong and selfish of me to adopt an accusing tone and scold you for not behaving as I wanted you to do; it was putting you into the impossible position of choosing between falling in with my wishes, against your own inclinations, and refusing so to do, which might seem ungentlemanly. I can only offer as an excuse the fact that I have suffered loneliness for many long months, and I came to England in the hope of making new friends and starting a new life. I was expecting too much too soon, or perhaps something where there is nothing, and I must apologise if my frustrated feelings came out in a demanding and shrewish way. I shall endeavour not to allow it to happen again, if only you will stay on good terms with me and my brother-in-law."

A turmoil of feelings inside the rector: a renewed warmth towards this woman who now seemed so vulnerable, and so reasonable; a rush of sympathy for her enforced solitude; a hope that her words really did imply a liking for him, with concomitant feelings verging on the sin of pride; a sense almost of shame that he had failed to be more positive towards her. Above all, an illogical feeling of illicit pleasure at simply being with her, which was more than the sum of the pleasure of looking at her deep tresses and deeper eyes, the pleasure of hearing the soft lilt of her voice, the pleasure of watching her elegant swaying motion, the pleasure of the unaccustomed intimacy between them. He had to restrain himself from saying more than he did.

"Madam, it is again I who should be apologising, for my behaviour at our last meeting. The only excuse I can offer is that I am unused to intimate conversation of that kind, and scarce know how to conduct myself. There was much truth in what you said about my being fearful, for I was fearful of presenting myself badly to one who I in turn hoped would be a friend and ally in this place so new to both of us. For you would be quite wrong to imagine that there is nothing in the place where you have turned your – interest."

As they stepped along the rough track round the field-edge, constantly adjusting for dips and sidestepping large stones, sometimes almost stumbling, they returned sidelong glances, smiling encouragement at each other, but said no more, for many minutes. They reached the far hedge, and mounted a stile alongside a patched-up gate rarely opened; on the far side, rough grass led to mere scrub as the land dipped into the hollow of the bog. The sun was now quite low behind them, and its beams were almost parallel to the slope, drawing out their shadows grotesquely. Far ahead of them to the east were raised fields, like the one they had just traversed except in belonging to the neighbouring farm; on either side, the ground sloped down from walls and hedges through furze and the remains of decaying fences to the scrub and rock of Lost Man's Bog. Maeve's step seemed to become more sprightly and her voice more excited as soon as the scattered waters and mighty tumbled boulders came into view; it was actually the first time Hale had seen the spot close-up, though he had of course heard much of the history and legend surrounding it. They paused in their walk, though Hale sensed that she was straining against an enormous urge, and it seemed to him that the urge was to hurl herself down the slope to the swamp. Having briefly taken in the main features of the scene before him, the rector half-turned to regard his companion: she looked strangely flushed and intense as she stared down with her eyes wide, as though she were seeing the scene for the first time and it were ten times more inspiring than it appeared. The motionless pause began to vex him.

"I understand that you come often to this place. The landscape here intrigues you?"

"Why yes, of course;" she tore her eyes from it for a moment; "does it not you?"

"It is certainly an unusual spot." He struggled for expression which did not lead him into lies about the bleak and sinister hollow before him but at the same time did not offend his companion's evident admiration for it, and came up with a word which he did not often use. "It is certainly very romantic, as the poets might say."

"Oh it is certainly that, and much, much more; it has seen epics, romances and tragedies, for countless generations!" Hale reflected that the Stanhope feud hardly merited such a description, but he let her continue as she seemed to become gripped by something which made her bob and sway slightly, wringing her hands. "Warriors built a great city here, centuries before the Romans came. They were mighty men, like Achilles and Ajax, except that they were Celts as I am, and they built with huge stones, high towers and strong gatehouses, lofty walls and rich palaces. They went out to battle in chariots and defeated all the peoples round about, bringing back gold and silver with which to adorn their wives and their city." She became still, and her voice quieter. "But then they offended their gods, or the Christian god overcame their gods, and thunderbolts from heaven struck down their proud towers and battlements, and a great storm flooded the ground so much that it will never dry out. The people were all slain in the ruin and the tempest, and nothing remains of their city but these tumbled stones."

After a moment of reflection, she seemed to become herself again. "Excuse my folly, Mr. Hale, but the place excites my imagination so! Do you think this might have been such a city?"

Relieved at being excused from the need to dissemble, Hale was forthright: "My dear madam, I hardly think so. These rocks show no signs of having been worked by man, and even an Achilles would scarcely wish to build a house out of blocks like that one, which must be fully ten feet square; he would have no need of such thickness in all dimensions, let alone the difficulty of moving such a piece."

"You are too literal-minded or not imaginative enough, Mr. Hale! Surely the heat of a great fire could have – what is the word? – fused several stones into one?"

"Even so, this hollow simply has the nature of a swamp, and one cannot account for that by reference to one storm. It must always have been so, and no-one would choose to try to raise great buildings in such a damp, unstable and feverous place."

"It was higher, on a hilltop, but the thunderbolts and storm reduced it to this depth. You see, Mr. Hale, you cannot get round by logic what I can sense emotionally and poetically to be the nature and history of the place! And now we two stand here and speculate on its past – another stage in that history."

These words suddenly made Hale aware of their situation for the first time: he was standing alone with an attractive young widow as the sun went down, in the most remote and unfrequented spot in two parishes. In a blundering and semi-articulate way he suggested to her that despite the attractions of the scene and the pleasure he took in her company, it was not a good idea for them to be alone together thus, in case they were seen and the situation misinterpreted. Mrs. Morton laughed, and being considerate and civil, unlike her brasher self of their last meeting, she allowed what he said. "But surely it would be much more reprehensible of you to abandon me here in this dangerous place with night drawing on?" Renewed laughter ended his sudden pain and confusion at this reminder of the social and moral complexity of his position, as she assured him that she knew the whole of the bog in detail in the dark, that she was safer on her own there than having to watch out for him too, and that in any case she would soon be going straight back to the farm to commence supper. Accepting all this gratefully, he withdrew and made his way back to where his horse was tethered.

The Mortons' musical gathering was set for three o'clock on Saturday afternoon, to be followed by an early light supper to enable visitors to get home before it was dark; it was understood that Hale would be amongst the first to leave, in order to take evening service in his village. A programme of items had been drawn up so as to provide variety of forms and styles, and copied onto cards in Maeve's elegant handwriting. Firstly, Baines the schoolmaster performed a keyboard suite by Handel on the fortepiano competently; he stayed on as accompanist for the Stephensons' young daughter, playing what amounted to little more than advanced exercises on the violin. Then Miss Price replaced him at the fortepiano to play a sonata by J.C. Bach, in a manner resolute but not always secure, rather than melodious; she was more at ease with the group of English and Scotch folk songs which followed. The finale to the first part was provided by Mr. Hale, who lived up to the honour with a beautiful performance of an unaccompanied sonata by Bach, followed by the contrasting Badinerie from the second orchestral suite, giving it a joyful bounce which made any accompaniment superfluous. After a pause for refreshment and words of praise for the performers, the Mortons obliged with the second half. The farmer produced an ancient bass viol, which he said three generations of his family had played in the church band in their former home village in Somerset; he himself had only recently started to teach himself the skill, but begged their indulgence, as he had worked on a few short pieces for this occasion. He made his way without too many strange noises or hesitations through a stately minuet, an old ayre and a lively jig. Finally, the highlight of the entertainment arrived, and it surpassed expectations: Maeve's talent for singing was already well-known from the previous gathering, but her performance this evening excelled that demonstration by a considerable margin, and one might even suspect that she had engineered the preceding items, even the whole meeting, so as to throw her own skill into even sharper focus.

At the interval, she had somehow found time, in between pouring tea and passing cakes, to change from her widow's black satin into a flowing dress of bright green, with a darker green silk scarf around her shoulders, onto which fell her red hair, the cap no longer in evidence. She seated herself on an armless chair in the middle of the assembly, with her harp on her lap – not the great free-standing instrument Mr. Hale had expected, but just a base, arm and arch of natural wood with seventeen strings stretched across. On this simple instrument, Maeve accompanied herself in a series of Irish songs, at times slow and melancholy, with the harp providing elaborate decorative motifs around the edges of her mysterious and evocative words, at times brisk and vigorous, with the instrument marking and complicating the steady rhythm behind the text. In conclusion, the spell-bound audience were roused to clapping and foot-tapping as she launched into a string of reels. The rector found himself swaying and keeping time with the rest, and for a moment felt profoundly silly when the music stopped. Silly, but also sad, when the direct communication between performer and listener suddenly ended; or was there more to it than that? Was the red-and-green vision of Maeve, sitting barely five paces from him, more than just an incidental addition to the emotional stirring of the music? Two encores, and he still felt profoundly cheated when she agreed to another and the latest possible moment for his departure had already arrived; but at the same time he felt some relief that his indecision about exactly how he felt would soon be irrelevant. He got up as she began to settle herself again, announced to the world that, much against his will, he had to get back to St. Mark's, apologised to their hostess for his rudeness, thanked both host and hostess profusely, and made his way out with Morton as quickly as might not seem impolite. The farmer saw him off briskly, so as to return to his more loyal guests, with brief thanks for his presence, and as Hale rode away he could half-hear, half-imagine the sister-in-law tripping through another ballad in what he now guessed, from her introductions and explanations, to be her mother tongue.

And so he continued for the following week, his thoughts so taken with Maeve that he could concentrate on little else; for the first time since his arrival at Stoke Armitage, he fell back on a college practice sermon, unrelated to the season, for his Sunday homily. And yet he felt that it would be wrong for him to force himself on her, as he feared his attentions might be seen: she was lonely and vulnerable after her bereavement, far from home, and he had the advantage of a cleric's favoured station. He was thus much relieved and anxious to comply when he received a kind of invitation from her – though the nature of the invitation would have scared him off a few bare weeks before. A note from her arrived wondering at his silence and indicating that she would be making the most of the last few days of what could still be just termed summer by walking up to the Lone Stone, in the late afternoon, before taking in the sunset at the "ruins". She hoped she might see him there before the dark evenings of winter drew in, if he knew the place.

Reverend Hale knew the Lone Stone well; it had stood on Lone Stone Hill on the edge of Stoke Armitage for centuries, perhaps a great many centuries, having been raised by men before history could record the deed. Local stories spoke of Romans or of Druids as its originator, but Hale's understanding was that monuments of this kind were even older than those venerable peoples. He had seen similar stones in several parts of the country, usually arranged in rings or small clusters, starting with the Rollright Stones near Oxford, but here was the single stone, its significance lost long ago; perhaps once its context had made its meaning clear, as marker, boundary, viewing point or place of power, but all that now remained was the solitary block, cut with the simplest of tools and dragged, according to local experts, from an outcrop five miles away to sit on top of a lonely cone-shaped hill. East to west it was a little over a yard wide, north to south perhaps two-thirds of that, and it stood about seven feet high; there was no telling how

275

much more might be below ground – not so much as to prevent it from nodding slightly towards the south, but too much for it so to fall over. Originally, Hale surmised, it might have been a regular rectangle, but now weather and time had scoured its surface, wearing down less resilient patches, peppering porous places with small holes, opening up inherent weaknesses into cracks and prising slivers off. The top in particular had been invaded by rain which had scored deep channels down the highest yard or so of the wider sides so that it had begun to look like a rudimentary hand with half-formed fingers, struggling from the tyranny of the rock like Michelangelo's slaves. Basically grey, at close quarters parts of it could look pink or blue or green, though the exact hues depended largely on the condition of the sky overhead and the grass roundabout. It was at the foot of Lone Stone Hill that the Reverend Hale had first met Maeve Morton.

The following afternoon saw the unaccustomed sight of Reverend Hale walking any great distance, climbing Lone Stone Hill an hour before sunset, his coat as yet unneeded and unbuttoned but worn against the coming cold. Because of the width of the flat summit, the stone can only be seen by an observer actually on top of the hill or, as an indecipherable dot on the horizon by one a long way from its foot. So Hale did not see the stone at all until he reached the top of the hill, and then there it was suddenly, leaning towards him. At first he thought he was alone, but after a moment he became aware of slight movements around the stone's edge; approaching it obliquely, he realised there was someone behind it, and when he had worked his way round sufficiently he was sure that it was Maeve Morton in her accustomed black and with her hair uncovered, but curiously lying back against the sloping stone, her arms above her head and spread so as to cover as much of its surface as she could. Her eyes were closed, and it was a moment before she realised that she was being watched. She pushed herself upright and took a pace forwards, smoothing down her dress. "Why, Mr. Hale, how long have you been watching me? You could have shown some courtesy in apprising me of your presence!"

He realised that this was part of the game, and saw that a laugh in her eyes belied the sternness of her expression, and so made only the mildest of oblique protests: "Madam, I assure you that I have just arrived here and was aware of your presence behind the stone only in the instant of you becoming aware of mine. But tell me, what were you doing there?"

"Only resting." This would have satisfied Hale, but she looked suddenly truly serious and went on, "Though a maiden resting here in this way can have dreams more potent than normal. In ancient times, young girls would sleep on such stones or in their shadows and dream images of their future lives, perhaps of the men they would marry. Such stones have powers." Before Hale could blunder in, she carried on. "I was resting here on the stone when I first saw you riding by, so many days ago now."

Hale turned, and looked at the edge of the hill-top; what he was thinking was obvious – that the path which skirted the base of the hill was far too far below the line of sight for her to have seen him on it, unless she had been standing virtually on the edge. She seemed to know what he was thinking, and said, "There are many ways of seeing, and not all depend on looking."

With that, she began to walk away, the way he had come, as though the subject had been closed. Hale fell in with her steps but was unwilling to leave the theme entirely.

"Mrs. Morton, I must confess that I find conversation with you less easy when you are speaking in certain modes or on certain subjects. To be more precise, I am less skilled in the employment of the Romantic idiom than you are, and must beg your indulgence when your use of it leaves me confused and perhaps struggling to distinguish between your imagery and the facts you wish to convey."

"Perhaps the distinction between them is not as great you imagine, Mr. Hale. But it is, I think, a situation due at least in part-measure to the racial difference between us. To the Celtic mind, the world of the imagination, the world of the past, the world of the future and the world of the spirits are all next door to each other and equally valid. One who understands this can, on certain conditions, see more than one of them at once, or even pass between them. I know this is hard for you to understand, as it is not part of your inheritance."

"I confess that your talk of spirits disturbs me somewhat, as they are very much part of my inheritance, as you call it, but I fancy spirits of a very different kind. Nevertheless, I wish to learn more of your Celtic world and so perhaps come closer to an understanding of what you say."

"Indeed, Mr. Hale, and it is my intention that you should learn a great deal more about it, and very soon, so that you should understand me perfectly."

An observer at the foot of Lone Stone Hill might now see the pair at the very edge of the summit, in silhouette against a sky already darkening as the sun descended to their left, over Lost Man's Bog. Almost as one, though in fact it was Maeve who led, they walked slowly round the rim until they faced the setting sun, and then she reached out with a quick action which caught him by surprise; she seized his left hand in her right and drew it to her side, pulling him awkwardly off balance so that he all but fell into her. For a moment, he looked straight down into her face, inches from his, into a wide smile and laughing mouth, and then he pulled himself upright and away. He stood, unsure what to do; she released his hand, and drew back, now laughing aloud. Before he could expostulate, she spoke: "I am sorry, Mr. Hale, you were clearly not prepared for that and it is entirely my fault that I misjudged the moment. Please do not think that I laugh at your discomfiture, but at the absurdity of the situation." And Mr. Hale was at once won back over, and for some minutes they stood in silence, the same hands now joined and her head resting on his shoulder. Perhaps it was the Irish custom that made her so forward; perhaps it was the fact of her having been married already; but whatever caused her to behave in such a manner (he chose not to think "unladylike"), he was content to forgive it.

"You may escort me down the hill and set me on the road to the farm, but then you must go. You may come back tomorrow at the same time, if you wish."

It seemed to Reverend Hale that he was leading two lives: one, which took up most of the day, involved taking services, writing letters and sermons, dealing with parishioners in a variety of ways, together with all the ordinary paraphernalia of living, and another one, which took up a tiny part of the day and most of the night both when he was conscious and when he slept, involved Maeve Morton. The former was the one for which he had prepared for many years, but now it had become as a dream world through which he drifted waiting for his next meeting with her; the latter was in fact largely a dream, but seemed the more real experience. He knew this was nonsense, but he could do nothing to change it, for he did not want it to change. As far as he was aware, no-one was yet aware of what had come over him or had seen them together in the remote places where they walked and talked, and although he was on one level aware that his conduct might be considered inappropriate in a pious young clergyman, even to himself, on another he was not bothered by it, and for the moment he was prepared to drift on.

The following afternoon inevitably saw him back on Lone Stone Hill; Maeve was again there before him, this time sitting on the ground in front of the stone to face him as he came up from the south; the forward slope of the stone prevented her from resting more than her shoulders and the back of her head against it. She was playing with a silver bracelet which she had evidently just slipped off, and as she greeted Hale she indicated that he should sit on the grass by her.

"Now," she said, "this is your first lesson about Ireland. You will have heard of the little people, the fairy folk of Ireland, from whom all the magic comes? Good; now in truth they are all that remains of a great race of heroes, warriors and wizards, who ruled in Ireland before the Celts came. They were called the Tuatha De Danann, the people of the goddess Danann, and they brought to Ireland the four great treasures. Here, look. This belonged to my grandmother, and her grandmother, and my mother gave it to me."

She held up the bracelet from which hung four charms of antique silver. With the thumb and first finger of her free hand she took hold of the first and held it up to Hale's eyes. It was a rough rectangle of the metal, with a surface roughened so as almost to resemble the stone behind them. "The Stone of Fal, which would cry out in recognition of a true king. Do you remember the stone from which King Arthur had to draw the sword to win the kingship? And the Stone of Destiny from Scone on which the ancient Scots kings sat? For the Irish and the Welsh and the Scots share the Celtic heritage."

The next she held up was a long pin with a leaf-shaped point. "The Spear of the god Lug, to wield which is to win victory." Then a tiny knife. "The Sword of Nuada, the De Danann king who conquered Ireland but in so doing lost an arm, which his craftsman replaced with one of silver. No enemy can escape this sword." Finally, a miniature round cooking pot on short legs. "The Cauldron of the god Dagda, from which no-one ever went hungry, for it refills as it empties."

Hale peered at each in turn and tried to take in her words. She replaced it on her wrist; it was a heavy thing, made for a considerably larger arm, and it hung down around her thumb joint with the charms almost amongst her fingers. Hale remarked that he had not seen it before; "Indeed no, for it is too precious to take it out and risk losing it. And one does not want its power to decrease by exposure." He would have queried that but for her putting out a hand and asking for assistance in rising.

When they walked down the hill this time, to the point at which their ways parted, they did so arm in arm. It did enter Hale's head that if word of this reached his congregation, any one of whom could have been passing by, it would have caused a scandal, but somehow that seemed an insignificant risk compared to the wholly unfamiliar pleasure he felt in Maeve's company. He had asked her if she had mentioned to anyone that they were meeting in this way, and her reaction convinced him that she had not, since she seemed to think it hilarious that he should even mention the possibility; she believed her brother-in-law understood from their public meetings that she liked him and would not be surprised if that were to develop further, but he did not know that they were meeting already.

The next day followed the same pattern: they met at the stone, and as they sat on the grass Maeve recounted the outlines of some of the ancient tales. Hale himself was largely silent, and at length she asked him what troubled him.

"Indeed, a matter which scarcely counts as a trouble, being more in the nature of a joy, but which does not admit of easy handling, and so vexes. In truth, there are things I would say to you which I have not said before to anyone, and so I am ignorant of what to say and even of whether they should be said at all."

Maeve cut him short by rising so as to move nearer, but he misunderstood and stood up as though to leave. She stood in front of him. "Does what you want to say concern the two of us?" He nodded. "Then perhaps this will make the saying of it easier, and give you some clue as to what the answer may be, if I understand you aright." And she pecked his cheek. He wrapped his arms around her shoulders and returned the kiss, on her mouth. She pulled back slightly and placed a finger on his lips: "Do not say it now, in the ordinary course of an ordinary day; on Friday it is the last day of October, the last and holiest day of the Celtic Year; that would be a better time to say something of such eternal importance. Would that be pleasing to you?"

He nodded. "That would be the eve of All Saints' Day, in the old calendar. Is there not some superstition of the country people attendant on it, to do with witches and phantoms? I know it is a night some old folks hold in dread."

She laughed. "Mere prejudice and a perversion of the old beliefs, in which all spirits not canonised by the Church and all ancient heroes were seen as demons! In Celtic times, that night was one of the utmost spirituality, which non-believers may take for evil. But Morton is going away on Thursday to visit an old friend and will take the chance to call in on a couple of his customers and suppliers on the way, and so will probably not be returning until Sunday. That makes it possible for us to meet so that you can say what you wish at midnight, the holiest moment."

Hale was more than a little taken aback at this suggestion, but as he had gone along with the bizarre plan so far there was no logic in choosing to pull out at this point. He nodded dumbly, and three days later he left the rectory long after the village had retired for the night. He was careful to put no more than the bare minimum of lights on as he made his final preparations and then slipped out almost in the manner of an escaping felon. They met at the foot of the hill to walk to the "ruins", which Maeve had chosen as the most romantic backdrop for his words. Her excited smile gave him courage and he immediately reached for her hand: as his tried to close around hers, he felt the localised but sharp pain of one of the silver charms hanging off her loose bracelet digging into his palm; for a moment he imagined that he had felt a deliberate jab, but at once dismissed the idea as absurd. He instinctively flinched and put the slight wound to his lips. Maeve stopped and asked him what the matter was, and he took her hand and held it palm uppermost: the miniature dagger lay across it. Next to it he placed his own hand, showing her the inflamed spot by moonlight, by way of explanation; she caressed it, with a pained expression, though she muttered, "The sword of Nuada, from which no-one escapes." He licked the wound again, seeming to sense something bitter, but thought no more of it.

Maeve took his arm in hers and set off more briskly across the wide field. At first they chatted as before, but gradually Hale was conscious of becoming quieter; he felt less inclined to speak, then realised that it was that he was actually less able to speak. As they approached the gate, he was aware that Maeve's voice was growing less clear, or rather seemed to be coming from a distance, and although she was right next to him he seemed to be conscious of the separating power of every inch between them, even of the yawning distance from the front to the back of his eye and the great expanse of the optic nerve through which her image had to drag itself wearily into his consciousness. He felt dizzy, and steadied himself against a fencepost; his mind seemed turned inwards, though he was dimly aware of her muttering about the effect of the night air and apologising for bringing him out in it when he was unused to it. She produced a phial from somewhere and held it to his mouth, urging him to drink; in other circumstances he would have been more circumspect and at least enquired as to its nature, but in his weakness, and especially the acute embarrassment it brought with it, he took it willingly. The bitter taste again, and he spat most of it out, though for a moment it did revive him as the small draught burned into his stomach; then she was almost dragging him through the gate, saying that exercise would hasten the effect, and he was staggering down the slope towards the bog, not willingly but without the power to stop. He now realised, in a muddled way, that he was drugged, though the idea that Maeve had drugged him came more slowly and was grasped less readily. He could barely move his arms now, and opening and closing the wounded right hand was impossible; his head seemed stuck slightly uplifted so that he could see directly in front of him only with an effort which was quickly becoming too great. His legs were faltering and he was moving only by the force of momentum built up over the downward slope; Maeve pulled him by the arms this way and that to steer him past the swamps and rocks as they entered the bog. There was no longer any concern about helping him; she was simply trying to get him to a particular spot, for what reason he could not imagine.

His shins and knees collided with a stone and he fell forward across it, with great blows to his limbs and trunk which he scarcely felt but which made him vomit up some of the poison, bitter in his mouth. He could not move; in fact, for a moment after the noxious matter had left him, he consciously wanted never to move again but to lie there doubled up and at peace. But she was pulling him upright again, by his collar, and she roughly got him into a slumped semblance of a sitting position on the stone. He was in a state closer to sleep than wakefulness, but was still able to see if not to look, and could hear, albeit indistinctly, and felt a sick coldness in his centre which made him want above anything else to crawl into a warm bed and sleep it off. Maeve seemed to realise all this, because in the speech which followed she bent down to speak loudly into his ear, and when necessary she pinched his face in her hand and twisted it so that he could see what she was talking about.

"I assume that you understand that you have been drugged. It is useless for you to try to move, though your state of consciousness remains, in impaired form. The sword of Nuala, from which no-one escapes." She dangled the charm in front of his eyes. "Now it is time for your last lesson in Celtic beliefs, Reverend Hale, and the subject is the human sacrifice." She paused a little as if for effect. "Before your god came and replaced my gods by force, they were honoured all over the Celtic world with the sacrifice of all kinds of animals, the better sacrifices being of the noblest creatures, such as the horse, but the best being of man himself. You should ideally, it is true, be a brave and noble warrior captured in battle, rather than a country clerk, but it is perhaps something that you are a priest of your god – I hope my gods will appreciate that point, as they will the day and time on which you will be offered, midnight of Samhain, the most sacred moment of the year, when dead and living are at their closest. They are hungry for blood, my gods: the great sacrifice has not been made to them for so many centuries, and the one who makes it will surely be blessed by them. Tonight I become one with the Tuatha, a warrior-priestess, and no more will I live the wretched life of a penniless widow. These ancient stones will become again a city and I will rule it, in exchange for the life of a Christian priest!" Even in his drugged state, Hale was aware that she was shouting, and from the glimpses of her that passed in and out of his sight he guessed that she was doing some kind of swaying dance. He could understand no more; perhaps she was reciting something in Irish; then she came and stood by him again, moving his face.

"The victim is garrotted and then buried or drowned. I have this cord ready, and shall attempt to strangle you; I may well succeed, so weak are you grown, but in any case the drowning will finish the job. The water behind this stone, into which I shall drag you, is a

285

full yard deep and completely overgrown. Then to keep you from rising I have this hurdle ready to cover you, and these stones with which to hold it down." She showed him a hurdle lying nearby, large enough to cover a body, and a half a dozen rocks just heavy enough for her to be able to heave about by means of the handles of the rough rope cradles in which she had wrapped them. She had planned it all meticulously, and it looked likely to succeed. People rarely came to this spot, and a few minutes after the struggle the surface of the swamp would look unbroken. No-one would think to look for him here; no-one knew he had ever come here. By the time the hurdle fell apart, months or years hence, his flesh and garments would have rotted away and the bones would have sunk into the mud. Nothing would ever be found. Laughing in her triumph, she threw his head back so that the jaws snapped together – just enough of a physical sensation to force a thought through the muddle in his mind. He had felt better after being sick; perhaps if he could vomit the rest of the poison up he might have a moment's energy in which to put up some kind of resistance. The sooner the better, before it all passed into his system. He had, after all, spat quite a lot of the dose out at first, and if she had measured it at all it was possible that he was not as incapacitated as she thought. The blow had done it before: he needed to suffer a similar shock in order to induce the vomiting.

Maeve had moved away; although he did not know it, she was sitting on another stone some feet away, watching the moon, waiting for the midnight. He slowly tried to establish contact with each of the far-flung provinces of his body, and to test out its capacity to help in the coming movement. His feet he could not answer for, but he felt that he might be able to bend his knees and push upwards from his thighs in a way which might get him half-upright; again, the lower middle part of his body felt able to carry this through, though his arms were all but useless; there was some flexibility in his left arm, and he might even be able to grasp weakly with the left hand. He prayed for help in his coming action, and for

286

forgiveness for what sins had brought him to this point. Two fears remained: that when he came to act, it would be in the form of imagined action only, a dream rather than reality, and that, even if he did succeed in moving, all that would be achieved would be to alert Maeve to his imperfect coma while demonstrating his inability to resist, and so draw her to attack him again. The one thing he did not dwell on during these seconds or minutes was Maeve's part in what was happening; no grief for lost love or pain of betrayal, or even puzzlement at her bizarre change, further clouded his mind, and all that concerned him was surviving the encounter. It would have been no different had he been the victim of a common footpad, and this was the surest proof of all that his feelings for her had been as flimsily grounded as hers for him, which had been wholly false. Mere sentiment, infatuation and naivety had overwhelmed him.

At last, he felt he had to act before the poison completed its work and he drifted off never to return to the living world. He knew he would have to haul himself up twice, firstly to try to induce more vomiting and then, being a little strengthened by that, to confront Maeve. The first action would only need to be a partial rising, but the second would have to be very quickly upon the heels of the first and much more committed. Trying not to draw attention, he pushed up from the knees and thighs and tried to untwist his body, making himself perhaps three-quarters upright; he then hurled himself down again across the stone, so as to catch himself across the stomach and adjacent areas, cracking a couple of ribs, and he managed to force up some disgusting matter which now burnt his lips. He was careful to let his head and neck fall far beyond the stone, so as not to injury himself too severely, and felt his face fall into brackish water which purged the horror from his mouth and nose. Almost at once he sensed Maeve above him, struggling in the dark and her heavy dress to find a foothold from which to push his head under and so finish it. He could not rise straight up – his middle was higher than his head – but was forced to roll the bottom half of his body off the stone and use the action to turn his face up for a delayed breath. Maeve slipped and fell crossways onto him; she clearly feared getting to deathgrips on the brink of the swamp, as she tried frantically to crawl away rather than stay to strangle him from above. This gave him his chance: he could never have risen from his back in less than minutes by his own efforts in his state, but by clinging to her shoulders he managed to get himself pulled over onto his front and dragged a couple of feet from the water's edge. He sensed rather than saw her stagger up and turn to face him, and then he made his tremendous, once and forever effort, cranking himself onto his knees, then laboriously planting his right leg in front of him and pushing up with all his remaining strength and determination. He rose unsteadily – a child of five could have toppled him again – and Maeve prepared to spring at him in a way which would have knocked the remaining consciousness from him. At this moment, inspiration came from somewhere, perhaps from where his prayers all went, and he cried out the very thing which would have the greatest effect: he tried to make it a stunning shout, but it came out as the equally inhuman screech of man with a partially-paralysed throat and chest: "Halloween, living and dead together!" And he staggered forward a couple of paces, making stiff-jointed grasping gestures toward her. His voice frightened even him as it cracked open again: "Living and dead together forever!" This was not her vision of the delicate shades of lords and ladies populating the background for warriors and bards; she looked briefly at the sodden, stained, stiff creature floundering towards her, with moss in his hair, craziness in his eyes and a deadly pallor in his cheeks, and she fled with a scream, hopping over stones and splashing through puddles.

Just in time she vanished into the darkness, as Theophilus came to the end of his energy and sank to the ground. At once a cloud blotted out the moon and brought on a light shower. He lay in the rain, his face on his arm, trying to find some relief from his pains in stillness. After quite a number of minutes – in fact he slept thus for nearly an hour without realising it – he stirred and decided that he was lying in far too open a spot, in case she came back to finish the job; in fact, now she had to carry her plan through merely to dispose of the evidence, namely himself. He stumbled and crawled a couple of hundred yards southwards as the rain fell more heavily, to the comparative safety of Hyde's farm. He fell rather than climbed over a fence and dragged himself into a bush which covered most of his body, and fell asleep again, praying that he should waken before folks were about. In that he was starting to worry about his appalling appearance, he could be said to be returning to the mundane concerns of life.

He need not have worried: the first streaks of light in the sky and the first sounds of animal and bird woke him early. As he stretched, he reviewed the damage: his stomach was very sore both inside and out, but he knew from experience that his cracked ribs would soon repair themselves; he had a very bad headache, and felt chilled from his wet clothes through to his bones; the original wound on his hand was throbbing slightly still. But that was all: he would have a bad cold for several days, but if he got home and dried and warmed himself, a few hours of more restful sleep would improve his condition considerably. His hat had long since gone, but he found his keys and a few coins still safe in their buttoned-down pocket. He set off as quickly as he could manage, keeping close to hedges in case he came upon early risers, and quietly let himself back into the rectory shortly after seven. A boiling kettle and a pan of hot water allowed him a hot drink and a brisk wash which served as much to warm as to clean, and he fell into his bed to sleep soundly for two hours before having to get up again for the All Saints' Day Eucharist – which he managed remarkably easily, despite some hoarseness, the occasional sneeze and the well-wishes of those who thought he looked as though he had been, with unconscious accuracy, "under the weather".

It was not until this point that he really had chance to think about what had happened the night before. The feelings about Maeve that had grown over two months had dissipated almost instantly, and a sense of having been a fool at letting the situation get so out of hand was now rather stronger. As to what would happen now, he could not guess: even though he had nearly been murdered, he really wanted the whole business to be forgotten. He doubted she would try such a thing again, and he certainly did not wish the details of his recent conduct to become public. Even though they lived so close, there was really no need for either even to visit the other's village, and it was by no means impossible that they would scarcely ever set eyes on each other again. It did cross his mind, however, that she might attempt to cover herself by contriving some tale against him – he had heard stories along such lines – and he resolved to return to the bog as soon as he could to see if he could recover his hat. He spent the rest of the morning on the unaccustomed task of washing clothes, and then, though he really wanted to sleep again, set out, coatless, on horseback.

It was one of the last truly bright days of the year, and the bog looked serene compared to how it had appeared the night before. He knew the point at which he had entered it then, and tied the horse there before descending the slope. He would not have remembered the way, but soon discovered some marks made by someone sliding which the rain had not obliterated, and followed them. He saw his hat first, floating brokenly on a pool, and made his way carefully towards it; in front was a stone which resembled the one on which he had come to rest. Having fished out his hat, he looked around for any more evidence of what had happened. The muddy ground was very much torn up, but it was impossible to say by what and a few more sessions of drying and soaking would remove the marks entirely. He caught sight of a length of cord also partly floating in the pool but caught against the edge; he pulled it out too, realising that it was the garrotte which she had intended using on him. Finally, surveying the ground around the stone, he noticed something glinting in the mud, and brushed the dirt away from it. A tiny silver sword. Wary of what still might be on it, he took out the pocket handkerchief which he was obliged to use from time to time and picked the emblem up – yes, he had to pull as the whole bracelet came up out of the mud which had almost claimed it. Always loose, it must have been shaken or rubbed over her hand when she was struggling to crawl away from him. He wrapped the two unexpected items up and put them in his saddlebag, tying the hat onto the saddle so that it might dry. When he arrived at the rectory, he was careful to treat the three things very differently: his hat he put in front of the fire to dry so that it could be brushed up to look at least respectable; the garrotte he put away handily in a desk drawer, in case he had to give an account of the night's events; the bracelet he buried in the corner of a well-turned flower bed, suddenly aware that however fantastical a story she might weave against him and however innocent he might be, his possession of that bauble would probably be taken as proof that the attack had been the other way round. In retrospect he wished he had stamped it into the mud, never to be seen again.

The rest of the day, and the next, he waited anxiously: he could not have said exactly what he was awaiting or why he felt so apprehensive. He did not seriously expect Morton and the constable to come to his door to arrest him, but neither did he rule it out, so badly did he feel himself to have behaved recently. Even less did he expect Maeve to appear, but given her insane behaviour even that could not be discounted. He took services mechanically, slept in his chair, gave his living-out housekeeper and his verger grounds for concerns over his health. It was not until Monday that Mrs. Blake ended his anxiety by passing on the latest gossip when she came to make his breakfast and lay the fire. It concerned the Mortons in the next village, whom she knew he had visited a few times; the brother-in-law, who had taken the penniless foreign widow in out of charity, had returned home the day before to find her gone, leaving no note or explanation. She had taken his second horse, her clothes and her few possessions, and had also helped herself to several of his valuables, including his mother's ruby brooch, as well as the housekeeping money entrusted to her and a few pounds kept in the house. He was frantic with both anger and concern at her well-being and would have set out at once to try to catch her had not the servants told him that she had been gone for fully a day and a half, having set off on the Saturday morning before anyone had risen. The rest of her story was speculation and generalisation about ingratitude and greed, and Hale ceased to listen.

Morton did call at the rectory the following day, not with constables and warrants but in a very subdued mood. He mechanically asked Hale if he knew of what had happened and then if he had any idea where she might have gone; he was visiting everyone who had known her at all, to ask the same thing. In all honesty, Hale could give him no helpful reply, though he did suggest that Ireland seemed a likely destination, which had of course already been thought of; Morton had sent an agent to make inquiries along the road to Bristol, where she might be supposed to take ship. Fortunately, Morton did not think to ask anything embarrassing about when Hale had last seen her, and he went away at once.

Eventually the agent found the ruby brooch in the window of a jeweller's shop in Bath; it had been bought from a young woman in black who struck quite a good bargain despite being obviously in need of a sale. Morton followed in person, but nothing further was discovered. A letter sent to the address from which she had come in Ireland was acknowledged by the new occupant, who knew nothing of the former tenant except that she had moved to England some weeks before. Nothing of Maeve Morton, née Healy, was ever heard again, and nothing of her was left at Stoke Armitage and Armitage Cross, except in the thoughts of two men and a small package buried in a flower bed.